BRIDE OR DIE

A CLAIRE HARTLEY ACCIDENTAL MYSTERY

MADISON SCORE

That's What She Said Publishing, Inc.

Bride

or

DIE

ISBN: 979-8-88643-939-7 (ebook)

ISBN: 979-8-88643-940-3 (paperback)

madisonscore.com

022424

For Mike. Without you, this story would still be scribbles in a notebook.

AUTHOR'S NOTE

I've always dreamed of being a writer. Well, unless you count kindergarten, where I briefly decided to be an artist or doctor before realizing I had no aptitude for either.

Literature was the lifeblood of our family growing up. My mom was a middle school librarian, and I spent many summers in our local public library devouring every Goosebumps book. We read at the dinner table, preferring the endless worlds of our books to the canned laughter of sitcoms. I loved them all—fantasy, young adult, mystery, humor, and eventually romance.

During my youth, I wrote all kinds of crap. Poems, short stories, Harry Potter fan fiction. You name it, I've butchered it. I even went to college for it (on purpose. I'll wait for you to stop laughing.).

After graduation, the crushing reality of adulthood set in. Writing is not a career for the fainthearted. You don't get health insurance. You can put thousands of hours into a manuscript and not make a dime. Even if you do successfully write a book (which is the second hardest thing I've ever done), there's no guarantee anyone will want to publish it. And even in the one-in-a-million chance you get published, there is always someone on the internet waiting to tear it to shreds.

So I entered the workforce. I moved to a new city while my then-boyfriend (now husband) finished pharmacy school. I tried and failed at marketing. I answered phones for a company that sold automated mail machines. I sold overpriced bras and buttery pretzels.

But all the while, in the back of my mind, there was the urge to write. I actually owe the idea for Claire's story to my mother-in-law. During one of our visits, she mentioned a news story. It was something about an elaborate marriage proposal and the person who planned it. I think she meant to encourage me to check it out as a career path. Instead, I thought, "Holy crap, that would be an amazing book."

And so I wrote. I dragged myself to my beat-up college laptop after the rigors of my 9-to-5. Slowly, painfully, the story took shape. A heroine emerged, then a love story, then a murder. Sometimes the book wrote itself. Other days it was like crawling over a football field made out of cheese graters.

Life got in the way again. I changed careers, bought a house, got married, moved. Writing fell to the wayside as I navigated these pitfalls and triumphs of adulthood. And still, as I wrote out checks for electricity bills and push-mowed our stupid little plot of land, Claire's story whispered in the back of my mind. Finally, I finished it. When the pandemic hit, I wrote the second one. A third one followed while I was pregnant and waddling to the bathroom every four minutes.

This book is the product of my lifelong dream. A three-part story that's been rattling around in my brain for a decade. Thank you for taking a chance on me. I hope you love Claire as much as I do.

Xoxo,
Madison

CHAPTER ONE

To Do:
- Call the caterer
- Buy portable fire extinguisher
- Don't think about J

"No. I will not marry you."

The curvy blonde stared down her nose at the man who knelt in front of her and held a three-karat diamond ring.

The man's mouth dropped open, and his cheeks flushed. His steel-gray eyes narrowed.

A group of dancers who had crowded around him stopped wiggling their jazz hands. The heart-shaped sparklers fizzled and died, leaving behind the smell of sulfur.

"What do you mean, no?" His voice echoed through the cavernous warehouse, bouncing off banners and props and filling the room with his disbelief. A bead of sweat traced a serpentine path from his forehead to the bridge of his nose. He wiped at it with the back of his hand, and the overhead lights flashed across the face of a gold watch.

Claire Hartley hopped down from her director's chair, stilettos striking the concrete floor.

"Barney, you can do better than that." She frowned and tilted her head to one side.

Barney's shoulders slumped, and he loosened his tie. A thick head of brown hair was slicked back with pomade, which made him look more like a middle-aged used car salesman than a twenty-seven-year-old hotel tycoon.

She lowered her voice and straightened the rose in his lapel. "This is the biggest question you'll ever ask in your entire life. You've already got all the fanfare and excitement you wanted," she said, waving a hand at the flash mob. "Now you need to make it personal and tailored just for Victoria."

Claire turned around and shot a stern glance at the mob behind her. "And guys, only half of you had your sparklers. What gives? I said this was a full *dress* rehearsal."

A slender brunette with pigtails frowned. "I thought we said jazz hands only because the last time you used sparklers, the future groom almost set his fiancée's hair on fire?"

"Yes, and that is why the groom no longer holds a sparkler. But as long as you guys keep your distance, we should all live to see at least thirty. Now take five and practice that lift sequence, please."

The dancers leapt to their feet and took turns dousing their still-smoking sparklers in a bucket of water. They gossiped as they retreated to the back wall, shaking out their limbs and stretching.

Claire tucked an unruly curl behind her ear and shifted

her clipboard to one hip. She reached for Barney's hand and pulled him to his feet. Rose petals clung to the knees of his khaki pants. He towered over her despite her four-inch heels.

"I know it's tough." She touched his arm. "But don't get discouraged. I know you can do this. Tell me about how you first met Victoria."

Barney took a breath, but Claire interrupted. "Chutney! I know you're new, but please do not wear a dress that short during the actual proposal. You are a gorgeous dancer with the grace and poise of ten thousand ballerinas, but no future bride wants to see another girl's hoo-ha when her boyfriend proposes."

A redhead with legs up to her eyeballs flushed and tugged the hemline of her sundress down.

"Sorry, Barney. Go ahead."

Barney smiled, brushing his thumb over the fabric of the ring box. "I was on my way home from an out-of-town meeting for my chain in Connecticut, and out of nowhere I have a crazy craving for some pie and coffee. The only place open was this little run-down diner called Stella's on the edge of West Haven."

"Oh, I know Stella's! Their rhubarb pie is amazing. I used to stop there after a run." She could practically smell the flaky crust. She hadn't run in months—not since a group of college boys hanging out the windows of a pickup truck had catcalled her for eight straight blocks. Pilates and yoga now filled the exercise void in her life.

"That's exactly what I got that night. Victoria was working the night shift. She was new, and she spilled my coffee all over the table and was so afraid I would yell at her." He chuckled. "We ended up talking all night, and at the end of her shift, she went home with me. I took her to

Laflin Park for a picnic the next day. We've been together ever since."

Claire bit her lip. Barney was royalty in the hotel world. His hotels were all over the eastern seaboard, but his headquarters and pride and joy was the Heirloom Hotel smack in the middle of his hometown, West Haven, Pennsylvania.

"Well, that's...good. You should definitely mention that in the proposal. Just maybe not the part about taking her home with you. Her grandparents will be there. Speaking of which, someone needs to make sure Grandpa Reed has an extra oxygen tank just in case." She pulled a pen out of her messy bun and wrote a note on her clipboard. "Want to try it again?"

"Sure, just give me a minute to think about exactly what I want to say."

She glanced at an oversized clock next to a photo booth. "Okay, we've got twenty minutes. Take a break to breathe and really think about it. And remember, keep it personal and meaningful."

Barney nodded and pulled a pen and a small notepad out of his jacket pocket. He scratched something out and started pacing.

She returned to her seat and crossed her legs at the ankle. Flipping through the pages of notes on her clipboard, she made notations and adjusted the proposal timeline.

Her phone rang, and she answered it without glancing at the number.

"Claire Hartley?" a pleasant-sounding woman asked.

"Yes, this is she."

"Miss Hartley, this is Becca from Rooted Catering. I'm calling because we haven't received your final guest count, and we need to put an order in for the chicken and fish."

A vice clenched her stomach. Claire gripped the arm of her chair so hard that her knuckles turned white.

"No, you haven't received the final guest count. As I mentioned several months ago, I will not be requiring chicken *or* fish because I'm no longer getting married."

As Becca expressed her condolences and rattled on about the non-refundable deposit, Claire took deep breaths and tried to slow the heartbeat hammering in her ears. After taking some notes and saying goodbye, she stabbed at her screen until the call ended. Cursing inwardly, she threw her phone into her bag as if it were a snake.

"You're still getting calls?" Mindy Harris, Claire's fastidious assistant and best friend, asked as she appeared at Claire's side. She cracked open a bottle of water and offered it to her boss.

"Thanks." Claire took the bottle and gestured at her willowy friend. "Oh, I like this! Is it new?" She twirled her finger, and Mindy obediently spun, showing off her simple black wrap dress, dangling gold necklace, and cherry-red lipstick.

Mindy struck a sassy pose and tossed her waist-length hair over her shoulder. "It is. Thank you. But don't deflect."

Claire frowned and drained half the bottle of water. "The venue called last week, the caterer called today. Aunt Sarah even called because she couldn't find the registry. She somehow missed the memo." Claire shook her head. It was business hours, and there was no time for personal nonsense. "Any crises I need to freak out about?"

Mindy slid her oval-framed glasses back up her nose and glanced down at her tablet. "Surprisingly, no. We have a morning appointment Thursday with the carriage company for Nicole's proposal. Oh, and I talked to the River Authority, and they said that for the Jet Ski proposal everyone has to wear a life jacket."

Claire groaned. "They're going to ruin the comedic effect of the guys wearing tuxedo wetsuits."

"I know. They clearly don't understand art. Also, I'm supposed to remind you to write a post about the 'something old' tradition for the blog tonight. Your mom called. Oh, and I got an email from Kyle's friend, Luke." At Claire's frown of confusion, she continued. "You know, the big-shot documentary filmmaker who just moved to town. He wants to meet with you about Nicole's proposal."

Claire sighed and stretched her arms over her head, rubbing the kink in her neck she had earned after a particularly intense yoga session the previous day. She closed her eyes. "I would rather put on a meat dress and be dangled over a pit of velociraptors than see even one more person today."

Mindy snorted. "He said it wouldn't take long. He just wants to discuss logistics."

"Ugh, fine. Ask him if tomorrow morning works for him. Actually, make that afternoon. I've got practice with Steve on the river in the morning."

"Fair enough. Should I tell him you'll meet him at his place? Kyle said his house would be perfect for the last stop." She tapped at the glowing screen.

"That's fine. Get his address for me? Oh, and I almost forgot." Claire reached into the oversized purse slung over the back of her chair and rummaged around, plucking out a small box wrapped in silver paper and adorned with a tiny red bow. She presented it to Mindy.

"What's this for?"

"For your birthday, duh." Claire smiled. "What kind of boss-slash-friend would I be if I didn't remember your birthday? And by the way, you're taking tomorrow off and then I'm taking you out later this week for drinks."

Mindy clutched the box to her chest. "This is peak season. I can't take a day off!"

"Stop. I'll be fine. Now open it."

She tore the paper off to reveal a pair of heart-shaped diamond studs. She tilted them toward the overhead lights. "Claire, what the hell is this?"

"They're earrings for the best assistant in the world."

Mindy drew her into a tight embrace. "I can't accept these. They're way too much," she said, but she was already plucking them from the box.

"If it weren't for you and your amazing aptitude for organization, Happily Ever Afters would still be based out of my one-bedroom apartment."

"You're so sweet. How do they look?" Mindy brushed back her ebony hair.

"Gorgeous and perfect, just like you."

"Stop. You're making me blush. Hey, want to go get a pre-birthday drink tonight? It's ladies' night at Rodano's."

"Wish I could, but I have a hot date." Claire wiggled her eyebrows suggestively.

Mindy gasped. "You've finally decided to call off your sex embargo? I've been telling you for months now that the best way to get over Jason is to just bang one out."

Claire glared at her.

"Sorry, I know, we don't say his name. Who is it? Tell me everything. I hope it's not that guy from the deli. Jodi said the size of his hands was disappointingly misleading."

Claire laughed. "Gross. No, the date is with my nephew. We're going to play *Murder Melee Three* and 'pown some noobs,' as he says. Am I saying that word right? Pown? P-own?"

"Please tell me you're not going to wear the goofy headphones."

"Min. It's *MM Three*. Of course I'm going to wear my headphones. How else do you expect me to get a three-hundred-and-sixty-degree sound field?"

Mindy took a step back and narrowed her eyes. "You wouldn't know it from looking at you, but there's definitely a teenage boy trapped in your body."

Claire shoved her playfully, nearly tipping her own chair over in the process. She glanced at her watch and pulled out her cellphone. "My mom is blowing up my phone. I'm going to call her back really quick and then we'll get started. Can you check on Barney?"

Mindy nodded and bent to adjust one of the cardboard shapes meant to mark a bush.

The phone barely managed to ring twice before Claire's mom picked up.

"There's my Clairebear!" Sweet as honey, Alice Alejo's voice flowed through the speaker.

"Hi, Mom. How are you?"

"Just fabulous, sweetie. Roy and I head to Palm Springs in a few days for my conference. We're thinking about heading to a spa afterwards and staying for another week. We'd love it if you would come along," she said, a hint of a plea in her voice.

The last time Claire had taken a family vacation with her mother and stepfather, they had wound up at a yurt in the desert, gathering quartz as an offering to a waxing quarter moon. Roy spent the entire long weekend sanding and re-painting the door of their (rental) yurt, and Claire had checked everyone's shoes for scorpions no fewer than thirty-seven times. She wasn't eager to repeat the experience.

"You know I'd love to, Mom. Work's so busy right now that there's no way I can get away. By the way, have you heard from Charlie? She won't answer my texts."

Alice sighed. "That's what I figured. Charlie told me on Sunday that one of her clients was having a crisis that needed real damage control."

"Jade Alexander's fourth infidelity scandal is so not more important than what I had asked her."

"Was it about the sale at Sephora?" Alice asked.

"No comment."

"Clairebear, there's another reason why I called. I got some bad news this morning. You may have already heard, and I didn't want to upset you, but...well, do you remember your freshman roommate, Courtney?"

"Vividly," she said, rolling her eyes. "Crazy Courtney" was an incessant party girl who regularly stumbled into their dorm room at four in the morning smelling like a bong.

"I still do regular tarot readings for her mother. She called me this morning. Courtney's gone missing, sweetie. She disappeared over the weekend."

A wave of goosebumps spread down Claire's arms. Her veins were ice.

"That's the fourth girl from your college," Alice continued. "The media keeps talking about this 'West Haven Wrangler' who's kidnapping newly married women and—"

"You mean the West Haven Widowmaker? Which, by the way, that nickname makes no sense. A widowmaker would be someone who is murdering men and leaving widows behind. But apparently 'Widowermaker' isn't a snappy enough moniker for Channel Eight News."

"Yes, the Widowmaker. They think Courtney's disappearance is connected. She just got married last summer.

Are you sure you don't want to move in with Roy and me for a while? You'll love Miami. You can see the beach from the new guest room. And you'd be so much safer here than in the city where you don't even have anyone to look after you."

"Mom, there are three universities and like 200,000 people in West Haven. A few of them are bound to go missing. Remember that girl who disappeared from Bridgeford University a couple of years ago? The community watch group organized a massive search party before a sanitation worker found her taking a nap in a Taco Bell dumpster."

"Clairebear, I think you're being a little too flippant. All four of the missing women were from either your graduating class or the one above you. I'm worried about your safety."

Claire rubbed at her temples. Talking to her safety-obsessed mother nearly always led to a pounding headache. "Nobody even knows if all those disappearances are connected. They've never found any bodies. Maybe they're all just newlyweds who got cold feet and took off. I can attest to the fact that Courtney was a flighty girl who was prone to dropping everything and leaving whenever it suited her. Her husband John is a good guy, but he's painfully boring. They were mismatched from the start. And besides, I am perfectly safe. I have Mindy and Nicole and a ton of nosey neighbors."

"But Claire, these disappearances *are* connected. I can tell. You know I have a very sensitive intuition."

Her mother was a self-proclaimed psychic with her surprisingly successful television show. She routinely performed aura readings for her live audience and communicated with spirits using a variety of methods. While several of her "premonitions" had technically come true throughout the course of her life, Claire didn't put much stock in her mother's career.

"I sent you a present in the mail," Alice continued. "Just be sure to open it very carefully."

"Okay, Mom. Thank you. I'm at a rehearsal so I have to go. I love you," Claire said, hanging up.

A weight settled on her chest as she remembered the few good times she had shared with her college roommate —late night tacos, occasional boy gossip, and mutual dislike of a certain business professor. They hadn't become lifelong friends, but they had certainly tolerated each other for a year. And now the girl who she'd shared that first year of adulthood with had disappeared.

She took a deep breath and composed herself. After a quick glance at her watch, she stood again. "Okay, everyone. From the top! Barney, come over here and pretend I'm Victoria."

The dancers took their positions around the room.

Claire turned to Barney. "Okay, so you just stopped the car in front of the park. What do you do?"

Barney walked to the opposite side of her and mimed grabbing a handle. "I get the ring from you, who will be hiding behind the bush next to my parking spot. Then I take Victoria's hand and lead her down the path," he said, grasping Claire's hand and helping her out of an imaginary car.

Ick. His palm was practically dripping with sweat.

"Good. Now you say the keyword."

"Victoria, I've been thinking, and there's something I'd really like to ask you."

The stereo mounted on the wall began playing the first few measures of a recent pop song.

"Baby, I've been thinking. There's something I gotta say."

The dancer in the fedora collapsed his newspaper and leaped in front of the large, taped-off circle that represented a park fountain. He handed a fake rose to the woman next to him and step-ball-changed several feet in each direction. The woman joined him, and they danced toward Barney and Claire.

The male dancer dipped the woman right in front of them, and she offered Claire the rose.

"Beautiful!" Claire laid the flower across her clipboard. "Greg, make sure you step just a little farther away from the fountain. Last time I planned a proposal in this park, the fountain broke and hosed down a small child. But they fixed that last summer. I think." She flipped through her notes.

"When I dream, I dream of you."

Another pair of dancers burst onto the scene, tossing their maps onto the ground and twirling around the makeshift park. Arms raised, they paraded around in a circle before carrying two more roses over to Claire.

"Gorgeous! Don't forget to pick up the maps. We don't want to litter." She pointed to the map of Pennsylvania on the warehouse floor. A dancer snatched them up and strutted away into the next dance sequence.

"The first photographer will be right over there," Claire shouted to Barney over the music. She pointed toward a piece of cardboard marked "bush." "He'll be able to capture that angle with the flash mob in the foreground. And the second one will be on our side, but behind us." She pointed toward another taped-off section of the floor.

"And the videographers?" Barney guided her around the edge of the fountain and past the speakers.

"As requested, there will be three. They'll be roaming around to get the best shot."

He nodded, apparently satisfied. Three videographers

seemed like overkill, but the client got what the client wanted.

The dancers formed a line and the remaining five couples shimmied, slid, and sashayed down the aisle. Each woman handed Claire another fake rose until her entire clipboard was covered, blocking out her appointments for the next week.

"John will release the doves from behind the fountain, and assuming they cooperate, it should be really lovely and completely over the top, just as you wanted."

"Say you'll be mine. You've been sent from above."

"I don't even know how to thank you," Barney said. His eyes were just a tad small for his face, but they were open quite wide.

"You're my forever, my one true love."

Claire waved a hand. "It's all part of the job. It's almost your cue, so be ready."

When the chorus rolled around again, Barney leapt into the group of dancers, matching their movements with his long limbs. His goofy grin lit up his face, and he gyrated and grooved until the song was nearly over, when he came back to Claire and dropped down on one knee. The other dancers whipped out extra-long sparklers from their sleeves and mimed lighting them, striking a pose as Barney began his speech.

"Victoria, do you remember what I said to you the night we first met?" He paused, awaiting his phantom girlfriend's reply.

"After you poured coffee in my lap instead of in my mug, I told you that you could spill coffee on me anytime. And I still mean that. I want to live the rest of my life with you, one long stream of hilarious accidents that bring us closer and closer together for all time."

He reached out and took Claire's hand. "I want you to spill coffee on the kitchen table where we're going to sit down and eat dinner with our future children. I want you to spill it on your keyboard so I can help you fix it. I want you to dump it on my work papers so we can fight and make love. Most of all, I just want you. You are the most patient, kind, and incredible woman I have ever had the pleasure of knowing. You're the only one for me, Victoria, and I would be so honored if you would agree to be my wife. Will you marry me?"

He looked up at Claire, worry lines creasing his forehead.

It wasn't the most romantic sentiment she'd ever heard from a groom, but it was heartfelt and that was what mattered. The chorus of bells at the end of the song began to fade out.

"I don't see how she could ever say no," she said.

The dancers broke out into cheers, and Barney cracked a smile.

At a nod from Claire, the dancer who held a cage labeled "doves" popped open the door. He reached in and began tossing the small pillows over the circle that marked the fountain, imitating the triumphant release of the birds.

Claire and Barney laughed, and he visibly relaxed.

"You really think she'll say yes?"

"I know she will. Don't forget, we have one more rehearsal on Friday. Then I'll see you on Saturday at six. I'll be hiding in the bushes next to your parking spot so I can toss you the ring." She handed him a small earpiece. "Turn this on and put it in before you get out of the car. I'll make sure you hit your cue and stand where you're supposed to be."

He grasped it like a lifeline. "I always feel better with you in my head. Thank you, Claire."

She waved one hand and headed for the door. "Min, can you lock up once everyone's gone? I have to go let Rosie out."

Mindy hurried over. "Just so you know, I think I saw You Know Who's car in the parking lot."

Claire's expression darkened, and she straightened her shoulders. "I'll take care of it."

She wrenched the exterior door open. It was a breathtaking spring day in Pennsylvania. The sky was so blue and cloudless that it almost looked fake after months of desolate, gray skies. The daisies Claire had meticulously planted around the exterior of her warehouse had poked through a layer of mulch, green buds primed to burst. The air was warm and smelled like freshly cut grass, and a puddle stood in the corner of the parking lot where a pile of dirty snow had been only that morning.

A Mercedes Cabriolet was backed into a spot behind one of the company vans. A woman sat in the driver's seat with an expensive camera pressed to her face. When Claire took a step toward the car, the woman dropped the camera and picked up her cellphone.

Claire's stilettos struck the pavement as she marched across the parking lot. She threw her shoulders back like she was preparing to ram the car and rapped on the driver's side window. Not today, Satan.

The woman jumped dramatically and rolled her window down. The smell of marijuana and cinnamon rolled out like a fog. "Hang on, sweetie," she said, her nasally voice too loud as she pulled the phone away from her ear. The screen was blank. She was talking to no one.

"Yes?" the woman asked, the picture of bewilderment.

"What the hell are you doing here, Wendy?" Claire stood with her arms crossed.

"I needed a place to pull off to take a call. It's the *boyfriend*," she said with an exaggerated smile. Her pin-straight brown hair brushed the collar of her all-white tennis dress, and her collarbones jutted out like dinosaur fossils under a desert floor. She lowered her massive sunglasses, then gestured at the phone screen, which was still blank. A diamond bracelet sparkled in the afternoon sunlight.

If only Claire had a cup of coffee in her hand. That virginal tennis dress would more accurately reflect Wendy's personality with some Café Bustelo splotches. Claire's hands balled into fists, and her fresh manicure bit angrily into her palms, leaving half-moon indents. She fought to keep her voice steady.

"Oh, really? So, it's just a coincidence that you were pointing a giant camera at my warehouse, then? I'm sorry it's so hard for you to come up with your own proposal ideas. Daddy's money can buy an awful lot of things, but I guess creativity just isn't one of them."

Wendy rolled her eyes and slid her sunglasses back on.

"Don't flatter yourself. I have no interest in whatever it is you're doing here. And where'd you get that dress, by the way? Plus Barn? You really should consider picking up something that disguises your hips a little more." Wendy rolled up her window and shifted into drive, peeling out of the parking lot.

Claire climbed into the driver's seat of her convertible and slammed the door behind her. She gripped the steering wheel with both hands until her knuckles turned white. She wouldn't allow that insipid, flightless vulture to get under her skin. Karma would come for her.

She tugged at her seatbelt and nearly swore when it refused to pull taut. It was going to be one of those nights. Finally, the engine cranked, and she swung out of the parking lot onto Market Street.

West Haven crawled past her windows. She loved the bustle of her city, the sidewalks that desperately needed to be resurfaced and the roads that had more potholes than asphalt. The mom-and-pop stores stood crammed up against big box competitors teemed with people who lifted their faces to the sky and blinked in the light of the sun as they exited. The Greek restaurant on the corner of Hemlock and 14th Street was closed again, probably from another health code violation. A city worker was hanging floral baskets filled with bright red petunias from the streetlights. The new beer garden a block from her apartment building was already hopping, dozens of couples crammed around small picnic tables underneath crisscrossed strands of Edison bulbs.

When Claire pulled into her parking garage, she slammed the door of her Audi, trudged up the four flights of stairs to her apartment, and pulled out her keys.

As soon as she slid the key into the doorknob, a skittering sound came from the interior of her apartment.

She flung the door open. A modest kitchen with stainless steel appliances, bar, and small island stood to the right. "Baby girl! Ouch." The hardwood was unforgiving on her knees when she lowered herself to the floor. Her rescue corgi, Rosie, launched herself into Claire's arms and licked her furiously. "Mommy missed you so much."

Rosie dove out of Claire's arms and performed a lap around the apartment before abruptly collapsing. She panted, and her tongue lolled out of a space where several teeth were missing. A scar slanted one of her eyes.

Claire cast an eye over her apartment. A pile of tousled blankets on the couch in the living room to her left revealed Rosie's nap location for the day. More dog hair littered the hallway that led back to the bathroom and only bedroom. She was definitely overdue for a deep clean. At least her rarely used dining area off the kitchen was still clean. Well, except for the row of super-dead plants that lined the windowsill.

"There was a time when this dress was black," Claire said, staring at the cloud of ginger-colored dog hair that had settled on it. "If you weren't so cute, I would absolutely shave you bald."

She snapped a leash on Rosie and led her out the door. The corgi pranced excitedly, jumping at Claire's legs and adding another scratch to the three she already had. She bent over and reached down to grab Rosie's right paw, which was missing a toe.

"Rosie. *No jump.*" She held up her other hand to the dog.

Rosie licked it, and Claire shook her head. She had rescued the dog six months ago from a local shelter. In all that time, the only command Rosie had successfully learned was "shake." Maybe she could get a personal session with a trainer after Barney's proposal. "Close enough."

After a brief encounter with a neighbor's German Shepherd and a convenient patch of grass, Claire led Rosie back to the apartment. Claire kicked her stilettos off and flexed her aching calves, then reached for a repurposed cereal box full of menus, accidentally knocking over a rolled-up yoga mat she had abandoned in the kitchen earlier. Blowing a strand of blonde hair out of her eyes, she flipped through the stack until she found the dog-eared menu of her favorite pizza joint.

"Yes, hi. Can I get a large pizza with sausage, onion,

peppers, and pepperoni? Yes. Delivery. Six-oh-one East Beaumont Street, Apartment four B. Claire. Thank you." She tossed her phone into a stack of throw pillows and groaned.

"Forty minutes is so long, Ro," she said, her voice echoing off the tiled backsplash. She opened a can of dog food and plopped it into a ceramic bowl adorned with crowns and scepters. "You're not going to judge me if I eat the whole pizza by myself, right?" She set the bowl down on a mat and scratched Rosie's rump for a moment before heading to the shower.

In her hallway, she ran a hand over a shelf that held three plaques, all boldly proclaiming "West Haven Chamber of Commerce Event Planner of the Year." A vacant spot sat to the right of the last plaque. It wouldn't be empty for long.

She bumped her bathroom door open with her hip and stepped onto the cool tile. Pictures of Paris, Prague, and all the other cities she desperately wanted to visit adorned the walls, captured in black frames. A small bowl of homemade potpourri sat on top of a wooden towel cabinet, permeating the room with the smell of fresh linen and lemongrass. The window was open a crack, letting in a warm breeze and a hint of spring.

Claire slid her dress off her shoulders and let it drop to the floor. She stepped under the shower's warm flow and attempted to banish the proposal details that swarmed around her head like a cloud of gnats. Business hours were over, and if she didn't disengage now, she'd be up all night. She buried her hands in her hair and thought about the War Hammer of Vladgar, a legendary item in *Murder Melee 3* that she and her nephew had not been able to find. The jets embedded in the wall pummeled her back.

She toweled off quickly and changed into a black silk

robe, twisting her hair up into a towel. In the living room, she turned on the gaming console and dug her headphones out of a cabinet, setting them on the coffee table out of Rosie's reach.

She tapped her nails against the back of the couch. It was no use. If she didn't listen to the song that was soon to be featured in the biggest proposal of her entire career, she'd never have enough time to plot out the eight counts. Maybe just one listen through. Then she'd stop for the night.

She connected her phone to a Bluetooth speaker, and an acoustic song filtered out, gentle piano and a voice as smooth as soft serve ice cream. She cranked the volume and pushed all her thoughts about her day away.

Claire bent over Rosie, who was gnawing on a slipper in the corner. "RoRo, people are going to sing this song to Auntie Nicole during her proposal," she said, scooping her dog up and holding her close. Rosie struggled as Claire waltzed them around the small living room, singing along loudly.

"Come on in... to my heart," she sang. She practiced some ballroom dance moves she had seen on YouTube. Maybe a step-ball change at the chorus?

Rosie frantically licked Claire's face and ears until she set her down laughing to mop her face with the sleeve of her robe. It wasn't until Rosie stiffened and growled that Claire glanced up and realized there was a stranger in her apartment.

CHAPTER TWO

To Do:
- *Change stupid locks*
- *"Something Old" blog*
- *Bribe the River Authority for S proposal*

A MAN STOOD IN CLAIRE'S DOORWAY HOLDING A VASE FULL OF flowers. There was no pizza in sight. The song still played serenely in the background, in stark contrast to the panicked heartbeat in her ears.

"What in the actual hell?" She grabbed an abstract sculpture off her coffee table and wielded it like a weapon. "Who are you, and how did you get into my house?"

"I knocked. You said 'come on in,' so I utilized this thing over here, colloquially known as a 'door,' to enter the apartment," the man said, setting the vase on the kitchen bar behind him and pointing at the front door.

"No, I didn't." She clutched at the neck of her robe. Her

heart thudded, and adrenaline coursed through her veins. The statue was heavy in her hand. What should she do? Hit him? Run? But no, she would never leave Rosie with a delusional madman.

"Come on in...to my heart," the song crooned again in the background.

"Oh," she said. Her face was hot, and her hair towel was on the verge of falling off. "I was..." She trailed off, shuffling backward until she was almost at the wall. The more distance between them, the better.

"Singing to your dog? You really should lock your door, you know."

Oh, hell no. She straightened to her full height, flinging the towel to the ground and putting her fists up in a defensive position, still clutching the sculpture. "You have five seconds to tell me who you are and why you're here, or I'm calling the police."

Her phone buzzed on the coffee table, and they both looked at it. She leapt forward and snatched the phone up. Her mom would kill her if she got murdered.

The man's sea green eyes flashed over her from head to toe. His head nearly cleared the top of Claire's hand-me-down china cabinet. Dark brown hair hung messily over strong eyebrows, matching a day's growth of beard. His jaw was solid but not severe, and his worn high-tops scuffed against the hardwood floor. He looked decidedly amused. Asshole.

The stranger took a step forward and fumbled in his pocket.

Rosie continued to growl, retreating until she was in front of Claire, and the fur on her back bristled.

"I swear to god I will crack your skull open with this if you take even one more step," she threatened.

The man pulled something out of his pocket. Oh hell, was it a gun? Was this the end—murdered while waiting for a pizza? Alice had been right all along.

She threw the sculpture in his direction before pounding on the wall next to her fireplace. "Mr. Lebowitz! Help! There's a man in my apartment!"

It would take Mr. Lebowitz at least three minutes to get out of his recliner and put some pants on, so she just needed to stay alive a few minutes longer.

"Whoa," the stranger said, catching the statue and gingerly setting it on the bar next to the vase of flowers. He laughed. "Sorry. I was shocked by the sight of you dancing with a dog. I'm Luke, Kyle's friend. Luke Islestorm. You're Claire, right?" He pulled a business card out of his wallet and flicked it across the living room. It landed on top of her fuchsia-painted big toe.

"Luke? Oh! The camera guy." She bent to grab the card. A breeze tickled her bare skin as the robe gaped, and she flushed and tugged the sash tighter. She plucked the card off her foot and stood up straight.

"The camera guy? That's my identifier? Not 'director of the critically acclaimed, instant classic *The Suburban Hustle*' guy?"

She lifted her chin and glared at him. She had begrudgingly watched the documentary just the week before with her friends Nicole and Kyle because Kyle claimed he was childhood friends with the director. The scandalous exposé featured bored Los Angeles housewives with secret meth labs.

"I'm aware of your credentials. That's why I agreed to work with you instead of my regular camera crew. However, I distinctly remember telling my assistant that our meeting is tomorrow afternoon."

He ignored her icy stare. "Oh, I got the message." He strode to her dining room table and picked up a vase covered in a dazzling array of brightly colored glass shards. "I just don't like to be kept waiting."

"Are you kidding me? You storm into my house at—" She swiveled to look at the oversized clock on her wall. "Eight o'clock at night on a Sunday because you didn't feel like waiting to have a meeting during normal business hours?"

He set the vase back down and walked over to the kitchen island.

She followed him. What the hell was he doing here?

"When I have a vision, I act on it." He turned a full circle in her kitchen. He rapped his knuckles on her granite countertop and bent to examine her toaster. Was he a home inspector as well as a filmmaker? And why the hell was he so damn nosey? "After seeing some of your work, I figured you would be similarly passionate, no matter what time of day. But maybe I was wrong."

Her mouth gaped. What kind of asshole broke into a coworker's apartment uninvited only to insult her work ethic? There was a whole list of camera crew she typically used for work. Who would be a suitable backup for when she was inevitably forced to kill Luke?

He reached for the roses, stroking a petal between his thumb and forefinger. "These aren't from me, by the way. They were sitting in the hallway. Your name's on the card."

The front door crashed open. They both jumped. Claire's thin, bearded protector lurched through the door with a shotgun at his shoulder. Behind him, rotund Mrs. Lebowitz, in her signature floral housedress, clutched a cast iron frying pan and panted under the weight of her considerable bosom.

Should she call them off? Nah. Claire had had enough of waiting for karma to take care of the egomaniacs in her life.

"You," Mr. Lebowitz shouted, waving the barrel of the gun at Luke. "Get down on the ground! Get behind me, Claire." The elderly man shuffled across the floor in tattered slippers and too-short pajama pants, exposing several inches of hairy ankle. He thrust the gun in Luke's direction.

Luke threw his hands up, eyes wide. "Whoa, hey. There's been a misunderstanding here. Claire knows me. We're working together." He pointed at her and backed away slowly, bumping into the stainless-steel refrigerator.

Claire sat on the arm of her chaise, a snarky smile beginning to spread. Judgey McJudgerson didn't look so large-and-in-charge at the end of her octogenarian neighbor's shotgun.

"I said get down! On the ground now! Shirley, call the police." Mr. Lebowitz's bald spot shone under the overhead lighting. Remnants of something he had had for dinner clung to the tufts of his beard.

Claire stood and laid a hand on Mr. Lebowitz's arm. There was no need to get the police involved. Surely, being threatened at gunpoint had given Luke enough of a scare. "Hold on. I'm sorry, Mr. Lebowitz. This man may be incredibly rude, but I don't think he's here to hurt me. He claims to be my new cameraman for an upcoming project, but we haven't met before tonight."

Mr. Lebowitz lowered his gun and glared at Luke. "Doesn't look like a cameraman. Doesn't have the shoulders for it. Boy!" Mr. Lebowitz boomed, bringing the butt of the weapon back up to his shoulder. "Throw your driver's license over here."

"Are you serious?"

"Do I not look serious to you, sonny?" Mr. Lebowitz audibly released the safety on his gun.

"All right, all right." Luke slowly removed his wallet from his back pocket with one hand and attempted to fish out his driver's license. "It's stuck."

"Then throw the whole thing over here."

Luke tossed his wallet across the room. It landed with a mighty *thwack* on the hardwood floor.

"Shirley," Mr. Lebowitz said simply, as though this was something they did every night.

Mrs. Lebowitz bent down to pick it up, grunting and using the end of the frying pan to stand back up. She flipped the wallet open. A scrap of paper fluttered to the ground.

"What's his name supposed to be?" her husband barked.

"Lucas Something-that-sounds-made-up," Claire said, picking Rosie up and stroking behind her ears until her low growl began to subside.

"It's Luke. Luke Islestorm. I'm twenty-six, and I just moved here from California. Actually, I moved back. I was raised here. I lived on Montrose Street in the Heights," he said.

Claire wrinkled her nose. The Heights was a notoriously upscale neighborhood. That sure helped explain his sense of entitlement.

"My best friend is Kyle Collins, and I'm going to be working with Claire to help him propose to his girlfriend," Luke explained. A flush crept onto his cheeks. Ha.

Mr. Lebowitz lowered his gun and glanced at the driver's license his wife held.

"It says on here you're a veteran." Mr. Lebowitz re-set the safety and handed the gun to his wife, who clumsily balanced it with the wallet and frying pan.

"Yes, sir. Four years of active duty in the Navy."

"Navy, huh? What'd you do?"

"Hospital corpsman."

Mr. Lebowitz took the wallet from his wife, folding it back up before striding across the room. He took Luke's hand and shook it enthusiastically. "Sorry about that. Can't be too careful when you've got a pretty young girl next door with no one to protect her. It's always a pleasure to meet another military man. I was Air Force back in the seventies."

Claire cleared her throat. "Um, hi. Still here. I think I can take it from here, Mr. Lebowitz. Luke doesn't look like he's much of a threat."

When Mr. Lebowitz patted Claire on the head with a liver-spotted hand, Luke frowned.

"Whatever you say, dear. Come along, Shirley. Our show's about to start." He took the shotgun back from his wife and rested the barrel on his shoulder.

"You let us know if you have any trouble, Claire. We're just on the other side of the wall," Shirley said, staring at Luke.

"Wait one second." Claire set Rosie down, crossed to the bar, and plucked two of the roses from the vase. "Please take these. Thank you for always being so wonderful." She kissed Mr. Lebowitz on the cheek and gave Mrs. Lebowitz a firm hug. "Have a good night, you two. Don't stay up too late." Claire winked and waved them into the hallway, shutting the door behind them.

"Well, now that we've established that I'm not a murderer, can we please get some work done? I want to talk about the final scene at my place. I really think we should have three cameras." Luke sank down onto the couch and laced his fingers together behind his head.

Egotistical asshat though he may be, he clearly spent some time in the gym. His biceps strained against the fabric of his T-shirt. When Claire didn't comment, he pulled a small notebook from his pocket and flipped to what appeared to be a crudely drawn floor plan.

Rosie cautiously approached and sniffed at his high-tops. He extended a hand to her and, after sniffing it so gingerly it seemed she thought he was a bomb, she allowed him to scratch her neck.

"First of all, you can kindly take your feet off my coffee table." Claire yanked the wooden table out from under his feet. "And secondly, tonight is the first night in weeks that I actually get to spend time with my nephew. So no, there will be no meeting tonight."

"Oh yeah? I don't see him. Is he a dog too?"

She threw a pillow at him. He caught it easily. "No, he's not a dog. And he's not technically coming over. But we have plans."

He leaned forward, holding the navy throw pillow between his large hands. "So, you're telling me you have plans with your nephew tonight, and yet it's almost eight o'clock on a school night. Are you video chatting with him? No, wait. How old is he?"

"He's twelve. Not that that's any of your business."

"Aha!" He grabbed the gaming headphones on the table and held them up. "You're gaming."

She crossed her arms and stared him down. "So what if I am? Can't a grown woman play video games? Am I threatening your male ego with my immense prowess at first-person shooter games?"

He threw his hands up. "I didn't say that. I'm just surprised. You don't seem like the video game type."

"We all have our vices. Mine just happen to be similar to those of a teenage boy."

He grinned and pulled Rosie onto his lap. She panted

and rolled over, exposing her belly. Traitor. "What are you going to play?"

"None of your business." Claire shook her head and walked into the kitchen. A tension headache held her skull in a vice grip. All she wanted was some pizza and peace and quiet. Even though Luke was the best-looking guy she had seen in weeks (okay, maybe months), she wanted to shove him out the door. What was it going to take to get him to leave? She wasn't sharing her pizza with this stuck-up film-maker, that was for damn sure.

The card from her flowers lay on the counter. "Clarabell" was scrawled on the outside. She scowled and slashed it open, scanning the contents for a second before tossing it back onto the table.

"I'm not a damn cow," she muttered as she plucked the entire bunch of flowers out of the vase and stomped back the hallway toward her bedroom. A thorn jabbed her index finger and drew a drop of blood. Figured. A prick from a prick.

"Hey," Luke called after her. "If I hop on and play too, then can we have our meeting?"

She fumbled with the latch on the window at the end of her hallway. "As I have already mentioned, our meeting is taking place tomorrow. I'm not sure what you're still doing on my couch. And now you're making me late for nephew time."

"Oh, come on. We could do split screen."

The window slid open with a resentful screech. She leaned over the rickety metal fire escape and tossed the roses outside, where they scattered on the sidewalk like matchsticks.

"What the hell are you doing?" Luke hovered at the end of the hallway.

"Just getting rid of an annoyance." She shut the window and latched it again, then breezed past Luke on her way to the kitchen. God, he smelled good. Like freshly mown grass and clean linen. "One of the two that showed up unwanted at my apartment this evening."

"Flowers are annoying? Man, have I been doing things wrong for the past decade."

Claire shook her head. "Flowers are not annoying. The person who sent them is annoying. If he wanted to impress me, he should have sent a pizza," she muttered.

He arched his eyebrows. "I assume he's an ex?"

"You assume correctly."

He let out a low whistle. "What'd he do?"

"That is also none of your business." She slung her headphones around her neck and pressed a button on her remote. Her TV flickered on. "Come on. I promise I'll come to the meeting tomorrow with a ton of ideas. You're going to struggle enough just trying to keep up with me." She opened the front door before returning to her seat.

Luke leaned down to scratch Rosie under the chin again. "You continue to underestimate me." He walked to her door and turned. "Claire?"

"Yeah?" she asked, already setting her mouthpiece in place and bringing her controller to life.

"I have to be honest."

"I can tell that's difficult for you," she quipped.

"I think what you do for a living is ridiculous."

She recoiled as though he had just slapped her across the face. How dare he? She raised the controller and debated about whipping it into his stupid, perfectly straight nose.

Luke plowed on, apparently either not knowing or not caring about the verbal bitch slap he had administered. He tapped a finger on a framed picture in which a team of skydivers spelled out "Marry Me?"

"These extravagant proposals are a waste of time and money. Why is this so important to you? Why did you build an entire career out of helping people ask a four-word question? Does there really need to be fireworks and dancers and celebrity guest appearances? It should be the easiest thing you ever ask."

Claire gripped the controller like a lifeline. A small *crack* split the air. She set the controller down on the coffee table and flexed her fingers. There was no need to take her stress out on an innocent electronic. "If you really need an answer to that question, I'm not sure you're the right man for this job."

He crossed his arms and stared at her. "I've known Kyle since we were kids. If he wants his oldest childhood friend behind the camera when he asks his girlfriend to marry him in a complete spectacle, I will find a way to do it, with or without you."

She stood and flung her headphones onto the couch. They bounced off and hit the floor. Rosie immediately sat on them. Claire crossed the room, face hot and hands clenched into fists. She jabbed one finger into Luke's chest. "Let's get one thing straight. I am in charge of this project. I am going to make all of Nicole's dreams come true and give her the most romantic day of her entire life, and they will remember it forever. If you want to be a part of that day, you will listen, and you will cooperate. And that means having meetings at their scheduled time, not in the middle of the damn night."

She drew a breath, and he made a noise like he was about to interrupt. Claire cut him off.

"Also, if you think filming a bunch of suburban crack

addicts is more poignant and meaningful than capturing declarations of lifelong love, that's fine. But when you are in my house on my time, you will be respectful and keep your opinions about marriage and my business to yourself. Are we clear?"

Luke stared at her for what felt like a full minute. Eventually, he smiled. "Oh, man. This is going to be fun."

"Goodnight, Luke." She shoved him out the door and slammed it.

His laughter echoed in the hallway. She leaned against the closed door. How dare he come into her house without an invitation and then insult the business she had painstakingly built with her own two hands? How was she going to work with this smarmy, narcissistic douchebag? This was worse than working with Wendy. If he ruined even one part of her vision, she was going to end him.

She locked her front door, then angrily grapevined her way back to the living room. Ever since she had heard that TED talk on mind tricks, she had performed a dance move after doing certain tasks—locking the front door, turning off the stove, unplugging her straightener. Since she started memory-dancing, she hadn't been forced to turn around and double check that those all-too-important tasks had been completed.

She stopped grapevining at the piece of paper that had fluttered out of Luke's wallet. She picked it up and unfolded it.

Change is in the wind.

Yeah, no kidding. She sat back on the couch and unlocked her phone. A message had come through while Luke was running his mouth. It was from her mom.

Change is in the wind, Clairebear. I feel it. Love you.

Well, shit.

THREE HOURS LATER, CLAIRE SAT NEXT TO A HALF-EMPTY pizza box, her gaming headphones hanging around her neck at a drunken angle. Half-asleep, she tapped away on her laptop. A can of seltzer sat on the table, and she reached over and shook it, but it was empty. She rubbed her hands over her tired eyes.

"RoRo, if you were getting married, I would totally hand-make your wedding dress." She yawned.

Rosie slept in the signature corgi fashion on the area rug, belly exposed to the ceiling. She opened one bleary eye at Claire and, seeing that she was not offering some sort of snack, grumbled softly and resumed her floppy-pawed position.

After two hours of gaming with her nephew, Ryan, who lived in Los Angeles, Claire had put in another hour of work on her blog. She had just finished a particularly touching article in which she had interviewed one of her previous clients, Ashley, whose mother and grandmother had hand-made her wedding dress out of scraps of their own.

Claire closed her laptop. Her bare feet slapped against the hardwood as she approached her hallway closet. Opening the French doors revealed an array of jackets, boots, and scarves. At the back of the closet hung a black garment bag. She reached in and pulled the zipper down a few inches, exposing a brilliant white dress. Delicate lace covered a sweetheart neckline and cascaded down to the floor, simple but beautiful. She should have glided down the aisle in this dress. She should have been on the cusp of her own happily ever after. Instead, love was on the back burner, possibly forever. All she could do was make sure true love won for her clients. No one would ruin that. Especially not that asshat of a cameraman.

She ran a hand over the fabric for a moment before zipping the bag back up and shoving it against the wall. She piled all her winter coats in front of it, obscuring it from view. There was no sense in holding on to the past. She slammed the doors and stormed back down the hallway to the kitchen.

The card from the flowers still sat on her island. Claire opened a drawer and withdrew a lighter. She held the card over the sink and flicked the lighter. The spark caught the corner of the card and quickly engulfed it. Flames ate away at the clumsy handwriting and empty apologies.

CHAPTER THREE

To Do:
- *Threaten J with a restraining order*
- *Double check Nicole's shoe size*
- *Ask Kyle to look over liability waiver again*

As Claire poured herself a cup of coffee the next morning, a familiar name on the local news drew her attention.

"A West Haven man is distraught after the disappearance of his wife, Courtney Stevens, from their home on Firestone Lane on Saturday. Stevens, a graduate of Venor University, worked at a local architecture firm. Stevens was last seen when she left for her morning run at seven o'clock Saturday morning. Friends and family have organized a search party and have canvassed the surrounding neighborhoods, but no sign of the newlywed has been found. Her family and police are asking for your help in finding her.

Courtney is a white female, approximately one hundred and twenty pounds, and has brown hair and blue eyes. Police have not confirmed whether there is any connection to the other recent disappearances or to the West Haven Widowmaker. Anyone with information is asked to call the crime tip hotline."

A picture of Courtney flashed across the screen.

A twinge of sadness washed over Claire. Courtney's family must be devastated. During freshman year, Courtney's mom sent monthly care packages with homemade cookies for both girls, and Courtney, who had a nearly constant case of the munchies, usually finished hers in the dead of night when she was famished after an evening of bunk-bed-shaking banging.

And her poor husband, John. Claire had crossed paths with him a handful of times at Venor. He had walked her and Courtney back to their dorm after parties several times, and he always carried gum. Would it be weird if she reached out to see how he was doing? Would he even remember her? Maybe she should send a care package or takeout gift certificates.

She turned the TV off and crossed to her dining room window to glance at the world outside. An elderly man shuffled down the sidewalk pushing a gray-muzzled pug in a stroller. The "open" sign flickered on at the café down the street. Was Courtney out there somewhere, blowing off steam? Or was she already gone—taken by the Widowmaker?

Claire texted Mindy to say they should consider tightening up their background checks for applicants and vendors. Their second-choice caterer had the manners of a drunken Russian sailor. If bits of murdered women showed up in Yuffie's pastries during a proposal, Happily Ever Afters would never recover.

Claire shivered and turned away. It was time to get back to work. She sat at the dining room table with her laptop and coffee. She added French vanilla creamer to the mug with one hand as she typed in her computer password with the other.

"Damn! Forty-nine comments on the blog already," Claire said to herself as she hastily scrolled through them and smiled at the onslaught of supportive and gushing comments. "Everybody loves a tradition. Oh, wait, here we have a troll."

She cleared her throat and read in the snotty valley girl voice she reserved for mean commenters. "*PrincessBride* says 'Tiaras are so last season. And I'm sorry, but a girl who's so thick in the thighs should *not* have chosen a mermaid gown.' Geeze. She sounds like a real princess. Deleted." She removed the woman's comment.

Rosie looked up from her bowl, flecks of dog food caught in her whiskers. With a noncommittal grunt, she went back to devouring her meal.

Claire set her laptop back on the coffee table and strode back into her bedroom. Tapping the unlock button on her tablet, she scanned the screen for her daily appointments. A coordination meeting and test-drive for the Jet Ski proposal was scheduled for this morning, and, she noted with disdain, the meeting with Luke Islestorm after lunch.

She slid the tablet into her purse and thrust open the doors of her walk-in closet.

How dare he barge into her home uninvited with his stupid muscular forearms and do-me grin? And that annoying swoop of hair hanging in his eyes. What color were his eyes again? Asshole-colored. It didn't matter anyway.

"I think proposals are stupid because I'm a slimy bachelor who is incapable of expressing love," she mimicked, making faces at the rows of shoes in front of her. She selected a pair of strappy turquoise heels. "I'm a dumb boy who thinks he knows everything because I interviewed some criminal housewives with secret meth kitchens. Nothing is real or worthwhile unless it's terrible. What an ass."

She laid out a hot pink wetsuit, black pencil skirt, silky white blouse, and a lightweight blazer before showering quickly. When she got out, she had a message from Nicole.

Nicole: *Wanna go out tonight? A girls' night is long overdue.*

Claire: *Yes, please! I'm meeting with a real "visionary" today so I will definitely be in need of a drink. Or five. Pick you up at 7. I'll tell Min. Any chance Kyle can pick us up so we don't have to rock-paper-scissors for designated driver?*

Nicole: *He won't mind! He's working late anyway. See you later.*

Frowning at her reflection, she inspected for rogue eyebrow hairs and lurking blackheads. She applied a light coat of waterproof makeup and pinned her hair back. She snaked one foot into the hot pink wetsuit and jumped and stretched her way into the neoprene. That would have to do for the day. She put her business clothes in a garment bag and bent down to scratch Rosie's head.

"Be good today, okay? If I find one more chewed-up Italian shoe in your dog bed, you get no treats for a week."

Rosie panted happily, looking thoroughly unchastised.

Claire closed the door behind her and rolled her shoulders. At best, it was going to be a very long day. At worst, she might end up in jail for running Luke over with her car.

"HEY, STEVE!" CLAIRE HUSTLED ACROSS THE PARKING LOT toward a handsome man leaning against a Jet Ski. The river, wide and a bit muddy for her taste, flowed sluggishly behind him. "Ready for your run-through?"

"You have no idea. I've been waiting to take this baby out since I got back." He patted the side of the purple and silver Jet Ski fondly and flicked a speck of dust off the handlebars. Steve was a professional stunt man in Hollywood, and he returned home to Pennsylvania to take care of his mother when he wasn't training or shooting films.

"Tell me what you have in mind." Spots of foam floated lazily on top of the slow-moving water. Ripples caught rays of morning sunlight and sent them dancing over the surface. The air smelled strongly of mud and vegetation.

"It'll be easier to show you if you come out on the water with me."

"I was hoping you would ask." She kicked her shoes off. "Let's do this."

Steve handed her a lifejacket, which she squeezed into and buckled over her wetsuit. Claire straddled the seat and slid her sunglasses on.

The engine roared as they flew over the surface of the river, bouncing in the wake of a nearby boat. She leaned as Steve took a hard left. The spray tickled her toes, and they chased a heron from his perch in a nearby tree. All thoughts of Luke, Courtney, and everything else wrong in her life spilled from her mind. They spent a few minutes racing along the river as he pointed out places he'd like to position ramps for tricks.

When they pulled back to the dock, Claire was sure her hair was a hopeless disaster, and her cheeks hurt from smiling so much. Totally worth it. After Steve had loaded his machine back onto the trailer of his pickup truck, he helped her unbuckle her lifejacket.

"What the hell is *this*?" a shrill voice called from across the parking lot. A woman wearing yoga pants and a neon pink crop top slammed the door of an SUV.

"Tara! Hey, sweetie," Steve called. "Shit, shit, shit. What do we do?" he muttered to Claire.

"Relax, I've got this," she said. She slid a plain silver band from her right hand to her left ring finger. Mentally, she ran through what she remembered from Tara's Pinterest boards and social media posts.

The woman's brown hair gleamed in the sunlight as she crossed the cracked asphalt to the dock. Oversized sunglasses covered almost half of her deeply tanned face. "I get a call from Justine saying she went past the marina and saw you showing some *floozy* a good time on the river." She stabbed one dangerously pointy hot pink nail in Claire's direction. "Would you care to explain yourself?"

"He's giving me lessons!" Claire blurted out. "You must be Steve's girlfriend. Tara, right? I'm Claire." She held out her hand, but Tara only stared at it disdainfully.

"Lessons? Lessons for what?"

"On the Jet Ski. I'm buying my husband one for his birthday and I wanted to surprise him by giving him his first ride." She brushed an imaginary hair off her wetsuit, conspicuously flashing the faux wedding band.

"Since when are you giving lessons? You never told me

that. Is this some kind of joke?" Tara asked, rounding on Steve and putting her hands on her hips.

"I put an ad up on Craigslist looking for an instructor, and Steve answered. He said he was hoping to make a little extra money on the side so that he could get his girlfriend a puppy." Claire's hand flew to her mouth in mock horror. "Oh my god. Was that supposed to be a surprise? Did I ruin it?"

Steve finally caught on and sighed, glaring in Claire's direction. "Well, it's certainly not a surprise anymore."

Tara's mouth opened and a smile slowly stretched across her face, revealing perfectly white teeth. "You're going to get me a puppy?"

"You bet. You can get the smallest, most embarrassing one you want, and I will walk her proudly."

Tara rushed into his arms. "Really? Any kind I want? Even a Pomeranian?"

"Even one of those little fun-size versions. What do they call 'em?"

"Teacup?" Tara's voice screeched to such an octave that she was dangerously close to being audible only to a teacup Pomeranian. "You are the sweetest thing. I love you." She buried her face in his chest. "I'm sorry for accusing you. You know I trust you. But you have to admit this is kind of a weird thing to hear about secondhand." She broke their embrace and turned around.

"I'm sorry I called you a floozy." She stuck her hand out and grasped Claire's warmly. "And thank you for taking lessons from my amazing boyfriend here, because you're apparently paying for my new puppy!"

Claire laughed. "It's my pleasure. I'm so sorry to ruin the surprise, Steve. And thank you for the great lesson! You're still okay with doing one more tomorrow?"

"Absolutely," Steve said, slinging an arm over Tara's

shoulders. "Want to get some coffee, hon? Maybe afterwards we can go get some toys."

"Toys for us or for the dog?" Tara asked, winking.

He flushed and laughed. "Not in front of the customers, babe," he said as his hand snuck around and pinched her backside. She shrieked and swatted at him.

"Have a nice day, you two." Claire waggled a few fingers at Tara's retreating figure.

Steve turned around and mouthed "thank you" over his shoulder.

Claire loathed lying to the fiancées-to-be, but sometimes it was necessary to preserve the surprise. The black garment bag in the back seat of her car caught her eye. Shit, the meeting with Luke. The Jet Ski adventure had gone on longer than expected.

She grabbed her garment bag so hastily that she dropped it on the ground before hustling over to the public bathrooms. Escaping from her wetsuit was like trying to shuck herself out of an ear of corn. She crashed into the toilet paper dispenser and nearly put her foot in the toilet before successfully removing the suit. Straightening the collar of her sensible button-down shirt, she triumphantly threw open the stall. A glance at her watch showed it was 1:30. She had five minutes to fix her hair and makeup before she had to leave for the meeting with Luke.

Good Lord. Her hair looked like she had been electrocuted while simultaneously flailing around in a wind tunnel. Pulling emergency bobby pins out of her purse, she attempted to make herself presentable. She could only imagine what Luke would have to say about her appearance. At least her makeup was still intact.

Tossing everything back into her purse and mentally preparing herself to deal with an opinionated asshole,

Claire gripped the door handle and tugged. It moved about a centimeter and then stopped. Something metallic clinked.

"What the hell?"

She pulled again, harder this time, but it stayed firmly closed. She pushed just in case, but there was nothing but the faint metallic sound. There was no lock on the inside of the door. A tickle of panic crept up her spine.

"Hello?" she called. "Is anybody out there? I'm trapped in the bathroom." She pounded the door with her fist. But there had only been one other car in the marina parking lot when she went inside.

"Okay, there's no need to panic. The park must just close the restrooms at..." She checked her watch again. "1:35 in the afternoon. Sure. That seems like a normal time to close restrooms."

She tried for another minute to open the door, pushing and pulling, even tugging up on the handle. As the panic rose, she stepped away from the door and took a few steadying breaths.

"You can do this. You are an educated, capable woman. What do we have here?" She scanned the small room. A narrow window with frosted glass sat above a radiator. Crossing the tiles with her heart hammering in her ears, she turned the dusty lock and pressed her palms to the window-pane. The window was definitely less than twelve inches wide, and it was clearly meant for nothing more than airing out the bathroom. It was her only choice. She gathered all her strength to shove against the glass that clearly hadn't been used in years. It squealed as it slowly rose.

"Right. I can do this." She stared at the window. The four slices of pizza she had eaten the night before may have been a mistake. Another watch check. It was 1:40 now, and if she didn't leave in the next couple minutes she would be late.

Being late was not an option, especially for a meeting with an egotistical asshat.

She climbed onto the radiator on her knees and gently tossed her purse out the window and onto the ground below. Great, now her birthday present from her mom was almost certainly scuffed. Should she exit feetfirst or head-first? Boobs or butt would surely be the point where she got stuck, but if she turned herself sideways and slid out feet-first, toes pointed like a ballerina... The wood scraped and bit at her legs, drawing the hem of her pencil skirt up. And now she was going to be arrested for indecent exposure. Awesome.

Her knees passed through the gap, and even her thighs. But when her under-butt hit the sill, everything came to a screeching halt. There she was, trapped half in and half out of the tiny, outdated public bathroom. Twisting her hips and flailing her legs, she couldn't go any farther. And her purse was now on the ground outside. She was an idiot.

She wiggled forward on the radiator, climbing back inside and curling her body until her knees cleared the window. Her heart hammered in her ears, and her hands shook. This was bad. This was very bad.

Spotting a vent above one of the toilets, Claire climbed up onto the tank without hesitation. The vent cover was nailed in instead of screwed in. She whipped a bobby pin out of her hair and jammed it between the vent cover and the wall. As she dug her fingernails into the vent cover and pulled it off the wall, a cloud of dust descended directly into her face. She sneezed so hard she nearly fell backward into the toilet.

"Oh, thank god," she said, coughing and choking through the dust. The vent was wider than the window and seemed to lead a short distance through the wall to the adjacent men's bathroom. Hopefully, that one wouldn't be locked. She hoisted herself into a seated position on the top of the stall. Calling upon every Core Crusher Pilates class she had taken in the past year, Claire gripped the stall and managed to slide one leg, then the other, into the vent.

Oh, fabulous. This vent probably hadn't been cleaned in the fifty years since it was built. Closing her eyes and praying that there wasn't a family of spiders taking up residence, she shimmied deeper into the vent and sneezed violently.

After a full yard of shimmying, her turquoise heels made contact with another vent cover. She slammed her feet against it, and it popped out of the wall like a cork from a bottle of champagne. Scooting like an inchworm, she lowered herself out of the vent, onto a urinal, and finally onto the tile floor.

She collapsed on the floor for a moment, breathing heavily. Her prim button-down shirt was so covered in dirt and dust that it looked like she had crawled out of the Paris catacombs. She climbed to her feet, checking her shoes for any damage. They, at least, emerged unscathed.

Holding her breath, she gripped the bathroom door and tugged as hard as she could. The door opened so quickly and so easily that it almost slammed into her face.

"Freedom!" she cried, staggering out into the sunlight.

She immediately zeroed in on the door to the women's restroom. A padlocked chain coiled around the door handle. A chill ran down her spine. Why would the park staff lock one door and not the other?

She didn't have time to speculate. Shoving all thoughts of this harrowing experience from her mind, she ran around the corner of the building and picked up her purse, which was thankfully still waiting for her in the dirt.

She sprinted across the parking lot as quickly as she could in her heels. There were no other cars in the parking lot. Who the hell had locked the door?

Unlocking her car and jamming her key in the ignition, Claire barely buckled her seatbelt before reversing out of her spot and careening for the park exit. Her vent escapade had cost her time. It was 1:50. She was going to be late to Luke's.

CHAPTER FOUR

To Do:
- *Call Marco about bow and arrow*
- *Send Ryan's care package*
- *Stop thinking about egotistical asshat and his pecs*

FOLLOWING THE BRITISH-TONED DIRECTIONS FROM THE GPS, Claire cut back through town and emerged into the surrounding countryside. As she zipped past trees, ponds, and countless cows, the air felt cleaner—at least until she passed a farmer fertilizing his field. She wrinkled her nose and rolled up her window.

"You can do this," she said to herself as she turned onto Stone Bridge Road. She glanced at her reflection in the rearview mirror and nearly drove off the road when she didn't recognize the person staring back at her. Splotches of dirt were smeared across her forehead and cheeks. She wiped at them frantically with her hand, but it was no use.

Resigning herself to the world's fastest Wet-Nap bath before heading into Luke's, she put her hands back on the wheel. "You may be covered in dust and dead bugs, but you are a professional. You just have to get through a one-hour meeting with this asshole, and then you can reward yourself with a scalding shower and some margaritas. A mysterious bathroom lock and an opinionated dickwad are not going to stop you from making the biggest proposal of your career flawless."

She slowed as her car crested a hill. She didn't often get the chance to leave the city during prime proposal season, and the emerald green fields that surrounded her filled her with a deep sense of calm. Wildflowers dotted the hill to her left. A herd of cows grazed on the right.

When she saw Luke's house number on a mailbox, Claire turned onto a paved driveway flanked by stone walls. Not ostentatious at all. The driveway wound nearly a quarter mile through the woods. She caught brief glimpses of landscaping projects—an unfilled pond to the left, a dilapidated garden shed up ahead, and what appeared to be a semi-constructed tree house set back from the drive.

"Interesting," she said, tapping her fingers on her steering wheel. It definitely needed some work, but she could already see possibilities for decorating the entrance and driveway for Nicole's proposal.

She brought her car to a stop on the asphalt and, for a moment, simply stared at the gargantuan structure in front of her. Beautifully finished wood and natural stone covered the exterior, bending in natural arches around the door and windows. A two-story turret rose majestically from the northwest corner. A stone pathway wound from the driveway through the lush grass, leading to the wide porch with its two turquoise Adirondack chairs.

"Holy crap," she said. This was where Camera Guy lived? Stupid rich jerk.

She snapped herself out of her trance and pulled another Wet-Nap out of the glove box. She was not about to meet Luke looking like she had just come from raiding an ancient Egyptian tomb. She wiped frantically at her face, smudging her mascara. Her blouse was still covered in dust. Maybe she should just put the wet suit back on? She glanced into her back seat, seriously considering it, when a knock at her window made her jump.

"You are almost fifteen minutes late," Luke said. Worn jeans hung loosely from his hips, and the black T-shirt he wore stretched over impressively defined pecs.

Claire threw her door open. "I'm sorry about that. My last meeting went a little long."

His green eyes swept from her toes to her rather disheveled hair. "What the hell happened to you? Playing some light rugby with your nephew?"

She glared at him. "No. He lives in California. This particular meeting happened to involve a Jet Ski and...well, let's not worry about the rest." She didn't owe him any explanations.

She slammed her car door and took a few steps into the yard. It needed a decent mow and some fresh mulch, but there was definite potential.

He raised his eyebrows. "You're doing a Jet Ski proposal? Seriously? Is everyone just made out of money here? Or maybe all your clients are determined to start their married life off in bankruptcy?"

She shot him a dirty look. "You're one to talk." She nodded at the mammoth house. "My client is a professional stunt man in Hollywood. He makes decent money, and he wanted to propose to his girlfriend in the place where they first met. He botched a jump when he was practicing on the river, and she saved his life."

She stared him down, daring him to find a way to mock one of the top five greatest meet-cutes she had ever encountered.

Luke considered this for a moment and shrugged noncommittally. "If he's a stunt man in Hollywood, what's he doing here?"

"He comes here to take care of his mom when he's between films. You know, something people with a shred of empathy and kindness do. You're probably not familiar."

There was nothing in their unofficial verbal contract that said she had to be nice to him. She rolled her shoulders back and glanced around. Was his heart still in his chest, or had it been replaced by an old paint can full of rusty nails and broken glass?

Luke cracked a smile. Maybe she could find a way to shove him into that half-filled pond down the driveway. He clearly needed to be taken down a peg.

She walked past him and turned a full circle, heels sinking into the grass. A simple wooden swing hung under a sprawling oak tree. In the flower bed, daffodils bobbed in the breeze.

"This is beautiful." She stepped lightly up the wooden steps and brushed her hand over one of the stone pillars that flanked the porch. Damn it, she had accidentally paid him a compliment.

He came to stand next to her. "You know, I think that's the first nice thing you've said to me since we've met. Thank you. It didn't look quite like this when I bought it, but I've been working on it."

"I didn't even know this was out here." She held her fingers in a frame formation and closed one eye. How would everything look on the final night? With enough decorations and a spruced-up yard before the big day, flawless. That is, if Luke cooperated and didn't fight her on every single aspect.

He raised his eyebrows. "Come on. I'm a filmmaker, and I don't even do the finger thing."

Filmmaker. Barf. She waved a hand to shush him and resumed her position. "The driveway is certainly wide enough to accommodate the carriage," she decided.

"There's going to be a carriage? An actual horse-drawn carriage? How much is Kyle spending on this?"

She hefted a binder labeled *W's Proposal* out of her purse. She shoved it toward him. "All my ideas are in there. See what you think. Oh, and don't lose it unless you want me to use your lifeless body as a prop for the proposal."

He ignored her threat. "Who's 'W'?"

"Huh?"

"It says 'W's Proposal.' Has Kyle been lying about his real name all this time?"

"Oh, no. I changed the initial in case Nicole came over and saw it. I want her to be completely oblivious until that day. By the way, if she ever asks you what we're working on, we're doing a proposal for your brother, Johnny."

"But I don't have a brother."

"For the next three weeks, you do."

Claire stared him down before turning to give the yard one final glance. For once, he didn't have a comment. It was time to get down to business.

"A few decorations could really enhance the romantic feel—some fairy lights in the trees. And here"—she indicated the meandering walkway—"I'll bring some solar-powered lanterns from the warehouse so no one breaks their neck in the dark."

"I'll handle it. I've been meaning to get some, anyway."

Sure he was. His idea of solar-powered lanterns was probably Christmas lights shoved in Miller Lite bottles. Not today, Satan. She made a mental note to keep that item on her To Do list.

She held her arms out in front of her and mimed dancing on the asphalt. "Everyone will be singing or humming this song that she loves—well, you heard it already. Last night. Anyway, I think it would be so romantic if her family held long, white candles while they sing. As long as you're okay with it, I mean."

He squinted through the window into his foyer. "I haven't tested how candlelight looks on camera in here yet. I'll give it a try and let you know if it fits my vision."

She bit her lip. Her hands balled into fists at her side. What a prickly, unwelcoming asshole. Would he even allow her to see the inside, or would estrogen in his toxic male space not fit his *vision*?

"Could I see the inside? This door is stunning." She reached out to stroke the iron swirls that blossomed over the glass.

Luke motioned for her to follow him inside and opened the doors.

"I'm still unpacking." He brushed a hand over the back of his neck as he led the way.

Inside, miles of hardwood floors stretched through the house, occasionally covered by surprisingly tasteful rugs. The kitchen stood to the right, all gleaming stainless-steel appliances and granite countertops. A sun-drenched break-fast nook practically begged her to whip up some eggs Benedict and read the newspaper.

The furniture was a bit sparse in the living room to the left, and cardboard boxes labeled in sloppy handwriting were stacked haphazardly. A grand piano sat imposingly in front of a huge bay window, and several guitars hung on a far wall.

"So, not only are you a wildly successful award-winning director, but you're also secretly a musician?" Perhaps a compliment and discussion of hobbies would help remove the stick that appeared to be lodged up his ass. Not that he deserved any praise.

He shrugged. "I dabble."

It was worth a shot. She ran a hand over a polished mahogany banister, marveling at the cathedral ceilings.

"This house is like if a castle and a rich man's hunting cabin got married and had an enormous baby." Stretching out in front of that fireplace with a good book on a chilly winter evening would be divine.

"Think it'll do?"

"Hmm?" She swung her attention back to him.

"For the proposal, I mean."

"It's perfect. Listen, I know we got off to a rough start what with the breaking and entering and the neighbor with the shotgun, but I really appreciate you letting us use your home for the engagement. It's going to mean a lot to Kyle and Nicole."

"Anything for Kyle. We grew up together and made it through some pretty rough times. He lived in the house next door, and we used to communicate in Morse code by flashlight after lights out."

"Interesting." She tapped her chin. "That does explain why Kyle was able to successfully spell out 'boobs' in Morse code during an obscenely underwhelming game of Truth or Dare at Omega Phi."

He looked unimpressed. "Greek life sounds riveting. Do you want to see the ballroom next or the patio?"

She was still smiling from the mental picture she had of a younger, even more awkward Kyle crouching on his bed with a flashlight. "You have a ballroom? Like a real-life room for holding balls? Who did you buy this house from, Scarlett O'Hara?"

He smirked. "You're going to be hell to work with."

She shot him a disdainful look as she brushed past him. "You have no idea. Do you mind if I...?" She pointed toward the hallway.

"Be my guest."

She poked her head in each door she passed. One room held nothing but a row of computers, expensive-looking cameras, and a cluster of boom microphones.

"This is an awfully big house for one person," she observed.

"It's an investment."

"You're not planning on staying here forever?" The sooner he left West Haven, the simpler her life would be.

He shrugged. "Who knows what the future holds? I go where my work demands."

She wrinkled her nose. He had all the roots of an air plant. What a lonely way to live. She glanced over her shoulder. He was staring at a framed picture of an older woman in a yellow dress. Maybe she was the person who had removed every romantic bone from his body. "Is that why you moved back? Work?"

Luke nodded. "When I was in the Navy, I was stationed in Afghanistan and then California. I decided to get into film when I got out, so I stayed in LA because I figured it was my best shot. Went through school, the whole thing. Then I realized that there's more freedom with my particular area of expertise, and if you're good enough, you can pretty much get away with doing it anywhere you want. Every place has a story. Even West Haven."

It was the longest string of words she had ever heard him utter. As much as she hated to admit it, she wanted to know more.

"And what is your expertise?"

"True stories. Gritty, real, shocking."

"You sound like a journalist."

He scoffed. "This is much more than journalism."

Claire turned around again and rolled her eyes. She glanced at the series of framed pictures lining the hallway above the pristine white wainscoting. Who were all these people to Luke? And more importantly, why did she even care? "What are you working on while you're here?"

"Sorry, I can't discuss what I'm working on. I don't share anything about a project with outsiders until we're ready to start marketing, especially with this story. It's going to be sensational."

"Well, I'm glad to see the move hasn't damaged your ego."

He ignored her dig. "Tell me more about yourself. I like to know who I'm working with."

She crossed her arms and avoided eye contact. She wasn't about to give him more ammunition to needle her. "There's not much to tell."

"How did you get into this whole ridiculous proposal business?"

Here we go again. She bristled, ready to lash out, but a picture of a teenaged Kyle and Luke on a boat caught her eye. She needed to remember why she was here. He had no power over her. She wasn't going to let him under her skin.

"It's a long story. Is this the ballroom?" She tugged on a set of French doors, but they didn't budge.

"That's my office," he explained. "I keep it locked."

"Oh," she said, quickly withdrawing her hands like a scolded child. "Sorry."

"I keep everything under wraps when I'm working on sensitive projects."

"You're really killing me with the anticipation here."

She slowed as she approached the last set of doors. She turned the lever handles, and the doors swung open to reveal a massive ballroom. Forty yards of polished marble floors gleamed. Arched windows stretched the entire length of the room and allowed sunlight to spill inside. Heavy, wine-colored drapes flanked each window.

Claire hadn't realized she'd been holding her breath until she exhaled noisily, turning another full circle just inside the door.

"Holy crap." Her footsteps echoed in the empty room as she crossed to the windows. "It smells a bit musty, but if we open up these doors for a while it should freshen up. We could add a few, small round tables along that wall, and there will still be plenty of space for dancing. This room is just perfection." She poked one of the drapes forcefully, releasing a cloud of dust. "Well, almost."

"I'm thinking about turning it into a gym."

She gasped. "And ruin these marble floors? That would be sacrilege. I mean, I hope you'll consider leaving it as is until after the proposal."

"What's your favorite flavor of ice cream?" he asked.

"What? Ice cream?" She stared at him. A dimple appeared in his left cheek when he smiled.

"You know, ice cream. It's cold and creamy and delicious. Ever heard of it?"

She walked away from him, examining the floor-to-ceiling empty shelves on the back wall. Dust catchers. "What does that have to do with anything?"

"I told you. I like to know who I'm working with."

"If I give the wrong answer, are you going to open a trap-door and drop me into a tank full of sharks?"

Luke leaned against the wall, a slow grin spreading over his face again. His jawline could chip a diamond. "Are you always so defensive? It's a simple question."

"Teaberry. My favorite ice cream is teaberry," she said.

"What makes you so interested in these ridiculous proposals?" he fired back quickly, as if trying to surprise her into answering.

Claire's hand flexed into a fist, and she took some deep breaths to stop herself from smashing it into his face.

"Proposals are *not* ridiculous. They are a pledge of unconditional love and commitment between two people, motivated by the purest of emotions. In sickness and in health. From this day forward, they will never again feel alone in this world."

His eyebrows rose, but she chose to ignore it.

"It's one of the most beautiful things in the civilized world. They're the first step in a couple's happily ever after."

"I'm sorry—what is the current divorce rate in the United States?" Luke interjected. "Close to fifty percent?"

"And do you know what is one of the primary causes of so many of these divorces?"

"Adultery?"

"No. Well, yes, but also because of a breakdown in communication. And what could be a better way to set a precedent of open and honest communication in a marriage than a beautiful, thoughtful, and romantic proposal that lets your significant other know exactly how you feel? Have you ever looked into the eyes of a woman who has just accepted a marriage proposal?"

Something in Luke's gaze hardened. "No."

"Just wait. Wait for Kyle and Nicole's proposal and watch her. Then you'll understand why I have such a love of creating these moments for people. It makes it all worth it. Every stressful moment, every bungled decoration, every encounter with self-centered filmmakers. All worth it."

"I'll take your word for it."

Claire walked over to him and placed a hand lightly on his arm. Her fingertips tingled where they touched his skin. "I'm sorry."

He looked bewildered. "Sorry for what?"

"For whatever happened in your past that turned you into this cynical person."

He scoffed but didn't brush her hand away. "I'm not cynical. I'm a realist."

She pursed her lips and took two steps back. She rolled her neck, trying to release some of the tension that was building up in her shoulders. "Fine. Can I *realistically* see the rest of the house so I can get out of your hair? Do you know much about the previous owners?"

That cool, off-putting demeanor disappeared, and he looked alert, interested again. "Harvey and Lorraine Davenport built it in the nineties." He rapped his knuckle on the wall.

"Sounds like a couple who would own a house like this," she observed.

"Harvey was the founder and CEO of—get this—Davenport Toilet Company."

She snorted and clapped a hand over her mouth.

"He started the company in the sixties. For whatever reason, Davenport Toilet Company grew to be the most successful toilet manufacturer on the eastern seaboard. He personally replaced toilets in the White House, in penthouses in New York. They were the first American company to offer built-in bidets and Japanese-style toilets. When I toured the house, there was a picture of him shaking hands with two different presidents."

"Have you seen the sheer number of Mexican restaurants in West Haven? Of course he became successful. People are probably cracking bowls left and right after having enchiladas at La Casa de Taco."

Luke laughed, a warm, velvety sound, and Claire couldn't help but smile in response.

"Why did they sell?" she asked.

"They moved to Colorado to be near their grandchildren."

"And you swooped in and secured the Toilet King's castle."

"I did. And now my best friend can ask his girlfriend to marry him while surrounded by a legacy built on human waste," he said, sweeping his hand toward the chandelier that clung to the cathedral ceiling.

"You're kind of putting a damper on my romantic vision here." Nicole would never learn about Harvey Davenport.

Luke winked and led her outside.

AFTER A THOROUGH INSPECTION OF THE REST OF THE HOUSE, including an outdoor pool, the first floor bathroom (which did indeed include a luxury toilet with a bidet and heated seat,) and what could only be described as a glorious man cave complete with a foosball table, dartboard, and screening room, Claire deemed Luke's house the perfect place for the last scene of Kyle's proposal.

Finally, she was almost done with this insufferable man. She just had to be professional for another ten minutes and she would be home free.

"If you need help moving the boxes upstairs for the party, please let me know, and I'll make my team available," she said as they returned to the front of the house. "I realize this is a little intrusive, but would you mind if I stayed here for a minute to write down some notes?"

"My place is your place," he said with a slow smile.

As he turned around to leave the room, she took a moment to surreptitiously check him out. The worn jeans hung low on his hips, accentuating a truly spectacular butt.

As he reached the threshold, he said without turning around, "Stop it."

About to perch on his piano bench with her notebook, Claire froze mid-squat. "Stop what?" she asked, bewildered. Maybe the piano bench was an antique?

"Stop checking out my ass. I'm not a piece of man candy."

She flushed. "Don't flatter yourself."

Luke poured himself a glass of water from a pitcher in the fridge and then disappeared down the hallway.

Mortified but determined to ignore it, she took one more appreciative look at the gorgeous hardwood floors and crown molding before opening her notebook.

After spending about twenty minutes scribbling thoughts and ideas, Claire gathered her things and made her way toward the front door.

"Luke?" she called out. "I'm going to head out. Don't forget we have a meeting tomorrow at the antique store to look for props, and then we're going to discuss the rest of the locations. Also, don't lose my binder."

"I wouldn't dare," he said from behind, startling her. He was tugging on a sleeveless workout shirt as he descended the stairs, and she caught a glimpse of a six-pack. Of course he had a six-pack.

"Good." She ignored the heat spreading from her stomach to the tips of her fingers.

"Are you really not going to tell me why you look like you crawled out of a combat zone? A girl like you is always prepared. I doubt a Jet Ski did that."

"A girl like me?" She arched an eyebrow at him.

"Woman," he said as his eyes dipped down before sliding back up to meet her gaze.

"Not that I owe you any explanation, but—well. It was weird. I went to the public restroom at the marina to change out of my wetsuit. While I was inside, someone locked the door with a chain."

"A park attendant?"

"I assume so. You'd think you'd check if someone was inside before locking a restroom, though."

"Especially in the middle of the afternoon," he said thoughtfully. "So, you crawled out the window?"

He turned away from her, pulling a protein shaker bottle from a cabinet and filling it with water.

"Too narrow. I ended up having to crawl through the vent into the men's restroom."

Luke whirled back around. "You crawled through a vent in a public restroom? Why didn't you just call someone?"

"I may have dropped my purse out the window prematurely."

He burst out laughing. "No wonder you were late."

She regarded him coldly. "I assure you it won't happen again."

"I know it won't. My time is very valuable, and professionals don't waste each other's time," he said, like a parent scolding a child. His biceps flexed as he screwed the cap back on his bottle.

Claire's mouth nearly fell open. A hundred half-formed retorts flooded her mind, but none of them were right. There were no words for a douchebag of this magnitude. She turned on her turquoise heel and stomped out the front door, closing it behind her far harder than was necessary.

CHAPTER FIVE

To Do:
- Buy first aid kit
- Pick up package at post office
- Update spreadsheet and cost analysis for S
proposal

"CAN YOU BELIEVE THIS GUY, ROSIE?" CLAIRE ASKED AS SHE drove down Main Street. "*Professionals don't waste each other's time.* Like it's so professional of him to harass me about ice cream and flash his stupid six-pack at me while I'm taking notes on how to create the most beautiful day of my best friend's life."

Rosie declined to comment. She was strapped into her seatbelt harness in the back seat, panting happily.

Still fuming, Claire crawled to a stop at yet another red light. At this rate, they would never reach the dog park. She drummed her fingers on her steering wheel, willing the light to change. The signpost next to the traffic light caught her eye—Firestone Lane. A lead balloon dropped into her stomach. Courtney's street.

Instinctively, Claire activated her turn signal. It would probably be more peaceful for everyone if they took a nice quiet walk on a residential street instead of the dog park. The last time they had gone, Rosie had spent the entire visit trying to herd a family of territorial dachshunds. It didn't go well.

After some quick Googling on her phone, she found Courtney's address then pulled to a stop in front of a red brick house with a picket fence and impeccably groomed yard. Glancing at the mailbox, she exited the car and extracted Rosie from her harness.

They walked down the sidewalk, enjoying the sunshine as they strolled past rows of small but well-maintained ranch homes. Rosie darted from one side of the sidewalk to the other, sniffing furiously as though it was her sole duty in life to pee on every blade of grass and lamp post on the block. An elderly woman in a straw hat and overalls waved at them as they passed. Children's giggles came from somewhere out of sight.

A house with sunny yellow siding and crisp white shutters came into view. Courtney's house. It looked smaller in person than it had on the news. An involuntary shiver ripped through Claire. She could imagine Courtney here, slamming her car door, hauling a reusable shopping bag full of wine bottles into the house. Stepping out the front door for a run.

As they were observing the house, a car slid into the driveway. *Crap.* Caught in the act of snooping. She bent down to untie and retie her shoe.

"Claire?" a man's voice called.

She shot upright, nearly banging her head on a garbage can someone had left by the sidewalk. The man had stepped out of the car and was clutching a bag of groceries. A baby carrot tumbled out of one of the bags, and Rosie darted for it, dragging Claire with her.

"Oh, John. I didn't know you lived here," she lied.

"Moved here two years ago," he said, shifting the bag of groceries to his other hand.

"It's a beautiful neighborhood. I was so sorry to hear about Courtney. How are you doing?" She reached out and touched his arm.

"As well as can be expected." He cast his eyes downwards. There were bags under his eyes, and the tan, cocky jock that had broken Courtney's bed freshman year was gone, replaced by a sallow, thin shell.

"Do the police have any leads?"

He shook his head. "It's like she just disappeared. She hasn't used her phone or her credit card. No one's heard from her. A couple of neighbors' security cameras caught her on her jogging route that morning, but the last sighting was about four blocks that way." He pointed north.

"I'm so sorry to hear that," Claire said. Gah, she was bad at this. What did you say to someone whose wife either ran away or was kidnapped? Did Hallmark have a card for that?

"I really hope they find her," she added.

"Me too. She was so excited that morning. She's up for a huge promotion at work. Her interview was supposed to be on Monday. Running helps calm her nerves. I never should have let her leave."

"You don't think someone at her work would have..."

"I don't know what to think. I just want her to come home."

She leaned in and wrapped John in a hug. They may not have been close in college, but he always shared his pizza.

"Well, we'd better get going. Here, take my card. Please let me know if there's anything I can do for you." She broke the embrace and pulled a pristine business card out of her wallet. "I'll be thinking of you."

"Thanks. It was nice to see you." He waved with one hand as he walked up the driveway and disappeared inside the house.

"Oof," Claire muttered, leading Rosie quickly down the sidewalk in the direction that John had pointed. She made a mental note to read some blogs about grief and how to be less painfully awkward around potentially widowed spouses.

She counted the blocks as they continued down the cracked sidewalk, stopping when she got to four. There was nothing remarkable or frightening about this block—no creepy, white kidnapping vans advertising free candy, no shadowy corners where someone with ill intentions could hide. Elderly men in white New Balance sneakers puttered around on riding lawn mowers. Women with headphones and jogging strollers nearly drove Claire and Rosie off the sidewalk.

They were passing by a weathered picket fence when a metallic *clang* rang out behind them. Claire whirled around, goosebumps running down her arms. Rosie growled, staring at the driveway of the house closest to them. Was that shadow beneath the minivan someone crouched down?

"What is it, Ro?" she asked softly, eyes probing the void under the van. Casting a glance around her, she crouched suddenly to the ground, fully expecting to see a pair of human eyes blinking back at her.

"It's just a damn oil pan," she said out loud, clutching a hand to her chest.

Rosie continued to growl, but Claire was less concerned. Rosie also growled at delivery men, other dogs on TV, and any household appliance that made a noise louder than eighty decibels. That noise had probably just been a wayward squirrel knocking over a trashcan.

"Come on," she ordered, tugging the dog back up the street. She couldn't quite get rid of the prickly feeling at the base of her spine. Was someone watching her? She was being ridiculous. Even if Courtney had been taken by the Widowmaker, it wasn't like he'd still be here, elbow-deep in a flower bed.

When they had almost reached the end of the block, Claire abruptly whirled around again, staring intently at the spot where they had heard the sound. Was it her imagination, or had a flash of black just disappeared around the corner of the house? It was probably just a cat. She was allowing her mom's jabber about the Widowmaker to get to her.

She pulled Rosie in a bit tighter and made sure her cell phone was in her other hand. She was being crazy, spooked by the disappearance of a notoriously flighty girl. Why was she even here? There was nothing she could do. Shoving the noise to the back of her mind, she led her dog across the intersection.

They walked up and down the block three times—just in case—but nothing seemed out of place. Claire wasn't sure what she had expected to find—a puddle of blood in the street that the police missed? A laminated ransom note?

Shaking her head, she turned around, tugging Rosie away from a piece of roadkill and heading back to the car.

Hours later, Claire wrapped her hair in hot rollers, still seething about her encounter with Luke. As she applied a smoky eye shadow to her lids, her phone buzzed. When she unlocked it, a text from an unfamiliar number appeared.

Remember we're meeting at ten tomorrow. I don't care how many Jet Skis you have to ride before noon—it's unprofessional to be late.

She flung her phone into her purse on the bathroom floor and nearly kicked it. Rosie looked up from her position curled around Claire's feet and yawned.

"Men!" She ripped the cover off her lipstick. "Me, unprofessional? I'm so professional that I crawled through a vent to make it to our meeting. He's the one who essentially broke into my house because he didn't feel like waiting for our scheduled meeting."

She applied a crimson lipstick and brushed mascara onto her lashes. The black dress she had chosen for the outing clung to her hourglass figure, and the boning in the bodice made her girls extra perky. Black stilettos and pearl studs completed the outfit. She may have sworn off men, but she wasn't joining a convent.

"You know what, Rosie? It's been a long day. I'm not wearing a bra tonight." She unhooked her strapless bra and, grasping it with one hand, yanked it out like a magician revealing a handkerchief. She tucked it back into her lingerie drawer in her bedroom. Bras were one of Rosie's favorite contraband chew toys.

"Please be a good girl while Mommy's gone," she pleaded as she unrolled her hair. "I better not find another poop in the closet when I get home. I love you." Rosie's puppy dog eyes nearly had her stripping her heels back off and sliding into pajamas, but she had made plans. A girls' night was overdue, and she needed to make sure that Nicole wasn't getting suspicious about Kyle proposing. The ring was hidden in the safe at the warehouse, but Nicole had an uncanny ability to dig up the truth. Claire bent down to Rosie's furry face and kissed her between the eyebrows.

Claire grabbed her purse and flung the front door open, then nearly kicked a package wrapped in brown paper. Her mom's return address in Florida was stamped at the top. What in the world had she sent her this time? Knowing her mother, it was probably loose-leaf, aura-cleansing tea or black tourmaline crystals. She had enough new age knick-knacks in her closet to open her own apothecary.

Claire gingerly set it on her kitchen counter and tugged at a corner of the packaging. A plain but sturdy cardboard box emerged. There weren't any airholes, so at least she hadn't tried to mail Claire a live scorpion to throw at anyone who dared to threaten her. It wouldn't be the strangest thing her mother had ever done.

Smiling at the mental image of a black scorpion dangling from Wendy's beak-like lips, she pulled a box cutter from her kitchen drawer and slashed the tape. A bright yellow stun gun sat formidably in a layer of cushioning. A deck of tarot cards was nestled next to the handle. Claire shut the box again, shoving it to the middle of the kitchen island where Rosie couldn't possibly investigate it, and pulled out her phone. She stabbed at the screen and dialed her mother's phone number.

"Hello, darling. How is your day going?" her mother's ethereal voice poured from the phone.

"Mom. What on earth did you send me?"

"Oh good, you got it. It's for your protection, Clairebear. You can shoot it from a distance so you don't have to get too close."

"Mom, I don't need a stun gun." She shivered at the sight of the box. "And what's with the cards?"

"They're tarot cards, sweetie. I was hoping you would let me do a reading. I keep seeing danger in your future, and I was hoping the cards would give us another clue. Oh, and by the way, Grandma says hello and she wishes you would wear some longer skirts."

"My dead grandmother thinks my skirts are too short?" Claire asked. She glanced down at her outfit, then up at the corners of her ceiling as if expecting to see the bespectacled ghost of her grandmother staring disapprovingly at her.

"Yes, sweetie. We had a nice chat the other day via spirit board. She finally gave me the last ingredient to that lemon cake she made every Easter. Would you believe it's bacon grease? I'll send you the recipe."

She shook her head, glancing at the small white vase that stood on her console table. She had bought it from the estate sale after her grandmother had passed away. "Thanks, Mom. We'll set up a video conference soon to do the card thing. I'll talk to you later."

The phone was heavy in her hand as she stared at the box again. There was no way in hell she was bringing the stun gun to the club, and Rosie had an uncanny ability to sniff out anything that could cause her harm. The stun gun would have to go in the doggie-proof, secret hiding spot. Claire picked the stun gun up with both hands and moved slowly, half expecting it to go off unprovoked.

She sank to her knees in her bedroom. The loose floorboard next to her bed groaned as she pried it open, revealing a small hole. She pinched the handle of the Taser between her thumb and finger and placed it in the hole. If it went off by itself, could it set her bed on fire? Vowing to do some research, she stood and brushed the dog hair from her legs.

"Grandma is crazy," she informed Rosie as she bent to say goodbye again. Even if there was a West Haven Widow-maker, it wasn't as if Claire was in danger. She wasn't married, so she didn't fit the profile. The deadbolt clanged as she locked it. No one was in the hallway. She put her hands out to her sides and did a few moves from The Charleston. Front door was definitely locked. She hurried out to her car, pushing the thought of her new weapon to the back of her mind.

She picked up Mindy first, throwing open her passenger side door as the car rolled to a stop. Mindy had ditched her glasses for contacts and was wearing a tight, red, sequined number. She nearly tripped on her gold heels as she got in.

"Holy crap, Min, you look hot! How was your birthday? Tell me everything."

Mindy laughed and buckled her seatbelt. The gold bangles on her arm jingled. "Thanks! It was great, actually. I met a guy at the club last night," she said, wiggling her eyebrows.

Claire lifted one hand off the steering wheel to give Mindy a high five. "You are my hero. I want to hear all about it, but I guess we have to wait till Nicole gets here." She pressed down on the accelerator as they exited the city limits. A sprinkle of stars was visible in the inky black sky now that they were away from the city lights. She was silent for about ten seconds. "Ok, just give me a hint. A little tidbit. I'm dying here."

"Well, let's just say that he was rather well-endowed, and he might have had a few interesting piercings."

"Piercings?!" Claire squealed. "Where, exactly?"

"Let's wait till Nicole gets in," she said with a knowing look as they pulled to a stop outside Nicole's house. Claire beeped the horn twice.

"Speaking of men, how did the meeting go with hot, obnoxious Camera Guy today?"

Claire pressed a hand to her forehead. "I have never worked with someone so infuriatingly egotistical and stubborn in my entire life. He keeps talking about how everything we do is ridiculous. And he chastised me about seventy-five times because I was a few minutes late to the appointment."

Mindy's mouth gaped. "You were late? What the hell happened? Did a meteor crash onto the highway?"

"No, but something weird did happen. I'll tell you later. But you're missing the point," Claire said. "We hate him. You'll see tomorrow. He's the worst. I'm too annoyed with him to even bother doing my usual internet stalking to see if he's fit to work the proposal. I don't want to know any more about him than I have to."

"Wow. He really got under your skin," Mindy observed. "Also, speaking of douchebag camera guy, tell me our cover."

"You know what it is."

"I know, but the more times we repeat it, the less likely we will accidentally tell her after three daiquiris."

"Fine. We're working on a proposal for Luke's brother, and Luke is helping with the camerawork."

"Perfect. Shit, here she comes. Hi, Coli!" Mindy called as Nicole flung open the car door. She slid into the back seat, a short, strappy black dress clinging to her athletic frame. Her shoulder-length brown hair was straightened into a sleek bob.

"You guys will not believe the day I had." Nicole immediately launched into a story with her silvery voice. "We were in this field that was just starting to bloom, and the sun was at this perfect angle. And I've got this toddler in a basket with this precious little hat on, and his mom is like *screaming* at me because I couldn't get him to look at the camera. I was trying to explain to her that he doesn't need to look right at the camera, but apparently, she thinks I'm some sort of department store photographer doing school portraits. So then when I tried to get him to actually look at me, I made him laugh with a cow puppet and he projectile vomited onto the little Calvin Klein outfit he was wearing."

"Oh my gosh." Claire inched the car away from the curb.

"Holy crap. What did she do then?" Mindy asked, turning around to face Nicole.

"She tried to kick my tripod out from under my camera, and then she left saying she refused to pay for such amateur service."

Claire gasped.

"I will crack that bitch like an ice cube tray." Mindy slapped the dashboard with one hand.

"Will you text me her address? I'm going to send that Neanderthal a self-activating glitter cannon. She'll never get it out of the floorboards," Claire added, making a mental note to make another, more aggressive attempt to vacuum the glitter that remained in the cracks of her floor after a particularly wild New Year's Eve party. She could only imagine what Luke would have to say about the professionalism of having glitter in her floorboards. Idiot.

"Thanks, guys. It just sucks. Customers like her make me wonder if I should even be a photographer."

Claire slapped on her turn signal and veered off the road. Mindy and Nicole screamed. Claire lurched to a stop in a parking spot outside a small bodega. With her car in park, Claire turned around to face Nicole and pointed her index finger at her.

"Do not ever let some bored, khaki-wearing helicopter mom from the Heights make you second guess yourself. You are a magnificent and accomplished photographer with the most diverse portfolio I have ever seen. Who was asked to shoot for the state championship football game when they were only seventeen?"

"Me," Nicole muttered.

"And who was personally contacted to take formal portraits of their photography professor's family? Which is literally the highest form of praise you could ever expect from a professor?"

"Also me," Nicole said with a small smile.

"And remind me. Who was contacted by the visitors' bureau to capture West Haven in all of its expansive, if slightly smoggy, glory?" Mindy broke in.

"Fine. I'll keep the studio," Nicole said, looking considerably happier.

"Good. Now let's dance our asses off." Claire activated her turn signal and pulled out of the spot.

She parked on the street a short distance from the raucous club. The heavy bass thumped so loudly from within that the building's windows shuddered with each beat. A line stretched down the sidewalk, cordoned off with a red velvet rope. She tugged the neckline of her dress down and pulled the hemline up a tad, fixing an enthusiastic smile on her face as they approached the bouncer.

"There he is! How did we know the most handsome man in the town would be working the door tonight?" She stood on her tippy toes and planted a kiss on each cheek of the hulking, six foot man clad entirely in black.

"Well, hey, if it isn't my girls," Carl said affectionately. "Come right in." He lifted the velvet rope and allowed them to bypass the line. Several hopeful patrons shot them dirty looks from the front of the line. Nicole gave them a cheery wave and tossed her hair over her shoulder as they passed.

They entered the dimly lit club. Pictures of celebrities who had allegedly visited the establishment vibrated with every thump of the bass, threatening to fall off the wall. They made their way through the throng of club-goers, dodging spilled beer and flailing elbows.

"Yeah, hi," Claire said to the bartender. "We're going to need three margaritas on the rocks, please."

"You've got it," the bartender said.

Once their drinks were in hand, they settled at a round table near the dance floor. The table had a sticky film on it, and the chairs had dings and cracks around the frame from being repeatedly knocked over. She perched on the very edge of her seat and did her best not to touch anything.

"Okay," she said after a delicate sip of her drink. "Min, you have to tell us about the guy from last night."

Mindy downed nearly a third of her drink in one gulp before slapping it back on the table. "Okay, so I was just dancing right over there by the DJ table." She pointed at the far corner of the room. "And he came up to me and said, 'happy birthday,' because, you know, I was wearing my birthday crown."

"Of course," Nicole said, raising her drink in a toast.

"He asked me if he could buy me a drink, and we started dancing, and he was just all over me and grabbing my ass."

Claire raised her eyebrows. "This guy sounds like every other red-blooded American male."

"He does, but there's one thing I haven't told you." Mindy paused dramatically.

"The piercing?" Claire took a long sip from her drink.

Mindy leaned in. "No. He was *British*."

Claire's and Nicole's mouths both dropped open. "You hooked up with a *British guy*?" they said in unison.

"Yep. As soon as I heard that accent, my panties were off. And I mean that literally. I took them off in the ladies' room and then handed them to him. I'm not really sure why." She paused, frowning for a moment. "It seemed like a good idea at the time. And it must have worked because I didn't even finish my drink before he dragged me into the bathroom."

"I am so unspeakably jealous. I have so many questions. Is he here with cute British friends? Can I have one? Will they recite Shakespeare for us in the bedroom? Wait here, I'm going to need to get us another round to fully appreciate the immensity of this story," Claire said. "Don't tell any more 'til I get back."

After shelling out an obscene amount of her hard-earned money for their customary second round of Cosmos, she carefully carried the drinks back to the table. She clutched them to her chest and side-stepped an obnoxious couple who were trying to make out and walk simultaneously.

"Okay," she said. "Spill."

"I think I'm getting too old to be mixing all these liquors." Nicole frowned at her Cosmo before shrugging and taking a large sip.

They weren't as young as they used to be. Hangovers were now turning into a two-day affair. But after the day Claire had, a stiff drink was in order.

Two drinks and several bouts of wild dancing later, Mindy had divulged that the mysterious British gentleman was a graduate psychology student at Venor University. She also shared that he had a Prince Albert piercing and knew how to work it.

Then it was Claire's turn to explain the trapped-in-the-bathroom incident and Luke's dismissive attitude toward proposals.

"What are the two of you working on, anyway? How did you even know he was here?" Nicole asked.

Claire had just taken a large sip of her drink and nearly choked on a piece of ice. She coughed into the crook of her arm until her eyes stopped streaming. She made eye contact with Mindy for a moment before beginning.

"Sorry, wrong pipe. Kyle recommended us, and Luke tracked me down when he moved here. His brother from Philly wants to propose to his girlfriend, and he saw the segment *Good Morning, Pennsylvania* did on the business. Unfortunately, his brother is a businessman and very busy, so I've been meeting with Luke as a proxy as well as getting his input on the camera situation," she recited carefully.

"I've never heard him mention a brother. What's his name?"

"Johnny," Claire said at the same time that Mindy said, "Liam."

Claire fought the urge to give Mindy the stink eye and quickly added, "His real first name is Johnny, but he goes by his middle name, which is Liam."

"Huh." Nicole stirred her drink. "I guess they're not very close. Luke's cute, though, isn't he? Does it run in the family?"

"It does. Fortunately for Liam, though, he seems to have missed out on the douchebag genes."

Nicole sipped her drink. "Kyle has kind of hinted a

couple of times that Luke is quite a ladies' man. Not the settling type."

"Good," Claire said forcefully, flailing her hand and nearly knocking her glass over. "Then I'll never have to plan a proposal for him because he will die of a frozen heart at age eighty in a hot tub full of twenty-two-year olds. Enough about him. Did you guys hear about Courtney?"

"Crazy Courtney?" Nicole asked.

"Yeah. She's missing."

"Are you serious?" Nicole pinched the top of her straw.

Claire nodded. "She disappeared this weekend while she was out for a run. No one's heard from her."

Mindy gasped. "Oh my god. Was she abducted? Or do you think she ran away? She was always so flighty. Didn't she change her major six times before graduation?"

"No clue, probably not, and I think it was only four times." Claire was pretty certain she'd answered the questions in order. "It's so sad, though. I actually ran into her husband today."

"You ran into Jumpin' John?" Mindy's carefully plucked eyebrows rose.

Claire cringed. The nickname had stuck after John jumped out the second story of the Phi Kappa Omega frat house on a dare and fractured his spine, effectively ending his football career.

"He seems devastated. The police don't have any leads so far." She stirred her drink with the metal straw she had brought along with her.

"That really sucks." Mindy noisily crunched through a piece of ice. "Didn't she get you candy nipple tassels for Christmas that year?"

Claire snorted. "She did! I never wore them for anyone though. I think I ate them during a particularly bad bout of

PMS. But enough sad stories. Mindy, has your gentleman texted you today?"

Claire reached into her clutch and dug around until she pulled out a small plastic monocle. She squinted and pinched it in place, now leaning heavily on the table despite its stickiness. She fished a cherry stem out of her drink and tried to tie it with her tongue.

"Old Timey Claire is here!" Nicole cheered.

"He has." Mindy smiled widely. "Here," she said, holding it toward Claire. "Look at the nice things he says."

Claire inspected the text carefully through her monocle. "I had a great time with you last night. Meet up again soon?" she read aloud through the cherry stem. "Prithee tell, you didn't text him back?"

"No. I mean, not yet. I don't want to seem too desperate."

"Mindy, it is unbecoming of a lady to behave like an asshole." Claire pounded the table. On the last word, the cherry stem flew out of her mouth and bounced off the head of a bald man at the next table.

"Do you know how rare it is to find a nice guy our age who actually texts you the next day? When you have that, you don't let it go. I mean, not in a creepy, clingy way. But you tell him he's the bee's knees." She straightened her monocle.

Mindy nearly knocked over her drink while reaching for her phone. "You're so right. Lemme see that. How about I say 'Heyyyy sexy!' But just one exclamation point because I don't want to seem desperate."

"Good thinking." Claire tipped an imaginary hat to her and finished the last of her drink. "This new-fangled technology is a real humdinger." She dragged out her phone. "Should I text Luke and tell him how mean he is?"

"Do it!" Mindy encouraged. "Shame that douchey braggart. Oh no, 'sexy' auto-corrected to 'stalactite.' How does that even happen?" she asked, frantically tapping her phone.

Claire laughed and leaned on one elbow. "Just tell him it's some American slang. Like he looks as sharp as a stalactite. He'll have no clue."

"You're so smart." Mindy pointed a finger at her friend. "Okay, next question, do I ask him if he went to Hogwarts?"

"Please don't do that. I bet every idiot American girl asks him that. Don't say anything until he responds." Claire said sternly. Her non-monocled eye was almost closed as she poked at her phone with one hand, bringing up Luke's text from earlier in the day.

"Dear Luke," she said as she started typing. "You are meaner than the business end of a shoehorn, and I'd like to bring my dog over to poop in all of your shoes. Sincerely, Old Timey Claire.' There." She pressed the lock button on her phone and dropped it back into her purse. "That'll teach him to besmirch my life's work. Nothing says shame like dog poop. Where's Nicole anyway?"

"Here," Nicole said as she sat back down at their table. "I noticed that our night was deteriorating into pouting about boys, so I called Kyle to come pick us up."

Claire grabbed Nicole's hand and looked her in the eyes. "You are more magical than a herd of Technicolor unicorns grazing in a cotton candy field at sunset."

"Thanks, Claire," Nicole said. She leaned over to give her a squeeze and gently patted her on the head. Nicole had the liquor tolerance of a sixty-year-old moonshiner. "Now drink the rest of your water," she said sternly, pushing the largely untouched glasses in front of Claire and Mindy toward them.

They obediently sipped for several minutes, talking about Nicole's upcoming photography gigs.

"Oh, Kyle's here already." Nicole jumped up. They shoved their glasses into the middle of their tiny table and stumbled to the front of the club, waving goodbye to the bartender. As they exited the building, Claire gave Carl a fist bump. "Tread warily into the great unknown, Carl."

"You too, Goldilocks," he said.

Kyle stood on the sidewalk, leaning against his Toyota Camry.

"Kyle!" Claire said. "Where's my pan flute? You are a gentleman and a slayer of many drunk dragons. Thank you for arriving with horse and carriage to transport myself and these damsels to safety. A shilling for your time." Claire performed a clumsy curtsy and struggled to open the butterfly clasp on her change purse.

"Sorry, babe. We made the mistake of ending with a Dirty Girl Scout. Old Timey Claire's here to stay." Nicole giggled.

"Your mom's a dirty Girl Scout," Mindy slurred as she stumbled off the curb.

Kyle was such a cutie—*dashing gentleman*, Claire mentally corrected herself in her Old Timey voice. He stood just under six feet tall, with black-framed glasses, kind hazel eyes, and neatly trimmed facial hair disguising his pear-shaped face. Tonight, he wore a gray and black baseball tee that flattered his slender build.

He drew Nicole into his arms and kissed the top of her head. She snuggled into his side. "Keep your shillings, Claire. Thanks for showing my girl a good time tonight."

Claire tipped an imaginary hat at him as they climbed into the car.

As Kyle settled into the driver's seat, his phone chimed.

He glanced at the screen before throwing the car in reverse. "Claire," he said.

"Yes, sir?" She swayed with the motion of the car and toppled over, laying her head in Mindy's lap.

"Did you text Luke and tell him you were going to bring Rosie over to poop in all of his shoes?"

"What? Does that even sound like something I would say?"

"Yes," everyone in the car said.

"He deserved it. You can't let an ego like that run around unchecked. What time is it?"

"Eleven," Nicole reported from the front seat.

"It's only eleven o'clock and I'm already this drunk and tired? When did I get so old?" Claire sat up and slumped in her seat. She unzipped her purse and glanced at her phone again. She swiped to reveal a message from Luke.

"Haha," she said. She threw her phone back into her purse and crossed her arms over her chest. The pleasant swimming sensation was receding, and her head ached. She should have drunk more water.

"What's funny?" Mindy asked.

"Nothing. That's all Luke's text said. Just 'Haha.' Have I mentioned that the only thing I hate almost as much as animal cruelty is when boys respond with 'haha'? It took him almost half an hour to come up with that brilliant response."

"Oh, we men do that on purpose to get under your skin," Kyle said as he turned onto Claire's street.

She groaned. "Figures. Min, will you pick me up in the morning? We have a meeting with a douchebag at the antique store at ten, and I don't want to see his stupid, smug face if we're late."

Mindy yawned and stretched out across the back seat as Claire got out. "Okay, whatever you say."

"Bye, Coli! Let me know if you have any more problems with the mayor of Twat Town. I'm serious about the glitter cannon. And Kyle, thanks for picking us up. You're seriously great," she slurred, before opening the door and stumbling up the dimly lit stairwell to her apartment.

CHAPTER SIX

To Do:
- Google stun gun instructions and safety courses
- Eradicate "haha" from the English language
- Take Rosie to the groomer

CLAIRE AWOKE THE NEXT MORNING WITH A POUNDING headache and a mouth that was as dry as a cotton ball cruising around the desert on a cracker. It was only seven o'clock. She rolled over and tried to fall back asleep, but her bladder wouldn't allow it.

"God, Rosie. I used to be able to stay out drinking every kind of drink under the sun until two in the morning and then roll into an eight o'clock class the next morning, fresh as a hot waffle. What has happened to us?" She rolled over to her bedside table and unscrewed the cap on a bottle of water that Drunk Claire had kindly left her the night before. A half-eaten candy bar she didn't remember sat next to it.

Rosie gave her a reassuring lick and let out a low whine.

"Ugh, fine." She seriously considered not putting on pants, but ended up finding dirty sweatpants crumpled at the bottom of her hamper and slid them on before staggering out of the apartment.

"Come on, Ro. It's so bright out here. This tree is just as good as that tree. You really don't need to investigate them all," she pleaded.

As annoying as the sun was to her bloodshot eyes, the day was warming up to be one of those breathtaking, transitional spring days full of promise and change. She would be so professional at this meeting that Luke wouldn't even recognize her. But maybe she should pack a screwdriver and some bolt cutters in her purse, just in case.

When Rosie finally did her business, Claire half dragged her back up to the apartment. There wasn't time for a morning walk today. She used her fancy, curl-defining shampoo in the shower and added an extra bit of makeup. She spoke to Rosie as she applied a layer of hibiscus-colored lipstick.

"He's so not going to catch me looking like a frazzled troll today, RoRo. And if he thinks he's going to get under my skin with that idiotic 'haha,' he's in for disappointment." She slid on a hot pink dress and a pair of boots she had been dying to wear.

It was almost eight thirty. Time to make sure Mindy was on schedule.

"Holy shit," her friend moaned into the phone. "Did I challenge a lumberjack to a chugging contest last night? Because I'm pretty sure I no longer have a liver. Or kidneys. Or even a life."

"Well, good morning, Princess Sunshine. Hey, listen, do you think you could come a little early to pick me up? I want to get coffee and donuts for us before the meeting with the asshole."

Mindy groaned. "You mean you want to give him coffee and donuts to show that his 'haha' didn't bother you last night."

"Please. I don't care what he thinks. I'm a professional. At least, as long as there isn't any vodka involved. And since we're collaborating on this project, I thought I would bring baked goods as a courtesy."

"Whatever. I'll be there at nine fifteen," Mindy said, hanging up abruptly.

When Mindy rolled up to her apartment building, Claire shut the car door as quietly as possible. She handed over two aspirin and a bottle of water. "If we can get through this meeting, we have time for a nap before Steve's rehearsal."

"You are a saint." Mindy took the aspirin and swigged them down with a mouthful of water. "Let's go get some donuts for an asshat." She lowered her oversized sunglasses back onto her face. She had managed to gather her tangled mane into a low side ponytail and throw on a gold braided headband.

"You know, even though we're old ladies now, we can still make hungover look good." Mindy added an extra dab of lip gloss before driving off.

———

THE GIRLS PULLED UP TO THE ANTIQUE STORE A FULL FIVE minutes before ten. Luke was in his beat-up truck in the parking lot, reading a newspaper that he propped up on the steering wheel.

Claire fixed her hair in the mirror before quietly closing

her door and sneaking over to Luke's parking spot. "You still read the newspaper?"

He jumped so violently that he ripped the sports section in half. "Jesus, woman, don't you know you're not supposed to just sneak up on people like that?"

"I apologize. I didn't mean to scare you. Coffee?" she asked politely, holding out a to-go cup. "I was tempted to get you a raspberry mocha swirl, but something tells me you wouldn't find that very *professional*."

He glared at her. "The only thing I'm afraid of is the fact that you're actually here on time." He took a sip of coffee and grimaced. "You should have gotten me a raspberry mocha swirl. That sounds delicious."

"Come on. You insisted on meeting here at ten, so let's get this over with. You're the one who's always so impatient to get down to business," Claire said as she opened his car door for him and made a mock sweeping gesture for him to exit.

He stepped out of his truck, bringing with him a hand-held camcorder. "You look...cleaner today," he observed as he flipped the camera open.

"You look equally egotistical today," she said coolly.

He smiled and pressed a button to start recording. "Today is April twenty-third, and these two fine ladies and I have traveled to this quaint antique store on the outskirts of town to procure some items for Kyle's proposal to Nicole," he said, swiveling the camera around to take in Mindy and Claire's faces.

"Last night was a little rough for these two. In fact, this one threatened to have her dog poop in all of my shoes because she can't handle criticism."

Claire turned away from the camera and groaned as Luke flipped the camcorder around to face him. "We're going to try not to kill each other." He stepped several feet away to take in the shop from a different angle before pausing the video. "All right, let's do this." He opened the door and allowed Claire and Mindy to walk in first.

If only she could fart on command and leave him stewing in silent fumes. Claire strutted inside, seriously debating stomping on Luke's foot on the way in. The entire store smelled of a confusing combination of shoe polish, dust, and mildew. "Marco?"

"Polo!" A balding man suddenly popped up from behind the counter, a jeweler's loupe trembling in place over mighty jowls.

Claire smiled. It was a long-standing joke between the two of them. Marco had been instrumental in discovering countless unique and romantic items she used for her proposals. "I was wondering if you could help me find a few things today."

"I could do that. We've got all kinds of crap in here!" He chuckled and leaned forward onto the glass counter. Beneath him were scads of antique rings, watches, and thimbles nestled in rows of velvet.

She glanced over her shoulder. Luke had switched his camera back on and was swiveling it around, getting a close-up of a pair of wooden clogs. He disappeared down an aisle that contained a clutter of ancient vanities, cabinets, and books.

"What are you looking for today, Miss Claire?"

"Well, I was hoping you might have an antique bow and some arrows?" She could have just bought one from a sporting goods store or the internet. But this particular item needed some history. Some legitimate wear and tear.

Marco considered for a moment, rubbing one hand on his protruding belly. "I know just the thing. Come," he said.

There was a spring in his step as he led her toward the back of the store.

"I'll be right back," Mindy said to no one in particular, clutching her stomach and running toward the front.

Luke tore up the aisle after her with his camera.

Ignoring the fuss, Claire examined Marco's modest selection of antique weaponry. "Oh! This one is perfect," she said, carefully picking up a slender wooden bow. "These arrows are amazing. Min, come see this." She clutched the bow and turned around.

She walked past an aisle of hope chests and nearly banged her head on a set of snowshoes that dangled from the ceiling. "Min?"

Luke came back in, closing the door gingerly behind him. "Mindy's a little indisposed at the moment. What did you find?"

"Do you have to film everything?" Claire asked, glaring at his camera.

"This is what you hired me for. You gave me free rein as a creative consultant, so I creatively decide to film whatever I want when I want."

She fought the urge to roll her eyes for the millionth time in his presence and instead presented the bow. "What do you think?" Surely he had an opinion. He had an opinion on everything.

He brought his eye away from the camera. "Wow." He set the camera down on top of a display of antique Coca Cola bottles and picked up the bow, hefting its weight in his hands. "This is for the second scene? The one at the archery range?"

"You actually looked at my notes?"

"Of course I did. I told you, I take my work seriously. I mean, that notebook is so creepily organized that I half expected it to belong to a serial killer, but you have a few genuinely good ideas."

Hmm, a serial killer binder. She filed that thought away for later.

He gave the bow back to her. His pinkie brushed hers, and he withdrew his hand quickly. Her cheeks burned at the contact. He needed to keep his pinkies in check. Next time, she would rip it off.

"You sound surprised." She tucked a strand of hair behind her ear.

"Not surprised. Just glad to be working with someone who's almost as passionate as me. Even if it is about something as ridiculous as marriage proposals." He shot her a cocky grin and picked up his camera again. He made it a whole two sentences without insulting her or her life's work. A new record.

The shop bell jingled in the background.

"Marco, would you mind taking this to the register for me?" she asked without bothering to check the price. As he obliged, Claire turned back to Luke. "Did you check on Mindy?"

He nodded. "I did. She's not feeling too great right now. Half of her drinks from last night and all of the protein bar she had for breakfast are currently splattered across the parking lot."

"Ugh. Please. I don't need those kinds of details." Her stomach twisted.

"She'll be all right. I left her with a bottle of water. She's sitting on the curb saying something about 'freaking tequila.' I guess that would help explain the message I got last night." He grinned over the top of the camera.

"Poor thing. She just needs a nap and my patented hangover cure."

"Which is?"

"A lady never reveals her secrets." Claire turned to examine a table full of arrows. There were so many, each more beautiful than the last. One had a tail that was made from real feathers.

"What do you think about these? Oh, and that quiver with the braided strap is perfect." She reached for it.

Suddenly, the quiver was snatched up by a hand weighed down by several gaudy pieces of costume jewelry.

"Hello, Claire." Wendy pinched the strap of the quiver between her thumb and forefinger. She examined Claire through narrowed green eyes on her overly tan face.

"Wendy."

"Wouldn't this just be *darling* for that outdoors-themed proposal I'm planning? You know, for the senator's daughter."

"I have no idea what you're talking about. And actually, I believe that's mine." Claire extended a hand for it. The quiver was perfect. She wouldn't allow it to fall into Wendy's acrylic talons.

Wendy ignored her and sauntered down the aisle, peering at a row of antique picture frames. "So this is the shop where you find all those kitschy little elements that enchant those tasteless reviewers. I should have known it would be in the Hispanic part of town." She ran one finger over the face of a miniature grandfather clock and wiped her hand on her shirt.

Marco appeared from around the corner and glowered at Wendy. "Excuse me, miss. If you have a problem with my store, you are free to leave it immediately."

"Actually, I'd like to buy this arrow bag, please," she said, putting on a sickly sweet voice. She held it toward him. "How much?"

"This particular piece has already been sold to another customer."

"Really? Who?" She arched a heavily penciled eyebrow.

"This young lady." He pointed at Claire. "She has reserved it. I am sorry." He snatched the quiver from her clutches. "This item is not for sale. But you are free to browse the rest of the store, or to leave."

Wendy shot Claire a piercing glare before turning on her Louboutins and cantering back down the aisle. She paused by a display and, with a nasty smile, knocked a poker set onto the floor, flinging chips across the store as she left.

Claire set her belongings down and kneeled, picking up poker chips and depositing them back in their case. "Overgrown stick insect doesn't even know the proper term for a quiver."

Luke set his camera down on a nearby trestle table and bent down to help. "Who was that? Satan's Bride?"

"Close." She blew a piece of dust off of a chip. "That would be my nemesis, Wendy Flutter. We've been pitted against each other for Planner of the Year Award for the last three years, and I always win."

While Claire had the satisfaction of a row of awards, Wendy had walked away from last year's ceremony with a different kind of win.

"Planner of the Year Award? People give awards for this nonsense?" He looked at her with raised eyebrows.

"Very prestigious awards. It's through the Chamber of Commerce." She shot him a dirty look. "The awards happen every summer, and she always loses because frankly she's not that good at her job. We also have a bit of a history." She snapped the case closed more forcefully than she intended. "So, we kind of hate each other."

"Whoa. Calm down there, killer. What kind of history?"

"Not one that I care to talk about. Marco, can I get these, please? Thank you so much for not giving her the quiver. She's like a toddler—she only wanted to have it because I need it."

"I despise that woman," Marco growled. "She once came in here snooping around after you left and tried to figure out what you bought."

"Seriously?"

"Yes. She asked my wife, but Adelaide wouldn't tell her. Before she left, she knocked over a chess set. That seems to be her thing." He shook his head at the door.

Claire glowered. "How is Adelaide? Do the doctors still have her on blood thinners?"

He launched into a ten-minute story about the state of Adelaide's health. Luke observed the exchange with his head cocked to one side.

"Thank you for everything, Marco," Claire said when he had finished. "These are for an extremely special proposal. Not only is it going to be my most elaborate one to date, but it's also for my best friend."

He clapped his hands together in pleasure. "And you will be Planner of the Year for the fourth year in a row." He smiled broadly. "Go, win your title."

Luke snapped his camera shut and took the bags before Claire could, carrying them out into the parking lot.

"Thank you," she said begrudgingly as she opened the door to the back seat.

He set the bags on the floor and carefully hefted the bow inside before he turned to face her. They were so close that she could smell the spice of his deodorant. She took a small step back.

"We'll have to test the bow out to make sure it works," he said. "She'll probably need a wrist guard too."

We? There was no "we."

"I'll handle it," she said. Surely there would be a way to safely fire arrows inside her apartment. Security deposit be damned. "Where's Mindy?"

"Over here," came a feeble call from the curb. Mindy had her head in one hand and a water bottle in the other.

Claire squatted next to her and gently patted her silky black hair. "Next time we stick to clear liquors only."

Luke stood a few paces back. For once he had set the camera down and was instead leaning against the trunk of Mindy's car.

Mindy moaned. "The only clear liquor I want is water, forever. By the way, I did manage to do one productive thing while I was out here throwing up everything I've eaten for the past twelve years."

Claire smoothed a flyaway strand from Mindy's face. "Oh yeah? What did you do?"

"I taped a sticky note to the back of Satan's window that says 'Honk If You Think I'm An Asshole.'"

Claire snort-laughed and glanced at Luke. Had he heard that noise escape her? Snort laughs were a far cry from professional. "Thank you for that. Want to go pick up my car and then crash at my house until our next meeting? I have a frozen pizza, and I will make you my top secret hangover cure."

"Ooh, the blue Kool-Aid? That would be so amazing! Let's do it." She climbed to her feet.

Claire helped her up and turned to Luke. "I'll see you tomorrow sometime? I have a few ideas to run by you."

"I have some interviews to take care of in the morning. I'll come over around three," he said, opening the car door for her. "And I do mean three, not three fifteen."

Would there be no end to the late-shaming? "That's fine.

Bring my binder." She climbed into the car and shut the door. Luke retreated to his truck. He didn't look nearly as obnoxious from behind.

"Holy shit, Claire," Mindy said after she closed the car door.

"What?"

"He is so fucking hot. You have to have sex with him. Please. Do it for me."

Claire scoffed. "First of all, absolutely not. Second, don't forget my sex embargo. I'm working on the business right now, and I can't afford any phallic-shaped distractions. And third, can you imagine Luke in bed?"

"Vividly," Mindy said dreamily.

Claire shook her head. "I have him pegged. No foreplay because that would be too romantic and therefore a waste of time. Doggy style exclusively so he doesn't have to look anyone in the eyes. And he probably wears a stopwatch to be sure that he doesn't go over his allotted time slot for fornication."

Someone rapped at Claire's window, and she jumped.

Shit. She buzzed the window down. Luke stood outside, eyebrows contracted, but an amused half smile played on his lips. How much had he heard?

"Just thought I'd get this back to you now," he said as he hefted the binder through the open window.

"Thanks," she said. Her heart was fluttering again. Maybe he hadn't heard?

"Anyway, I'm off to buy a stopwatch. Gotta make sure I'm using my time wisely." He raised his eyebrows before turning on his worn high-tops and walking back to his truck.

"Oh my god," she moaned, yanking the lever on her seat

and dropping it until she lay flat on her back. She pressed her hands over her face and screamed.

"It wasn't that bad." Mindy patted her leg.

"I'm supposed to be the professional one. So far during our encounters I arrived uncharacteristically late and looking like I had just crawled out of a vacuum cleaner, and now he overheard me insulting his penis."

"To be fair, you insulted his personality more than his penis."

"That's not better."

"You're really letting him get to you," Mindy observed as she turned the key in the ignition.

"He's not getting to me. Just drive." Claire righted her seat and slid on a pair of cat's-eye sunglasses.

TWENTY MINUTES LATER, THEY TRUDGED WEARILY INTO Claire's apartment. Claire took Rosie out and picked up her mail from the mailbox on her way back inside. Mindy was already making Kool-Aid as Claire flipped through her mail.

"Bill, bill, bill. Oh, what's this? Probably another save the date," she said as she turned over a plain white envelope. She ripped it open and pulled out a picture.

"What the hell?"

Chills ran up and down her spine. The picture was grainy and shot in bad lighting. A small, dimly lit room was barely visible through the haze. A set of bunk beds was pushed to one side, and both beds were covered in colorful polka-dot sheets. A sleeping figure was in each bed.

"Holy shit," Mindy said as she came to stand next to Claire. "Is that—"

"My dorm room. From freshman year," Claire said. Her

hand shook, and the photo wobbled. She collapsed onto a bar stool. "And that is Courtney and me, asleep."

"Who in the hell would send this to you? What does it mean?"

She picked up the envelope again. There was no return address. Her heart hammered in her chest.

"Claire, you have to call the police."

"And tell them what? Someone sent me a picture from college?"

"Courtney disappeared. This could be evidence. I saw an episode of *Mysterious Murders* where a cold case was solved because of DNA on an envelope."

She dropped the picture on the counter and jumped back, nearly knocking her stool over. She crossed the kitchen to the window and glanced outside. Nothing seemed out of the ordinary, but she slid the curtains shut anyway.

The back of her neck prickled. Goosebumps shot down her arms. "Do you think someone could be watching me? I took a walk with Rosie yesterday, and the whole time it felt like someone was watching us. It wasn't the first time either. I swear last week when we walked in Buchanan Park, I heard a camera shutter snap. I never see anyone, though, so I just figured I was letting my mom's chatter get under my skin."

"I don't know, Claire. But we need to take this to the police station. Whoever sent this to you knows that you have a connection to Courtney, and they know where you live. The police need to know." Mindy pulled a pair of rubber gloves and a gallon-sized plastic bag from a kitchen drawer. She put the gloves on and carefully picked up the picture and envelope, sealing them in the bag. She handed it to Claire.

"You should take a picture on your phone, too, so you have a copy."

Claire glanced at the picture in her hand. Was this the Widowmaker at work? Was he trying to tell her she was next? Or was this some weird gift from Courtney's husband? But he didn't know her address.

"Of course this would happen to me," Claire muttered to herself as she walked up the concrete steps to the police station an hour later. "I'm planning the biggest project of my entire career, my wedding is off, Wendy is determined to strike me down, and now I'm going to be involved in a missing person case for a girl who vomited in one of my socks."

She pulled open the glass front door and stepped into a chaotic office. A portly, bald police officer manned a front desk and yammered into a phone. A stressed-looking female officer walked by clutching a mountain of paperwork.

Claire walked hesitantly to the front desk and waited while the officer finished his conversation.

"Can I help you, miss?" His eyes flicked over her and zeroed in on the envelope in her hand.

"Uh, yes," she said. Apprehension tingled at the nape of her neck. What was it about cops that made her so uncomfortable? "I might have some evidence pertaining to a missing person case. Could I turn that in here?" She held the picture toward the desk.

"Which missing person case?" the cop asked flatly. He didn't take the picture.

"Courtney Stevens." She laid the picture on the desk and slid it toward him with one finger.

Several officers in the surrounding area looked up from their desks. A man in plainclothes walked over and offered his hand to Claire. His ice-blue eyes narrowed as though he were looking into the sun. Stubble spread over a firm jawline, and his ears were slightly too large for his head.

"I'm Detective Smith." He made clear eye contact and shook hands firmly, as though he were meeting a politician. He wore a crisp, white shirt with a starched collar and a stony gray suit jacket and slacks.

"Claire Hartley."

Two uniformed officers came to stand behind Detective Smith as he picked up the picture and studied it.

"I received this picture in the mail this morning. Courtney was my roommate during freshman year at Venor University. That was our dorm room," she said, nodding toward the image. "There was no return address and no note. I thought it might be relevant to the investigation."

Detective Smith flipped the bag over and looked at the front of the envelope. He exchanged a glance with the policeman to his left and nodded at the officer behind the desk, who pulled out a form and slid it across the counter.

The detective snapped the paper into a clipboard and handed it to Claire. "Miss Hartley, I'm going to ask that you please fill out this statement form with as much detail as possible. Get this to Jeff," he said to the officer who stood to his left. The officer disappeared into the chaos as Claire took a seat.

She filled out the form with painstaking detail including an accounting of the weather and which shoes she was wearing when she opened it, and signed at the bottom. Detective Smith's eyes burned into her as she dated the form.

"Please let me know if I can be of any additional help," she said as she handed the clipboard over.

"Thank you, ma'am. We'll be in touch if we need

anything else. Don't hesitate to call us if you come across anything else. Be careful out there."

"I will." Maybe it was time to schedule a stun gun safety class. She thanked him and turned to leave. As she pushed the doors open and felt the sun on her face, she instantly felt better. The heavy doors closed behind her. This would be the end of her involvement in Courtney's case. It was time to get back to work.

———

TWO HOURS LATER, CLAIRE SHOUTED INTO A MEGAPHONE AT the edge of a river. A boombox blaring a seventies rock song sat at her feet. Steve and four of his soon-to-be groomsmen sped across the water on their Jet Skis, motoring in circles and flying up the floating ramps that a local sports shop had agreed to rent out. Claire held up a blue card as the verse melted into the chorus, and the four friends began driving in circles around Steve, who mimed singing into a microphone.

"Okay, and here's where we'll fire up the floating disco and strobe lights," she said to herself as they transitioned into the final verse. "Hopefully, none of the attendees are epileptic. Oh, and we really need to make sure to bring in some softer lighting onshore. She deserves spectacular pictures."

She made a note on her clipboard. "Ready for your finale, Steve?" Claire shouted into the megaphone.

After a brief nod from Steve, Claire flashed the last card —orange—and Steve made a wide arc and went full-speed at the biggest ramp floating in the river. A spray of water trailed him as he approached, his face set in concentration. He hit the ramp so fast that before she could even blink, he was airborne. Droplets flung out in a near-perfect circle as he expertly manipulated the Jet Ski into a backflip. When he landed safely a dozen yards away, Claire slowly exhaled the breath she had held the entire time.

He roared back into shore, pulling up in front of her and jumping off. "How was that?" he asked, a silly grin on his face.

"That was *amazing*. Seriously. Like, flawless. I think my heart nearly stopped while you were upside down though. If only we could get you a giant, flaming hoop. That would just take this thing over the top. Great job, guys," she called to the men who were crawling out of the water.

Steve's eyes lit up. "Is that something we could really do?"

"Unfortunately, I made it a policy not to allow my clients to play with fire," she said with a smile.

His shoulders slumped.

"Steve, I just want to say thank you." She tossed her clipboard back in her bag. "You have been so dedicated to this. It's really made my job so much easier. Tara is a really lucky girl."

He smiled. "It's been rad working with you. I just can't wait to make her my wife."

"Oh, I forgot. I have one other thing for you. Now, you don't have to do this if you don't want to, but I think it would be a fantastic addition to the proposal. Especially if it's cold." Claire opened the trunk of her car and pulled out a garment bag. "Go ahead."

Steve unzipped it, revealing what at first appeared to be tuxedos. He pulled one out, rubbed the material between his fingers, and let out a triumphant roar like his team had just scored. He held them out to his friends, who mimicked his roar, all swarming around and taking wetsuits.

Before Claire knew what was happening, she had been lifted up onto their shoulders. They jogged her around the parking lot chanting "tux-es, tux-es!" Claire laughed and put her hands on their shoulders, trying to keep herself steady. Shit, had she shaved her legs this morning?

The river wound lazily away from them to the east. Cars flew over the bridge to their right. Graffiti littered the side. It was too bad she couldn't get that cleaned up in time for the proposal. Maybe if she snuck down here at night with a pressure washer, she could get some of it off. What city official could get upset over some light vigilante pressure washing?

Two of the men deposited Claire by her car while the other two immediately stripped to try on the wetsuits. She pulled her clipboard back out and walked over to Steve. "Although this was absolutely excellent and probably the most unique proposal I've ever had the pleasure of planning, I have a few concerns. First, what do you want to do about the ring? We can't have you losing it while you're doing a backflip over a river. I could hold it for you until after you're done, but then I'd have to throw it to you." Hand-eye coordination wasn't exactly her forte.

He considered this for a moment. "Yeah, that's fine. I'll give it to you. Actually, is there any way I could give you the ring today? I have it in my car right now, but I'm afraid that she's going to find it."

She smiled. "Normally I charge ten dollars a day to keep a ring secure for a client, but I like you, so I'll do it for five."

"Awesome," Steve said. "Give me a second and I'll grab it." He hoisted himself into his pickup truck and brought back a small black box.

Claire wrote his name, the proposal date, and the

current date on a label on her clipboard. She slapped it on top of the box. "Don't worry. It'll come off."

He handed the box over. "Would you take a look at it?"

"Of course." She tilted the top on its hinges and revealed a large, emerald-cut peach sapphire with a diamond halo. She clutched a hand to her heart. "You got her the one she circled from the magazine. Excellent call."

"You think she'll like it?"

"She'll love it. It's perfect." She flipped the lid shut and walked it to her car to secure it in the fireproof safe in her trunk.

"Are you nervous about not having it on you?" she asked.

"To be honest, it's kind of a relief. I was so worried that I'd get pulled over when we were together and blow the whole thing."

"Yeah, a lot of my clients run into that problem. I usually tell them to hide it in someplace they know she won't be interested in looking, like in a loose ceiling tile or in a video game case. Of course, if you make her mad before the proposal, she might try to give away all your video games and lose the ring. And that," she said, pointing at him, "is why we always do what?"

"Get insurance on the ring," he recited like a schoolboy.

"Excellent. The sports store and river authority have given us clearance to keep the ramps out until the big day, so keep practicing as often as you can. If Tara asks, you're practicing before your next movie starts filming. Thanks, guys," she called over her shoulder as she got back in her car.

As she was backing out of her parking spot, the public restrooms appeared in her backup camera. A chill went down her spine. Her eyes swept down the parking lot, but the only cars in the marina lot were ones she could attribute to Steve and his friends. Shifting into drive, she left the restrooms and her thoughts in the dust.

As she made a right turn onto Market Street and swerved to avoid a truly gigantic pothole, her phone rang through Bluetooth. "Hey, Min. Are you feeling better after a nap?"

"Tons, thank you," Mindy said. "Did you go to the police station?"

"I did."

"Were you interrogated? Did anyone say 'forensics'? Did you see any perps? Tell me everything."

Claire stopped at a light. She glanced behind her. Had that black sedan been following her? She could have sworn it had been back there for a good half a mile. "They just had me fill out a statement form and took down my information in case they need anything else."

"Really? That's it?" Mindy sounded disappointed.

"Yep. I told you, it's weird, but it's no big deal."

Despite her words, Claire's stomach tightened. The light turned green, and she inched forward, eyes flashing to the rearview mirror. The black sedan turned off down a different road, and she breathed a sigh of relief. One silly picture and she completely dissolved into hysterics.

"I'm not convinced," Mindy said. "The person who sent you that knows where you live. Remember what I told you. You need to vary your routine, take different routes. Visit different grocery stores. Just in case."

Claire shook her head. "You sound like my mother."

"Hey, Alice Alejo is a gem. Also, in case you forgot, you have an interview with that morning show tomorrow. I already sent the footage in, so all you need to do is show up."

"Ugh. I forgot. Where is it at again?" Claire's eyes

flicked to her rearview mirror again. There was a cop behind her, but surely that was a coincidence. Ordinarily, she would go straight down Market Street until she hit Beaumont Street. Maybe there was some truth to what Mindy was saying. She moved into the turning lane at the next red light.

"In Harrisburg. But hey, this is going to be great for the business and the blog."

"You're right. I just hate giving live interviews. I always sound like a rambling idiot."

"Hey. You are spectacular and amazing, not to mention the very best. That's why they came to you. They don't choose Planner of the Year by drawing it out of a hat. You have plenty of valuable insight. And before you know it, you'll be such a big deal that you can demand they send you the questions in advance."

Claire drummed her fingertips on the steering wheel. "Come with me?"

"I want to, but I don't think I can. I'm doing a virtual meeting with a potential client for the second round of interviews tomorrow morning."

"Oh, that's right. Which one, the army guy with all the tattoos?"

"Yes! Sergeant Sexy."

"I love him on paper. I really hope he doesn't turn out to be a scumbag. There is so much potential for a patriotic proposal. Oh, speaking of sexy, did you hear from mystery British boy last night after you called him a stalactite?"

"Not yet," Mindy said.

Claire pursed her lips at her friend's dejected tone. "You know he's probably just waiting because you took so long to respond yesterday. I swear boys do this thing where they take the amount of time it takes you to respond to them, set a timer for double that amount of time, and then only reach out when it goes off."

The sun disappeared as she entered the parking garage.

"Should we put that theory to the test?"

"I think we should!"

"Okay, so if he texted you at eight in the morning yesterday and you didn't text him back until thirteen hours later, that means you should hear from him tonight at nine. I'll bet you a round of drinks that he texts by nine thirty."

"You're on. I'll keep you posted."

Men.

CHAPTER SEVEN

To Do:
- *"Something new" blog*
- *Drink more water*
- *Order more sheet protectors*

THE NEXT MORNING, CLAIRE STUMBLED INTO HER SHOWER just after four without bothering to turn on the light.

As the warm water washed over her, she leaned against the wall and closed her eyes, falling into a light snooze. When her face started sliding down the slick vinyl, her eyes flew open and she jumped, losing her footing in the slippery tub and crashing to the floor. Her elbow slammed into the edge of the tub as she blindly grasped for purchase. A burst of colors shot across her vision as the left side of her face collided with the unforgiving vinyl. She came to rest in a tangle of limbs on the floor.

"Mother fu—" she gasped in pain and clutched her

elbow, which throbbed as though she had just botched a professional wrestling move. When she attempted to stand, a shooting pain stabbed through her hip. She fumbled for the light switch under her mirror, flooding the bathroom with light, and wiped the wet strands of hair out of her left eye, which already felt tender.

She cleared a circle in the condensation on the mirror.

"Oh, no."

An impressive black eye was blossoming. Her eye already started to swell shut. "No, no, no! Shit!"

She half-blindly dialed Mindy.

"For fuck's sake, Claire. It's four thirty in the morning. I'm not on duty yet. Is someone dead?"

"I'm sorry, it's an emergency. Do you think *Marnie in the Morning* would let me reschedule?"

"I doubt it. They said this was the last opening for another two months." Mindy yawned.

"Min, I just gave myself a black eye."

"How in the hell did you do that?"

"I kind of fell asleep standing up in the shower."

"Oh god. You're killing me, Claire. Okay. We can spin this. Whatever you do, do *not* make any domestic violence jokes."

"You still think I should go on looking like this? I look like I've been in a turf war."

"You have to. Tell the truth if she asks and turns it into a joke or a talking point about the industry and the perils of working in secret. Hopefully, the makeup artist will be able to cover up the worst of it, but maybe put some frozen peas on it in the meantime. I'll be watching when you come on at eight. And don't worry, nobody really watches that show anyway."

Claire dried off and shuffled into her bedroom, touching

her swollen eye gingerly. She picked up a thick, stretchy headband before wandering into the kitchen. She flung several frozen TV dinners onto her countertop before she located a bag of peas. Groaning softly, she wrapped it in a washcloth, put the bag on her face, and secured it in place with the headband.

She snapped a picture and sent it to Nicole with a message reading, "This is how my morning is going so far. How are you?"

Not even the svelte pantsuit she had picked out the night before could distract from her face. Nevertheless, she added a pair of sassy, bubblegum-pink high heels and a dangling gold necklace. She slid on two rings and a set of earrings that matched her shoes and deemed herself as acceptable as she could get considering the circumstances.

"Maybe I can get them to only shoot me from the right," she muttered to herself, pressing a hand to her tender cheek. It seemed like a reasonable request.

After a final glance in the mirror, she abandoned her appearance. During her last interview, the makeup team had scolded her for pre-styling her hair and not coming in with a fresh face. Their opinions on topical application of frozen vegetables remained to be seen.

She gathered her belongings, rushed Rosie out to pee, and walked out the door with the largest mug of coffee she could find. Then she had to turn around halfway down the hallway to lock her door. She put her thermos down to do the foxtrot and finally left. The lone stranger she passed on the way to the garage gawked at her headgear, but she walked on with her head held high.

On the way to the studio, she didn't have time to practice the vehicle counter-surveillance techniques she had begrudgingly looked up the night before. Surely if someone was following her, they wouldn't get up at five in the morning to do so. The risk was worth it. When she arrived at the TV studio just over an hour later, the sun hadn't yet peeked over the tops of the buildings scattered in downtown Harrisburg. She strapped the bag of peas back onto her face before entering the lobby.

"Hi," Claire said to the receptionist sitting behind a sleek, glass desk. "I realize I look ridiculous right now, but I'm going to be on the show this morning. Claire Hartley."

"Of course." The receptionist didn't even blink as she dialed a number on her office phone. "Claire Hartley is here. Can we get an escort to hair and makeup, please? Thank you. Someone will be down in just a minute, Miss Hartley. Would you like some coffee or tea while you wait?"

"I've already got some," she said, hefting the quart-sized travel mug. "I mean normally there would be an entire bottle of wine in here, but considering the early hour, today I opted for something a bit more rejuvenating."

The receptionist smiled politely. "Let me know if you change your mind." She turned back to her computer and tapped away on the keyboard with French-manicured nails.

Claire sat in one of the chairs that lined the far wall. "Tough crowd," she muttered to herself. A pissed-off horde of butterflies seemed to be crashing around in her stomach. The receptionist already thought she was a freak. Claire might as well practice some of her calming techniques. She closed one of her nostrils with the index finger of her right hand and inhaled slowly. She then covered that nostril and exhaled deeply out of the other one. She repeated this process for several minutes until her heart rate slowed.

"Claire?" someone called as she was mid-nostril breath.

"Oh." She jerked her hand away from her face, feeling as guilty as a thirteen-year-old boy caught in the bathroom with a handful of tissues. "I'm sorry, I was just doing some alternate nostril breathing to calm down," she babbled. "It's a yoga thing."

"Don't worry about it," a tall, thin Black girl with a pink-streaked mohawk said to her. "I've seen much weirder rituals. However, I don't see many vegetables being used as fashion accessories."

"Oh, that." Claire released the headband and revealed her eye. "I kind of fell asleep in the shower this morning and smashed my face on the tub."

The woman whistled and pressed the bag of peas back onto Claire's face. "I have got my work cut out for me this morning. Come on." She grabbed Claire's uninjured arm and guided her into the depths of the studio.

"All right, everyone," she called to a small crew around her. "This is Claire, and this morning she thought it would be a great idea to give herself a black eye. But we love her anyway, so we're going to fix this mess."

"Thank you," Claire whispered to her as someone nudged her into a chair. A swarm of people descended on her, plucking, blotting, fussing.

After what felt like hours, they wheeled her chair around so she could inspect herself in the mirror. Although the discoloration around her eye was far less noticeable, it was still considerably more swollen than the other.

"Any chance we could put me on stage left?" Claire asked a producer who was hanging out nearby.

He looked up and saw her face, clapped a hand to his forehead, and started yammering into the black headset he wore. "We need to move the set around. We have an interviewee with a black eye. That's right. We need her chair moved to stage left. Just move Marnie's chair into the middle. Yes. For god's sake, just move the planter offstage. I don't care how heavy it is." He stormed off down a dimly lit hallway and disappeared.

"I guess I'll take that as a yes," Claire said. Her phone lit up with a message from Nicole.

Nicole: *Ouch! Please tell me that's the accidental result of some crazy sex with Luke and not evidence of you being mugged this morning.*

Claire: *Whoa, hey. At this point I would rather strangle Luke than see him naked.*

Not entirely true, but she left it and added:

Claire: *I hit my face off the tub, so sadly this was a strictly non-consensual injury.*

Nicole: *Come on. We both know you're dying to find what lies below the belt of those tattered rich boy jeans.*

She was not going to dignify that with an answer. Claire ignored the text until Nicole sent another a few minutes later.

Nicole: *Sorry about your eye. Hope it doesn't hurt too much. Good luck this morning! I'll be watching before I head over to the studio.*

Claire: *Thank you! What are the odds that no one will notice?*

Nicole: *Slim to none. But you've got this.*

Nicole signed off with a kissy face emoji.

Her makeup artist reappeared. "You're on in ten minutes, honey. Come with me." She helped Claire down from the chair and led her back down the hallway.

———

"OUR NEXT GUEST HAS CAUSED QUITE A SENSATION AROUND town for the past three and a half years," a woman with a toothpaste commercial smile and blazing red hair gathered back into an elegant bun said to the camera. She sat under the sweltering studio lights, not even breaking a sweat. "Her name is Claire Hartley, and her full-time job is something that, until earlier this week, I didn't know existed. Let's show you a clip of some of Claire's most recent work."

The camera zoomed in on a sign that said Camp Susquehanna before cutting to a video with a handsome young man in a camp counselor shirt.

Backstage, Claire took deep breaths as the giggles of a cabin of campers filled the studio. She turned to the monitor on her left and watched a young man wearing a counselor shirt cut through the crowd of middle school students putting on a play. He got down on one knee in front of another counselor, a pretty brunette who was holding cue cards for the campers onstage.

The feed in the studio cut off just as the woman gave a tearful "yes." It was the proposal that had earned her Planner of the Year last year. She had gotten two tick bites and a laceration from a tree branch after fleeing from a copperhead snake that had surprised her mid-pee, but it had been worth it.

The studio audience clapped and cheered.

"And now let's meet the mastermind behind this and

dozens more joyful unions." Marnie held out her hand to Claire.

Someone behind Claire gave her a gentle shove, and she emerged under the unforgiving lights of the set. She stood as tall as she could and waved to the dozen bleary-eyed people hanging out in the audience. They applauded politely.

Marnie, the ever-smiling host, greeted Claire with a perfunctory hug. Claire perched on the edge of her seat, wringing her hands in her lap. The lights were worse out here. She should have brought sunglasses. The butterflies were back, dancing a jig in her abdomen.

"Claire, it is so exciting to have you with us today," Marnie said.

"Thank you so much for having me."

"It's definitely our pleasure. Now, Claire, why don't you tell the audience a little bit more about what it is you do?"

"Absolutely. I'm an event planner, but I specialize in crafting marriage proposals. I started my business just over three years ago. I actually started while I was still in college, but the business really took off after graduation. People say the marriage rate is declining, but you wouldn't know it if you looked at my planner. We're busy year-round."

Marnie laughed. "I can't imagine a happier job. Are all of your proposals like this?"

Claire smoothed a wrinkle in her pantsuit. "Well, each proposal is very different. There are definitely some trends going on lately that a lot of my clients are really interested in, like flash mobs and lip dub proposals. Usually, though, I try to make each proposal as unique to the girlfriend—or boyfriend—as possible. In the proposal you just saw, we initially wanted to go with something ice-skating themed because Jackie loves the sport. But after talking to Chris and seeing him with Jackie, I realized how much Jackie loves the kids from camp, which is where they first met as counselors. Chris agreed a camp-centric proposal would be the most meaningful declaration of love, so we decided that the proposal should take place where they met, surrounded by their family and the kids whose lives they're changing."

There was a collective "aww" from the audience.

"Now you said that you tailor each proposal to the girlfriend. Or, as you mentioned, boyfriend. Have you had many cases of that?"

"I wouldn't say a lot. I think I've only planned two proposals where a girl wanted to be the asker. Those actually end up being really fun to plan because the guy has absolutely no clue what's going on. Even though it's the twenty-first century, I think it's still sort of an important thing to a lot of men, though, to be the one who asks. But hey, women wear the pants too." She flashed a grin at the crowd, who cheered again. "I've also planned proposals for men proposing to men and women proposing to women as well."

"I was hoping you would bring that up. That was how your business took off, wasn't it?"

"Yes," Claire said, leaning forward in her chair. "Matt, one of my good friends from school, wanted to propose to his boyfriend at graduation. We managed to get the entire graduating class involved, and it went viral in less than a day."

"I think everyone's seen it by now," Marnie said as a still frame from the video appeared on the screen behind them.

Claire smiled at the memory. "Thanks to that engagement and the attention—and the ad revenue—I received, I was able to start my business after graduation. Matt never lets me forget it either." She laughed.

"And how is the happy couple now?"

"They're wonderful. They just adopted a baby girl."

The audience applauded again.

"So, Claire, I have to ask. Our makeup crew told me this morning that you gave yourself a black eye. Did that happen at work?"

Damn it.

"You know, being in the event planning business can be surprisingly dangerous on occasion. But no, actually. Believe it or not, I fell asleep in the shower this morning and hit my face. I was up late last night working on my blog. A proposal planner never sleeps." She touched a hand to her tender eye. "Except in the shower, I guess."

Marnie laughed and asked a few more questions about the shower incident before asking, "Have you ever had a proposal go really wrong? Has a girl ever said no?"

"Never. I have a really strict application process, and I only officially accept applicants who I'm ninety-nine percent certain will have a successful, consensual engagement and happy marriage. That's the secret to Happily Ever Afters' unblemished track record."

Wendy, on the other hand, must have been closer to a 60% success rate in getting couples down the aisle.

"Word on the street is that some of your clients call you the 'Mistress of Yes.'"

Claire laughed and leaned back in her seat. Her heart rate had slowed. Her hands had stopped shaking. This wasn't so bad. "They do, actually. I think it makes me sound like a dominatrix, though, so we don't exactly advertise it."

Marnie smiled. "What's your application process like?"

"Well, first, I have the prospective asker fill out a questionnaire about why they want to get married, why they know their partner is the right one, and to provide links to their partner's social media profiles.. I call it evaluating, but really it's some super-intensive stalking. I examine their online presence to make sure they appear ready for this commitment. If I see a wedding-themed Pinterest board with one hundred-plus pins on it, that's a pretty good sign. If possible, I'll also observe the couple together out in public. When I decide that they're both in it to win it, I agree to take on the asker as my client, and we start the planning process using the data I gathered while essentially stalking their partner."

The audience tittered again.

"Have you turned a lot of potential clients down?"

"Some. There have been a few cases of men wanting to propose because they're being pressured, or even as an apology for cheating. I only commit to planning for people who I believe are genuinely in love and want to get married for no reason other than they can't stand to spend another day apart."

"That is truly amazing. If only all men would take such care when they propose. Tell me, Claire, how exactly did you get into this business?"

Oh, boy. There it was. She unclenched her fists and wiped her sweaty palms on her skirt.

"Well, there's a bit of a story to explain it. You see, in my senior year of college, my boyfriend of three years asked me to marry him."

There was another chorus of "aww" from the audience.

"But," Claire said, "he did it in the absolute worst way imaginable." She felt the penetrating gaze of the entire audience staring at her left hand and noticing her bare ring finger.

"And although I was happy to say yes at the time, I felt kind of unfulfilled. Lots of girls, myself included, imagine the day that someone proposes, years in advance. I was hoping for romance, for someone to go the extra mile, or even just for a ring. You know, something to show that he had put some thought into asking me to spend the rest of my life with him."

Marnie leaned forward in her chair. "But he didn't, did he?"

"No," she said. "It was truly awful. So, I decided from that day on that no girl—or guy—should ever be proposed to in such a thoughtless way. I mean, it's one of the biggest questions you'll ever ask in your life. If I was the one doing it, I would spend months planning and finding just the right way to ask."

"I can't help but notice that you don't have a ring on your finger today. Are you still engaged?"

"I'm not," Claire said. A few members in the audience sighed. Were they sighing in sympathy or at the irony of a proposal planner who was, apparently, profoundly unmarriable?

"It sounds like your ex wasn't worth marrying," Marnie said sympathetically. "Is there any chance you'll tell us how he did it?"

Claire gave her a small smile. "I guess it's been long enough now that I can tell the story. In college, my then-boyfriend was in a fraternity."

"Uh-oh," Marnie said. "I already don't like where this is going."

"Exactly. During homecoming weekend of our senior year, our football team won and everyone was celebrating, and his fraternity had a party at their house." She glanced at the camera.

"I hope my parents aren't watching this morning. I never told them the story." She winced. "It was a huge party.

Everyone was there. My boyfriend was playing beer pong and doing keg stands. I was just hanging out with my friends for most of the night. At midnight, though, he made the DJ turn off the music. He stood on the dining room table and screamed at the top of his lungs, 'Hey everyone! We're awesome. And I can't think of a better way to celebrate our being awesome than asking this girl right here to marry me.' And he kind of drunkenly pointed at me and asked me to come up. He proceeded to get down on one knee and propose to me with a beer bottle cap."

The audience gasped.

"I said yes because I was young and an idiot. And perhaps slightly intoxicated myself. I actually had to ask him the next day to make sure he really meant it. And that's not even the worst part."

"What could possibly be worse than that?" Marnie asked, clutching a hand to her chest.

"Right after he asked me to marry him, he stood up to kiss me and then threw up. All. Over. Me. He ruined the Jimmy Choos my mom gave me for Christmas."

Marnie's mouth dropped open. The crowd groaned.

Claire gripped the arms of her chair. She could still smell the stink of beer and sweat.

"Seriously. It was like an endless wave of vomit. I was so humiliated that I ran out of the house into the street," she said, clasping her right hand over her left. "It was there, in the middle of the street, covered in my fiancé's vomit, that I decided no woman or man should ever have to go through that again. So, I made it my job to help people in love craft the perfect proposal."

Marnie nodded sympathetically.

"Thanks to that experience, I spent the rest of my college career learning how to start a business and market myself as an event planner with a specialty for proposals and weddings. I helped three of my guy friends propose to their significant others before graduation, and that's when Matt's proposal went viral. And that's how I got here." She opened her arms at her sides.

"Was it worth it?" Marnie asked.

"Worth getting barfed on? Definitely. I may not have gotten my happily ever after, but I can make sure as many other people as possible get theirs."

Marnie's perfectly bleached teeth reappeared in a smile. "That's very sweet. Thank you so much for being our guest, Claire."

The audience roared for her a final time. She waved and tried not to rush off the stage, beyond ready to go home and lay in bed for a few hours.

CHAPTER EIGHT

To Do:
- *Watch some TED talks on public speaking*
- *Go to Sephora and beg for help covering black eye*
- *Contact Scott about pool rental*

CLAIRE'S CHEEKS BURNED THE ENTIRE RIDE HOME. *MARNIE IN the Morning* didn't have a huge viewership, but she had still shared her humiliating engagement story with thousands of strangers. Her eye twitched and pulsed the whole trip. When she finally trudged into her apartment, she tossed her camera-ready outfit in the hamper and pulled on a baggy band t-shirt.

She climbed into bed with Rosie and picked up her laptop. Floods of comments still needed to be moderated, and the budget spreadsheet for Kyle's proposal wasn't going to take care of itself. As she updated figures and policed the comment section of her blog, a wave of fatigue threatened to drag her under.

Her fingers hesitated on the keyboard. Bleary-eyed, she glanced around as if expecting to meet a judgmental gaze from her dog. Closing her work windows, she typed Courtney Stevens's name into the search bar.

There were dozens of articles on the disappearance online. Some were from reputable newspapers and media, and others were posts on internet sleuthing message boards. She read article after article for the better part of three hours. Most users on the sleuthing board agreed that Courtney had been kidnapped by the Widowmaker, but others argued that the government was somehow involved in her disappearance.

Exhausted from spiraling down the rabbit hole of theories, Claire ate a packet of crackers from her bedside table and decided she had time for a nap. There would be plenty of time to get ready before the king of douche mountain darkened her doorstep. Setting her phone alarm with one half-crossed eye open, she tossed her phone onto the covers and snuggled in.

A knock at her front door jerked her out of sleep. She sat up like her bed was on fire. Rosie barked and jumped off the mattress, feet skittering in place for several seconds before gaining traction and rocketing off in the direction of the door.

Claire glanced at the bedside table beside her and saw that it was already 2:55 p.m. Why the hell hadn't her alarm clock gone off?

"Holy crap!" She leapt out of bed and ran to her vanity mirror, attempting in vain to fix her hair that had been perfectly styled by professionals only a few hours ago. Why was it that every time she saw Luke, she looked like day-old ramen noodles?

"Shit, shit, shit." She nearly stabbed herself in the eye with her mascara brush. Half her hair was yanked back in bobby pins. She sprinted to the door, where someone was still knocking. She flung the door open.

"Sorry to keep you waiting." She clutched a hand to her heaving chest. "I fell asleep."

Luke stood in her hallway, wearing black dress pants and a teal button-down shirt that brought out the green in his eyes. Two of the buttons at the top were open, revealing a hint of chest hair. Damn him.

"You look nice today," Claire said, without hiding the surprise in her voice.

"Thank you." He flashed her that unnerving smile. He stepped inside and then took another look at her. "Same goes to you. I notice you're not wearing pants."

The bottom dropped out of her stomach. She had been so worried about mascara and smoothing the pillow creases from her face that she had forgotten that the only thing she was wearing on the lower half of her body was a pair of her most comfortable granny panties. Of course it couldn't have been one of her dozens of pairs of cute underwear. Damn it to hell. She pulled the hem of her T-shirt down and crouched.

"Excuse me for a minute." She scuttled into her bedroom.

Today she had divulged her most embarrassing story on live television, and now a douchey narcissist with a body carved from a block of marble who already thought she was unprofessional had seen her answer the door in her granny panties. Had she not suffered enough?

In the bedroom, she stabbed at her phone. Why the hell

had the alarm not gone off? She specifically remembered setting it for 2:35. Scrolling through her list of alarms, she stopped. It was set for 2:35 a.m.

"Damn it, Claire," she hissed, slamming her phone down on top of her gray down comforter. What the hell was wrong with her? Things like this didn't happen to her. She was always organized, always professional, always on time. Something about Luke made her brain shift into idiot mode. Or maybe it was the Widowmaker paranoia, or the stress of Nicole's proposal. That was probably it.

When she emerged several minutes later, she was wearing pants and a proper blouse, and Luke was tugging Rosie through the kitchen and living room with a rope toy.

"I apologize for my lack of professionalism." Claire sat primly on the edge of her couch. She would be so professional that all thoughts of her floral granny panty greeting would be erased from his mind.

He had tugged his way back into the living room while she was talking, and suddenly he was sitting next to her. He moved quietly for a man over six feet tall.

"You can save your apology." He leaned in close and peered at her face.

"What are you doing?" She leaned away.

"Stop moving. I'm trying to make sure you don't have a concussion." A small flashlight appeared out of nowhere, and he shined it directly in her eyes.

"I don't really want to play doctor right now. I thought this was a business meeting? I've made us start late, so I'm sure you're eagerly waiting to drag me over the coals for that."

He grunted and reached into the briefcase he brought with him. He drew out some gauze and a bottle of vinegar.

"Can't make sound decisions about my best friend's

proposal if you're concussed. Though I'm not sure I trust your judgment either way."

Dick.

He gripped her chin and tilted her face toward him. She clamped her mouth shut, praying that she didn't have toxic nap breath as he leaned in close and gently lifted the lid of her afflicted eye. "Just hold still."

The fresh, clean scent of his soap engulfed her. A long, thin scar ran down his neck and disappeared beneath his collar. A spark of desire grew in her belly, and she balled her hands into fists. Stupid, sexy, vinegar-toting bossypants.

He shined the pocket flashlight into her eye and then flicked it away. Maybe he was blinding her so he could run away.

"Any double vision?" he asked.

"No." The word barely escaped her tightly pursed lips. He was so close there would be no escaping her nap breath.

"Any change in vision at all?" He shined the light in her other eye.

She shook her head.

He repeated the procedure with the other side and went back and forth a few times before flicking it off.

"I just wanted to make sure you didn't damage your eye." He set the flashlight down and unscrewed the cap on the bottle of vinegar. "I need you in fighting shape if we're going to pull all this off."

Pull all this off? Her gaze drifted down to his dress shirt. It would look even better on the floor.

Focus, you hormone-fueled idiot. Great, now she was going to be aroused every time she smelled vinegar. Boardwalk fries would be off limits for life.

"I'm guessing you saw the show this morning." Did that come out as casually as it sounded in her head?

Their knees touched ever so slightly as he doused the gauze with vinegar. Even this minimal contact sent her heart racing. She frowned and crossed her arms over her chest. Her body needed to get its shit together. As panty-droppingly hot as Luke was, she wasn't going to get involved. Her sex embargo was non-negotiable.

"It happened to be on while I was making breakfast," he said noncommittally. "Keep your eye closed tight." He held the back of her head with one hand as he leaned into her, pressing the vinegar-soaked gauze gently onto her eye.

She melted under his touch, fighting the urge to moan at the gentle pressure of his calloused fingers. It had been a long time since a man had handled her so tenderly.

"All of a sudden I'm really hungry for boardwalk fries."

He smirked. "Old Navy trick. Just keep it squeezed shut because it'll sting like hell."

"Navy as in the armed forces, or did you learn this trick while selling reasonably priced flip-flops?" She flinched and squeezed her eye as some vinegar crept under her eyelid. The skin was tight and tender, but the warmth of his hand gently applying pressure distracted from the pain.

"Huh?"

"Never mind."

Luke picked up her hand and put it on the gauze covering her eye. "How about some coffee?"

"Make it yourself," she said, almost welcoming the instant sensation of annoyance. "Pot's in the kitchen. Bring me some too. Then we can get down to business if you don't have any other condiments to apply to my face. Some ketchup in your briefcase, perhaps? Whole grain mustard in your sock?"

He walked into the kitchen without comment. A suspicious number of cabinet doors opened and closed.

"They're in the cabinet above the coffee maker," she called, fighting the urge to swivel around and watch.

"Oh, I figured. I was just snooping," he said. Two mugs clinked onto the counter. "You don't see many leopard print slow cookers."

She rolled her eyes. "Don't judge my appliances. There's creamer in the refrigerator."

The refrigerator door creaked open. "You should call the police. Someone seems to have stolen all your food."

"Very funny," she said. *Police*. Her stomach twisted. Somewhere in an evidence locker was the picture of her and Courtney sleeping. Vulnerable, unaware. Whoever took the picture knew exactly where she lived. He could be outside right now. Claire shuddered. If someone was after her, surely they wouldn't attack while she had company.

"I have everything I need. Running water, coffee creamer, sugar. I'm a minimalist," she continued, pushing the thought of the picture and its mysterious sender to the back of her mind.

"I can see that. Do you ever actually cook?"

"Actually, I love to cook." She turned to look at him from one eye. "I've just been crazy busy lately with prime proposal season. That and since it's just me here now, it's hard to find the motivation to cook for one person."

"Just you here now? Meaning you used to live with someone else?" he probed.

"Yes." Her face immediately grew hot. She turned back around and picked up her binder for Nicole's proposal.

She cringed as Luke banged around her kitchen, filling her coffee pot. He was possibly the slowest coffee maker in the world. She should have done it herself.

That "Pin the Junk on the Hunk" game on the far side of her refrigerator had gone out with the trash last week, right?

It had been clinging to the fridge by a single piece of tape since the last game night she had hosted. She aspired to have a pristine apartment, but proposal season had shattered her cleaning motivation.

"Interesting business you keep," he said as he re-entered the room. He handed her a mug with a penis-shaped cactus on it. "Very professional."

Damn it.

"This is my home, not my business. I didn't mean to offend your masculinity by displaying another unattainable male beauty standard." She took a long sip from the mug, maintaining eye contact with the one eye that wasn't obscured by a horticultural phallus.

The thin line of Luke's mouth twitched. Almost a smile. "Do you have any sort of over-the-counter pain meds here?"

"There's some aspirin in the kitchen," she said.

He frowned. "Do you have any NSAIDs? Aspirin could increase the bleeding around your eye."

"Any what now?" Claire asked.

"Non-steroidal anti-inflammatory drugs. You know, like ibuprofen."

She took a shallow breath and cursed her vagina. Nothing was sexier than intelligence. Even when it came from the mouth of an egotistical iceberg.

"I think I have a bottle of that in the bathroom. I'll be back." She stood and left him in the living room. He wasn't going to get an excuse to snoop in her medicine cabinet.

She popped the cabinet open and shook two tablets from the bottle. Gripping the sides of the sink, she studied her reflection.

"Okay, Claire," she whispered. "Remember your sex embargo. You don't need any more distractions or douchebags in your life. Work is all you need right now.

Pull yourself together and keep it professional. You can do this."

She tossed back her medicine with a swallow of water from the faucet and marched back to the door before abruptly turning around. She dug some mouthwash out of the medicine cabinet and swished violently. Just in case.

When she returned to the living room, Luke stood in front of her bookcase, holding a binder from one of her previous proposals.

"You actually commissioned an ice sculpture that looked like the couple?"

She nodded. "It was part of the theme."

"What was the theme? Spending mountains of cash on frivolities so some guy can get his girlfriend into bed?"

Just like that, the embers of desire that had kindled in her stomach extinguished as though they had taken a blast from a fire hose. Claire clenched her teeth and took deep breaths through her nose. "Did we not just have a discussion about showing each other professional courtesy and respect during work hours?"

He shut the binder, then tucked it back into its place on the bookshelf. "You're right. I *apologize* for my lack of professionalism," he said, raising his eyebrows as he parroted her words back at her.

"Oh, shut up." She sat cross-legged on the floor next to the coffee table and pulled Nicole's binder toward her. There was no sense in sitting primly on the edge of the couch all night when her professional illusion had already been shattered.

Luke disappeared into the kitchen again, presumably to snoop some more. For someone who was so antsy to talk about his ideas, he seemed to have zero impulse control.

She reached under the couch and carefully drew out the

archery bow she had stashed for Nicole's proposal. She leaned it against the coffee table for inspiration. Her arms ached with effort as she hefted the proposal binder onto the table.

Luke reappeared with a lumpy washcloth. "Put this on your face." He sat the bundle in front of her. Ice cubes clinked inside. "But only for ten minutes, and then you need to take it off."

"What happens at minute eleven?" The hard edges of the cubes jutted into her cheeks and poked her in the eye.

"Your body needs sufficient time to warm the tissue back up before you put the ice back on. Let's talk business." He sank down next to her. Heat radiated from him.

Rosie came over and sniffed his shoes for a moment before settling down between the two of them. He scratched her behind the ears, and she laid her muzzle on his leg and closed her eyes. Traitor. Again.

"Tell me more about the movie this whole thing is based on." He leaned over and picked up the bow. He held it in his lap and drummed the string with his fingers as Claire spoke. His forearms clenched with the movement, tanned skin tensing and releasing. God help her.

"Sure. The entire proposal will revolve around Nicole's favorite childhood movie, *The Princess and the Arrow*. The main character, Avellana, is a fisherman's daughter who is actually a princess. Basically, her war-torn kingdom loses their king in a siege, and they fear that there are no heirs left to take over the throne. The queen, however, confesses on her deathbed that they have a daughter who was entrusted to a family of loyal peasants when she was just a baby."

Luke nodded, so Claire drew a deep breath to continue.

"Then Avellana is plucked from her humble beginnings as a fisherman's daughter and is brought to court. She is a kind and fair ruler, but she is not by any means a stuffy royal. She participates in archery and sword-fighting competitions all while learning how to run a country. And of course, at the end of the movie there's a ball."

"Of course."

"The movie opens with her diving into the ocean in a storm to save her 'father's' apprentice." Claire flipped the laminated pages of the binder with one hand until she got to the first of the series of scenes she was planning.

She pointed at a picture of a large indoor swimming pool. "For the first scene, I want it to be nautical-themed. Nicole usually swims at a local gym after work before she heads home, and I have already contacted them to ask about renting the entire pool and setting up an obstacle course." She wiggled her eyebrows.

He let out a low whistle. "You know this is insane, right?"

She paused. How did you explain romance to a cynic? "You know how Kyle and Nicole are always doing these elaborate, themed date nights and posting them on Instagram? And how everything has to be a 'thing'?"

"Oh, yeah. Like 'Pasta Carbonara Tuesday' and that time they hunted for Easter eggs while skydiving?"

"Exactly. Do you see why it would be ridiculous and disappointing for Kyle to just roll over in bed one morning and be like 'Hey, wanna get hitched?'"

"Point taken. So, the first scene?"

"Right. She'll run the course, and then I hope to have her dive to the deep end to rescue a dummy. So that's going to be your first major challenge—filming Nicole underwater."

Luke raised his eyebrows and set the bow down. "You are determined to make this as difficult as possible, aren't you? We'll need rebreathers, underwater ambient light, camera housings, and a whole score of other things. And the fluorescent lighting in those indoor pools is going to be a nightmare." He raked a hand through his hair. He almost looked flustered. Good.

"This is not going to be cheap. Or easy." He pulled a small notebook out of his back pocket and started scribbling.

"Are you afraid of a challenge?" she asked politely.

He looked up from his scribbles. "Never."

"I'm sure you can handle it."

"Are you sure this is something Nicole will really want to do on the same day she'll be putting on a princess dress and dancing at a ball?"

She snorted. "Clearly you haven't spent much time alone with Coli. She is the most competitive and adventurous person I know. I have gone skydiving no fewer than three times because she insisted I come along. The only thing she loves more than this movie is adventure. Trust me, she will love this."

"Fair enough. But for real, how much money is Kyle spending on this? He's a lawyer, not a sultan."

"He's been saving up for a long time." She smiled. In fact, he had saved a portion of every paycheck since graduation—even while he was still working at the Pretzel Palace and studying for the bar. "Luckily for him, he has a great job and a friend who's willing to give him an excellent discount. Plus, with all my connections with suppliers, we locked in the lowest prices for everything. And, as I'm sure you know, his parents are loaded."

Luke laughed. "That is certainly true. I remember for his twelfth birthday he got a tree house that was a near exact replica of the Death Star."

That got her attention. "No freaking way. Do his parents still have it?" She took a sip of coffee.

"They do. His dad got it behind his mom's back, and his mom was furious about it because it wrecked her vision or whatever for their backyard. But she let them put it up because it made Kyle so happy. They even ran power to it and everything. We would go up there on summer vacation in college and get drunk on Jack Daniels and play *Murder Melee Two*."

"Shut up." Claire put her pen down.

"Sorry," he said. "You're right, we should be talking about the proposal."

"No, I mean—" She jumped up and hurried over to the cabinet underneath her TV. She dug through a few drawers before pulling out a video game and slapping it down on the table in front of him.

The words *Murder Melee 2* in blood-red lettering hovered over a troll holding an axe. The body of a decapitated wizard was being crushed under one of his hairy feet.

"Is this—"

"The re-release of the compatible version for the newest gaming system. Which I also have." She indicated the sleek black console in the media cabinet.

He put a hand on her cheek. It burned where he touched her. "I'm almost starting to trust your judgment."

She laughed and swatted his hand away. Her sex embargo was looking less attractive by the second.

"Maybe once we finish up the meeting, I could be persuaded to kick your ass. If you don't have other plans this evening, I mean." Was that too eager?

He snorted. "You don't understand. *Murder Melee Two* is my favorite game, period. I played it every day of my teen years."

"It's my favorite too. It was seriously torture waiting for the third one to come out." She glared at her cabinet. "And then when it did, it was a complete disappointment. My nephew loves it, but the second one will always be the best."

"Thank you!" He banged his hand on the table. "Kyle and I argued about this for like five years. He loves the third one because of the whole siege at the end, but I wasn't impressed by the storyline."

"Seriously, it was so generic and unimaginative. I hate that they changed the creative directors after the second game."

"That was exactly the problem," Luke said, staring into her eyes.

"Anyway..." Her face was hot again. She was losing focus. She didn't want to like him. There was no reason to like him. He was a pompous, self-important dingus. And yet, her apartment felt warmer, safer with him here. The possible presence of a murderer outside her window suddenly wasn't as daunting.

"What I need you to tell me is how much I need to rein in my creative vision so that it still comes off well on film. For this first scene, anyway."

He opened his mouth to respond when there was a knock at the door.

Claire stood. A glance through the peephole only showed a blur of pink. "Who's there?" she asked.

"Waverly's Flowers," a muffled voice called. "Got a delivery for you."

Luke stepped up behind her.

She opened the door, revealing a pair of legs and a torso-sized flower arrangement. Flowers of all types in varying shades of pink exploded out of a large vase. "Where would you like this, ma'am?" the voice behind the flowers asked.

"Oh, um, in the kitchen is fine." She held the door open and allowed him to enter.

The man deposited the flowers on her kitchen island, smiled at her, and then left.

"You sure get a lot of flowers," Luke said. "These from the ex too?"

"I doubt it. He never paid attention to what I actually like." She walked around the arrangement. "Huh. I can't find a card, which also means they aren't from him. In the unlikely event that he actually did something nice, he always made a huge deal about it. Maybe they're from the show this morning or a client? But I can't remember telling anyone what type of flowers I like. Must be a lucky guess." She leaned forward to sniff a stargazer lily before shrugging and returning to the coffee table.

He walked over to the bouquet and examined it carefully. With a frown, he pulled his notebook out and wrote something down.

"What's wrong?" she asked. What was he writing? She would have bet her last dollar that he wasn't writing down her flower preferences. He wasn't interested in her, and he definitely didn't seem like the kind of person to put stock in something that would die in a matter of days.

He shook his head. "Nothing."

And just like that, he was back to being annoying by refusing to share more dumb secrets.

They talked for another two hours, going over the specs of the gym's indoor pool and discussing logistics for renting the horse and carriage. Occasionally as they talked, his gaze drifted toward the bouquet of flowers. Why was he so obsessed with them? Surely, he wasn't jealous. Maybe he was allergic and too polite to ask her to move them? Unlikely.

"You don't need to mansplain aperture to me." She rubbed her temples with her fingertips. "Nicole basically taught me a 500-level course on all things camera when I job shadowed her last year."

"You job shadowed a contracted employee?"

"Some of us try to learn a little about all the aspects of our businesses. Let me just show you the damn scene." She rescued her laptop from the bedroom and opened it, quickly entering her password.

"Whoa," he said.

A dozen tabs with various Courtney Stevens headlines littered her browser. *Damn it.*

"She was my roommate at Venor," she explained, closing tab after tab of articles and conspiracy theories. "I was just..."

"Doing some research?" he suggested.

"Worried about her," she refuted. "I actually—" The picture she had received hovered at the tip of her tongue. Should she tell him? No, he would probably tell her she was being paranoid. And maybe there was a logical explanation for the picture.

"Never mind."

His penetrating gaze burned into the side of her face, but she refused to make eye contact as she found the video clip and played it. By some miracle, they finally reached full agreement on the first stop of the proposal. Luke was still insistent on visiting the pool in person before he would give his final approval, but at least the fights over the details were done.

He leaned back, stretching his spine and rolling his neck out. He slung his arms behind his head, causing his biceps to bulge against his dress shirt. Not that she noticed. "I would call that a successful meeting. How's your eye feeling? Still tender?"

She pressed her fingertips to her eye and winced. "It's still there. That's something."

He pressed a gentle hand to it. Her toes curled. "I think you can stop icing it now. It should start to heal quickly."

She opened her afflicted eye. His stormy green gaze bored into her. She glanced away, searching for something —anything—to avoid meeting those stupidly handsome eyes.

"Thanks." She addressed the tiny purple stain on her rug from a memorable pomegranate cosmo party. There was silence. He was definitely still staring at her.

She lifted her eyes to meet his. They were only inches apart.

"So," she said.

"So," he said, his expression neutral.

She leaned in closer. He moved in too (*aha!*), but then she reached past him and picked up the gaming controller that sat on the floor behind him.

"Excuse me, just needed to get this." She smiled innocently at him and turned on the console. Business hours were over. Why shouldn't she have a little fun and torture Luke while she was at it? "Business Claire has now closed." She tugged her hair from the topknot she had tied it into. It fell around her shoulders, releasing a waft of her coconut shampoo.

"I wasn't aware she had ever been here," he quipped. "Just to clarify, 'Business Claire' is the Claire that doesn't wear pants to business meetings?"

She picked up a pillow and smacked him in the face.

"Do you want to talk, or do you want to get your ass kicked?" She handed him a second controller.

"Please, you'll be wallowing in the Mysterious Myre in the first five minutes."

"In your dreams." She crawled on her hands and knees over to her cabinet to put the disk in. As she closed the drive, she glanced over her shoulder at him. "I can't play *Murder Melee* in business casual. I'll be back."

She left her bedroom door open a crack while she changed. "Hey, it's almost dinnertime. Want to order pizza or Chinese or something? My treat."

"Sure," he said. "Which are you in the mood for?"

"I just had pizza yesterday, but I love pizza more than some people love their own children. Chinese is always fantastic too, or—ooh! What about—" She paused. Maybe she needed to mix a salad in there every once in a while.

"Subs?" Luke asked.

She returned to the living room in yoga booty shorts and a soft white T-shirt.

"How did you know I was going to say subs?"

"I didn't. I just decided that they sound amazing."

"Agreed," Claire said. "There's a great place on Seventh that delivers." She went into her kitchen and stood on her tiptoes next to the refrigerator. Her arm contorted as she groped. Why did she keep putting the menu box on top of the fridge?

A rather muscular forearm entered her visual field as he pulled the box down for her.

"Thank you." She leafed through the papers, plucked one from the stack, and held it up to him.

"Oh, no way. Two Boys is still open? I haven't had them in years."

She raised an eyebrow and smirked. "You haven't had two boys for years?"

Luke snatched the menu. "Don't you have a Jet Ski to fall off of somewhere?"

"Wow, you will dig up any excuse to keep me from beating you at this game."

"You're not going to beat me," he called as she walked into the living room.

"Turkey sub, everything on it. Call it in. And stay out of the living room until I say so. Oh, and do me a favor and take Rosie out?"

"What are you doing to the living room?"

"Don't worry about it." The rarely used pocket doors creaked as she tugged them out to hide the room.

Twenty minutes later, Luke and Rosie were impatiently pacing the kitchen. "Can I come back in yet?"

"Almost. Not yet."

"Are you rigging my controller so that you can win?"

"Please. Like I need a rigged controller to beat you. There!"

She paused with her hand on the door. What was she doing, fraternizing with the enemy? Exposing her dog daughter to that toxic, judgy, masculine energy? This was supposed to be a penis-free year while she re-examined her priorities and grew the business. She hadn't even made it to June yet, and she was already salivating over someone's forearms. Not that she was going to do anything about it. Her mind was made up. Forearms or no forearms, she was not going to sleep with Luke. They could be friends. Well, coworkers who occasionally hung out.

She slid the pocket doors open a crack and stepped out sideways before closing them again. Luke stood at the window, cradling Rosie like a baby. He pointed to something on the street. Rosie's ears perked up. Oh, no. Was that the sound of all the remaining eggs in her ovaries screaming at the same time?

She cleared her throat. He turned around. "It's about time."

"For your information, I was creating an immersive gaming experience. Think of it as an icebreaker between coworkers."

His eyebrows rose. "An icebreaker? You don't think you broke the ice sufficiently earlier when you answered the door in floral underwear?"

Great. He had seen the granny panties. "Do you want to see it or not?"

He put Rosie on the floor.

"After you." Claire pushed open the doors.

Luke walked in and turned around slowly. "Did you just build a blanket fort?"

Her heart thudded. This was stupid. Now she was the weird girl who planned proposals and made blanket forts on Wednesdays. "Maybe. My nephew and I do this every time he visits, even though he's now twelve and pretends that he's too cool for it. It enhances the video game experience."

He dropped to his knees and crawled underneath the edge of the blanket fort. "Nice," he said.

The coffee table was gone. Tons of pillows and blankets were stacked at the foot of the couch so that they could lean against it as they played. The linens surrounded them like a nerdy cocoon.

She crawled in after him, holding a corner of the fort open and whistling for Rosie. The dog wiggled her cute butt through the hole and immediately started sniffing everything in the vicinity, thrilled by the new living quarters.

"I don't care if you think it's stupid," she declared. "This blanket fort is corgi-approved."

"Stupid? Are you kidding me? This is the coolest thing I've done since I moved back." He looked her up and down again. "I'm jealous that you get to be in pajamas." He tugged on the end of her shirt.

"Don't you have a T-shirt on underneath your button-down?"

"Nah. It's too hot for that."

"I would offer you a shirt, but something tells me you and I are slightly different sizes," she said.

"That's all right. I'll just take it off anyway."

"Oh, well—" Claire was immediately distracted by the slow unveiling of a nicely chiseled torso one button at a time.

She tried not to stare. "Do you want me to hang that up for you?"

"Nah." He tossed it on the floor. Rosie walked over to investigate. After a moment or two of sniffing, she lay on her back and rolled around on it.

"Rosie, don't do that!" Claire scolded. She went to shoo Rosie off his shirt, but Luke grabbed her wrist.

"Don't worry about it. She's cute, she can do whatever she wants."

Her wrist burned beneath his gentle touch. Where was the asshole who consistently insulted her life's work? Who had replaced him with a reasonable, agreeable, shirtless human being? Oh, no. The sex embargo. Remember the sex embargo.

He smiled and leaned against the pile of pillows. He patted the spot next to him.

She was just about to sit when the doorbell rang. "That must be the food." She knelt to exit the fort again.

"Stay. I'm paying for this," he ordered.

"I don't need you to pay for my meals." She was nearly out of the flap when he grabbed hold of her ankle and tugged, yanking her back inside. "Ouch! Thanks for the carpet burn."

"It's not about need." Luke left the fort. She crawled out after him.

He answered the door shirtless and pulled out his wallet. The delivery man handed over the food without blinking and happily accepted the tip.

"I'm giving you money." She refused to owe him anything. Her vegetable drawer clinked as she opened it. She drew out two beers and popped the tops.

He took a beer and followed her back into the fort. "This is not how I expected to be spending my evening." He settled back against the pillows and took a swig of beer.

"I'm sure it's much more exciting than whatever you were planning."

"You're right. I was thinking about unpacking some boxes tonight and doing some editing on my project, but I guess if the alternative is arguing with you about work and schooling you in *MM Two* all evening, I'll take it."

"Tell me about your project." The smell of freshly baked bread filled the blanket fort. She hadn't realized that she was starving. The packet of saltines had long since digested.

"I can't." He lofted the sub in his strong, calloused hands and took a bite.

Claire had never been jealous of a hoagie before.

"I never talk to anyone who isn't on my team about the project until it's ready for release," he explained.

"Technically, you're on my team, which means that by the transverse property, I am on your team. So spill."

"Absolutely not. All I can tell you is that it's going to be huge."

"Huge, huh? Is there a secret underground marijuana garden on someone's estate in town?"

"Nope."

"Okay," she said pensively. "Is there some kind of evil demonic clown on the loose terrorizing children?"

"Close," he said, smirking.

"Well, that's terrifying," she said. "Let me go make sure the door's locked."

"I don't think you need to worry about killer clowns. Killer showers, though, those you might need to watch out for."

She shot him a dirty look with her good eye. "Is there a brothel underneath the library on Edgecombe Street? The last time I was there, a suspiciously attractive librarian checked me out. My books, I mean."

He smiled. "Not that I know of."

"How about if I beat your total kills first round, you give me a hint?"

Luke let out a hearty laugh as he finished the last of his sandwich.

"You could grow eight more thumbs and not be able to beat me. You don't understand. This game *was* my childhood."

"Someone's awfully cocky. Do we have a deal?"

He stared her down. "You're not going to win. But fine. If by some miracle you manage to beat me, I will give you a small hint about what I'm working on."

Claire held the pinky of her right hand out to him. "Pinky promise."

"Are we in second grade?"

"We're in a blanket fort." She held her pinky out more

forcefully. "You can't break a pinky promise. And if you do, I get to dump hot sauce in your boxers."

He sputtered in his beer. "Since when?"

"Luke, I don't make the rules. I just enforce them. Blame society. So come on, give me your pinky. Unless you're scared."

"I'm not scared."

He glared at her and slowly extended his finger. They ceremoniously hooked pinkies.

"You better start warming up those thumbs." She rolled her shoulders back and pulled out a hair tie. She threw her hair up in a messy bun and got ready to kick some ass.

CHAPTER NINE

To Do:
- Break into L's office and figure out what his stupid
documentary is about
- Get quote on cocktail table rentals
- Sound check on Bluetooth speakers

"Yes! Suck it!" Claire triumphantly threw down her controller and rose onto her knees, doing a wild celebratory dance as she hunched under the ceiling of the blanket fort. Rosie, who had been laying on her back dead asleep, jumped to her feet and barked.

Luke looked utterly dumfounded. The controller was in danger of falling out of his hand. He mouthed wordlessly at the screen. "I can't believe this. This has never happened to me before."

She had won by just one kill.

"You are a *looo-ser*. You are a *looooo-ser*," she chanted, still dancing. She collapsed on the floor and turned to him. "Drop the hint."

"I demand a rematch. There was no way that was anything but beginner's luck." His arms were crossed and his mouth—that mouth—had hardened into a solid line.

"Why do you insist on underestimating me? I told you. I. Rock. At. Video. Games." She jabbed him in the stomach with each word.

"You just wanted an excuse to touch my abs."

She crossed her arms. "Don't change the subject. You owe me a hint."

He threw up his hands in exasperation. "Okay, fine. Let me think."

Her phone vibrated somewhere outside the fort. *Shit.* She really should have kept it on her. What if a client had called? Had that fall in the shower knocked her brain out of her skull? Maybe she did have a concussion. "You can think while I get this."

She crawled halfway out of the fort and grabbed her phone from her purse. Her feet were still inside the tent, and she tapped them on the floor as she talked.

"Hey, Min. What's the status on the guy from this morning?"

"Tyler passed. I'm going to start working on some of the initial stuff now and let you know my ideas tomorrow."

"Awesome! Promise I'll be along for the next meeting. After that performance this morning, I'm sure I won't have people banging on my door for another interview."

"You did great! Your eye was barely noticeable. I thought you handled everything really well, especially when she started asking about Jason. How much did it suck to relive the story?"

"Only slightly less humiliating than it was when it actually happened."

Mindy had been there on the evening in question, and she had helped Claire rinse her party dress and destroyed shoes in the bathroom.

"I'm sorry. But hey, at least you were able to build an amazing business out of his stupid, drunken behavior."

"I guess you're right. Thank god I wasn't on Jerry Springer or something, or they probably would have surprised me by bringing him in and having him redo the whole—Hey! Knock it off," Claire said, kicking her foot at the hands that tickled it. She drew her feet out of his reach.

Luke laughed.

"Who's that?" Mindy asked.

"No one," Claire said.

"Um, is that Luke? Wasn't your meeting supposed to be over like two hours ago?"

"It ran a little late. We'll talk later." The hands were tickling again.

"Are you having dinner? Is he going to stay over? Are you going to do him?" Mindy screeched.

"I'll call you later. Bye, Min." Claire ended the call and threw the phone back in her bag. He probably hadn't been able to hear Mindy, right? She was loud, but he was sandwiched in a blanket fort.

"Sorry about that." She slid back inside. "Mindy wanted to brief me on a new client."

Luke was holding Rosie in his arms like a baby and making kissy noises as he rubbed her belly. Her tongue flopped out of her mouth, and she appeared to grin at Claire upside down. "So, are you going to do me?" he inquired, a mischievous look in his eyes. His black pants were now covered in dog hair.

Her cheeks burned. "Mindy has an active imagination. Now tell me your hint, and it better be a good one."

"What's the proposal for your new client going to be like? A fleet of yachts bobbing in a swimming pool full of champagne?"

"For your information, he is a Purple Heart recipient who is proposing to his girlfriend, a critical care nurse in the Army. Frankly, they deserve a swimming pool full of champagne. Now stop changing the subject and tell me the hint."

He sighed. "All right. Your one and only hint is that my new project deals with women."

"With women. Oh, good. What a great hint. You've only eliminated half of the seven billion people on the planet. Are you doing one of those sleep-your-way-across-the-United-States documentaries where you document differences in sexual preferences by state?"

"No, but that's a pretty badass idea," he said. "I should write that down." He leaned to one side, still holding Rosie as he pulled a mini notebook and pen out of the back pocket of his pants.

"You have a tiny notebook," Claire observed.

"I do. It's nowhere near as ridiculous as one of your binders."

"Why don't you just use your phone?"

"I like the feeling of physically writing something with pen and paper. It feels more concrete."

"Hmm." She got what he meant, but she wasn't going to admit it. She wiggled the controller at him. "Are you ready for another ass whooping?"

"I am, as long as you stop asking me questions about my project."

"If you weren't being so damn mysterious about it, I probably wouldn't even care. I've got enough things to worry about. But since it bothers you so much, there's no way I'm going to stop asking you. I'm going to find out." She pressed the start button.

"Yeah, we'll see," Luke said, leading his troll lord into a pack of wolves.

THE SUN HADN'T QUITE PENETRATED THE BLANKET FORT THE next morning when Claire awoke to the sound of rhythmic hoofbeats. She stirred but wasn't willing to open her eyes yet. What was she lying on? Why was it so warm? And why did her neck hurt so much? Her eyes flew open. She was lying on Luke's bare, muscular chest. His arm was curled around her, and his nose nuzzled her hair. Holy shit.

He had fallen asleep with the controller in his hand, which was causing his horse to gallop directly into a castle wall. She groped with one hand and managed to pluck the controller out of his grasp.

Rosie was splayed on her back next to Claire. She nudged Claire's hand and whined.

As she peeled her cheek from his skin, a small puddle of drool was left behind. So embarrassing. *Please stay asleep.* She gathered a corner of a nearby blanket and dabbed at it.

When he didn't stir, she extricated herself from his arm and slid backward out of the blanket fort. She slipped a pair of shoes on before grabbing Rosie's leash and tiptoeing out the door.

Rosie immediately set to her sacred dog duty of sniffing every tree in a three-block radius. A car door slammed, jolting Claire out of her accidental sleepover fog. Luke was the first man who had stayed over at her apartment since her projectile-vomiting turd bucket of a fiancé had moved out eight months ago. What did it mean? Nicole's words echoed in her mind. Luke was a *ladies' man*. A tingle of anxiety sprouted in her stomach. Despite all her firm self-talk about respecting herself and disengaging from the male sex this year, she had woken up to a stupidly sexy, half-naked ladies' man on her living room floor. The last thing she needed was an egotistical coworker/known manwhore douching his way into her life. Him staying over was an accident, an oversight. It didn't mean anything. Luke Islestorm would not break her sex embargo. He was a coworker by necessity, nothing more.

After Rosie did her business, they trotted down the street to a café with a walk-up window. Claire ordered two raspberry mocha iced coffees and chocolate chip muffins. As she waited, the back of her neck prickled and she glanced down the street. Was it her imagination, or was there someone staring at her? She probed the storefronts across the street. Half of the shops weren't even open. The few people on the sidewalk didn't glance in her direction. She was imagining things again. Juggling the food, coffees, and leash, she headed back home, glancing behind her every couple of feet, but there weren't any trench coat-wearing creeps following her.

Halfway up the flight of stairs, she set the coffee and pastries on the windowsill and attempted to fix her smudged makeup and haystack hair in the window's reflection. Her skin would surely rebel after neglecting her cleansing routine last night. Deeming her appearance a lost cause, she let herself back into the apartment. A startled Luke was shoving his foot into a sock. His shirt was back on. Good.

Rosie sprinted straight for him as though she hadn't seen him in a century.

"Well, good morning," Claire said calmly. "I brought you the girliest coffee I could find."

He rubbed the back of his neck. "Thanks. I hate to start the day with my masculinity intact. Sorry about all this. I didn't exactly expect our business meeting to turn into a video gaming sleepover. I don't even remember falling asleep."

She smiled. "Clearly. When I woke up, you were riding your horse directly into the wall of Castle Maverick at full gallop. You must have been exhausted from getting your ass handed to you. Poor thing." She held out a coffee.

He grunted and took a sip. "What *is* this?"

"That is a raspberry mocha iced coffee."

"This is amazing."

"There's a muffin in here for you too," she said, opening the bag and tossing it to him. "Want butter?"

"Is there any other way to eat a muffin?"

There was an innuendo in there somewhere, but she didn't take the bait. He followed her into the kitchen, arms full of their cups and plates from the previous evening. As she dug out the butter, he began filling up the sink with water and pineapple-scented dish soap.

"You don't have to do that," she said. "I have a dishwasher."

He didn't respond. Typical. Her dishwasher probably wasn't up to his unreasonably high standards.

She set a plate with a freshly buttered muffin next to him and took over drying duty.

He washed, she dried, and when the evidence of the previous night had been erased, they stood at the kitchen island and ate their muffins in silence. He took her plate from her as soon as she finished and washed it too.

Somewhere in the apartment, her phone beeped. *Shit.* What if it was a client?

"I'll be right back." She rushed back into the living room. Where the hell was it? She kicked around a few pillows until she found her phone and then ran down the hallway into her bathroom. She shut and locked the door before perching on the edge of her bathtub.

There were two texts from Mindy and one from Nicole. Mindy asked if Luke was still there along with a series of eggplant emojis and then detailed her agenda for the day. Mindy must have relayed the incident to Nicole as well, because Nicole sent a page-long message asking questions about her evening with him.

Claire's hands trembled as she texted Nicole back.

Claire: *Sorry, fell asleep early last night. Luke accidentally stayed over and he's handwashing my dishes as we speak. I was perilously close to throwing my sex embargo to the wind and mounting him in a blanket fort last night, but nothing happened.*

Seconds later, the phone vibrated.

Nicole: *He stayed the night?! Is he the first since Jason?*

She flinched at the name of her ex-fiancé.

Claire: *We were playing video games together and fell asleep. It hardly counts as "staying over." Besides, he's a ladies' man. I'm NOT getting involved.*

Nicole: *It sure sounds like you're getting involved. We need to talk about this later.*

Claire: *Agreed. Meet up for dinner after work?*

Nicole: *Sure, if you and Prince Charming over there aren't having another all-night meeting.*

Claire: *Shut up. Text me later.*

Claire quickly fired off a similar message to Mindy, who responded with a line of fifteen question marks. Claire swiped a brush through her tangled hair and stabbed a toothbrush into her mouth.

Mindy followed up by demanding to hear more about the evening and then told Claire that she had been exactly right. The mysterious British gentleman had texted her after eight o'clock the night before. Men. So predictable.

Claire walked back down the hallway with half a mind to ask Luke if her text timing theory was correct. He stood in her kitchen, messenger bag bulging with the notes he had taken the night before. He was frowning at the giant flower arrangement again. Maybe he had a flower fetish.

"Are you headed out?" she asked, leaning against the back of the couch in a way she hoped looked casual.

"Yeah, I have to jump in the shower and then meet an interviewee this morning." He lugged the bag over his shoulder. He sounded distracted. "Thanks for the coffee. And that muffin."

"No problem. Let me know when you're ready to schedule the next meeting," she said. "And thanks for dinner last night."

He bent over to scratch Rosie under the chin before opening her front door and stepping into the long, beige hallway. He even looked good under the harsh fluorescent lighting after a night of sleeping on the floor. She followed him, expecting him to make another joke about her admiring his ass.

"I'll call you later. About the meeting, I mean. Keep your door locked, okay?" he said, suddenly more stern. He offered nothing but a small wave as he walked away.

She tilted her head. What was that weird noise? Some kind of mechanical clicking coming from the end of the hallway? Strange. Probably a new mechanical failure coming from that death trap of an elevator.

"Okay," Claire said slowly, watching as he disappeared down the stairs.

As she turned to enter her apartment, a flash of red disappeared around the corner by the elevator—the same place the noise had come from. It was probably Lucky, her neighbor's notoriously curious cat that was regularly forced to wear colorful sweaters. She shrugged and shut her door.

Back in the living room, she drummed her fingers against the back of the couch. Why had Luke suddenly changed his demeanor so drastically? Was it his upcoming interview? And why did he keep staring at her flowers?

She picked up a corner of the blanket fort and tugged it toward her, collapsing her creation.

CHAPTER TEN

To Do:
- *Consider hiring a freelance bookkeeper*
- *Take Bertha for an oil change*
- *Contact landlord about leaky ceiling in the south-west corner of the warehouse*

CLAIRE THREW HERSELF INTO HER WORK. THE STRANGE, sexually charged sleepover had no place in her mind among the details of Barney and Nicole's proposals. She spent the morning on the phone negotiating deals with lighting vendors. After haggling over prices for what seemed like hours, she had successfully reserved enough battery-operated lights to make Luke's yard look like a dreamy fairytale. Maybe she should have asked permission, but it was too late.

The rest of the day passed in a daze of talking details and logistics with customers, vendors, and Mindy. She dragged out her receipts from various purchases the last week and updated the running tabs on the shared spreadsheets she used to keep her clients in the loop on costs.

She reached out to multiple bridal stores to get quotes on recreating the dress from *The Princess and the Arrow*. Throughout the day, she had kept her phone next to her on the couch. Although she had several messages from Nicole and Mindy, and even one probing text from her mom asking if she had recently cleansed her apartment with sage, she hadn't heard from Luke. Not that she wanted to talk to him.

"He's probably busy bossing someone around," she said to Rosie, who was standing on her hind legs, staring at the pigeons on the fire escape. Rosie cocked her head skeptically before going back to watching the winged rats.

"What?" Claire said. "He said he had a big interview with someone for his top secret project this morning. Or maybe he dragged his big blue balls over to the home of some poor girl with no self esteem. Good for him. I can wash my dishes all by myself."

She stood and stretched, pulling out her phone to check the time. "I'm getting in the shower. Don't eat anything."

Claire showered away the previous evening. Why had he washed her dishes though? He could have just grabbed the muffin and headed out. Surely, he wasn't trying to spend more time with her. Whatever. She refused to continue thinking about him. Instead of blow-drying her hair, she twisted the curly mass into a sleek topknot and brushed a heavy layer of concealer over her black eye. She pulled on a red floral sundress and paired it with some strappy sandals.

As she locked her apartment door behind her, her phone rang. Jason. For the third time today. She ignored the call and rolled her eyes. How had he not learned after eight painful months that she wanted nothing to do with him?

On the way to the restaurant, she opted to take a long, meandering route. No car seemed to linger behind her for long, but better safe than sorry. She pulled up with five minutes to spare and waved to the chronically early Nicole, who was in the car next to her.

They were seated in their favorite booth by the window. When the waiter arrived, they both ordered a hard cider and a bacon cheeseburger without opening the menu.

Nicole unfolded her napkin and put it on her lap. "Tell me everything about last night."

Claire scanned the rest of the restaurant before leaning in closer and dropping her voice. "I will, but first I have to tell you something really weird that happened earlier this week."

"Earlier this week? And you waited until now to tell me?"

"I don't like to think about it, and I'm hoping the situation will just go away. But anyway, I got a really weird piece of mail this week. Remember how Courtney and I had bunk beds freshman year until she started sneaking all those guys in and waking me up in the middle of the night with the bed slamming off the wall?"

Nicole groaned. "How could I forget?"

"Someone sent me a picture of Courtney and me in our bunk beds fast asleep."

Nicole choked on her cider. "What do you mean? Like someone was spying on you? What the hell?"

Claire slid her phone across the table and showed her friend the picture she had taken.

"It looks like someone was standing outside your window."

Claire nodded. "We were on the first floor that year."

Nicole sat back in her seat and folded her hands in her

lap. Her eyebrows furrowed and her lips pursed.

Claire braced herself. Nicole was almost certainly winding up to ask a slew of questions Claire didn't have the answers to.

After a few seconds of silence, Nicole spoke. "First, why would someone take pictures of you while you were sleeping? And second, why would they hold on to that picture until now? Do you think it was whoever took her? Have they been following her since college? And how do they know you? And how do they know where you *live*?"

Claire's stomach hardened into a fist. This was exactly why she had waited so long to tell Nicole.

"I honestly have no idea. I don't really want to talk about it, but I wanted you to know. I took the picture to the police station, but they didn't seem overly concerned. I haven't been able to stop thinking about it. I haven't checked the mail in days because I'm afraid of what I might find."

Nicole propped her elbow on the table and rested her chin in her hand. "Well, shit."

"My thoughts exactly."

"I'm so sorry that happened to you. I really hope it was just a random, onetime thing, and that's the end of it." Her tone was casual, but she set her glass down harder than necessary. Her expression had not relaxed, and her gaze kept darting to her phone.

Claire took a large gulp of her cider. She might as well unload the rest of the crazy. "I'm not sure that it was. Sometimes it feels like someone's following me. Usually, it's when I walk Rosie. I can't figure out if it's real or all in my head."

Nicole reached across the table and grabbed one of Claire's hands. "Do you want to stay with me for a while? For a change of scenery? Maybe it would bring you some peace of mind."

Claire shook her head. "Thank you, but no. It's better for me to be within city limits for work right now. Can we talk about something else?"

"Yes!" Nicole said enthusiastically, but her worried expression didn't disappear. "Tell me about what happened with Luke."

Claire groaned. She didn't really want to talk about him either. But Nicole would never let her rest until she heard every detail.

Nicole sipped her drink thoughtfully as Claire described the evening. When she finished, Nicole tapped on the table with one short, unmanicured nail. "Throughout the whole night and the morning, he never really made a move?"

"No. Or at least, I don't think so. He tickled my foot, but that's pretty far away from my vagina."

Nicole snorted. "So, you're really not interested in him?"

"No," Claire said firmly. "He's a coworker."

Nicole stared at her with her eyebrows raised.

"And I have a sex embargo, remember?"

Nicole put down her napkin and stared at Claire. "When are you going to give up this embargo thing? Jason was a real fuckin' dick. There's no denying that. But are you going to let him sabotage the rest of your life? Your business is built around your belief in true love. It's literally your job."

"Not everyone finds true love, Coli. I was a delusional idiot who thought that I had found it, but I couldn't have been more wrong. I can't even trust my own judgment. I refuse to get hurt again. Especially not by an egotistical maniac with the body of a Greek god. It's so much easier and more fulfilling for me to plan other people's happily ever afters."

Nicole pointed a finger at her. "You are not a delusional idiot. You deserve love. I'm not saying Luke is the love of your life, but you have to be open to the possibility of meeting whoever that is. Maybe he's here right now." She lifted her eyes and scanned the restaurant.

Claire glanced around the room. A man in a trucker hat at the bar belched and rubbed his beer belly.

"Yes, that must be him. It's easy for you to say. You and Kyle are the most obnoxiously perfect couple ever. You guys barely even argue. This project isn't really even underway yet, and he's already argued with me about every single aspect of the proposal."

"Really? Like what?"

Claire froze, and she immediately blurted out the first thing that came to mind. "Dragons."

"Dragons?" Nicole raised her eyebrows.

"Dragons." Claire affirmed.

"Okay. Is he pro-dragon or anti-dragon?"

"Luke is anti-dragon. But I told him that he clearly doesn't know his brother very well, because it's not an Islestorm proposal unless there are some dragons involved."

Nicole frowned. "This sounds like a really weird case."

"It is. He met his girlfriend at a Dungeons & Dragons tournament," she lied.

"Huh," Nicole said, sipping her cider. "Well, it will certainly be unique. Probably not Planner of the Year material, though."

"Probably not. Luckily, the budget is small, so it'll be quick and simple."

"Except for the dragons." Nicole raised her eyebrows.

"Right, except for the dragons. But anyway, enough of this Luke drama. How are things at the gallery going?"

"It's so great! I actually had a buyer come in from New York. He bought like ten pictures and wants me to come up to the city to do a photo shoot for some models."

Claire's mouth gaped. "You're joking. When did this happen?"

"This morning. He said he read some reviews about me online, so he wanted to stop by to check out my studio while he was in town for business."

"Holy crap. That's amazing, Coli. I'm so proud of you!" Claire reached across the table and squeezed her arm.

"Thank you! I'm just thankful that turning my grandpa's store into a studio-slash-gallery wasn't a complete disaster."

"You are unstoppable," Claire said through a mouthful of burger. "Before long, they're going to be begging you to move to New York and shoot for all the big magazines. Just don't turn into one of those creeps who abuses their subjects and extorts them into sleeping with them. I can't imagine Kyle would be happy about that." She winked.

Nicole laughed. "No, I can't imagine he would." But then she sighed.

"Uh-oh. What's the matter? Trouble in lover's paradise?" Kyle hadn't mentioned anything during their planning sessions.

"Not exactly, I guess. Lately, I've just been really ready to move forward with our relationship and, you know, move in together and maybe even start talking about marriage." Nicole smiled sheepishly. "But every time I bring it up with Kyle, he just gets kind of weird and changes the subject. You don't think he's going to break up with me or move away, do you?"

"No! Definitely not," Claire said, almost too fervently. "He's so crazy about you. And he just started a new job with a huge law firm. Some guys are just weird about things like this. Like they don't want to make a commitment that big until they feel they're ready and they have all their financial ducks in a row and everything. Doesn't he still have some crazy student loans from law school?"

Nicole nodded. "That's true. But I told him, you know, we'd save money if we move in together or get an apartment of our own because we wouldn't be paying for two rents and two sets of utilities. Not to mention his apartment is closer to the studio, and I'm there most of the time anyway."

"And what did he say?" Claire rolled her neck. Sleeping propped on Luke's chest had given her a crick.

"That he agreed, but that he wanted to get his feet underneath him at work before he started making any other big life changes." She sighed again.

"That's hard. Are you unhappy?"

"Not exactly. I'm just tired of waiting around for the rest of my life to begin. I don't know why I'm getting so impatient about this. It's not like either one of us is going anywhere. He'll ask me when he's ready. I don't want to push it."

"Why do men have to be so difficult?"

"Seriously, sometimes I wish we could have been lesbians."

"Tell me about it. I feel like I have a better understanding of women than men. We'd be up front with each other and be like, 'Hey, want to move in together?' and 'Hey, just so you know, I'm handwashing your dishes because I'm trying to make amends for acting like your profession is a sham.'"

"I doubt that was why he was washing your dishes. But amen to that," Nicole said, and they clinked their glasses.

It was after ten when Claire finished the final accounting work for Barney's proposal. She closed her spreadsheet and rubbed her hands over her tired eyes. Making a mental note to talk to Mindy about hiring an accountant, she opened her internet browser to check the news and the weather for the next day. Sunny with a high of seventy, no chance of rain.

She typed in the website for a local newspaper and skimmed the headlines. She stopped when she saw one that referenced her missing roommate's case. "West Haven Widowmaker Claims Another Victim?" read the headline.

"Widowermaker," she corrected out loud, shaking her head.

She clicked on the link, which opened up with a large picture of Courtney on her wedding day. She skimmed over the first few paragraphs that detailed Courtney's disappearance but stopped when she got to a paragraph about the Widowmaker.

Stevens' disappearance is tragic but not unusual. In the past five years, four other West Haven area women have disappeared and were never heard from again. Although police have yet to confirm a connection between the multiple disappearances, many citizens believe that one person is responsible.

"The Widowmaker has her, I guarantee it. Courtney told me the week before she disappeared she kept seeing this strange car in the neighborhood—a four-door sedan with tinted windows, all black. Nobody in this neighborhood drives a car with tinted windows. I heard from my friend in the police department that those other girls were stalked by a black sedan too. And three of them went to the same college as Courtney. Mark my words, this is the work of one man," said Martina Cutchen, one of Stevens' neighbors.

A black sedan. Had there been a black sedan along Firestone Lane when she and Rosie had investigated? Lots of people owned black sedans though. At least now she had an idea of what to look out for. Unless he read this article and changed his vehicle. Hmmm.

She stared at the list of victims attributed to the Widowmaker. Courtney Stevens, Kayley Herrold, Shawna DeLong, Jennifer Heiser, and Ariel Pullizi. Something stirred in her memory, and Claire crossed the living room to her bookcase. Dropping to her knees, she hunted on the bottom shelf for the yearbook from her freshman year of college.

She leafed through several pages until she found Courtney's picture. She circled it with a red marker and kept going. One other girl, Kayley Herrold, was also in their class. She marked her as well and kept flipping. Claire found Shawna and Jennifer one class above them and circled them as well. Ariel, it seemed, had not attended Venor University.

Claire turned back to her keyboard and typed each girl's name into her search engine. Her wireless printer spat out article after article as she scoured the internet for details on each disappearance. One article fluttered to the floor, and Rosie jumped on it, sinking her teeth in before Claire could save it.

An hour later, Claire forced herself to step away from the keyboard. A stack of articles stood nearly as high as her coffee cup. She pulled out her three-hole punch, mercilessly stamping the sheets. She slid them all into an empty binder and left it on her coffee table.

"Don't look at me like that," she said to Rosie, who was lying on her back with her tongue lolling out. "I'm not going to get involved. I just want to know what happened to these girls."

CHAPTER ELEVEN

To Do:
- Start training for 5k for stopping animal cruelty
- Ariel research—diner location?
- Write thank you note to Marnie

THE NEXT MORNING, CLAIRE AWOKE TO THE OBNOXIOUS clattering of her phone vibrating against the headboard. Rosie barked at it until Claire picked it up.

"Hello?" she said blearily.

"Claire, you need to turn on the TV immediately. Like right now." Mindy's voice was urgent.

"Oh god, what happened? Are they closing our Sephora?"

"Worse. Just turn on *Marnie in the Morning*."

She fumbled in her blankets for the remote control. The channel was already set to that station, and she gasped when she saw who was Marnie's guest this morning.

"That she-devil! Of course she'd try to get on the show after I was. She doesn't have an original thought in her head. How in the hell did she get in there so quickly? You said they were booked for months."

"I would bet anything that she paid today's guest off or pulled some kind of sabotage. Oh, and that's not even the worst part."

"How much worse could it get?"

"In the commercial for the show, Wendy was teasing a huge secret about you."

"What the hell? What could she possibly know about me? Maybe she found out Jason has been sending me all those flowers and is going to say we're getting back together and play the victim card."

"Please. If she knew Jason was doing all that, she would kill both of you."

"Shh. It's coming back on."

The camera zoomed in to two women sitting on the set. Wendy wore a black pantsuit with no shirt underneath and a dangly necklace that drew attention to her exposed cleavage. She looked orange underneath the studio lights.

"Good morning, Pennsylvania! We were expecting local *New York Times* best-seller Sharon Keim on the show this morning, but she unfortunately came down with the stomach flu. So instead, today we have Wendy Flutter. Wendy, tell us a little about yourself."

"Well, I plan proposals for a living." She preened toward the camera like a peacock in heat.

"Just like the guest we had earlier this week, Claire Hartley. Do you know Claire?"

"I know her very well," Wendy sneered.

"I imagine you would, since you've been the runner-up

for Planner of the Year for the past three years. Is that correct?"

Wendy's expression darkened. "Yes, despite the fact that my proposals are more unique and creative, the judges can't seem to look past her cheap tricks." She rolled her eyes, and one of her false eyelashes was so long that it temporarily got stuck in her bangs. She blinked until it dislodged.

"I think we have a clip for one of the proposals you planned, actually. Can we roll that, please?"

A sports arena appeared onscreen. A buzzer signaled halftime, and a pack of sweaty basketball players traipsed off the court. An emcee walked out to the mid-court line with a microphone.

"Ladies and gentlemen, it's time for tonight's halftime contest. Five hundred dollars if you can make five baskets at halftime. The lucky winner of this contest is..." He paused dramatically, drawing an index card out of his back pocket. "Emily Thompson!"

The camera sought a horrified-looking girl halfway up the bleachers. She shook her head fervently, but security guards pulled her out of her seat and guided her down to the court.

Emily stood next to the emcee. Her face was bright red, and her hands trembled. The emcee put an arm around her.

"Emily, tell us where you're from."

"Sweet Valley," she whispered almost inaudibly.

"What was that, Emily? You look a little nervous. I think she needs some encouragement. Em-i-ly! Em-i-ly!" he began chanting. The entire crowd joined him until her name was echoing off the walls. He handed her a basketball and led her to the free-throw line.

"All right, Emily. All you have to do to leave here today with five hundred dollars in your pocket is make five free throws in a row within the five-minute time limit. On your mark. Get set. Throw!" The announcer's voice thundered off the walls of the arena.

Emily looked dubiously at the hoop that was ten feet off the ground. She bounced the ball a few times on the line, squatted in position, and threw the ball in an arc. The ball bounced off the rim and nearly hit a referee in the back of the head. She missed her second and third shots. Her face grew redder by the second, her hands shaking as she clutched the ball.

The ball rolled around the rim for what seemed like an eternity before sinking through the net on her fourth shot.

"That's one!" The emcee said encouragingly. "If you can make four more in a row, this stack of cash is yours," he said, waggling several hundred-dollar bills.

The crowd went wild with cheers and encouragement. Emily looked like a day-old tomato who was about to vomit.

She threw again and missed the hoop by a mile.

The audience groaned and clapped politely. As Emily turned around, red-faced and clearly disappointed, she nearly stumbled over a man kneeling behind her. She clapped her hands to her mouth and stared at him with bug eyes.

When he drew out a box, opened it, and held it toward her, the girl went from beet red to incredibly pale. The man slid the ring on her finger before she could respond and reached forward to hug her. The camera panned away from them and showed the crowd cheering. The couple walked off the court, the woman clutching her fiancé's hand, looking several shades too pale.

The video feed cut off and focused back on the two women in the studio. Wendy was leaning back in her chair, looking smug.

"That was—nice," Marnie said delicately.

"It was very nice. Roger was able to declare his love in front of over two thousand people. Everyone in the audience was saying how incredibly romantic it was."

"Were you invited to their wedding?"

Wendy shifted in her chair. For a second, her thousand-watt smile dimmed. "No, actually. They didn't end up going through with the wedding."

"What a surprise," Claire muttered to herself.

"I'm sorry to hear that." Marnie cleared her throat. "Wendy, tell us what makes you think you deserve to win the Planner of the Year Award this summer."

"Well, in addition to providing more cost-effective services for the community, I also have a much stronger moral backbone than my competitors."

Claire snorted. "You've got to be freaking kidding me."

"What do you mean by that?" Marnie asked.

"Well, I know for a fact that Claire Hartley is sleeping with one of her employees. A cameraman, in fact."

Claire gasped as the live TV audience did. "That insipid, heartless *bitch*."

"She did not just freaking say that," Mindy said, furiously enunciating each syllable.

Marnie looked uncomfortable. "I see. And you feel that sleeping with one of her employees—"

"Compromises her moral integrity, which makes a mockery of the work that she does. How can you have respect for and plan proposals if you yourself are slutting around in such a non-monogamous way? I mean, she was engaged to a man and was supposed to get married, and now she's sleeping her way through her staff? I find it despicable."

"I'm not sure I'm following your logic," Marnie said.

"You say that she has no respect for marriage because she, as a single woman, may or may not be sleeping with another man after breaking off an engagement?"

"Exactly," Wendy said.

"Do you feel there's some sort of time limit of mourning that must be met after a broken engagement before you can move on?"

"Well, yes. It hasn't even been a year and here she is, already sleeping around. I can't help but wonder if that's why her engagement ended." Wendy shot a look at the audience.

"And you feel that her personal life should influence the judges' opinion of her work?"

"Yes, because she's mixed her personal and business life by sleeping with an employee."

Marnie crossed her arms. "Do you even have any proof that she's been doing these things?"

"Actually, I have pictures of him leaving her apartment early in the morning," Wendy said snarkily.

Marnie raised her eyebrows. "How did you get those?"

"Who cares? Put them up on the screen! Show everyone who she really is." Wendy flung an arm dramatically at the screen on the wall behind them.

"Just to be clear, you stalked your competition and waited in her apartment building in the morning just to see if you could catch her doing something? I'm sorry, but that's about the creepiest thing I've ever heard." Marnie recoiled from Wendy. "And I work in daytime television."

Wendy leaned forward in her chair and looked right at the camera. "You're missing the point here. The point is, Claire is a big slut, and she doesn't deserve to be Planner of the Year."

"Oh, am I a slut, Wendy? Am I? I'm not the one who

slept with an engaged man and *broke up the engagement*," Claire shouted, throwing her remote to the floor. The back popped off and the batteries sprung out like a jack-in-the-box.

"You could call the show," Mindy suggested. "Tell them all what really happened. God, you're not even sleeping with Luke. I mean, you should be. But you're not."

Claire took a deep breath and stared at her television, into the eyes of the woman who had slept with her fiancé. She clutched her comforter in a vice-like grip. Her ears were ringing. She forced herself to take a breath. "No, unlike Wendy, I am a lady. Ladies do not fight on TV. This is not *Stepwives of Secaucus*. I will beat her the old-fashioned way."

"With a baseball bat? There's one in my car."

"Tempting, but no. I'm going to get an early start, maybe go for a run. I'll call you after my first cup of coffee."

Claire hung up and threw her covers off. She paused for a moment, then viciously ripped her sheets off and tossed them across the room, accidentally burying an unsuspecting Rosie.

Marnie was still talking on the TV, but Claire was angrily ripping open her closet door. She spotted her spare sheets and yanked them into place at the end of the bed, folding them into stern hospital corners.

The pillows were getting a violent fluffing when she suddenly heard Mindy's voice in the room. Confused, she looked at her phone and confirmed she had hung up the call.

"Hi Marnie, I'm a big fan. I just had a question for Wendy."

Marnie responded, "Okay, go ahead."

Claire dropped her pillow on the floor. Rosie jumped on it and began humping it.

"How did you meet your current boyfriend, Wendy?"

"That is nobody's business but my own," Wendy sneered at the camera.

"Oh? Isn't it? So, you can come on the show and try to assassinate my best friend's character because you're jealous of her success, but you won't tell the world that you slept with her fiancé and broke up her engagement, and that's why she's single right now?"

Marnie gasped. "Is this true, Miss Flutter? Did you sleep with Claire Hartley's fiancé?"

"Oh, sweet Jesus." Claire buried one hand in her mane of hair. Could this week get any worse?

Wendy slapped her hands indignantly against the armrests of her chair. She uncrossed her praying mantis legs and leaped up, shouting at the ceiling as though Mindy were floating above her.

"You don't know anything! Jason loves me! We were meant to be together."

"Would you have even looked at Jason if he wasn't dating your nemesis?" Mindy asked.

"I—Jason and I—" A vein was standing out on Wendy's forehead. "We were destined to be—AAARGH!" Wendy shouted. She put her hands underneath the coffee table that sat between her and Marnie.

"Miss Flutter," Marnie began, a warning in her eyes.

Wendy paid no attention and promptly flipped the table over. It narrowly missed Marnie's chair and instead crashed into the large planter that a production assistant had moved earlier in the week for Claire's black eye. The planter split down the middle, and the fake palm tree tipped, thwacking the back of Wendy's chair and rolling onto the floor.

Wendy stepped closer to a camera and stared directly into it, inches from the lens.

"Jason is mine. I won. You hear that, Claire? I won your fiancé, and I will win the award this year. You are nothing. You hear me? *Nothing.*"

At Marnie's behest, a muscular man in a black polo strode across the stage and took Wendy by the elbow. He dragged her backward, away from the cameras. She cocked her fist back to hit him and then apparently thought better of it.

"Get your hands off me! I'm not finished with my interview," she demanded as she was led backstage.

The audience gasped, and for a long moment, there was dead silence. Even Marnie took a few seconds to recover.

"Uh, well," she said awkwardly. "We've certainly had some interesting developments this morning. We'll be back after the break with turtles—should we really be moving them out of the roadways? Find out next." The camera faded out.

Claire dialed Mindy immediately.

"Min, what the hell?"

"You didn't seriously think I was going to let her assassinate your character and the business into which we have poured three years of our blood, sweat, and tears."

"Now the whole world knows Wendy slept with my fiancé," Claire said, dramatically collapsing onto her freshly made bed like a teenager who wasn't allowed to go to a party.

"Sure, if by 'whole world,' you mean a handful of early risers who choose to watch a local morning show instead of real news."

"You have a point," Claire begrudgingly admitted.

"Plus, no one will even remember the Jason thing. She flipped a table on live TV. She openly admitted to stalking you. That clip will probably go viral before the end of this conversation."

Claire sat bolt upright again. "You're right! She purposely waited outside my apartment to see if I would do anything nefarious. I know she's been staking out the warehouse, but this is next level. Who does that? Do I have grounds to get a restraining order?"

"This is unacceptable," Mindy agreed. "I wonder how long she's been doing this. I'll ask my cop friend if we have any grounds to apply for a restraining order."

"Thanks, Min. I wonder if she's the one who sent me that picture. I didn't know her in college, though. Ugh. Whatever. I'm already done with this day. Are you meeting me for Barney's final rehearsal this afternoon?"

"Yes, ma'am. I'll be there and I'll bring coffee. And you're meeting Kyle at that jewelry store at eleven?"

"Ten forty-five. Thanks for the reminder. I'll see you later if I haven't died from humiliation," Claire said and hung up. She fired off a quick text to Nicole asking if she had seen the show that morning and fell onto the bed again, staring up at the ceiling.

When her phone buzzed a moment later, she expected it to be Nicole, but instead she saw a text from Luke. Her stomach clenched. Surely, he hadn't watched the show. Why was everyone she knew such an early riser? She frantically flicked her finger over the screen, holding her breath as she waited to see what he had written.

Luke: *Let me get this straight. Satan's bride from the antique store is stalking you?*

Claire: *So, it would seem. I mean, she's always kind of followed me around a bit and showed up at my office in the warehouse, trying to spy and figure out what proposals I'm doing. But it seems that she's progressed to full-on stalker mode. Sorry you were caught in her crosshairs.*

Her thumb hesitated over the send button as she debated if that was too much detail for a text but sent it anyway.

A moment later, her phone buzzed again.

Luke: *It's a shame she didn't catch anything juicier. Maybe next time.*

Claire read it once, fought the urge to call Nicole and ask her what she thought, and then read it again. "Sex embargo. Be cool."

Her thumb trembled over the winky-face emoticon at the end of his sentence. An idea struck her like a bolt of lightning.

"Rosie, I'm about to enact some serious karmic justice. Are you ready for this?"

Rosie whined in response, sitting at the bedroom door and clearly ready to go pee on every leaf in a ten-mile radius during her morning walk.

Claire intertwined her fingers and flexed them in front of her, getting a good stretch before picking her phone back up. She typed four letters and hit send.

Claire: *Haha.*

CHAPTER TWELVE

To Do:
- Price moving companies
- Collect cardboard boxes from neighbors and vendors
- Stomp Wendy into the ground during the awards

CLAIRE AND KYLE EMERGED FROM THE JEWELRY STORE, blinking in the bright midday light. She glanced inside the bag once more where a slender silver bracelet and a handful of silver charms clinked together.

"I almost forgot," Kyle said, reaching into his back pocket. "Here are the trivia questions on our relationship you wanted."

"Perfect! Thanks so much. She's going to love this." She tucked the paper in the outside pocket of her enormous purse. "Now, you're absolutely sure you want me to move Nicole's things into your place the day of the proposal?"

"Definitely."

"Great. I'll call the movers today. And don't worry, I'll personally handle all of her embarrassing things rather than have some stranger pawing through her underwear."

He laughed. "I appreciate that. Let me know if you come up with anything else."

She gave him a quick hug. "I'm going to take these things over to Luke's tomorrow. Is there anything else you want me to take while I'm there?"

"Yeah, how about a box of condoms? I'm getting sick of hearing him talk about you."

She held her breath. *Remember the sex embargo. Remember the business.* But her curiosity interjected. "He's been talking about me?"

"Yes. He tried to bring you up in a way that I'm sure he imagined was casual, and then he just kept asking questions about you. We were trying to have dinner and drinks, and I swear he wouldn't shut up."

"What was he asking?" Not that she cared.

"Where you're from, how you know Nicole, where you went to school, basic stuff. And then he asked if you were seeing anyone."

"Did he?" Oh boy. She was in danger.

"Yeah. He said he knew you had a crazy ex-boyfriend who keeps sending you flowers and unwanted gifts. Is Jason still harassing you?" Kyle's expression turned serious.

"Not really. He sent flowers earlier this week. At least I think it was him. He usually calls at least twice a day, but I never answer. He'll get tired of it eventually and give up."

Kyle glowered. "Let me know if he doesn't. Oh, and Luke also mentioned something about 'accidentally' staying the night at your place?" He formed air quotes with his fingers.

Claire stared innocently back. "I have no idea what you're talking about."

He crossed his arms. "Just be careful, Claire. Luke's like a brother to me, but he's never really been much of a relationship guy. I don't want you to get hurt."

Claire held up her hands. "I have no intentions of having anything but a professional relationship with Luke. Well, except maybe some friendly competition here and there. Did he tell you I beat his kill count on the first try in *MM2*? It was super embarrassing."

"I probably should have warned him about your crazy prowess with a crossbow, but it's fun to see him lose. But anyway, don't tell him I told you any of that. You know, bros before smart, ferocious businesswomen and all that."

"Right." She laughed. "Call me if you need anything else. See you later."

———

SHE MADE A QUICK STOP FOR LUNCH AT A LOCAL CAFÉ BEFORE hurrying over to the park, trying not to think about Luke grilling Kyle. He was probably only looking for a story, searching for another Toilet King anecdote to tell at parties. He once knew a pants-less girl who planned proposals for a living but couldn't hold down a relationship. It wasn't as exciting as underground meth labs, but the irony would certainly appeal to him.

At the park, she met prospective groom Barney and her team. After doing a full run-through three times, she decided that everything was ready.

"It's going to be so great," she reassured Barney, who was starting to look a little nervous. "Are you ready to sweep her off her feet tomorrow?"

"I think so." His voice trembled as he swiped at the sweat on his forehead.

"Of course you are. Remember, park next to this bush..."

"Right. I remember," he mumbled.

She laid a hand on his arm. "Your delivery was flawless. She's definitely going to cry. And say yes, of course."

He stiffened his upper lip and nodded.

"Get some sleep tonight. Tomorrow's a big day." She patted him on the shoulder.

As Barney got back into his red Corvette, she praised her dancers and whipped out a box of chocolates for them to share. As they argued over the various mystery chocolates, Mindy sidled up close.

"Sooo, what did he say?" she asked, nudging Claire in the ribs.

"Who, Barney? He seems nervous, but I think it'll be fine."

Mindy slapped her on the arm. "No, Luke."

Ugh. Luke again. She had heard his name enough today. "What did he say about what?"

Mindy stared at her like she was an idiot. "Did he see the segment this morning?"

Claire shuddered. "Yes, unfortunately."

"What did he say?" Mindy repeated, staring into Claire's eyes intently. She held her hand out and wiggled her fingers.

Claire shook her head and unlocked her phone before handing it over.

As Mindy read, her eyebrows arched higher and higher. "No, he didn't. He didn't put that winky face. Oh my god. Claire, he wants it."

"Even if he does, which I'm sure he doesn't, I'm not interested," Claire said, pulling out her checklist for Barney's proposal and skimming it for the hundredth time that day.

"How can you not be interested? I would give up caffeine for a month to take a ride on the Luke Express."

Claire wrinkled her nose. "He's a bossy, high-strung douche."

"A douche who nursed your black eye back to health. I can't believe you hit him with a 'haha.' Savage." Mindy held her hand up for a high five that Claire obliged.

"He deserved it. I do, however, have a meeting with said douche next week. I'm planning on asking for his help with the choreographed dance. It would be too weird to do it with Kyle."

"Ooh, what are you going to wear?"

"Pants, for sure. I won't make that same mistake again."

Mindy tutted. "Okay, we're going to your place right now, and I'm going to help you pick out what to wear while I brief you on the new clients."

"Clients?"

"Yep, scored another prospect this morning. Even though Wendy is trying to assassinate your character, business is seriously booming right now from all the TV spots. I have fifteen more requests in the queue."

Claire bit her lip. "Wow. That's a lot. Min, are you sure we can handle all this? My mom keeps talking about how we should expand and hire a few more people and—"

"Don't worry about all that right now. Chances are half of those applicants won't make it through the screening process. Right now, you and I are enough. We can do this," she said firmly. "Now let's go find an outfit, Mistress of Yes."

Claire laughed and shook her head as she got in her car. She glanced around the parking lot before pulling out, but none of the surrounding cars were black. Nevertheless, she took the long way home.

An hour later, Mindy had scattered half of Claire's wardrobe across the living room. Her friend held up a short and clingy red dress.

"I don't want to sweat in that. I should probably just wear leggings, don't you think?"

Mindy rolled her eyes. "I know you want to keep things professional with Luke. Do you really think leggings are professional?"

"They are if they're conducive to the meeting activities. He'll find something else to judge me for, don't worry. Can we deal with this later? I want to hear about our new clients." She picked up a miniskirt Mindy had dragged out and tossed it in the pile by the TV to make space. It was going to take her hours to get everything sorted by color and season again.

"Fine. I still think you should wear something hot, though. Anyway, so we've got Tyler, the charming veteran with a wheelchair who is transitioning from the Army to a career in chemical engineering after his injury.

Claire clutched a hand to her heart. "I love him already."

Mindy nodded. "And his girlfriend is the Army nurse who stabilized him and nursed him back to health after his injury a year ago. She's still deployed, but she'll be home in June."

"Stop it," Claire said. "First, let's snoop through her social media and make sure she's not a Jason. I'll check for her on all the online dating sites and apps." She whipped out a legal pad and started making notes on it. Mindy did the same.

"All right. How did he do on the preliminary questionnaire?"

"He killed it. Judging from the results, it seems that he's ready for marriage. They are planning on living together once they're both home, and according to him, they've had the necessary conversations about kids, finances, and household roles and expectations."

"Great! I'll start researching her preferences on Monday. Did he have any initial requests from us?"

"No. Here's a binder with some of my ideas so far" Mindy dropped a book onto the table. "They're both really patriotic, so I'm thinking fireworks and a marching band and—"

Someone knocked on Claire's door.

"I didn't order a pizza," she said as she walked to the door and peered through the peephole. She gasped and recoiled as if the knocker had been a brain-eating zombie.

"Who is it?" Mindy whispered.

"Claire? Come on, I know you're in there," a man's voice called from outside the door.

Rosie growled and the hair on her back bristled. She stood tense and alert at the door.

Claire held a finger to her lips and tried to tiptoe away.

"You can relax. It's not the Widowmaker," he called sarcastically. "Come on, I can hear that music you play when you're brainstorming. Open up."

"Damn," Claire whispered. She took a deep breath and turned the knob.

"Jason."

"Claire," he said. He stood just under six feet tall and was dressed in a tailored suit. His face was baby smooth. He had never been able to grow more than a few thready patches of facial hair. The blond hair that she used to love running her fingers through was a little longer and messier than the last time she had seen him. "Please, I just want to talk. Just hear me out. I'm so sorry for everything that happened."

She folded her arms over her chest.

"Can I come in? This used to be my place, too, you know."

"I am in the middle of a business meeting," she said coolly.

"Can't it wait?"

Was he serious? "No, it can't wait. You never understood how important work was to me."

Jason stared at her, looking genuinely hurt. "You never used to speak to me that way."

"That was before I grew a set of balls," she said with a steely glare.

He looked down at the floor, where Rosie was hiding just behind Claire's ankle. She bared her teeth and growled at him. "You got a dog?"

Claire declined to comment.

He took a deep breath and continued. "Okay, so listen. I came over here to tell you that I have a job offer at the museum on Blanche Street."

"Doing what?"

"Curation."

"You found an art history job? With your grades?"

"I did. I wanted to show you that I'm independent, and I'm willing to work hard. And I'm so sorry for what I did to you." He reached out for her hand, but she snatched it away.

"I'm glad you found a new job. That's great," she said. "But I really am in the middle of a meeting right now." She opened the door wider so he could see Mindy bent over an open binder.

"Really? Because it looks like you're in the middle of a

slumber party." He gestured at the piles of clothing and shoes strewn all over. "Hey, Mindy." He waved.

Mindy set her jaw and hissed at him.

"Mindy was looking for an outfit to borrow," Claire said and then shook her head. "I don't owe you any explanations. Please leave. We have nothing to discuss."

"Come on, Claire. I told you I'm sorry. We were in a bad place when that whole thing happened." He tried to take a step into the apartment, but she put out a hand to stop him. She should have gotten an ankle holster for the stun gun her mother had sent. It did her no good hiding under a floorboard with ex-boyfriends coming over uninvited.

"Oh, you mean when you got drunk at my award ceremony and then ended up having sex with my nemesis in the men's bathroom?"

"Yeah, that. I'm sorry, but you telling that story about how I proposed to you always pisses me off. It makes me look so bad." He rubbed a hand over the back of his neck and stared at her, pale blue eyes penetrating in a way she once found endearing.

Something was bubbling up inside her, hot and dark. "If you really, sincerely wanted to propose, maybe you should have put a little more thought into it. And then, oh, I don't know, *not cheated on me?*"

"No matter how hard I tried, I was never good enough for you."

"I thought you were good enough," she whispered. "That's why I said yes. I loved you so much. But you know what? You ruined us. I was ready to be your wife, and I was doing everything I could to build a life for us while you sat around the house all day, watching TV and eating chips."

Jason bowed his head, his cheeks flushed. There was a ring around the white collar of his button-down. "I was lost after graduation. Your business was taking off, and I couldn't find a job. I felt useless."

"You couldn't find a job with a major in art history? Gee, who would have thought?" Claire spat. "It wasn't fair for you to put the entire burden of supporting us on me. You could have flipped burgers or worked at the mall or done anything to help around here at all. For god's sake, I sent in a check for your student loan payment the night before you cheated on me." She was squeezing the doorknob so hard it was a miracle it didn't snap off.

"Well, it didn't help that every day you became more successful and kept telling our story, and people would laugh and look at me like I'm a piece of shit. I was always Claire's lazy fiancé."

"Yes, you were," she said. "You need to go now."

He put his hand on the door. If she had a weapon in her hand, she would have used it. "Please listen to me. I still love you, Claire. I'm so sorry for what I did. I still think we can make this work."

"This is not going to work. And I know you're living with Wendy. I'm not an idiot. Maybe I should call and tell her you keep sending me flowers and calling me fifty times a day. I can't believe she doesn't already know since she's been actively stalking me."

"Damn it, Claire. Listen to me." His eyes narrowed. He stepped over the threshold, frustration sizzling off of him.

Her stomach clenched. She took a step back. She had never seen him this angry before. Something plastic brushed the tips of her fingers. She gripped it and hoisted it in Jason's direction. The end of a broomstick almost hit him in the nose.

"You're not welcome here, Jason." Her voice trembled when she said his name.

"She said you need to go." Mindy threw the door open the rest of the way and held Claire's DustBuster over her shoulder like a baseball bat. "Do we need to call the police?"

He ignored both of them. "Wendy means nothing to me, Claire. Maybe we could go to counseling? I would be willing to do it if you'd go with me. We could work out these issues and be happy again. Like we were in school." He pulled a bouquet of roses out from behind his back. "I brought you your favorite flowers."

She stared at the cotton candy pink blooms. "My favorite flowers are lilies," she said, shoving him with the broomstick until he stumbled backward into the hallway. She slammed the door in his face and locked her deadbolt. After a quick bout of angry dancing, she re-joined Mindy in the living room and ignored the pounding on the door. Mindy turned up the stereo even louder, and they returned to their discussion about their new clients until the knocking finally stopped. She really needed to change the locks.

WHEN MINDY LEFT SEVERAL HOURS LATER, CLAIRE NEEDED A moment to take her mind off work. She dug under her couch until she found the binder with articles about the missing women. She went through all the information she had collected and separated it by victim, added binder tabs, and secured it all neatly back into place. Then she began to read.

Her eyes started to glaze over after she finished the first section. She pulled out a yellow legal pad and took notes. As the media had already noted, each woman disappeared shortly after getting married.

Four women had attended Claire's university, while one,

Ariel, had only completed high school. She had disappeared while Claire was still in high school. Claire printed out a map of Pennsylvania and searched for Middletown, where Ariel had attended high school. She marked it with a red dot, noting that it was about an hour northeast of West Haven.

Ariel had married her high school sweetheart right after graduation and had quickly become pregnant. She disappeared when she was only three months along. Her husband grieved for his wife and unborn child.

A server at the diner Ariel worked at gave an interview to the police. The girl, Candy, noted that Ariel had previously mentioned feeling as though she was being watched when she walked her dog.

Chills ran down Claire's spine. A coincidence, surely. Creeps were everywhere.

Several regulars corroborated Candy's report that sometimes a black sedan with heavily tinted windows would sit across the road from the diner on weekends for hours at a time. Anytime someone got up to investigate, the driver would speed off. The license plate was always covered up.

Ariel disappeared after closing the diner on Christmas Eve. The diner had no security cameras, and police found no sign of a struggle.

Claire sat back on the couch and hugged her knees to her chest. What kind of a monster kidnapped a pregnant woman and made her disappear forever?

CHAPTER THIRTEEN

To Do:
- *Pick up doves*
- *Pack mini blow torch for sparklers*
- *Don't forget emergency umbrella*

CLAIRE HAD BARELY TAKEN HER FIRST SIP OF COFFEE WHEN HER phone buzzed.

"Hello?" she asked, half-asleep as she leaned against her headboard, work papers for Barney's proposal on her lap. The world was dark outside, the city still asleep.

"Claire, it's Jerry. I can't make it to film today."

"*You what?*" She shot up and nearly dumped her coffee on her lap. It was Barney's proposal day. This was not happening. "Why the hell not?"

"I'm in the friggin' hospital."

"Oh, no," she said. Shit. Barney would lose his mind if there were only two videographers. Why today of all days?

And who could she call on such short notice as a replacement? "I'm so sorry. What happened?"

"My appendix ruptured last night. I have a few numbers of other camera guys who might be able to take point on the gig today if you want them." He grunted in pain.

She flipped over one of her Barney papers and hastily scrawled a note about sending Jerry a card.

"Don't worry about it. I have someone I can try first and if I can't get a hold of him, I'll call you back," she said. "Feel better and keep me posted on how you're doing."

After Jerry thanked her and hung up, she frantically searched through her contacts. "Shit, shit shit." She would give her last dime to avoid making this phone call. But she had no choice.

"What's wrong?" Luke answered, gruff and straightforward as always.

"Oh, hey. I'm sorry. I figured I would get your voicemail."

"Well, whenever someone calls before sunrise you know it's not going to be good news."

Claire laughed sheepishly. "I have a huge favor to ask. Do you have any meetings this afternoon?"

"No, why?"

"Is there any way you would be willing to take point on filming a proposal with me today? I'll pay you of course. We've been working on this for months, and it's one of the biggest ones I've ever done, and my cameraman called off just a minute ago with a ruptured appendix and—"

"Whoa, slow down. Yes, I can do it. What time do you need me and where are we going?"

Thank god. Even though it meant spending several hours with Luke that were sure to be frustrating, she wouldn't be disappointing a groom-to-be on one of the biggest days of his life.

"The proposal's at sunset, but there's a lot of setup to do. If we could meet up around two, I'll give you the rundown and show you the location. I'm sorry for springing this on you."

"Two is good. You're lucky you're cute," he said, yawning loudly.

Something twinged in Claire's belly, but she ignored it. "Sorry for waking you up so early. You were the first person I thought of."

"I'm glad," he said. "Meet you at your place?"

"That's perfect. Thank you so much, Luke. You're a lifesaver."

He hung up, and she breathed a huge sigh of relief. Too jittery to focus on the paperwork, she dressed quickly and headed to the stairwell with Rosie. A long walk would calm her nerves. The sun rose slowly, turning the world a beautiful shade of gold. They passed mothers pushing crying babies in strollers, dog owners stumbling around half-asleep with poo baggies in hand, and an early-morning outdoor Pilates class.

If she was being honest with herself, there was another reason for her long walk. The haunting headshots of the Widowmaker victims hovered in her mind as if burned there. Every couple of steps, she pivoted to take in the street. There weren't any black sedans with tinted windows yet, but if she spotted any, she was going to write down the license plates.

As they walked down the asphalt path at their favorite park, a twig cracked behind them. Claire whirled around, keys threaded through her fingers, breath hitching in her chest. A squirrel scampered across the path. Rosie lunged, nearly ripping Claire's arm off in her haste to chase the woodland creature.

"Get it together, Claire," she muttered as they resumed their walk. But the back of her neck remained prickled, and she couldn't shake the feeling that she was being watched. She glanced over her shoulder several times, but nothing was out of the ordinary. A paper delivery boy flitted past on his bicycle. More people had crowded the park, but no one seemed to be paying close attention to them. None of the cars in the lot were black sedans with tinted windows. She slipped her earbuds in and drowned the paranoia under a guttural scream from her favorite metal band.

"Wendy's probably stalking me again," she said as she bent down to untangle the leash from Rosie's tiny legs. "Maybe she's hoping that I'll squat down next to you and pee on that tree too, since she didn't get what she wanted during that interview. Then she'd have something really juicy to take to *Marnie in the Morning*."

On the drive home, the dorm room picture resurfaced in her mind. She glanced in her rearview mirror. Maybe today was a good day to get that deadbolt her mother had been pestering her about. Luke had mentioned it too—not that she cared what he thought about her personal safety. She turned toward the hardware store, her eyes flashing repeatedly to the rearview mirror.

Was that a black sedan behind her? Of course it was, everyone and their mother drove a black sedan. Tingles ran up and down her spine. She practiced some deep breathing and forced herself to relax. Surely it would turn off soon. Maybe she'd catch a glimpse of the license plate as it turned. There were still three blocks until the hardware store.

She pulled up to a red light. The sedan rolled to a stop behind her. The sun was shining directly into the mirror, obscuring the driver's seat. The car lurked behind her for the next three blocks, even though she went slower than the speed limit. Should she call the police? And tell them what —someone was driving behind her? Who would try to attack her in the daytime? But Courtney had disappeared mid-morning while on a run. Her heart hammered in her throat as she swung into the hardware store parking lot.

The black car pulled in beside her and parked. The windows were tinted. Anyone could have been inside. Claire hesitated, her hand on the keys dangling from the ignition. She could make it to the door of the hardware store before someone took her. She was certain.

"Stay here," she ordered to Rosie, as though she was suddenly going to sprout thumbs and let herself out of the car. She rolled all four windows down partway—it was a chilly morning, only in the fifties, but she couldn't be sure how long it would take to hunt down a deadbolt. Especially if she was grabbed by a serial killer.

She thrust the door open, slamming it behind her and threading her keys through her knuckles like her mother had taught her even before she had her own keys.

The driver's side door of the black sedan opened a crack. She held her breath and froze, key knuckles drawn back in a fist. A slender piece of wood descended, thudded heavily onto the asphalt. What the hell?

A pair of slip-on Sketchers dropped to the ground next. An elderly woman with platinum white hair shuffled out from behind the driver's side door.

Claire laughed out loud, then clapped a hand to her mouth. She was being foolish. No one was out to get her. The picture was probably a fluke.

"Good morning," she said cheerily to the old woman, holding the front door of the hardware store open.

"Thank you, dear," the old woman said, not pausing to remove her sunglasses before crossing the threshold. "Hank,

I need another plunger. Harold clogged the damn toilet again, and he snapped the other plunger in half," she called as she walked inside.

Inside, Claire started down the first cramped aisle. The store smelled like grease and metal, and seventies era rock poured out of ceiling-mounted speakers.

She finally found the deadbolts at the back of the store. She glanced over several of them before choosing a heavy-duty looking one. She brought it up to the cash register and, seeing no one around, rang the bell that sat on the countertop.

A hefty, lumberjack-looking man made his way out of a back room. His name tag read Hank.

"All set?" Hank asked. As he spoke, his lengthy beard bounced up and down, tickling the front of his shirt.

"I think so. Will this work for a standard apartment door?" she asked.

"Yes, ma'am. You know how to install one of these things?"

"I'm sure I can figure it out." She tapped her foot on the concrete floor. She didn't need a big, judgy lumberjack mansplaining deadbolts to her. That's what YouTube was for.

"I only ask because you have to make sure this is installed properly to ensure that your door's secure. You're going to want a pack of these too." Hank reached underneath the counter and slid a pack of long screws toward her.

"Replace the ones on your strike plate," he continued. "These'll go straight through the door frame and into the studs in the wall. Much more secure."

"Right. The strike plate." She vowed to Google it the moment she got to the parking lot.

"If you have any problems, give us a call here at the store." He handed her a business card.

"Thank you." She tucked the card in her purse.

On the way home, she blasted her angry metal music until the stress slipped away from her shoulders. The sun was bright, the music was great, and the black-sedan-driving granny was all but forgotten. It was a perfect day for a proposal.

West Haven's business district flashed by her windows. A gaggle of women holding rolled up yoga mats exited the Starbucks on the corner. A group of men in suits hurried down the sidewalk, arguing over something and brandishing a piece of poster board with a chart on it. Flowers bloomed from apartment building window boxes, and people on the street were tugging at their collars, clearly as surprised as Claire was by the sudden change in temperature. She swerved to avoid one of West Haven's signature potholes—this one so deep that the brick underneath the road was exposed.

With a pang, she realized that if she went straight another ten blocks, she would be entering the edge of Venor University. She hadn't visited since Homecoming two years prior. She, Nicole, Mindy, and Jason had painted their faces blue and yellow and tailgated in the parking lot where Mindy had once run a cheetah-print bra up the flagpole on a dare.

When Claire pulled into her parking garage, she glanced at her watch. There was plenty of time left before she was supposed to meet Luke. She could go over Barney's proposal timeline once more and finally bang out the blog post she had been putting off on engagement gifts. Maybe there would even be time to install this damn deadbolt. Inside the apartment, she dumped her purchase onto her dining room table, shoving the bouquet of lilies out of the way. Its overwhelmingly sweet floral scent was almost nauseating.

She filled the coffee pot with water and walked once around the planter, trying to spot a gap in the dense collection of stems at the center. Seeing none, she dumped the whole pot on top. Good enough.

———

HOURS LATER, SHE WAS AS PREPARED FOR THIS PROPOSAL AS she ever would be. Her latest blog post was up, she had managed to shower without giving herself another black eye, and her day-of-proposal bag was packed and stocked with emergency essentials. A travel umbrella brushed against mini torches for the sparklers. Packets of tissues were squashed next to a bottle of ibuprofen and a first aid kit. Lint rollers fought with emergency mascara and lipstick samplers for space. She had twenty minutes before Luke was due to arrive. Surely that was enough time to install this deadbolt so he didn't have another reason to judge her.

The deadbolt slid out of the bag and wobbled on her kitchen island. Heavy-duty blister packaging surrounded it like Fort Knox. She made several attempts to cut the binding with kitchen scissors. No dice. She moved on to stabbing it viciously, but the plastic still didn't budge.

"Arg!" She threw the deadbolt across the room. It bounced off the couch and landed on the hardwood floor with a heavy *thump*. What was the point of selling a deadbolt for safety if consumers couldn't even get it out of the packaging?

A second later, someone knocked on her door. She walked over with hands still balled into fists in frustration.

The peephole showed a smirking Luke, looking cool and unbothered as always. She opened the door.

"What was that thump?" he asked as he crossed her threshold. Rosie sprinted to him and jumped up, putting her front legs on his. He scratched her behind the ears.

"What thump?"

"The one I heard right before you opened the door. It sounded like you threw something," he said, peering around her living room. "Aha! What's this?" He bent over and picked up the deadbolt. "I see you took my advice."

She shrugged, refusing to admit the real reason for her sudden interest in personal safety. "My ex showed up yesterday. I kind of forgot that I never changed the locks after he moved out."

"You didn't change the locks after he moved out?" he asked incredulously.

"He's not dangerous." She fought the urge to roll her eyes. "He just can't keep his dick in his pants."

"Do you know how to install this?" He raised his eyebrows. What was with everyone doubting her ability to Google directions? She was an independent, college-educated woman who had managed just fine living on her own for most of a year.

"I'm sure I can figure it out."

"As soon as we're done with the proposal today, I'm installing this."

She bristled. She had made it almost thirty seconds without getting annoyed at Luke. A new record. "I don't need your help."

"I know you don't. It's selfish, really. I'll sleep better knowing that you won't wake up to Wendy crouched on top of you, staring at you."

"Thanks for that horrifying imagery. And for the offer to

help," she said begrudgingly. Her hostility downgraded by a degree. He was doing her a huge, last-minute favor after all. "I don't know how to install the damn thing. I can't even get it open."

He smiled. His eyes crinkled at the corners. "Got a can opener?"

"You have a can of ravioli you need to heat up?"

"Do you always answer questions with questions?" He was still smiling.

"Do you—never mind." She stopped, bit her lower lip. She yanked open a drawer in her kitchen island and handed it to him.

He clamped the can opener down on the edge of the plastic and twisted the crank. A vein stood out in his right forearm as he forced the can opener around the packaging. *Good lord.* Twenty seconds later, he had the deadbolt and all of the accompanying hardware spread out on the dining room table.

"That's amazing," she admitted. "I never thought to try that."

He tossed the plastic packaging into her recycling bin. "Now that we've solved the great wrap rage crisis of our age, should we head out?"

She glanced at her watch. "Yes. I'll drive. Do we need to stop at your car and get your equipment?"

He spun around and showed her the backpack he was wearing.

"You squeezed it all in there?" she asked.

"I'm a professional."

"So you said," Claire muttered. She bent down to give Rosie a kiss but kept her distance. Claire's all-black outfit wouldn't be black for long during shedding season.

"You don't crate her when you leave?" he asked.

"No, I can't keep her cooped up," she said. "I hate to think of her whining and being unhappy in a tiny little cage."

"I see. And how many of your shoes has she destroyed while you've been out?"

"Only about half before I got smart enough to start hiding them before I leave." She bent to pick up the sneakers she had discarded after her hardware store trip and tucked them inside a kitchen cabinet. She ushered Luke out the front door, shutting and locking it behind them, then squatted and started gyrating her hips in a clockwise direction.

He burst out laughing. "What are you doing?"

Claire froze mid-squat. Damn it. She straightened and crossed her arms. "Oh. Um. I heard in a TED Talk that if you do something weird and random when you're doing an important task, it helps you remember that you did it. Now, when I turn off my stove or lock my door, I dance to help remember that I did it and didn't just imagine doing it. Now I don't have to freak out and whip my car around to make sure the door is locked."

"You're insane." Luke shook his head and started down the hallway. He paused at the end and hit the button to call the elevator.

She gripped his arm and tugged him away from the elevator doors. "Wait. Don't take the elevator."

"Why not?"

The doors slid open, revealing scuffed flooring and wall panels, several mysterious stains, and a sinister, flickering light. Though most of her apartment building had been renovated in the last decade, the elevator looked as though it hadn't been touched since the seventies.

"Straight out of a horror movie, got it. Let's go," he said, sticking his arm out.

"I'm taking the stairs. You go ahead." She turned away from the doors. It would serve him right to get trapped in a creepy murder elevator.

He caught her arm, spun her to face him. "You're not seriously afraid of an elevator, are you?"

"I'm not afraid." Her heart tripped in her chest. Were the palpitations from impending doom or from Luke's intoxicating scent? "But we're wasting time. I just prefer the stairs. I can always use more cardio."

"Come on." He tugged her into the elevator before she could protest. "Sometimes you have to do what scares you. It makes life interesting."

The doors slid shut like a coffin lid being lowered. Her heart thumped in her ears. She gripped the handrail for a moment, then opted to cross her arms instead. Luke crossed his arms as well and leaned against the scuffed wall panel, watching her with a slight smile.

The elevator lurched into action, dropping inch by inch like it was taking great, shuddering breaths. The overhead light flickered ominously. A groaning noise roared all around them. The number three illuminated above the doors. If she had taken the stairs, she probably would be in the garage already. She glared at Luke.

As the number two illuminated, the overhead light buzzed loudly and shut off altogether, plunging them into darkness. She yelped and jumped sideways, crashing into him. Was this the end? Trapped in an elevator with a bossy, sexy asshole?

He steadied her, chuckling. He left a hand at the small of her back, its warmth radiating through her T-shirt. Was it normal for someone's fingertips to be so hot?

The lights kicked back on, and the elevator continued to descend. She stepped as far away from him as she could and focused on breathing deeply until the doors finally slid open, revealing the dingy parking garage.

"That's why I don't take the damn elevator." The elevator wobbled as she stomped out of the death machine. Her skin burned where he had touched her. She shot him a dirty look and kept her eyes forward until she got to her car.

Luke looked comically large in her passenger seat. His head grazed the roof, and he had to clutch his backpack to his front as though it was an infant.

"Your car is ridiculous."

"Don't pout. You can put your seat back." She pointed at the lever.

"What? A whole two inches before I hit the back seat? How do you even fit anything in this car?"

She rolled her eyes as she turned the key in the ignition. Their ears were immediately assaulted by a bellowing scream, heavy guitar, and double bass. She jumped and clapped a hand to her chest before twiddling the dial to quiet it.

He put his hand on hers and stopped her. "You listen to Nightsmear?"

Claire shrugged. "It relaxes me. Rosie likes it, too."

"I've never known a girl who likes metal."

"I can appreciate every type of music. I love the intensity and the emotion, even though half the time I can't understand the words. I also really appreciate that nobody uses the word 'bae' in metal music."

Luke frowned. "I can't figure you out."

"I'm an enigma in yoga pants." She threw the car into reverse and snaked her arm around the back of his seat. "And sometimes no pants. You listen to Nightsmear too?"

"I've seen them in concert three times. I got a concussion at the last show after a mosher kicked me in the head."

She shuddered. "I'm too old for that general admission crap. I prefer to enjoy my music without getting kicked in the face."

"It's part of the experience," Luke insisted. "Speaking of which, your eye is starting to look better."

"It's just this concealer." She took a left turn, then reached into her center console and pulled out a pair of sunglasses. She slid them on. "It still looks like I went three rounds with the Hulk underneath it. How's your top-secret project coming along?"

"Really well, actually. I had a pretty big breakthrough thanks to that one interview."

"Sounds exciting. Are you going to tell me what it's about yet?"

"Unless you break into my house, you won't know until I'm ready to release it."

"That sounds like a challenge," she said, staring at him over the rim of her cat's eye sunglasses. How hard would it be to break into a house that size? If he was upstairs, she could break in and throw a kegger in the ballroom and he probably wouldn't even notice.

"Forgive me for not being more intimidated. You can't even open your own deadbolt. I doubt you're secretly a master lock picker," he said.

She frowned. Frustration prickled again. Who cared what his stupid documentary was about?

"Here we are." She pulled into a parking spot at her warehouse, then leaned over the center console to reach for her clipboard in the backseat and accidentally brushed her chest against Luke's left arm.

Oops. May he have the bluest of balls.

She led him to the side door and slid her key into the lock. As she turned the key, Luke bent down and pulled a weed from her flower bed and tossed it into the parking lot. What a jackass.

The warehouse shelves loomed large to their left. As she flicked on the lights inside, she heard a gasp and frantic shuffling. Luke immediately grabbed Claire's wrist and pulled her behind him. He picked up a wooden oar that was near the door and held it like a baseball bat. She picked up a bedazzled yard flamingo and held it by its spindly legs when she stepped out from behind him. No one was going to break into her business on her watch.

"Who's here?" she called out, voice deeper than usual. They moved across the taped-off circle that represented the fountain in Barney's proposal.

"Claire?" a voice called from the back office to their right.

"Mindy? Are you okay?" Claire relaxed, and Luke dropped the oar.

"Uh, yeah," Mindy said. "I'll be out in just a second." A minute later, she appeared in the doorway, her hair sticking up as though she had been electrocuted, and the button-down shirt she wore revealing several large gaps where she had missed the holes.

"So." Claire cocked her head at Mindy. "Did you come to work dressed that way, or were you having sex in my office?"

Luke turned away, shoulders heaving in silent laughter.

Mindy walked over to Claire, rebuttoning the top. "I'm so sorry. I didn't realize you'd be here this early," she whispered, dragging her fingers through her wild hair.

"Who is it?" Claire whispered back.

"Gavin from the club," Mindy mouthed.

"The British guy?"

Mindy nodded.

Claire gave her a quick high five. "I just need to grab a few things out of my office, Min," she said at a normal volume. She walked into the office and came face to face with a large Black man with an exceptionally chiseled frame. He whirled around, still in the process of buttoning his jeans.

"Oh, hello there. You must be—"

"Gavin," he said, turning back around and extending a hand to Claire.

She stared at it for a moment. "You know, I would love to shake your hand, but I'm pretty sure I know what you were just doing with it."

"Oh, right." The offending hand dropped to his side. "This is your office, then?" he asked, rapping a knuckle on the wall. Even his short, terse sentences sounded smarter with his British accent. Maybe she should take a trip abroad.

"Mindy and I share." She smiled and then turned her back to him. She covered the keypad to the safe with her body as she typed in the passcode. The door popped open, and she pulled Barney's engagement ring out of the safe. "I'll leave you two in a minute. I'm just here to pick up some speaker equipment." She opened the top drawer of her desk and pulled out another set of keys.

"Sorry about all this." He rubbed his hand on the back of his neck. "We didn't expect to run into anyone else."

"It's not a problem. Unless, that is, you don't call Mindy tomorrow. Then we'll have a problem." Claire waved at him and was about to exit when she noticed that a sock dangled from her ceiling fan. She stretched and stood on her tippy toes and plucked it from the blade. She pinched it between her thumb and forefinger and tossed it at him. "I'm assuming that's yours."

"Ah, yes," Gavin said. "Lovely to meet you! Great business you have here. Very creative." He followed her out into the main room.

"Thanks," Claire said. *He's cute*, she mouthed at Mindy as she passed by her.

Luke frowned.

"Are you still coming to the park today to help me monitor?" Claire asked.

"Yes! I was planning on heading out in about an hour to make sure everything is going smoothly." Mindy tugged at the hemline of her shirt. "I picked up the doves this morning. They're over in the corner."

"Thanks, Min." Claire walked to a cage with a blanket over it and peeked inside. When she lifted the blanket, several beady eyes stared back at her.

Thank god. They didn't have time for another Dovepocalypse. The warehouse was just beginning to smell normal again.

"I'm sorry, little guys. I promise you'll be free and back in the wild in just a few hours. Luke, can you help me with the speakers?" She pointed at a stack on the end of a shelving unit. As much as it pained her to ask him for help, it was better than throwing out her back hefting them alone. "I have a sound girl coming to help me with setup in half an hour."

"Uh, Claire?" Luke asked, staring at the mountain of speakers.

"Yes?"

"How are we going to fit all of this in your Malibu-Barbie-sized car?"

"We won't. We're going to take the company van." The keys in her hand jingled.

"Even better. Is it one of those creepy ones that doesn't

have any windows in the back?" He picked up one of the speakers and carried it toward the door.

"You bet. Every time I drive it, children run away in fear. We'll see you later, Min," she said. "By the way, disinfecting wipes are in this cabinet. Please use them."

Mindy walked right up to Luke. She was only a few inches shorter than him. She jabbed one finger into his chest. He nearly dropped the speaker. "Two things before you go. First, this is one of the biggest proposals we have done to date, so we don't have time for snarky comments about marriage. Second, Claire is the creative genius and beautiful human being behind this company, and I expect you to be respectful of her vision while you're on location. Am I clear?"

"We're clear. Nothing but business today."

"Good," Mindy said, taking a step back but maintaining eye contact.

"Anyway. It was nice to meet you, Gavin." Claire waved.

Gavin smiled, revealing dazzling white teeth, and returned her wave. Claire glanced at his crotch as she passed by. How did a Prince Albert piercing work, exactly? She was fairly certain that as soon as she went out the front door, the couple immediately grabbed at each other again. Whatever. At least someone was getting some action.

She set the doves down in the bucket seat of the van and crossed the pickup off her to-do list. She stretched a seatbelt through the handle of the cage and secured them. Next, she opened the safe in the back of the van and deposited the ring inside. She marked the transfer on her clipboard and spun counterclockwise with her arms lifted above her head. Luke hauled several more speakers out of the warehouse and piled them in the back of the van. For once, he didn't comment on her idiosyncratic memory technique.

"So," he said in a hushed voice. "You and Mindy are super protective of each other."

She glanced at him. "She can be pretty intense. We've been through a lot together. Don't worry, your testicles will return to their normal position eventually."

He scoffed.

She climbed into the driver's seat. "Thanks for your help. All set?"

"I'm looking forward to seeing you drive this." He slammed his door.

"Not so hard. You'll wake the birds," she scolded.

"That's what she said," he said quietly.

She snorted as she pulled out of the parking spot and began the short trip to the park. All the black sedans in the world couldn't bother her today. She was about to make some dreams come true.

"What, no death metal in this van?" he asked.

"I usually make Mindy drive, and she tends to lean more toward the pop garbage side of the music spectrum." Claire turned the radio on, and the voice of a breathy popstar exploded out of the speakers with choruses of *baby*s and *ooh*s. He leaned over and turned it off.

"Thank you." The car pulled to a stop at a red light. She mentally ran through the rest of the tasks on her list in silence. Minutes later, they pulled into a parking spot near the park's entrance.

"Nice location."

"Yes, the city does a pretty great job of keeping it maintained. I've actually done several proposals here. See that fountain over there?" She pointed to a beautiful pool of cascading jets in the southern corner of the park.

"That big one?"

"Yes. Every once in a while it'll go completely haywire

and start spraying outside the edge of the fountain like crazy. The last time I did a proposal here, the future ring bearer got nailed by the spray and went down like he was hit by Mike Tyson."

"Oh shit. How old was the poor kid?"

"Seven."

"He's going to have all kinds of nightmares."

"Definitely. He was doing this sweet little dance with the soon-to-be flower girl and all of a sudden *wham*—water fist straight in his left ear."

Luke shook his head. "Why do you keep doing proposals here then?"

"Well, because it's gorgeous. And in this particular case, my client brought his girlfriend here for their first date. Most people are willing to flirt with danger a little to get the pictures. Nicole's usually my photographer, and she's so good at getting the angles and the lighting just perfect. She'll be here today, hiding behind that bush." Claire pointed at a rather bulbous shrub near the fountain's edge.

The van's back doors creaked as they opened. She rummaged inside for a moment, then placed a fluorescent traffic cone on the asphalt behind her.

"Okay, here's what you need to know about today. Barney is going to come along this road and park right here in this spot." She cordoned off the space with cones. "I am going to be behind this bush so that I can toss him the ring, which is currently in that safe," she said, pointing to the built-in safe in the back of the van.

"Why doesn't he just carry the ring himself?"

"Clearly, you've never proposed to anyone."

Luke reddened and shoved his hands in his pockets. Interesting...

"If you're dating a really touchy-feely girl, as Barney is,

she will find that giant lump of a ring box before you even make it into your car."

He nodded. "I never thought about that."

"That's one thing I always warn potential grooms about. Now, after I hand the ring off to Barney, he's going to say a specific keyword and our sound girl is going to cue the music. That's why we need speakers placed down the whole length of this path. They're all Bluetooth-enabled."

He let out a low whistle. "You must have invested quite a chunk of change."

"We did. But it was worth it in the end to not have to pay rental fees all the time. Shall we?" She started down the path.

When he extended his arm to her, Claire took it begrudgingly and together they walked toward the fountain.

"Okay, so basically this entire proposal is a flash mob."

"How original," he remarked.

She shrugged. "Barney insisted. Victoria likes to dance. And it's my job to make clients happy and give them exactly what they want."

He scoffed. "I've never been so grateful to not have clients to appease."

"What do you mean?"

"When I make films, I'm the boss. All that matters is my vision and telling the story I want to tell. All this frilly pomp and circumstance would drive me insane." He stared pointedly at a bucket full of sparklers she had placed on the sidewalk.

"There he is. I was wondering when arrogant Luke would join us," Claire said. She stopped dead in her tracks and turned to look at him. "I realize that you're doing me a favor by being here today, and I appreciate that. I know you think what you do is more important and more noble than anything else on the planet. But you're in my arena today. I need you to shut up and do your job. And maybe, if you can dig around in that ice box of a chest of yours and locate your heart, you could watch Victoria's eyes when Barney proposes. You might learn something."

"Okay, okay. Sorry." He didn't look sorry.

She stomped off, covering only a few feet of pavement before whirling around again. "Anyway, here's where our first couple will be stationed."

He stopped and turned a full circle.

"Here?" he pointed at a patch of concrete.

"Yes," she said slowly. Was he having trouble grasping the concept?

"Just standing still?"

"Yes."

"You don't think it would lend more of a dramatic flair if they entered with some movement? For example, on a tandem bicycle?" He nodded down the road at a small kiosk where bikes were available for rent.

She took a deep breath and exhaled slowly. "This is the way we rehearsed it. And where would they put the bike when it's time to dance?"

"It's a bike. It has a kickstand."

Claire's hands curled at her sides. She was going to murder him. "There is no room for tandem bicycles in this proposal less than five hours before it's due to start. But thank you for your input."

They continued walking, pausing every few steps for Claire to explain another detail. She performed a dramatic example of one couple's dance moves and tripped. He gripped her arm to steady her. She snatched it back from him.

"This is where your second camera man will be stationed." She came to a stop halfway down the path.

"No, it's not."

She turned and glared at him, her hands balled into fists at her sides. At this rate, they were going to get stuck that way. "Luke. This is a huge day for me. Unless you would like me to dismember your body piece by piece and tuck every limb into an individually labeled barrel in the back of my windowless kidnapping van, I'm going to need you to stop challenging me on every single thing. Our usual camera guy is the one who helped me choose these spots."

"Then your cameraman is a dunce. If he shoots from here, the angle is way too wide. He could get all kinds of unnecessary crap in the background and ruin the illusion."

"It's not an illusion. It's a real thing that's actually happening."

He shook his head and looked at the sky. "Think of it this way. What if every time you saw a real movie, the cameraman had neglected to crop the frame close enough to cut out the gawkers who are there to watch them film? Would that not pull you out of the experience? If your camera guy shoots from this angle, you'll probably see a soccer team running around in the background." He pointed toward a group of children in the distance.

The stress weighed so heavily on her shoulders that Claire could have sworn she sunk an inch into the ground.

"Where would you have him stationed?"

He guided her to a different part of the path.

"I'm going to borrow your cockamamie visualizing technique for a moment." He stood behind her and stretched his arms out over her shoulders. She might as well have been wearing his biceps for earmuffs. Had she applied enough deodorant that morning? He held his hands in the shape of a frame and showed her the path the camera would track.

Damn it. He was right. Not that she would admit it. "Did you just use the word 'cockamamie?' Are you eighty-seven years old?"

He ignored her.

Heat radiated off him again, shrouding her and clouding her judgment.

"Whatever." She extricated herself from his limbs and moved away. She needed a yard stick to keep him at a safe distance.

"Nice spot," he said when they approached the fountain. "This is the end of the road?"

"No. This is where the magic happens." She held her hands out wide at her sides and twirled in front of the fountain. The mental image of Victoria's joyous "yes" sent a wave of goosebumps down her arms.

Six different geysers threw hundreds of gallons of water high into the air before it splashed into the penny-scattered pool below. She sat on the edge of the fountain, staring up into the sky for a moment, admiring the tiny rainbows that sparkled in the mist. She glanced around the park in both directions. There was a candy bar wrapper on the ground. Unacceptable. She strode over and snatched it from the ground, deposited it in a trash can. Much better.

"I'm not going to lie," Luke said, interrupting her trash purge. "A third videographer is unnecessary. With the limited scope of the ground we're covering, two is more than enough. In fact, I'm worried that the third will get in the way of the shot."

"Barney insisted on three." She shrugged.

"He sounds like a control freak." A soft breeze ruffled his

messy hair. He smoothed it back and tugged on the zipper of his backpack.

"He, like you, has a 'vision.'" She sat back down on the fountain and took a moment to close her eyes before the madness descended. "I almost said no to him as a candidate because at first I thought he was more interested in the spectacle than the engagement. But then I spied on them when they went on a date."

Her eyes snapped open. Luke looked at her with one eyebrow raised.

"It's part of my process. You could see the depth of feeling that they both have for each other. That's what convinced me. But anyway, I think Victoria will be good for Barney. He's the CEO of Heirloom Hotels, inherited from his dad who passed away. Sometimes I worry he's got more money than sense. Victoria, on the other hand, comes from humble beginnings. She was a server when they met, very down to earth, and has a good head on her shoulders. He encouraged her to go back to school and get her teaching degree. Now she teaches kindergarten at West Haven Elementary. I think she'll be able to keep him grounded."

"Damn. A CEO. No wonder he can afford a camera-wielding army, a cage of doves, roses, and what I'm sure is an impossibly huge engagement ring." Luke checked the battery on his camera and peered through the viewfinder.

"You guessed correctly. It's a princess-cut Tiffany. Four carats."

He whistled quietly. "Guess he doesn't have to worry about her saying no, then." The camera lens squeaked as he buffed it gently with a microfiber cloth.

"She's a really nice girl. I don't think she's a gold digger. Oh, good—Debbie's here to handle the sound," Claire said, standing up just as Luke was about to sit next to her. She sped off down the path, waving at the new arrival.

An hour later, Debbie the sound technician had successfully stashed all the speakers behind trees and rocks and had hooked them all up to her tablet via Bluetooth. After several sound tests, they deemed that everything was ready to go for the main event.

Nicole had arrived in the meantime and was taking some test shots while asking Claire probing questions about Luke's presence.

Luke chatted with the other videographers, who had been (begrudgingly) instructed to take his lead. Darren, the third videographer, stared at him with narrowed eyes. If Luke messed up, there would be hell to pay.

Dancers pulled into the parking lot, meeting up in their pairs and stretching against tree trunks. A florist truck drove up. The delivery girl saw Claire, waved, and presented her with an oversized bouquet of red roses. Claire handed her a tip and then began the process of passing out the roses to each couple.

"Jesus." Luke held his camera up to his face as Claire appeared with the bouquet. "How many couples are there?"

"Ten," she replied, passing them out three at a time each time she passed a couple. It was all coming together. The excitement in the air was almost palpable.

"Anna, I love your scarf," she said as she passed one of the dancers. "Oh, Antonio, you look like sex on a stick with that sweater vest." She pretended to fan herself. "You better not get too close to Victoria or she might try to marry you instead."

Antonio grinned as he caught Anna and flipped her over his back. Chutney, fortunately, had opted for jeans instead of her hoo-ha exposing sundress. Everything was as ready as it could be.

Claire turned to ask Luke a question about the white balance with the impending sunset only to see him rolling a bright red tandem bike toward her.

The smile died, and the barely concealed rage bubbled up again.

"What the hell is this for?" she asked through gritted teeth.

"Just trust me."

She clutched her clipboard so tightly to her chest that it splintered and snapped in half. She picked up the pieces and flung them into a trash can, clinging to her crumpled paper timeline. Mindy handed over her clipboard and put a hand on Claire's shoulder.

"I will hit him with my car if you want me to," Mindy whispered in her ear.

"It's the only way. I'll apologize to Kyle later."

Luke pedaled over to the first couple, Hannah and Eric, and got off the bike. He said something to the dancers, who got on the bike and took a few seconds to test the balance. Hannah set the roses gingerly in a basket on the front of the bike. They rode in a wide circle around the parking lot and crossed right in front of Claire. The breeze blew back the dancers' hair, and their cheeks were flushed. As much as Claire hated to admit it, it was more interesting than watching them pretend to read a map.

"Now," Luke said, sauntering over to her. "What if they weave in and out of the frame during the solos until the group dance starts, add some continuity to everything?"

"Luke, I am two seconds away from murdering you and stuffing your lifeless corpse in that trashcan. This proposal has been planned down to the second for the last month."

"Can we just give it a try? We have time."

The inside of her elbows hurt from clenching her arms to her side. She shook them out, held her new clipboard in a gentler grip. Just because he had been right about the camera angle earlier didn't mean he knew everything. But what if it did make it better? She glanced at her watch.

"We will give it one try. If it doesn't work, it's not going in the proposal. Barney doesn't even know about it, and he doesn't like to be surprised."

Hannah and Eric cheered from their seat on the bike. The sun was slowly slipping through the trees, elongating the shadows of the dancers. They had twenty minutes until Barney was due to arrive.

"Mindy, I need you," she called to her friend, who had walked away from the conflict to plant the cage of doves behind the fountain. "We're going to do a quick test and a final run-through to make sure everything is working. And I need you to schedule a good day for me to murder Luke after Johnny's proposal," she hissed. She glanced over her shoulder. Nicole was too far away to overhear.

"Consider it done." Mindy poked a finger through the bars of the cage and stroked the beak of one of the doves.

Claire hurried back to the parking lot with Mindy. "Places, everyone," she called as she mimed getting out of a door.

The dancers flocked to their individual positions, some studying maps, others playing guitars, and still others lounging in the late afternoon rays. She opened an imaginary car door for Mindy and took her arm before walking across the parking lot.

"Okay, and as soon as I get here, I'll say 'Victoria, I've been wanting to ask you a really important question,' and—

perfect! Thanks, Debbie," she said as the song thumped energetically from the hidden speakers.

Hannah and Eric crossed in front of their path, and Hannah smoothly whipped the roses from the basket and handed them to Claire.

"Nice job, Hannah. Head photographer should be on the right, and video one on the left behind that bush —perfect. Excellent job everyone. And now—oh shit! He's here! Shut it down!"

CHAPTER FOURTEEN

To Do:
- Send fruit basket to Jerry
- Ask Kyle how to get diplomatic immunity and murder (legally—can you run a business from prison?
- Ask vet about Rosie's gas

AT THE SIGHT OF A RED CORVETTE CRAWLING DOWN THE PATH to the parking lot, everyone scattered, the music shut off, and roses were hidden. Mindy and Nicole crouched behind one bush as Claire frantically cleared the cones from the parking spot and dumped them behind another bush. She crouched and pulled the ring out of a box in her pocket. They were ready for handoff.

Seconds later, Barney pulled into the parking spot. After a long moment, he popped open his car door, revealing a pissed-off Victoria.

"You've been so weird lately," came the voice from inside the car. It echoed in Claire's earpiece. She had nearly forgotten she had given Barney the other one. "You're never home, you don't call me at lunch anymore, and then you made me miss Pilates to come to the park. What are we doing here, Barney?"

Barney covertly hovered his hand over the top of the bush, and Claire passed him the ring. He put it in his breast pocket and buttoned it.

Barney opened Victoria's door and smiled, extending his arm. "Take a walk with me? Please?"

Victoria climbed out of the car, visibly annoyed. Her white lace sundress blew playfully in the breeze. It was going to look perfect with the fountain as a backdrop. She took his arm reluctantly and began to walk toward the fountain.

"You know, Victoria, I've been thinking, and I wanted to ask you something."

On cue, the pop song began to beat out of the hidden speakers. Victoria stopped for a moment, confused. "Is there music at the park tonight?"

Barney shrugged. The tandem bike rolled into sight, and he looked panicked for a split second before recognizing Hannah, who effortlessly made the rose handoff. Victoria looked down at the roses in confusion. Claire almost gasped. She had *not* given permission for the bike to be used in the real proposal. What if something happened?

"What on earth—" Victoria said. "Barney, what's going on?"

Another couple about six feet in front of them started dancing. The girl took her partner's hand and pirouetted, tossing the map up into the air and grabbing it before it hit the ground. The man spun around to reveal three roses behind his back. The couple sashayed up to Victoria and presented her the blooms.

Barney continued to lead her down the path. Shutters clicked and Claire spotted Luke hiding behind a tree with a tripod, filming the couple's progress. He glanced up and made eye contact with a second videographer before scurrying across the lawn, ducking behind trees as he went.

Claire clutched a hand to her heart as she watched the tandem bike roll into the view again. She wanted to stand— to shout—to insist they back out of the frame. However, the couple glided smoothly between the dancers in time with the music.

She fumed. Who the hell did Luke think he was? How dare he change her proposal minutes before it started? How would he feel if she came to a screening of his new documentary and picked it apart seconds before it aired? Actually, that wasn't a bad idea.

A small group of people gathered around the outskirts of the fountain, drawn by the music. Victoria seemed to spot her family just as another couple strutted up to them to present a rose. Tears sprang into her eyes, and she looked at Barney, who just smiled and rubbed her arm encouragingly as he guided her down the walkway.

Claire stayed crouched and snuck along the path behind them. She ducked behind trees and shrubs until she made her way to the fountain, then set a bag of emergency lighters and mini propane torches at her feet and waited.

There was cameraman one, a couple paces behind the couple. Luke was securing a position in front of the fountain. But where was cameraman two? She shot a look of pure hatred at Luke. Barney was not going to like this. Hopefully, he was too distracted to notice.

By the time Barney and Victoria reached the fountain,

Victoria had a massive armful of roses. She was now openly weeping, wiping at her eyes with her free hand. The light was perfect. Her emotional reaction was perfect. Nicole stood to her left, standing halfway up a stepladder to get the perfect angle. These were sure to be some of the most beautiful pictures Claire's blog had ever featured.

As the chorus kicked in for the last time, Barney jumped into the circle of dancers who now surrounded the fountain. He lunged and spun, pausing for a quick pelvic thrust before moonwalking across the front of the fountain. Victoria clapped her hands delightedly, nearly losing a few roses.

As the song hit the last few bars, a slightly out-of-breath Barney walked up to Victoria and got down on one knee in front of her. The dancers whipped long-stemmed sparklers out of their sleeves and lit them. Phew. Emergency torches were not necessary.

Forming a semi-circle in front of the fountain, the dancers arranged the sparklers to spell out "Marry me?"

At a signal from Claire, the music quieted until it was nothing but a soft background blending into the Starburst-colored sky.

"Victoria," Barney began as he kneeled before her. He took her left hand and kissed it. "Do you remember what I told you the very first day we met?"

Victoria nodded. The glow from the sparklers illuminated her tear-stained cheeks.

He launched into a rather long-winded description of the night they met. Claire crossed her fingers, hoping he remembered her advice about leaving out the sex.

Finally, he held the ring up to Victoria. As he raised it, the geysers in the fountain began to spurt. One faltered.

Dread clamped down on Claire's stomach. "Oh no," she

whispered. "Please hold off for just a few more minutes."

"Victoria, my love, my life, my destiny. Will you—" Barney was cut off by hundreds of gallons of water thundering down on his head.

The camera shutters clicked wildly. "Damnit! Damnit! Damnit!" she whispered. The ill-timed flood prematurely extinguished several of the dancers' sparklers.

Victoria gasped in astonishment as the water splashed onto her sundress. For a moment, she looked horrified. Then, she started to laugh. She dropped to her knees and hugged Barney under the torrent of water, laughing and kissing him.

Oh boy. Hopefully, Victoria's sundress had a liner beneath the lace. There was no room for suddenly see-through dresses and wayward nipples in this proposal. Claire grabbed the travel umbrella from her emergency bag and threw it in Barney's direction. He caught it in one hand and opened it over their heads.

"I love you, Victoria," he concluded, shouting over the rushing water. "Is that a yes?"

"Yes!" she exclaimed. As Barney slid the ring onto his fiancée's wet finger, one of the dancers opened the cage of doves and gave it a shake. The cameras snapped again and again as Barney and Victoria kissed under the clear, bubble-style umbrella, which was still being battered by the tumultuous downpour from the fountain. A gorgeous sunset warmed the sky behind them, the perfect canvas for the flock of white doves that soared overhead.

Victoria smiled and pointed at the birds, clasping a hand to her heart and saying something to Barney that Claire couldn't quite hear.

After another moment, the geysers quieted, revealing a thoroughly soaked but happy couple. Barney pointed out the hidden videographers and camera crew. He gave the signal to Victoria's family, who descended in a crowd of hugs that brought a new wave of tears to her eyes.

As Luke was still getting some footage of the newly engaged Victoria hugging her family, Claire ran to the van and grabbed some towels, a blanket, and a large box. She approached Barney cautiously and tapped him on the shoulder.

"I'm so, so sorry about the fountain." She handed him a stack of towels.

"We'll discuss this later," he said, giving Claire a hard look. There was anger in his eyes.

Her stomach twisted as he turned around to address the family. She hated disappointing clients. It almost never happened. No more proposals at this stupid fountain.

Barney took a deep breath and smiled, but it didn't reach his eyes. "Victoria, darling, I'd like you to meet the person who made this whole thing possible," he said.

"The fountain malfunctioning was not part of the plan." Claire bit her lip.

The whole family applauded, and Victoria came up to hug Claire. "It was perfect, every part of it. I don't even know you, but you planned such a perfect proposal. How did you do it?"

"Barney planned it all. I just helped execute it," she said. "And, as a final surprise, you should open this." She placed a large, flat box in Victoria's hands.

Victoria set it onto the ground and lifted the top off, revealing a strapless, shimmering, midnight-blue gown. "Oh, it's gorgeous." The fabric rustled as Victoria slid it out. She held it up to her chest. "How did you know to bring another set of clothes?"

"That was actually part of a surprise for both of you.

You're going out to Chez Louis with Barney and your whole family."

"The restaurant where we had our second date?" Victoria asked.

"Absolutely. And if you come with me, I have a hair and makeup team waiting to get you ready," Claire said. "Barney, I'm so sorry again," she whispered as Victoria stepped away at someone's call. "I'm going to give you a big discount on my consultation fees to make up for what happened."

He took a deep breath, his shoulders slumping back to their normal position. "You don't have to do that. It's fine. I was just really hoping everything would go perfectly."

"Did you see the beautiful smile on your fiancée's face? That's the surest sign that she just had her perfect proposal."

Barney turned around to glance at Victoria, who was showing off her ring to her family. He smiled.

"I'm sorry I don't have a change of clothes for you. Give me your measurements and I will run somewhere and—"

"As luck would have it, I picked up my dry cleaning this morning and accidentally left it in the car."

"Perfect. Don't worry. I will make this right," she said as she led Victoria to her van where a makeup artist and hairstylist waited patiently. They recoiled when they saw that Victoria was absolutely soaked.

"Sharice, do you think you can get her hair dry? Or maybe a nice, sleek topknot?"

"I will do my best." The hairdresser pulled out a blowdryer and plugged it into an outlet in the back of the van.

Claire left Victoria to be pampered and primped, and then skirted around Luke, who was filming Victoria getting ready, to go find Mindy.

"I'm dead. Our business is ruined. That was a disaster."

"I don't think so. He doesn't look too upset." Mindy looked

in the direction of Barney, who appeared to be telling the family a hilarious joke, judging by the chorus of laughter. She hefted the dove cage and dragged it down the sidewalk toward the van. "How do you think the pictures will turn out?"

"I have no idea. I'm scared," Claire said, waving at Nicole, who was capturing Victoria's uncle doubled over with laughter.

Nicole lowered her camera and scanned the crowd before coming over. She gave Claire a quick squeeze and said, "That was so great! You did such an amazing job."

"Were we both here for the same proposal? Did you see that our client nearly drowned?" Claire groaned, unable to shake off the feeling of failure.

"Trust me, nothing is ruined," Nicole said. "Just look at these pictures." She held the screen out and flipped through the images, each one more stunning than the last. Nicole caught the geyser as it splashed off the umbrella, the couple mid-kiss underneath.

"Oh my gosh, these are gorgeous." Claire gingerly took the camera and clicked through a few more. "Nicole. These are just flawless. I'm so relieved." She clutched a hand to her chest. All was not lost. She handed the camera back and walked a few feet away, collapsing onto the grass. The street lights flickered on over the path.

After an all-too brief moment of solitude, Mindy's waterfall of dark hair appeared. It tickled Claire's arm as she sat on the ground next to her.

"You okay?" She cocked her head.

"I'm fine, just mentally and physically exhausted."

Mindy poked her. "Everything's fine, you know. They both looked thrilled. You are Claire Freakin' Hartley. Don't you dare forget it."

Claire smiled. "Speaking of physical exhaustion, how was the early morning desk sex with the British hunk this morning?" Claire whispered.

"Phenomenal," Mindy responded in an overly loud voice. "I don't know what it is about that piercing, but it really—"

"Min." Claire raised a hand to stop her. "Quieter. Victoria's grandparents might still be hanging around. But I would love to get all the dirty details over drinks later this week."

"Fair enough. I have a date with Gavin to get to anyway. Do you need me for anything else? Everything that's ours is packed away in the van."

"Thank you. I'm all set. See you later."

Claire waved her off, not really wanting to be around anyone for a minute or two. She lay on her back, watching the last of the pink in the sky fade into a deep purple. The fountain tinkled gently in the background. Sure, now it was calm.

"I didn't know you were submitting this to *America's Funniest Home Videos*." Luke appeared out of the darkness and sat down beside her.

She sat up and hit him in the arm. "Where in the hell was the last cameraman?"

"I told you, he would have only been in the way. I sent him to the fountain from the start to take some warm fuzzies from Victoria's family."

She sputtered, unable to form words. "And you didn't even tell me? Luke, I planned this for *weeks*. Every single moment was carefully calculated."

He held up a hand to stop her again, a habit that was becoming annoyingly familiar. "I know this goes against every instinct, but just trust me. I will show you the footage when I get it from Bruce."

"And don't think I didn't see the fucking bike you snuck in without even a full rehearsal." She jabbed him again. It was a relief to transfer some of the blame. "You owe me an apology."

He grabbed her hand and put it back on her lap. "An apology for making your proposal better? I think I'll pass."

Fire coursed through her veins. Slamming her hands into the ground, she propelled herself up and stomped over to the fountain, cursing Luke with each step.

"Wait." He grabbed her wrist.

She snatched it back and spun around. "Go to hell."

"You're right. I'm sorry. If you had done this during one of my projects, I'd probably be upset too."

She scoffed. *Probably*.

"It wasn't professional, and I won't change anything on the next project without talking to you first." There was a smile hiding behind his apologetic mask.

She wasn't going to bite. "Who said there's going to be a next project?"

He shot her a dirty look. "Do you want to see the footage first and then decide if you want to fire me?"

She crossed her arms. It was over. There was nothing she could do about it now. And to be honest, she was dying to know how it looked on film. "Show me."

He took her hand and pulled her over to a bench beneath a streetlight. Why did her heart stutter every time he touched her? His douchebag energy must be shorting her circuits. They sat, and he pulled his camera out of his backpack, then flipped open a tiny screen and selected a video file. He fast-forwarded through some of the B-roll he had taken of the park and the ring. She would never admit it, but even in the raw footage, Luke had an undeniable talent for placement, angle, and light. The scene did look better without the soccer field in the background, and the couple on the tandem bike added an element of cohesiveness that wasn't there before. That son of a bitch had come in for less than a day and improved something she had planned for weeks.

When the water thundered down on Barney's head, she groaned and closed the screen. "It was supposed to be perfect."

"Real is always better than perfect." He tucked the camera away.

"Not in a marriage proposal. Luke, if you try to pull any last second changes like that during Kyle's proposal, I will snip your testicles off with a pair of garden shears and fashion them into a coin purse. And then I'll fill that coin purse with the world's heaviest currency and punch you in the face with it."

"So, this means I'm still on the project?" He grinned.

"It's too late to find someone else who can pull off the underwater portion," she conceded.

"I think you've had enough stress for one day," he said, stretching his arm over her shoulders. "You must be hungry. Want to get some food and install that deadbolt?"

"Don't you have something else to do? Another event to commandeer?" She rubbed her arms. A misty chill was settling over the park.

"Nothing important. I have some questions about our next project anyway." He turned toward her. Their faces were inches apart.

"What sort of questions?"

He brushed a hair out of her eyes and tucked it behind her ear. Her skin warmed under his touch. What was he doing? Hair stroking wasn't professional. And he had just risked the entire proposal by throwing in a tandem bike. Without her permission. She should slap his hand away. Or saw it off.

A shiver ran up her spine that had nothing to do with the chill of the night. *Shut it down, Claire.* She hated the effect he had on her, how striking he looked under the glow of the streetlight. The angle of his jaw, the thin scar that disappeared beneath his collar. How had he gotten that scar? Probably got stabbed for insulting someone's life work.

He opened his mouth to speak but stopped when Nicole hurried over to them. He pulled his arm back.

"Claire! There you are. Is everything okay? Mindy said you were having a self-esteem crisis. Oh, sorry." Nicole must have noticed the weird energy.

Claire pointed at the camera Luke still held. "We were just watching some of the footage. Everything's fine, I just had to sit down for a minute to process how much I screwed up. What's up?"

"Everyone officially left. I wanted to see if you needed help cleaning anything up."

Claire sat up straighter and looked around. She held her hand out to Nicole and allowed herself to be hauled up. "Actually, everything looks pretty good," she said. The sound technician must have packed the speakers up after Victoria and her makeup team had left. "You're so sweet, Coli. Remind me to tip Debbie extra. I think we're going to get some food. Want to come? We could invite Kyle," Claire said.

"Sorry, tonight is Make-Your-Own-Fortune-Cookie Saturday. Thanks, though!" Nicole turned to Luke.

"I hear you don't like dragons."

Luke stared at her like she was crazy. "I'm sorry?"

"Dragons! For your brother's proposal?"

"For my brother's—Oh. Yes. Claire and I have had some creative differences of opinion on Johnny's project."

Nicole stopped fiddling with her camera lens and stared at him. "I thought your brother's name was Liam."

Claire froze. *Shit.* Which name had they decided to go with? She was almost positive there was a flash card that read Johnny Liam in the front of the proposal binder. Would Luke remember?

Luke looked panicked for a moment. "Right, he goes by his middle name, which is Liam. Luke and Liam. My mom loved 'L' names. I just call him Johnny because it drives him nuts. I'm still saying no to the dragons, but Liam loves the idea."

"Told you," Claire said as she picked up her bag. She had come perilously close to faking a medical emergency to end the conversation.

"Okay," Nicole said slowly. "I'll see you guys later. I'll start editing tonight if I can and send over some proofs," she said, leaning in to hug Claire.

"Love you. Have fun with your fortune cookies." Claire waved goodbye and started back to the van with Luke. She opened the back doors. All the speakers, wireless headsets, and other props were tucked safely in the back.

"Dragons? What the hell?" he asked, waving with a strained smile as Nicole drove away.

"Sorry. She asked me the other day what the theme was and I panicked."

"And out of the whole world of possibilities you picked dragons?"

"Yes, and in case Nicole asks, your brother met his girlfriend at a Dungeons & Dragons tournament. Did you seriously not read the updated notes? I emailed them days ago."

Luke scoffed. "I had more important things to worry about."

"Learn the cover story," she commanded as she slammed the back doors. They should have taken separate vehicles. How could she even fit in the same car as Luke's ego?

She climbed into the driver's seat and collapsed against the head rest. "Normally, I feel pretty good after a proposal. But right now I feel like all of my carefully laid plans were just shat on by a vindictive god. No more proposals at this park. I might as well just hand Wendy the award right now." Claire shook it off and shifted the van into reverse. There was still hope for Nicole's. But if Barney made a stink online, her reputation could be irreparably damaged.

Luke stared out the window. "Judging by what I've seen from this Wendy character so far, she'll never win that award. She doesn't take the time to get to know her clients, and her ideas are overdone and unimaginative. How many people have proposed to their girlfriends at sporting events? Did that couple even really need a planner?"

She opened her mouth to agree, but he plowed on.

"And from that video—very poorly shot, by the way— you could see that girl was embarrassed and terrified even before her boyfriend came out with the stupid ring." Luke shook his head. "Maybe if she would have paid attention to her personality and planned for a smaller, more intimate proposal, they'd still be together. That's one of the reasons why you keep winning—you care. You pay attention."

Claire stared at him as she stopped at a red light. "Did you just pay me a compliment about the 'ridiculous' thing I do for a living?"

He shrugged. "It might not be the most useless waste of money in the world. Victoria looked really happy."

"I think she was. Do you want to hear about my next project?"

"Tell me." He crossed one leg over his knee and turned toward her.

As she drove, she gave him the full story on Steve, Tara, and the Jet Skis.

"Wow. There really is a Jet Ski proposal," he said when she finished.

"Yep. It should be pretty epic if we manage to actually pull it off. And if I don't get locked in the bathroom again." After shifting into park and pulling her keys from the ignition, she absorbed a second of silence before hopping out and opening the back door of her van. A prickle of fear ran down her neck. She swept the scene, but nothing was out of place. There were no black sedans parked in the lot, no shadowy figures hiding behind the fence. "I'll just be a minute. You can sit in my car if you want." She held her keys out to Luke.

"I'd like to have a few minutes to stretch my legs before I climb back into that sardine can."

"Hey. It's a pretty sardine can."

"I'm not saying she's not pretty." Luke held up his hands defensively. "I'm just saying she was built for short people like you." He picked up a speaker in each hand and carried them to the building. He could have waited for her to get the hand truck, but okay.

She glared at him as she unlocked the warehouse door. "I'm not that short," she said, pushing the door open. She flicked the lights and stomped her feet on the threshold. "Min? Are you in here?" There was nothing but silence.

"Thank god. I'm not in the mood to be surprised by any more half-naked men today." She set the dove cage down on the concrete floor.

"There go my plans for the evening." Luke brushed against her as he passed to set the speakers down in the corner.

"Very funny." A thrill slid through her belly, but she ignored it. He changed her proposal. She still hated him. She peeked into the dove cage. "Ick, that needs to be cleaned out. I'll have Mindy do that on Monday as penance for getting frisky in our office. And probably on my desk." Claire shook her head. "I believe I owe you a dinner. What sounds good?"

A short debate ensued. Chinese was the victor. She placed an order with the restaurant down the street from her apartment, and they piled into her car once again. Half an hour later they pulled into the parking garage, collected their plethora of camera gear and Chinese food, and hauled everything upstairs. Luke didn't try to force her into the elevator this time. Her stomach grumbled as they walked down the long hallway, all the way to Claire's apartment door at the very end. As they approached, Luke stopped dead in his tracks, holding his arm out to stop her.

The apartment door was hung open a crack, tilting on its hinges. The door handle itself was mangled, and it sagged against the screws that barely kept it in place.

Panic ripped through her like a wildfire, and she dropped the bag of takeout on the ground.

"Oh my god. Rosie!" She started to enter the apartment, but Luke gripped both of her arms and moved her several feet away from the door.

"Stay right here and call the police." His green eyes bored into hers. "Do you hear me?"

"But—"

"No," he said firmly. "If you hear or see anything, I need you to run. This is not a discussion."

CHAPTER FIFTEEN

To Do:
- *Change the freakin deadbolt already*
- *Research security companies*
- *Don't panic*
- *Send B & V engagement/apology gift*

As Claire dialed 911, Luke kicked her door open the rest of the way. It bounced off the wall as he flicked on the lights. He grabbed a pink umbrella that stood next to the door and crept inside.

"Nine-one-one, what is your emergency?" the operator said in Claire's ear.

"Hi, yes, this is Claire Hartley calling from Six-oh-one East Beaumont St, Apartment four B. I just got home, and my apartment has been broken into. The door is hanging off its hinges, so it was definitely forced entry."

"Okay, miss, are you inside the apartment?"

"No, I didn't go in."

"Good. Do not go inside. I need you to go to a neighbor's. I'm dispatching a unit to you right away. Would you like me to stay on the line with you until they arrive?"

"No, that won't be necessary," Claire said. "I'm sure whoever did it is long gone by now."

"All right, ma'am. Sit tight until the police get there."

"Thank you," Claire said, hanging up the phone. "Luke?" she called tentatively.

There was silence. Her stomach lurched, and her hands went numb. *Oh, god.* Was the perpetrator still in there? Had they incapacitated Luke? As much as he drove her insane, she didn't *actually* want him to die. Should she run to a neighbor? The Lebowitzes were visiting their children in New York, and she didn't want to get roped into a forty-minute discussion about cat dandruff with Mrs. Roberts across the hall. Should she just go inside?

Luke reappeared in the doorway, clutching the umbrella in one hand and Rosie in the other.

"Oh, thank god." Claire collapsed to her knees in the dingy hallway. She gathered Rosie into her arms and clutched her to her chest, waiting for her heart to stop racing.

Rosie whined and licked her face reassuringly.

"What took you so long?" Claire demanded. "And why didn't you answer when I called? I thought someone ripped your entrails out."

"I was being cautious. I checked everywhere and didn't see anyone. Everything is trashed though. I took some pictures in case your insurance company needs them. You have renter's insurance, right?"

She stared at him. "Who do you think you're talking to?

The cops are on their way." Sirens wailed in the distance, but it was impossible to know if it was for them or if someone had plowed into Denny's with their car for the third time this year.

They were quiet for a moment. Luke sat cross-legged on the ground next to her.

"Who would have done this?" She stroked Rosie between the ears and clutched her furry warmth close. Someone had broken into her home and touched her baby girl. There would be hell to pay.

He shrugged. "Wendy? Your douchebag ex? How many other enemies do you have?"

The mysterious picture in the mail slithered into her mind. Her heart pounded. "Who knows?"

Luke reached over and wrapped his arm around her. She shivered despite his warmth.

"There's something I didn't tell you." His voice was quiet, and he seemed hesitant. "When I found Rosie, she was tied up to the radiator."

"What does that mean? Whoever broke in here wanted to make sure she didn't run away? How uncharacteristically thoughtful."

"She was tied up with this." He drew a coil of rope out of his pocket. It ended in a loop.

"Is that supposed to be—"

"A noose," he said, letting it dangle from his hand. "I think someone is trying to threaten you. And they already seem to know how important Rosie is to you."

Claire slapped the rope out of his hands. It fell to the carpeted floor. She couldn't wrap her mind around someone breaking into her apartment, let alone tying her dog to a radiator with a noose. All she could do was scold the person in front of her. "Luke, that's evidence. You're not supposed to touch it. Shouldn't you know that? You're the true crime guy."

He took a deep breath like he wanted to continue but stopped when flashing police lights rolled up outside the building.

The elevator doors slid open, and two policemen came out with their guns drawn. After Luke handed over the rope and explained how they found the place, the police entered the apartment. Claire peered through the partially open doorway as they canvassed her apartment, taking pictures of the destruction.

Rosie was still clutched in Claire's arms when she was eventually allowed back inside. Her eyes widened. She didn't recognize her own living room. Her couch was flipped upside down. Throw pillows were torn apart, their stuffing littered throughout the room. Even Rosie's bowl was knocked over, leaving food to intermingle with the shattered remnants of Claire's favorite teal mug. Luke hovered behind her, silent, like he was waiting for her to have a mental breakdown.

On her fridge, a corgi-shaped magnet held a piece of plain white paper covered in crude handwriting.

You'll find out when it's your turn. Stop going to the police or mommy dearest will pay.

She gasped. Scattered underneath the note were reams of paper ripped from her binder with the Widowmaker research and a dozen candid pictures of her mother— grocery shopping, getting out of her car, laughing as she danced in the kitchen with Roy.

Claire stumbled backward, and Luke caught her. Rosie flailed, but Claire clutched her even closer. Luke held them both as tightly as if the world had just inverted and he was the only thing keeping them from falling into the sky. Her limbs trembled uncontrollably. Not even her new proximity to Luke's pecs could distract her from the dread that threatened to overwhelm her.

The tall, slender officer with steely blue eyes rubbed his neck as he came over to Claire. "Miss Hartley, my name is Detective Smith. I don't know if you remember me."

"From that day at the station." She nodded and extracted herself from Luke's arms to shake the detective's hand. Her heart still hammered like she had just run a marathon.

"Do you have any idea what this might mean?"

"That's my mother in the pictures." Tears were choking her throat. "It looks like they were taken at her house in Florida. Someone's watching her. And he's watching me. It has to be the same person who sent me the picture of Courtney and me sleeping."

Luke's eyes bored into the back of her head. *Whoops.* She had neglected to mention that to him. He would probably find a way to be angry about it even though it had nothing to do with their working relationship.

"The picture is still under investigation," Detective Smith said gently. "What's the binder for?"

"I was doing research on the West Haven Widowmaker." She frowned at the partially dismantled binder. All that carefully organized research ripped to shreds. "There are newspaper articles, maps, that kind of stuff in there. I was looking for similarities between the victims, descriptions of the killer, anything really."

The officers exchanged another glance, and Detective Smith nodded. The taller one stepped away and got on his radio to request backup.

Detective Smith scribbled something else in his notebook. "The FBI and state police have yet to confirm that any of the disappearances are connected," he said in a dull tone, as though it was a phrase he had recited hundreds of times. "The current official position of all law enforcement agencies is that this 'West Haven Widowmaker' does not exist. Is anything missing from your apartment?"

Why did it feel like he was scolding her? "I'm not sure. Let me look."

Before she left the kitchen, she glanced behind her. Detective Smith and the other officer had their backs turned to her. She snapped pictures of the note and the photos of her mom. In the living room, her laptop, TV, gaming consoles, and safe where she kept her clients' rings were all untouched. Luke followed her like a shadow, occasionally lifting furniture for her to look underneath. She checked her drawers, but all her jewelry was still there. She reviewed her bookcases, her shoe collection, and her makeup stash, but nothing was missing.

Whoever broke in wasn't there to pawn her expensive items for drugs. They were here to send her a message. Unless she was mistaken, she had pissed off a serial killer.

Burying the thought to deal with later, she opened her coat closet and took a brief glance inside. Was it her imagination, or was it less full than usual? She clicked the overhead light on and checked the back of the closet. The black garment bag containing her wedding dress was gone. She checked the floor and surrounding area, but there was no sign of it. That didn't make sense. Where had it gone?

"Did you find something?" the detective asked.

"My wedding dress is missing," she said slowly, pointing to the closet. "It was in the back in a garment bag."

"Hand me that fingerprint kit, Mark," Detective Smith

said to the officer who was setting up evidence markers in the kitchen.

Claire stumbled back down the hallway toward the front door, feeling sick. She had visions in her head of the wedding that she had called off—walking down the aisle on the country club lawn, clutching Roy's arm as he led her to Jason. She would have twirled in her perfect dress during their first dance. Who would break in and take only her wedding dress?

She took a deep breath and leaned against the kitchen island. Jason attended Venor University—that's where they had met. Every Widowmaker victim but one had gone to Venor. The girl who didn't attend the university lived up north, in a town barely twenty minutes from Jason's hometown. Could Jason be the Widowmaker? He certainly had the motivation to break into her apartment.

The possibility of being targeted by the Widowmaker had been in the back of her mind since she received the picture in the mail, but she had refused to look directly at it, to give it truth. She couldn't ignore it any longer. She was being hunted.

Nowhere felt safe. She hesitated between her living room and kitchen. Something seemed different. What was it? The dining room seemed emptier somehow. The flower bouquet had disappeared from the island.

"Detective Smith?" Claire called.

He hustled down the hallway. "Did you find something else?"

"A giant bouquet of flowers showed up at my apartment earlier this week, and there was no note on it. The bouquet is missing," she said, pointing at the bare spot.

"How carefully did you examine the bouquet?" He asked

as he flipped his notebook open and began jotting something down.

"Not that carefully. It was just flowers."

"How big was it? And what kind of flowers?"

She estimated the size with her hands. "Stargazer lilies. My favorite."

Detective Smith wiped sweat from his brow. "Do you have a clothing hamper?"

"Yes, why?"

"You should check that, too," he said.

Her heart thudded in her ears. "Why?"

"Just check."

Her mind raced as she twisted the doorknob to her bedroom. Was he trying to tell her that someone might have stolen not only her wedding dress, but her clothes? How did someone leave the apartment unnoticed while holding a garment bag, a giant bouquet of flowers, and dirty laundry?

She took a deep breath and lifted the lid of her wicker hamper.

"Oh my god." Her stomach lurched. It seemed half as full as it had been that morning. She pawed through the pile.

"Is anything missing?"

"There must have been six pairs of underwear in there. They're all gone. What kind of a sick freak steals dirty underwear?"

The detective made another note on his notepad.

The nausea reared its ugly head. She backed away from the hamper and sank down on her bed. Luke sat beside her and rubbed her back. Rosie whined as she nosed Claire's hand.

"Do you live here alone?" the detective asked. He looked

intently at her face. What was he staring at? Oh, right. Probably her giant black eye.

Claire nodded, tears stinging her eyes.

"We need you to stay with a friend or family member for the night," he told her. "We have to declare your apartment an active crime scene. Our forensic team is on the way. We'll be in touch to let you know when it's safe to return. Shouldn't be more than a day or two."

"Mark," he called over his shoulder. "Get in contact with the landlord. And start interviewing the tenants on this floor."

"No security footage?" the other cop called.

"No," Claire and Detective Smith answered at the same time. The landlord had promised for years to install security cameras but had never gotten around to it.

"Have Jenkins check with the businesses across the street when he gets here. One of them must have a camera. I saw in the kitchen that you had a newly purchased deadbolt." Detective Smith turned back around to face her. "Was the package open before you left?"

"Yes."

"I would take that back and get another one in case the intruder copied your keys," the policeman said, flipping his notebook to a new page and scribbling before he tucked it in the pocket of his jacket. "Don't hesitate to give us a call at the station if you need anything. Stay with a friend tonight, and don't forget to get a new deadbolt," he said.

They were kicking her out of her apartment. Her safe space. It wasn't so safe anymore.

"Can I pack a bag before I leave?"

Detective Smith shook his head. "I'm sorry, we can't disturb the crime scene." He looked around at the destruction before his gaze settled back on her. "We *will* find out who did this."

Luke picked up Rosie's leash. "She's coming home with me." His tone left no room for argument.

"You don't need to do that. Plus, frankly I'm still mad about you slipping a tandem bike into my proposal. I'll call Coli."

"If you call her, you'll spend the whole night making lists and trying to hunt down who did this on your own. I don't have time to rescue you again."

"Rescue me?" Claire sputtered. "I didn't ask for someone to break into my apartment and—"

"All right." He held up a hand to stop her. "I'm sorry. I'm already here, and we have a bag of room temperature Chinese in the hallway. Let's go."

Claire rubbed her right temple with her free hand. A tension headache pounded. Kicked out of her apartment due to an active crime scene investigation. These were not the circumstances she imagined for spending another night with Luke. "Fine."

She clicked the lock button on her phone and then groaned.

"What's wrong?"

"How am I going to tell my mom about this?"

Luke slid his arm around her waist and pulled her in closer. "You don't have to tell her right now. Just come home with me, and we'll take things one step at a time. I won't let anything happen to you. Or Rosie."

She didn't have the energy to respond. She let Luke help her up and guide her back down the hallway. Four more cops had shown up. Some took pictures of the destruction while others examined the note.

Claire picked up her purse and Rosie's leash before the

police could forbid it. She also snatched the bag of Chinese food from the hallway. No panty-stealing creep was going to make her miss out on General Tso's. As Claire, Luke, and Rosie left, one of the officers sealed off the apartment door with yellow caution tape.

Tall buildings and the glow of endless storefronts blurred past as Luke drove them through the shopping district. A faded pine tree air freshener dangled from the rearview mirror of his pickup truck. Claire adjusted the mirror and glanced into it regularly, mentally cataloging the cars that followed them even for short distances. It was hard to tell in the dark, but she didn't see any black sedans.

Could it really be the Widowmaker? Was he watching her now, laughing at the terror he had caused? What did he want from her? She wasn't married. She didn't fit the profile. Other than Courtney, she didn't know any of the victims well. Had she unknowingly done something horrible at Venor? But what about Ariel, who never went to college? It didn't make sense.

Luke must have sensed she was not in a talking mood and simply rubbed her knee as they traveled. His touch was a nice distraction from the violent chaos that had entered her life. Rosie frolicked in the backseat, running from window to window and barking at the streetlights as they flashed overhead. The truck seemed to shudder when they approached stop signs, but it didn't stall. Why did a semi-famous filmmaker insist on driving a shitty truck?

Buildings slowly melted away into single-family homes and gas stations, and eventually faded away altogether as they drove deeper into the country.

Detective Smith's words echoed in her mind. How could the police not believe that the disappearances were connected? Someone had literally handwritten a message to tell her to stop researching a serial killer, and they acted as though it was of no consequence. Could she even trust the police?

She had to stop these spiraling thoughts. Keeping her hands busy was probably not a bad idea, so she typed out brief messages to Nicole and Mindy to let them know what had happened. She slouched into her seat as Luke turned into his driveway.

At least the landscaping was improving. The empty pond was now filled and lined with rocks. The grass had been freshly mowed. Even the dilapidated treehouse had been disassembled. The yard was much closer to fitting her vision for Nicole's proposal.

Her phone pinged, and she glanced at it. A text from her mother. Her heart nearly stopped.

Alice: *Everything okay, Clairebear? Something feels off.*

A second later, a picture with a "prayer for protection" appeared.

Claire: *All good, Mom. Just finished a proposal. Call you tomorrow.*

She put her phone away and opened her window a crack as they traveled up the winding driveway. She tapped her fingers on the armrest, desperate to think about anything other than what had just happened. "I never thought I'd miss the sound of crickets. They used to drive me crazy when I was younger, but now they just feel like home. Maybe I'll move out of the city once my lease is up," she mused. "It might be worth the drive."

"You could probably rent a bigger apartment out here for the same amount of money."

"I've been thinking about buying a house," she said.

"Really? You want to stay here? I kind of thought after tonight you'd be ready to pack up and move to Florida with your mom. Or at the very least get a roommate."

"No way," Claire said, rolling her window back up as they came to a stop. "I've seen mosquitos the size of trashcan lids down there. And can you imagine a Florida proposal?"

"Hurricanes, alligators, brown recluse spiders. There's potential there."

She rolled her eyes. "Besides, as silly as it sounds, I love Pennsylvania. It's home. My actual hometown is about an hour south of here in the middle of nowhere. But when I came to Venor for school, I fell in love with West Haven. It has everything—great food, nightlife, a near constant stream of young people settling here and wanting to get engaged. I don't have to worry too much about earthquakes or hurricanes or tornadoes. It's safe—or was, I guess. And apparently, there's also inspiration for top-secret documentaries here, so added bonus." She stared at him pointedly.

"When did your parents move to Florida?" he asked, blatantly ignoring her probe into his work.

"Mom and Roy moved not long after I moved to the city after graduation. Roy's family is from Miami."

"Big family?"

She nodded. "I have twenty step cousins on that side. They're great. They taught me how to swear in Spanish when I was ten."

"A valuable skill to have."

"It is. You don't want to talk about what inspired you to return to this area?"

"I told you before, my work brought me back," he said

slowly, though it sounded like a calculated response. "And like you said, this area is home." He whistled to Rosie, who jumped over the center console and into the front seat.

Claire frowned and cast a glance around at the rustic scenery. That wasn't entirely truthful. Luke and Kyle both hailed from The Heights, a notoriously ritzy sub development full of mega mansions and eight foot gated privacy fences on the outskirts of West Haven. Was the subject of his documentary lurking somewhere in The Heights? She silently vowed to scour his place for clues after he fell asleep. She could use the distraction.

"Are people using cows to move drugs across state lines?" she fired at him as she opened her door. She picked Rosie up and turned her phone flashlight on, inspecting the corners of the dark yard before deeming it safe. Rosie had potentially been face to face with a serial killer today. She didn't need a run-in with a wayward woodland creature too.

Luke raised his eyebrows. "Not that I know of."

"Is that taco stand on Cypress Ave laundering money for the mob? Their tacos are an offense to Mexican food. There's no way they should still be operating."

"I'll check into it," he said, locking his truck and glancing around his yard.

"I will guess the subject of your project." She hefted Rosie back into her arms and started for the front door. The quarter moon didn't lend much light to the yard, and any one of the shadowy trees along the perimeter could conceal a deranged serial killer.

"Doubt it," he said as he pushed his front door open.

"You didn't lock your house when you left? After your many lectures to me on personal safety?"

He frowned. "I must have forgotten because someone dragged me out of the house on emergency proposal business. Let's get you inside." He glanced around the yard again as he ushered her in. He locked the deadbolt behind them.

Claire shook her head and set the bag of Chinese on Luke's breakfast nook. It was almost a relief to be annoyed again.

After flicking on the pendant lights above the kitchen island, he went from the kitchen to the living room systematically shutting curtains. More boxes had been unpacked since Claire's last visit. Furniture was now scattered through the expansive rooms.

Her phone pinged for the fifteenth time in two minutes. She sighed deeply and gripped the countertop like a lifeline.

"Are you okay? I mean all things considered." Luke had arrived silently at her side. His stormy eyes searched hers. He reached out one hand but stopped short of touching her.

"I'm fine. I guess." She laughed to herself. "I'm just worried about my mom. And worried about what she'll say when she finds out. And wondering how I'm going to clean up my apartment. And what I'm going to do if that psycho comes back while I'm there alone."

Luke held both of her shoulders in his rough, work-calloused hands. Rosie was squished between the two of them. "I swear to you, I will not let anything happen to you. I mean, we. Nicole, Mindy, Kyle and me. We'll keep you safe."

"I bet you wish you knew what you had signed on for before you agreed to help me with Nicole's proposal." She slid out from under his hands and walked into his living room to inspect the new couch.

"You can put her down, you know." Luke ignored her comment.

"Oh." She looked down at her dog. "I guess you're right."

As soon as Claire set her down, Rosie began running

from room to room, excitedly sniffing everything in sight. Claire followed her down the hallway and shut all the doors before returning to the front of the house. The last thing she needed was for Rosie to chew through an expensive A/V wire.

A tall, four-legged stool stood in the middle of the living room, and Luke's guitar rested on a stand beside it. "You were playing?"

He nodded. "It helps me clear my head sometimes."

"I get that." She ran a hand over the smooth veneer of the piano, then settled on the polished bench. "Would you play for me?"

Luke reddened and scratched the back of his neck. "I don't really play in front of people often."

"What did you say to me earlier? Sometimes you have to do things that scare you," she paraphrased. She glanced pointedly at the stool.

"I don't know," he hedged and wandered to the other side of the room to straighten a picture frame.

"Come on, don't make me play the victim card. If you play, maybe it will distract me from the fact that a crazy person broke into my—"

"Okay, fine." He sat on the stool and picked up the acoustic guitar by the base of its neck. The guitar hummed as he plucked a few strings, and then he adjusted some tuning pegs. He leaned forward and closed his eyes, placing his fingers lightly on the strings. He took a deep, audible breath and began to strum.

A slow melody resonated, bouncing off the curved ceiling and filling the entire room with a palpable sorrow. The music welled up inside her, filling her with both sadness and wonder at the same time. She watched, entranced, as Luke strummed. For a moment, all the terrible events of the past week just faded away as she allowed herself to do nothing but listen.

Even Rosie came to see what the fuss was about. She sat on the floor next to Luke's stool and watched him, head tilting back and forth as he changed notes.

When his fingers slowed and then stopped, Claire couldn't speak, only then noticing that tears had welled up in her eyes.

He hung his guitar back on its stand and came to sit next to her on the piano bench. He reached one hand up to her cheek and held it there, rubbing away one of her tears with his thumb. They looked at each other for a moment, nothing but moonlight separating them.

Claire leaned in. His warm, woodsy smell welcomed her like an embrace, promising warmth and comfort and security. She shouldn't be doing this. They were coworkers. Reluctant ones at that. The cocktail of hormones bouncing around her system from the break-in was making her stupid.

He moved his hand from her cheek to the back of her neck, gently cupping it as she leaned in, his hand buried in her curls. Their lips were only a breath apart when Claire's phone vibrated on the piano bench. They both jumped. Claire slipped off the edge of the bench and crashed to the floor.

She swore and held up a finger when Luke tried to help her up. Still on the hardwood floor, she mouthed *sorry* as she answered the call. "Hey, Coli."

"Are you okay? What the hell happened?" Nicole demanded.

She recounted the story.

"The guy who sent you the picture? Now he stole your dirty underwear? Are you kidding me? Claire, I think you should move in with me. Are you staying with Luke tonight?"

"I am." Claire glanced at him.

"Good." Nicole hesitated. "I will seriously clear some closet space tonight. Move in with me."

"You live in a one-bedroom apartment."

"So what? It'll be like college all over again. We could even get bunk beds."

Claire laughed for the first time since she had walked into her destroyed apartment. "That was a terrible joke."

"You're right, that was awful. I'm sorry. Stay with me tomorrow then. And with Mindy the night after. We'll set up a schedule."

"Thanks, Coli. I'll call you tomorrow." Claire disconnected and shoved her phone into her pocket. "Sorry, that was Nicole just checking on me."

Luke stood up from the bench and helped her to her feet.

"Can I ask you something?"

"Sure." She brushed off the seat of her pants.

"You mentioned another picture to the police. This wasn't the first set you received?"

She took a deep breath and crossed her arms over her chest. It was surprising that it had taken him this long to ask. "There was another picture. That one was mailed to me last week. It was of me and Courtney, my freshman roommate. The one who disappeared. We were asleep in our bunk beds."

He shuddered. "Was there a return address? Did they test the envelope for DNA? Did you notice anything unusual about the handwriting?"

"I don't know, Luke," she said. Had he been watching the same true crime show Mindy was obsessed with? "I turned it in to the police. I'm too tired and hungry to think about it right now."

"You're right. Sorry." He relaxed his stance and walked to the kitchen.

She frowned after him, certain the gears in his head were still whirring away.

He dumped the rice and chicken into bowls. "How do you feel about sweet and sour sauce?" he asked.

"Easily makes my top ten favorite sauces."

"There's a literal, handwritten list in a binder somewhere, isn't there?" he asked as he put the first bowl in the microwave.

"Maybe," Claire conceded.

"What else falls on your list of favorite things?"

She considered for a moment as she climbed into an iron-backed swivel chair at the island. She drummed her fingertips on the countertop as Luke filled two glasses with water. He slid one over to her.

"You already know most of my embarrassing favorite things, like video games and weird eating habits. Traveling would be another one, but I'm usually too busy to do it. Reading. Cooking. Gummy bears. Sorry, I keep coming back to food. Yoga and Pilates. I used to run, but not anymore. How about you?"

"Film, first and foremost." He plucked some napkins from a holder and folded them neatly. "I've been making movies since I was a little kid. Most of them were absolutely terrible. Music is a close second. I wrote a couple of instrumental tracks for my last documentary, actually. Boxing. Beef jerky. Travel, of course. I like to build things and make things with my hands. I guess mostly I love to create. Oh, and watching cute, strange girls do yoga. That's another one of my favorite things."

"What a coincidence," Claire said as Rosie settled at her feet. She ignored the dig. "I could walk you through a sun salutation later. You could use some flexibility."

He shook his head and passed her a bowl. "It's the least you could do after waking me up at six in the morning, demanding that I work for you, making me load and unload a van like a Metallica roadie, and then forcing me to defend your honor with a pink umbrella."

"Shut up. That song you were playing," she said, leaning back in her chair, "was it a Luke Islestorm original?"

Luke turned around to face the microwave and shrugged. "It was. There aren't any lyrics or anything. I just like messing around."

"At the risk of inflating your already record-breaking ego, it wasn't just messing around. It was beautiful."

Though he shrugged, there was definitely a ghost of a smile underneath his five o'clock shadow. He joined her at the island with his bowl of Chinese.

Claire ate a fork full of chicken and moaned with pleasure.

"Old, microwaved Chinese food is that good, huh?" he said.

"Shh. I'm having an experience." She didn't speak again until her bowl was empty.

"Are you tired?" he asked, taking her bowl from her and rinsing it in the sink before depositing it in the dishwasher. Apparently, he didn't hand wash his dishes at home.

"I'm still kind of wound up from this whole ordeal." The bar stool creaked as she climbed down. "You must be exhausted though. I'm sorry for waking you up so early. Thank you for being willing to help last minute, and for being there for me when... you know. Would it be weird if I hugged you?" She held her arms out from her sides.

"It might be a little bit weird," he said but stepped closer to her. "But I'm willing to overlook that." He bent down and hugged her around the waist before leaning backward and picking her up off the floor.

Claire laughed and flailed her legs. He leaned forward after a moment, allowing her to slide slowly down his torso until her toes reached the floor again. They locked eyes. Her heart thumped erratically, but this time it didn't have anything to do with danger. Or did it? Luke was a different kind of danger.

Rosie sneezed. Claire jumped and sheepishly withdrew her hands. She inspected the floor so she didn't have to look him in the eye. Her cheeks burned as she took a step back.

"This doesn't mean that I'm not upset about the bike. I haven't forgotten." She stabbed the air between them with her finger. Her sex embargo was crumbling around the edges. What was it about him that made him so irresistible even though he tried to ruin everything?

"I am fully prepared to never hear the end of it." He shot her a smile as he wiped the kitchen island down with a dishrag. "Want to try watching a movie and see if that helps you wind down?"

"That sounds nice. Does this mean you will allow my estrogen in your man cave?"

"Just this once." He opened the door that led to his basement.

"Are you sure you're not taking me down here to kill me? Because that's how my day is going." She held on to the lacquered railing as she stepped down the carpeted stairs. Rosie catapulted past them, nearly knocking Claire down the steps.

"Considering today's events, that joke is in extremely poor taste."

"You have a point."

As she descended, more of the basement revealed itself. Wall-to-wall cream carpet covered the floor. A set of doors on the far wall led outside into darkness. A fireplace stood at one end, flanked by armchairs and bookcases. There appeared to be another full kitchen on the back wall, and to its right, an actual screening room. Rosie was already rolling on the large sectional sofa that faced a projector screen.

"Is it exhausting being this high maintenance?" she asked.

He shrugged. "I needed a space for impromptu screenings."

"You live a rough life." She flopped onto the couch. "Okay, this is heaven."

Luke opened the media cabinet and glanced inside. "What are you in the mood for?"

"Let's rent *The Princess and the Arrow*. Then you can get the full picture for Nicole's proposal," Claire said, sprawling across as many cushions as possible.

"Do you ever stop thinking about work?" He slid a movie out of its case and put it in the Blu-Ray player.

"Is that—did you—"

"Yes, I bought it the other day. But if anyone asks, I'll deny it."

Almost instantly, a rumbling roar erupted, vibrating the couch. She jumped and nearly sprang up.

"Sorry, surround sound," he explained as he turned the volume down. "Beer?"

"Please." She gratefully accepted a bottle of a local craft beer. Hops danced with hints of blueberry and citrus. "Good choice. The summer brew is my favorite."

"Mine, too. Am I still a man if I admit that I enjoy the taste of blueberries in my alcohol?"

She pretended to think for a moment. "I guess you still qualify, but tread carefully. Everyone knows that masculinity is derived from alcohol preference."

"I thought it was coffee preference." He raised his bottle to hers.

She clinked bottles with him and ran a hand down Rosie's furry length. Luke's spotless couch was going to be buried under a cloud of dog hair. It served him right after the bike fiasco.

"I'll be right back," Luke said. He disappeared up the stairs and returned moments later with a T-shirt.

"You can wear this to sleep in if you want." He tossed her the soft gray shirt. "I don't think any of my shorts will fit you."

"Thanks." She stepped into the basement bathroom next to the wet bar. She emerged seconds later wearing just the T-shirt, a thousand times more comfortable. It dangled down to mid-thigh. Rosie's nails would surely shred Claire's legs before the night ended.

His eyes tracked every move as she sat down next to him on the sectional. She glanced at the doors that led outside and shivered.

"What's wrong?"

"It's just the doors. I feel like anyone could be watching from out there in the darkness."

He immediately walked over to a box near the sliding doors and pulled out a drop cloth, throwing it over the bare curtain rod and covering the door from top to bottom.

"Better?" he asked as he returned to the couch. He sat close, but they weren't touching.

She nodded. "Thank you."

The movie started, and she inched closer to Luke. Why was she suddenly craving human contact? She had survived eight months with no man in her life with absolutely no struggle. It must be the stress from the break-in. He might drive her to the edge of insanity, but this house felt safe. He felt safe.

Apparently reading her mind, he pulled her against his side and let her head fall to his shoulder. This time, their contact wasn't charged with sexual energy. It was warm and comforting. Her mind quieted, and her breathing slowed.

She saw about fifteen minutes of the movie before her eyelids drooped.

CHAPTER SIXTEEN

To Do:
- *Call phone company and get them to block J's number*
- *Distract mom from break-in news by asking questions about crystals*
- *Send apology card to Barney*

WHEN HER EYES FLEW OPEN THE NEXT MORNING, CLAIRE expected to see an intruder leering at her. Instead, she spotted Luke sleeping on the couch next to her, arm tucked under his head. Memories of the previous evening came flooding back. She sat up and glanced around, clutching the blanket to her chest. Rosie lay in a nearby pool of sunlight. Everything was quiet.

Was that a yellow legal pad on the coffee table? Maybe it was notes on his project. It was pretty unprofessional of him to leave them lying around. Glancing at him, she leaned forward. The sheet was covered in small, messy handwriting. She squinted. A few words jumped out at her.

Apprentice. Ball. Bookshelves. Mead. Turkey legs. He had taken notes while watching the movie. Something tingled in her stomach. Pulling the blanket off, she draped it over his sleeping form. Then she scooted off the couch and tiptoed across the carpet and up the stairs with Rosie on her heels.

The kitchen was filled with glorious morning light that made the granite countertops gleam. The break-in the previous night wasn't as scary in the light of day. Who was to say the Widowmaker was the one who broke in? West Haven had a crime rate just like any other city. It could have been a junkie or Jason looking for something she had neglected to throw down the fire escape when she kicked him out.

But the photos. An average, run-of-the-mill drug addict wouldn't know her mom and certainly wouldn't have the time or motivation to stalk her in Florida. Ugh, her mom. She really needed to call her. Claire stretched her arms up to the ceiling and stood on her tippy toes, limbering up for what was sure to be a migraine-inducing conversation with her mother. Luke's T-shirt skimmed her thighs, buttery soft. Would he notice if she didn't give it back? None of her T-shirts were this comfortable.

She needed to refocus on the task at hand. Rolling her shoulders back, she pressed the power button on her phone. *Shit.* It was in low battery mode. How could she be so thoughtless? What if a client needed her? A glance around the kitchen showed it was bare of the charging cords that littered her entire apartment. She dug through her purse and withdrew an emergency cord, allowing her phone to charge a bit while she gathered her thoughts.

Should she be completely honest with her mother and become responsible for the DEFCON Level One meltdown that would occur? Or should she shelter her from the truth until they had more information?

"Rosie, what would you do?"

Rosie looked up for a moment and sneezed before turning back to her bowl of water.

"Bless you. But that wasn't helpful."

It wouldn't do any good to tell her the whole truth until they knew more. The intruder's only interest in her mother was her relationship to Claire—surely she wasn't in any real danger. He could have just as easily threatened her favorite Uber driver.

Claire held her breath and dialed her mom's phone number.

Over the course of twenty minutes, she fended off several attempts her mother made to convince her to move to Florida. Claire unplugged her phone. A dead battery would at least be a legitimate reason to end the call. She paced as she talked, moving to the front porch to let Rosie out as she glossed over the more heinous details of the crime. Positioned near the front door, she watched her dog like a hawk.

Luke's yard was a bright emerald green dotted with the occasional dandelion. It was the perfect place to roll out a yoga mat and do a sun salutation, but she didn't feel like twisting herself into a pretzel this morning. Once she crossed the threshold into the outdoors, she sensed imaginary eyes staring at her from behind every tree.

"Yes, Mom," she said into the phone as Rosie attacked a wildflower. "I promise to check in with you every day. I'm going to take care of the deadbolt today, the police are observing the place every few hours, and I'm going to be staying with friends in the meantime. The police will figure this out. It was probably just someone looking for drug money." She whistled for Rosie, who trotted up the porch steps and followed her into the kitchen.

Claire opened Luke's fridge and pulled out an egg carton. She slid it onto the granite countertop and clamped the phone between her shoulder and ear.

"I know, Mom. It really sucks. No, it definitely wasn't the West Haven Widowmaker. If he even exists. I'm not married, remember? I'm safe." A prickle of fear tickled her spine as she set a jug of milk next to the eggs.

How did he choose his victims? Recently married girls who had attended Venor University? Did he look through the engagement announcements in the newspaper to select his victims?

A thought struck her like lightning. When Nicole and Kyle got engaged, would that put her on his radar? Was she sending Nicole right into the hands of a serial killer? But no, people didn't get murdered for no reason. There must be some person, some common thread that linked all the girls. There was no reason to suspect Nicole had pissed off the same person Courtney and the others had. Claire vowed to scour the victims' social media accounts when she got home. There was something there. She could feel it.

She pushed the thoughts to the back of her mind and pulled some shredded cheddar cheese and bacon from the refrigerator. Further investigation revealed an onion, a single red pepper, and spinach.

"I still think we need a safe word," her mom insisted.

Claire jumped. She had been so immersed in her thoughts, she had almost forgotten she was speaking to her mother. "A safe word? Like one that I would say to you if I was in danger? Shouldn't I be calling the police if I'm in danger?"

Kitchen drawers banged as she opened and closed them. Half of them were empty. Eventually, she unearthed a cutting board and knife and set them on the island.

"Well, if I call you and he's holding you captive, you could use the safe word and I'll know to call the police."

"Sure, Mom." Claire shook her head. "If it makes you feel better. How about 'platypus'?"

"Platypus. Platypus. Platypus," her mother repeated. There were some shuffling noises on the phone. Her mom also subscribed to Claire's theory that doing a dance move helped you remember important things. She sounded slightly out of breath when she returned. "Okay. I've memorized it. So, next time you're being held captive and I call, we're all set."

"Great. I have to go, Mom. I'm making breakfast. I'll call you later, okay?"

"Every two hours, Clairebear. I need to know you're safe."

"No, not every two hours, Mom. You know I won't remember. I'll call you tomorrow."

Her mother hemmed and hawed but finally agreed. "I love you, sweetie. Be safe."

"Love you too. Bye, Mom." Claire ended the call and dropped her phone onto the counter.

"It could have been worse," she said to the dog, who had rolled onto her back, exposing her belly to the sun. Rosie cocked her head.

Pushing the conversation with her mother out of her mind, Claire focused on making omelets, stuffed to the gills with cheese and vegetables. She covered them up and left them in the pan with the burner on low. It would be rude to eat before Luke was awake.

She scrambled a couple of eggs for Rosie, plating them carefully and adding a bit of spinach for garnish. It wasn't exactly Instagram-worthy, but Rosie wasn't the pickiest critic. She set the plate on the floor. The dog scampered over and immediately devoured her breakfast. The spinach was left behind.

Claire glanced around the kitchen again, drumming her fingers on the island. How long would it be until Luke woke up? He was her ride, and she had things to do. She was scheduled to post a blog entry this morning, and she really needed to start on an apology gift for Barney and Victoria.

Should she make some noise—maybe drop something in the kitchen? She picked up her purse and dangled it from one hand. It was certainly heavy enough to do the job. But she snatched it back and hung it on the back of one of the barstools. There was no sense in sacrificing a scuff-free Kate Spade tote to wake up a slumbering cameraman.

Hang on a minute. Luke was asleep. Was his office unlocked? Could she finally learn the subject of his annoying super-secret documentary?

She tiptoed down the hallway toward the office. *Creak.* She froze. Apparently, the Toilet King had skimped on his floorboards. There was no indication of movement from the basement, no footfalls on the carpeted steps. She crept along as quietly as she could until she stood in front of the French doors. After a glance in each direction, she tugged at the silver handles. They refused to budge. *Damn it.*

Burying a hand in her tousled mane of curls, she dug until she found a single bobby pin. People on TV did this all the time. How hard could it be? She bent the bobby pin until it was straight, jammed it into the lock and wiggled it around. The lock didn't budge.

The basement door crashed open with a bang. Rosie yelped. Claire jumped, banging her elbow off the wall behind her. A picture frame fell off a floating shelf and landed face-down on the hardwood floor. The glass shattered.

"Claire?" Luke sounded panicked. He whirled around the corner.

"Hey, I—"

"What the hell are you doing? Why didn't you wake me up?" There was a dangerous glint in his eyes. Great. Someone had gotten up on the wrong side of the couch.

"I'm sorry, I didn't want to disturb you. You scared me." She clutched a hand to her chest. Her heart hammered in a staccato rhythm.

He stormed over to her with a scowl. His confident, douchey attitude was gone. "*I* scared *you*? Some creep steals your underwear, and I bring you home, and then you disappear without waking me up? Do you know what I thought when I woke up and saw you were gone?"

She stopped clutching her chest and raised an eyebrow. "You weren't clued in by the smell of breakfast? Did you think someone broke in and murdered me and then casually whipped up some omelets?"

"You can't just disappear like that." He turned away from her, pressing a hand over his eyes. She had never seen him look so rattled. This was a different Luke altogether.

"I'm sorry I didn't wake you up," she said, bending down to pick up the picture frame that had shattered. She turned it over, revealing a woman in a yellow dress on a swing.

"Shit. Let me get the vacuum." Luke disappeared down the hallway.

Her face was hot as she picked up the larger pieces of glass. Her eyebrows furrowed. Why was he treating her like a child? She hadn't done anything wrong. Well, apart from trying to break into his office. But he didn't even know about that.

Rosie tried to approach the blast radius, but Claire ordered her to stay. For once, she listened.

He reappeared with an expensive-looking vacuum. He said nothing as he fired it up, rolled it over the shards. Claire stepped out of the way, trudging down the hallway with a handful of broken glass and a picture of a mystery woman. She spun around in the middle of the kitchen. Damn rich people and their hidden trashcans. Where the hell was it? She opened several cabinets until she found the correct one.

The glass shards sparkled in the bottom of the trashcan, mixed with coffee grounds and food scraps. *Mmm, coffee.* Surely a little caffeine would improve Luke's mood. She approached the coffeemaker. The machine was much bigger than her one at home. A half dozen knobs and vials glowed. She tapped her foot impatiently. What did a girl have to do to get a little bean juice?

Slap. Something smacked the counter behind her. She whirled around.

"Forget something?" He asked, eyebrows raised.

Her bent bobby pin sat on the countertop.

She froze, mind racing with possible excuses. Luke was many things, but he wasn't stupid. "Fine. I tried to pick the lock on your office."

For a moment, they simply stared at each other. A smile cracked the contours of his face. "How'd that work out for you?"

"It didn't, obviously." She gestured to the picture frame.

She turned around so she wouldn't have to look at him or the mystery woman and pulled the lid off the omelets.

She opened a cabinet next to the stove. Pint glasses and wine glasses took up the entire space. Shutting that one, she moved on to the next. How many cabinets were in this damned kitchen?

He crossed the kitchen and popped open a cabinet next to the refrigerator. He came back with two plates. Who stored plates next to the refrigerator and cups next to the stove? She shook her head. He needed a kitchen storage makeover.

Claire slid the omelets onto the plates and sat at the breakfast nook. Luke joined her, handing her a fork. She had a full view of the yard and driveway, and her eyes darted up every time something moved outside. Rosie, seemingly sensing her distress, came over and laid down on top of her feet.

"I called my mom," Claire said after a full minute of silence. The omelet would have been better if it was still fresh. She frowned. Of course this would be Luke's first exposure to her cooking. He would probably consider it a waste of time to even eat it.

"And?"

"As expected, she lost her mind."

He nodded. "She sent you a one-way ticket to Florida?"

"Probably. I haven't checked my email yet."

"You're safe here, you know."

Apparently, she wasn't hiding her anxiety as well as she thought.

"I have security cameras, motion detectors," Luke continued. "The whole nine yards. Kyle's buddy Sawyer installed them for me when I moved here."

"Oh," she said, turning back to her breakfast. "That's

good to know."

The night before came rushing back. The pictures of her mother scattered on the floor, her furniture flipped over. Her missing wedding dress. She didn't even want to think about the underwear.

Claire stabbed her omelet but found that she had lost her appetite. She set her fork down with a clatter. "Can I say something crazy?"

Luke nodded as he chewed.

"I don't care what the police say. I think the West Haven Widowmaker is real, and I think he's responsible for the pictures and the break-in." The words came out in a rush, like a cork had popped off a champagne bottle.

He set down his fork and put his hands on the table. As he looked at her, his expression turned serious. "I don't think that sounds crazy at all."

"No?" How uncharacteristically empathetic of him.

He wiped his mouth with a napkin and leaned back. "I mean, I'm the true crime guy, so no theory sounds too far-fetched to me. Can I show you something?"

He stood and offered her his hand.

She took it, ignoring the electricity that ran up her arm at his touch, and followed him back down the hallway to the set of locked doors. *Holy crap.* She was finally going to learn what all the fuss was about. He must be trying to distract her from her shitstorm of an evening.

He turned to face her. There were bags under his eyes. "Do not freak out. Give me a minute to explain." He took a key from his pocket and unlocked the door. He pushed the doors open and allowed Claire to step over the threshold.

She fumbled for the light switch. What was he hiding? A stolen Rembrandt painting? Ten kilos of cocaine? A complete collection of Beanie Babies?

She flicked on a light and revealed what at first seemed to be an ordinary office. A large walnut desk stood in the middle of the room. Computer monitors lined the outside walls. Papers were scattered all over the walls and desk. About what? She walked over to the closest wall.

"'Widowmaker claims another victim'?" she read from the headline of one news article.

"Pregnant newlywed missing," read another. It was like staring into her own murder binder.

Realization struck. Her heart jumped into her throat. She grabbed the nearest object—a wireless keyboard—and lofted it into the air like a tennis racket.

"Is it you?" The words felt like ice cubes as they tumbled from her lips. Her mind raced a mile a minute. It would be too perfect. A true crime fanatic, a storyteller. A murderer investigating his own murders.

"What? No, Claire, I told you not to freak out. I'm not the Widowmaker."

"That's exactly what the Widowmaker would say." She inched closer to the door. The wireless keyboard felt flimsy in her hands. It would inconvenience him at best. She needed something heavier, but she couldn't take her eyes off him.

"The Widowmaker is my project. And the break-in couldn't have been me, remember? I was with you all day. Not to mention I was in Afghanistan when you were in your freshman year. I couldn't have taken the picture either."

"He might not be working alone," she said, but she lowered the keyboard. He was right. Surely, she would know if someone she was working with was a psychopath. She put the keyboard back and took a deep breath, then turned to investigate the wall behind her.

An Asian woman with a slightly crooked smile and beautiful black hair had a corner of the board to herself.

"That's Ariel," Luke said. "She was first, and the farthest away."

Ariel's eyes seemed to stare into her soul. Claire shivered and moved on to another bulletin board that hung between two windows.

A map of Pennsylvania was spread over the far wall. A small cluster of neighborhoods in the central and northeast part of the state was thumbtacked, each with a line leading to a picture of a girl. So, this was what had brought Luke back home.

She stared into the faces of the women she had obsessively researched. Demographic and biographical information was listed underneath each person's picture. Ariel Pulizzi. Kayley Herrold. Jennifer Heiser. Shawna Delong. Courtney Stevens. Their names ran together like a morbid cadence in her mind. Chills ran down her spine as she read.

Underneath Kayley's name, he had placed another picture. The girl looked like a cherub, with wide, honest eyes and plump, rosy cheeks. Her blond hair shone in a ponytail. Claire remembered her from the biology class she had been forced to take freshman year.

Jennifer's picture was a candid one of her mid-jump in a Venor basketball uniform. Photocopied journal entries were taped underneath her picture. "Feelings of being watched on evening runs," said a hand-scrawled note.

"How did you get her journal entries?" she asked, barely above a whisper.

"I interviewed her husband. He kept copies of everything he gave to the police."

She moved on to the next victim. Shawna stood in front of a painting, regarding the camera without a smile. A copy of a police report was stapled underneath her, topped with a handwritten statement reading, "break in two months before disappearance."

Courtney's headshot from her architecture firm stared back at Claire. She was still amazed that someone as flighty as Courtney was allowed to design buildings. "Flowers with no sender" was written underneath her picture. A pang of sadness struck her. She could practically smell the fast-food tacos that were responsible for her freshman fifteen.

Though the victims were similar in age, they couldn't have been more different. Courtney was an architect with a drinking problem. Kayley was a NICU nurse. Jennifer had coached high school basketball. Shawna had moved to Scranton and opened an art gallery.

Interest tugged at Claire even as the true scope of the Widowmaker's horror spilled over her for the first time. The lines on the map spread like a spider's web. The girls were frozen in time, trapped in their youth. Their unrealized potential stared back at her.

Her head swam. Why didn't Luke open the windows? It was so stuffy in here.

He stood in the corner silently as she took in his new project.

Files and folders were spread all over the desk, containing police reports and missing person alerts. Claire stepped back and bumped into the desk, clutching it as she took in the splintered fragments of women who had gone missing, never to be heard from again.

She glanced at the bulletin board again, and noticed that another, much smaller picture and piece of paper were stuck to the board next to Courtney. She walked over to inspect it and recoiled when she saw her own face smiling back at her. She was dressed in all black and talking to one of her former clients from a proposal she had done the previous year. The photo had come from her blog.

Her temper flared like gasoline on a fire, and she fought for control. She pointed at her picture with a shaking finger. "Luke. What. The. Fuck?"

"I didn't have any proof." He held his hands in front of him.

Claire stabbed at her picture. "How long have you known?"

"I never knew. I only suspected. That night when you got the giant bouquet of flowers—I had an inkling. All five victims had flowers with no sender sent to them in the weeks before their disappearances. Then I found out you and Nicole and Mindy all went to the same college as these girls. I was afraid for your safety."

A hysterical laugh escaped her.

"You were afraid for my safety? When were you going to tell me that you think I'm the target of a serial killer? When I get kidnapped and stuffed in a trunk?" She shouted now, voice pitching in hysteria.

"I just wanted to keep you safe until I had some proof. I've been interviewing the family members of the victims and talking to the police, trying to figure out all the commonalities. Trying to see if you really are in danger."

"You thought the police should know your suspicions, but not me?"

Luke reached for her, eyes flashing with anger. "You're right. I should have told you."

"You fucking think?" she spat. Adrenaline coursed through her veins. She could have ripped the head from his shoulders and punted it down his stupid driveway. *Nobody* kept a secret like this.

"I didn't want to worry you before I had anything

concrete, something the police couldn't ignore."

She shook her head and straightened. She had half a mind to pick up the wireless keyboard again and crack him soundly over the head. "No. Fuck you. You took advantage of me when I was vulnerable because you saw an opportunity for an in for your documentary. You weaseled your way in and listened to my sob story and thought 'Oh, great, this psycho's next target just fell into my lap. Maybe if I play nice, she'll let me in, and I'll get the biggest scoop of my life.'" Her fingernails bit into her palms. She needed to escape this airless murder room.

"Claire—" He reached for her, but she ran past him into the hallway.

Rosie ran up to her and whined. Claire stormed up the hallway and snatched the dog's leash from the kitchen. She clipped it on Rosie and ran to the front room. She almost turned back for her outfit from the previous day. When Luke's footsteps fell behind her, she decided she could live without it and burst through the front door with Rosie. Wearing only Luke's gray T-shirt, she trotted barefoot down the driveway.

Hot tears of anger pricked her eyes, and she burned with humiliation. How could Luke have suspected that she was a target and kept it from her? He just wanted a front-row seat for the next disappearance. Fucking asshole.

Rage coursed through her, propelling her down the stone driveway. She barely felt the gravel as it bit into her feet. She wasn't going to disappear. She was going to kick Luke's ass. And then she was going to find the West Haven Widowmaker and destroy him. They'd both underestimated her, and she'd show them. She'd show everyone.

She hated herself for getting close to Luke. For getting close to anyone. She was better off alone.

Halfway to the main road, her cell phone rang.

"*What?*" she barked without looking at the caller. If it was Luke on the other end, she was going to lob her phone into the forest.

"Miss Hartley? This is Detective Smith."

"Oh." She stopped dead in her tracks. Her heart hammered. "Did you find something?"

"Not yet, ma'am. I just wanted to let you know that we now have everything we need. You can return to the apartment. We had your landlord install a new door frame, but you'll want to get yourself a new deadbolt."

"Thanks." At least she had her apartment back. Even though it was trashed from top to bottom.

"And, Claire, if you run into any trouble, give us a call. We will continue to have officers checking the property periodically, but I would still recommend having a friend stay with you for the time being."

"What about the threat against my mother?"

"Law enforcement in Miami has been informed."

"Have they told her anything?"

"Not yet, but they'll be keeping a close eye on her and the property."

"Thank you, Detective."

The phone beeped in her hand, and she looked down at it.

Dead battery.

"Damn it!" She had wanted to call Nicole, who lived just a few miles from Luke's house, for a ride.

Claire resigned herself to a lengthy walk and tugged Rosie along with her. They hadn't quite made it to the end of the driveway when Luke rolled up in his truck.

"Claire, get in the truck. You're not wearing pants," he said through the open window.

"I have nothing to say to you right now," she said, staring straight ahead as she walked. She stepped on a particularly sharp rock and winced.

"I know you're upset, and I *apologize*." He emphasized the last word. She wasn't in the mood to hear him mock her own words. In fact, she wasn't in the mood to hear him say anything ever again.

"Really? You're going to mock me after not telling me that I'm the target of a serial killer?" she asked, turning to stare at him with anger flashing through her.

"Okay. Fine. I'm SORRY!" The brakes on the truck screeched as it lurched to a halt. "I should have told you sooner. I didn't want to scare you until I knew for sure. But then the break-in happened, and it was too late. At least let me give you a ride home."

She ignored him, continued to walk. What was a couple miles walk barefoot and pants-less? It would probably be invigorating.

"Did you tell your mom about the pictures?"

She stopped and turned to face him. "No."

"Then you understand better than anyone why I couldn't tell you the truth. You protect the people you care about."

She was too mad to kick holes in his theory right now. But as soon as she worked up a logical argument, she'd text it to him along with a middle finger emoji.

He threw open the passenger door. "What if Wendy's out here with her camera? You want this to be on *Marnie in the Morning*?" He stared pointedly at her bare legs.

She opened her mouth to reply, and then clamped it shut again. As much as she hated to admit it, the lying sack of shit in the driver's seat was right. Her running pants-less down a country road would not do much for the image of

Happily Ever Afters. Her anger transformed into frustration. Luke and the Widowmaker were compromising her professional integrity.

Stupid, stupid, stupid. How could she let her phone die? What if a client was trying to call? And where the hell were her emergency spandex shorts that fold up to the size of a quarter? They were always in her purse. *Shit.* Mindy had borrowed them after a night at Gavin's. Claire needed to get herself together. It was prime proposal season. There wasn't time for her to lose it.

She took the handle and was about to climb in when her mouth dropped open.

"Oh my god," she said. "I never did my dance."

She let go of the truck handle and sprinted toward Luke's house with Rosie in tow.

"Shit, shit," she said to herself as she ran back up the gravel drive.

"Claire? What dance? What are you talking about?" he called from inside the truck.

She ran up his porch steps and pushed the front door open, rushing into the kitchen and over to the stove. To her horror, the knob was still turned to "L." She quickly spun it to "Off" and collapsed against the counter, breathing heavily after her half-mile run.

Luke bolted in through the door and stopped when he saw her in the kitchen. "What the hell? Why did you run?"

"I forgot," she said, panting as she clutched her side.

"Forgot what?"

"Forgot to turn the burner off. Could have burned your house down. I'd say I'm sorry. But I'm not, because you're an asshat and frankly, you would deserve it."

Luke stared at her for what felt like an eternity. "Claire Hartley, you are one of a kind."

CHAPTER SEVENTEEN

To Do:
- Find Widowmaker, convince him to go after L
instead
- Shoot L in testicles with Taser
- Pick up dry cleaning

CLAIRE REFUSED TO SPEAK TO LUKE THE ENTIRE RIDE TO THE hardware store. The all-black outfit she had worn the night before was thoroughly covered in dog hair, but it was better than running around pants-less while being stalked by a serial killer. She didn't want to do the guy any favors. Luke's gray T-shirt was folded neatly in her purse, and she wasn't sure whether to get it dry cleaned or burn it. She wordlessly picked out a new deadbolt, paid for it, and climbed back into the truck.

He made a few attempts to strike up a conversation on the way back from the store, all which she ignored. Rosie crawled from the back seat onto her lap and curled up like a furry cinnamon bun. When the truck pulled to a stop on the street outside the apartment, she leapt out with the dog and slammed the door behind her. Her stomach twisted as she plodded up the stairs with Rosie.

When they exited the stairwell, Claire's heart staggered in her chest. The hallway seemed to stretch forever. She took a deep breath and strode toward her door as if this was an ordinary trip—coming home after a business meeting. Luke followed behind her. The caution tape was gone, but the place still felt strange, as though she shouldn't be there. She slid the key in and swung the door open. It was worse than she remembered.

Her skin prickled, and she barely suppressed a full-body shudder. Broken glass crunched underfoot as she entered her kitchen. She clutched Rosie to her side as she stared in dismay at the destruction. Every surface was coated in what looked like an inch of loose flour. The island that had held the threatening pictures was the only clean surface—the police seemed to have taken the pictures as evidence. Good thing she had taken a picture. Cabinet doors hung open, some dangling from their hinges, and knives pulled from their butcher block littered the floor. Completely unnecessary destruction. So rude.

Other than the missing underwear, the bedroom was the least disturbed of all the rooms. Claire crated Rosie in the bathroom with some food and water. Sidestepping some broken picture frames in the hallway, Claire returned to the kitchen. Where the hell should she even start? She grabbed a garbage bag and a pair of rubber gloves and started picking up the bigger pieces of broken glass.

Luke turned around triumphantly, holding up his cordless drill in victory.

"Deadbolt's in," he said, setting the drill on the bar. "Care to test it out?"

She nodded and picked up her new key. Stepping into the hallway, she shut the door and inserted the key, locking and unlocking the door successfully.

"Thanks," she said flatly. She had no desire to speak to Luke, but her mother's firm teachings in manners wouldn't allow her to withhold an acknowledgment of gratitude.

"You're welcome." He stared behind her at the couch and the coffee table, which had been flipped over by the intruder. He strode over and righted them before turning back to her.

"How did your neighbors not hear all this going on?" he asked as she swept the small pieces of glass into a pile.

"Mr. and Mrs. Lebowitz are visiting their children. And I think the apartment directly below me is vacant."

"Still." Binders in her bookcase wobbled as he shoved it back against the wall.

She ignored him and dumped a dustpan full of debris into the trash. Claire's neighbors usually kept to themselves, and she generally preferred it that way.

Luke cleared his throat. "Listen, I know you're upset with me, and you have a right to be. I know that saying I'm sorry doesn't fix what happened. There were a hundred times when I wanted to tell you what I suspected."

He reached out and tucked a strand of hair behind her ear.

Her skin warmed at his touch. *Stupid vagina.* She slapped his hand away. When was he going to leave?

"I know it's going to take some time for you to trust me again. But I will make this right. And I get that I'm the last person you want to see right now, so I'll leave. Do you think

Nicole or Mindy could come over? I don't want you to be alone."

Claire nodded and picked up her now-charged phone. Thankfully, there hadn't been any missed calls from her clients. She texted Nicole, who responded right away.

"Nicole will be over in twenty minutes. You can go."

"I'm not going to leave you here alone," he said as he gathered the fluff from her torn-open throw pillows. "It's not safe."

She sighed. An image of the Widowmaker crawling up her fire escape burst into her mind, and she glanced out the window. "Fine. Shit!" She clapped a hand to her forehead and sprinted back down the hallway. The doorknob was cold in her hand as she wrenched her bedroom door open.

"What? What's wrong?" Luke called after her.

"Oh crap, oh crap," she said to herself as she rounded the corner of the bed.

She dropped to the floor and clawed at a floorboard.

"What are you doing?"

"Checking to see if...oh, thank goodness." Her Taser emerged from the hole. The Widowmaker hadn't taken it.

"Whoa, that looks like what law enforcement carries." He shifted so that he was partially concealed by the bedroom door.

"Relax, I'm not going to fire it. Although frankly you deserve thirty thousand volts straight to your nipples." The weapon clattered against the wood as she dropped it into the hole and slid the board back into place. "My mom bought it for me. You can go now." She stared pointedly at her bedroom door.

"Do you even know how to use it?" he asked. She ignored him until he left the room.

She moved to the bathroom, where she could lock

herself in away from Luke. She vacuumed up the glass first and then allowed Rosie out of her crate. A weariness settled over her as she disposed of her carefully curated lanterns. So much senseless destruction. And a threat against her mother. The Widowmaker would pay.

A few minutes later, there was a knock at the front door. The cavalry had arrived, and the treacherous Luke had no choice but to leave. She walked down the hallway to see that Luke had already answered it. Nicole was giving him some serious side eye as she dropped a pile of trash bags, cleaning supplies, and ice cream on the floor.

When Nicole saw Claire, she ran to her and wrapped her arms around her.

"Coli, you're strangling me."

Nicole pulled back with tears in her eyes. "I can't stop thinking about what would have happened if you had been home when it happened."

Claire squeezed her hand. "But I wasn't. And now I will apparently never be alone again, so we have nothing to worry about. Luke, you can go now."

He replaced her last knickknack on the top shelf of a bookcase and dusted his hands off.

He started to head out the door but turned around as he reached the threshold. "When I leave, you need to lock this door behind me, okay? Don't open it for anyone without a visual and vocal confirmation of who they are. If you don't know who it is, you call the police immediately. And then you call me."

"Why, so you can take notes and put it on the wall?" Claire retorted.

"Wait," he said, reaching through the door before she could close it.

She thought about slamming the door and snapping his

arm off like a hotdog in a guillotine. Luke stepped back inside and wound his arms around her. He held her tight and pressed his lips to her ear.

"Be safe," he whispered.

She went rigid under his grasp and shoved at his chest until he backed off. She should have kept the Taser.

He left, and Claire shut and locked the door behind him. She turned around and faced the disaster that was her apartment. A huge, drawn-out sigh escaped her lips. She was going to be a professional sigher at this rate.

Nicole came to stand in front of her and gripped her by both arms. "I know you're freaking out right now, but we can do this. You are Claire Freakin' Hartley. This is a tiny blip on your radar. We can control this." She swept her arm at the disarray. "Now breathe, stay calm, and then tell me everything. And why is Luke dead to us? Your text wasn't very clear."

As they talked, they cleaned, straightened, and organized the chaos until it began to resemble her apartment again. Hours later, satisfied with their efforts, they collapsed onto the couch, utterly exhausted.

Claire pulled the cork out of a second bottle of wine and poured a generous amount into two glasses.

"Want to just stay here for the night? I don't really feel like driving," she asked, stifling a yawn.

Nicole nodded. "That's fine with me. I just didn't want you to be alone."

"I doubt we're alone. This psycho's probably watching us right now." She flipped off the kitchen window.

Nicole scooted over and put her arms around Claire. "I know you're super tough and everything, but you don't always need to be so brave," she said, words muffled by Claire's voluminous hair.

"I'm not being brave. I'm just mad. I'm mad that someone broke in and messed up my already messed up life. And that they think it's okay to steal my dirty clothes like a freaking pervert and knock over my furniture and smash my grandmother's vase. Seriously, what the hell did I do to deserve this?"

Nicole stood and walked over to the window, drawing the curtains shut. She repeated the process for every window in the apartment.

"You didn't do anything, sweetie. Do you really think it's the West Haven Widowmaker?" Nicole sat on the arm of the couch. She hugged her knees to her chest.

Claire sipped her wine. "It's the only thing that makes sense. There are too many similarities in the disappearances. Too many coincidences. I think it's someone from Venor, maybe someone we once knew. I mean, he clearly knew Courtney. This is crazy. I know it's crazy. But do you think it could be Jason?"

Nicole's eyes flew wide, and she choked and spluttered. "Seriously? You think Jason could have done all this?"

Claire shrugged. "Probably not. I've never seen him act this violently. But I've been learning more every day about how little I actually know about him. We were together for five years, and he didn't even know my favorite flowers. He knew where I lived. He knows my mom and went to her house in Florida with me a couple years ago. The pieces fit."

"Hang on." Nicole picked up her phone and started tapping away. After a minute, she locked her phone again and shook her head. "I spied on his Instagram. It doesn't look like he went to Florida recently. Maybe he didn't act alone. That Wendy chick is super crazy, so maybe she had a hand in it. What would his motivation be, though?"

"Well, he took my wedding dress and my underwear.

Maybe he doesn't want me to move on with anyone else. Maybe it's one of those ridiculous, macho 'If I can't have you, then no one can' kind of things."

Nicole swore. "I could see that, I guess. But does that mean Jason's responsible for the deaths of all those other girls from Venor too? Why would he do that?"

Claire exhaled and shook her head. "I have no clue. I didn't even know most of the other victims. I don't know what they had in common or if they even knew each other."

"Where's your yearbook? We can figure this out."

"It's over there, but it hasn't been much help so far."

Nicole crossed the room and returned with the yearbook.

"If it's really Jason, and Jason is really the 'Widowermaker,' the only thing that doesn't fit the profile is the fact that I'm not married," Claire said pensively. "Every other victim was recently married."

"Right, hence the 'Widowmaker' nickname. You were engaged, though."

Claire cringed. It wasn't the time for a grammar lesson. "That's true. I still can't believe he took my wedding dress. What a dick. I loved that dress."

Claire's phone vibrated against the coffee table. She flipped it over to reveal Jason calling. What the hell? Without hesitation, she turned on the speakerphone.

"Jason?"

"Clarabell! It's so good to hear your voice. Listen, I just wanted to say—"

"Did you break into my apartment?"

"What? No. Why would I do that?"

"You didn't come in here and trash everything and steal my dirty clothes and my freaking wedding dress?"

"No! Of course not. Someone broke into your apartment? Who the hell was it?"

"If I knew, I wouldn't be answering your fifteenth phone call of the day. I think it was you. And you know what else? After seeing how crazy and stalker-ish you've been since we broke up, I wouldn't be surprised if you were the one who killed those other girls. Courtney, Kayley, all the Venor girls."

"Are you seriously accusing me of being the West Haven Widowmaker? Claire, we lived together. You know I'm not a monster. I may not have always been the best boyfriend, but I'm not a murderer, for fuck's sake."

He had a point. But how well did she really know him? Jason couldn't hold down a job for most of the time they lived together. Other than his weekly poker night with his fraternity brothers, he had nothing but free time. He could have been driving around on his moped, stalking and murdering women left and right.

"Are you also going to tell me that you didn't send that picture of me and Courtney sleeping in our bunk beds from freshman year?"

"I didn't even know you freshman year. Remember? We started dating when we were sophomores."

Claire opened her mouth to protest but stopped. She had nearly forgotten she had a blissful, Jason-free year when she first came to Venor.

"That doesn't change the fact that I know it was you who broke in here. No one else would have a reason to take my wedding dress. And if it wasn't you, then it was your psychotic excuse for a girlfriend. Either way, Jason, I'm done. If I catch you watching me, following me, or calling me, I will turn you in to the police. They're very interested in who broke into my apartment."

"I didn't do it!"

"Whatever, Jason. Stay away from me."

"Is someone staying with you? I'm worried about you."

"Yes. Someone is always staying with me, thanks to your stupid ass. So, you're shit out of luck if you were hoping to kidnap me. Goodbye." She hung up the phone and threw it at a pillow. It bounced off and hit the floor. Rosie came over, sniffed it, and immediately laid on it.

"Do you want to go silly string Jason's house?" Nicole asked softly.

"He's not worth it."

"Something else is bothering you." It wasn't a question.

"I've got a laundry list," Claire muttered.

"Seriously, what is it? Something with Luke?"

Claire sat up and slammed her glass down on the coffee table. "You know how I had to call him to help with the proposal yesterday? Because of Jerry's appendix?"

Nicole nodded.

"He came in with no knowledge of the entire project, and he just changed everything. He cut a cameraman, he added a freaking bike onscreen. He didn't even ask. I didn't have time to tell the client about the changes. And then he had the audacity to tell me that he 'improved' the proposal."

Nicole was silent.

"And the worst part is," Claire continued, a slight tremor in her voice. "He was right. I saw the footage. The third cameraman would have been in the way. The bike made everything more vibrant, more interesting. I planned this proposal down to the second, and he came in out of nowhere and 'fixed it.'"

Nicole set her wine down and grabbed Claire's hand. "He just has a different specialty, that's all. He's good with visual stuff. That's his job."

"And my job is to make everything perfect. How many other proposals have there been where I unknowingly cut corners or didn't provide the best experience possible? And, more importantly, how dare he do any of that without consulting me?"

"Would you have been this angry if it had been Mindy who suggested the bike?"

Claire frowned. "Well, no. But Mindy would know better than to add something in thirty seconds before the groom-to-be arrived."

Nicole nodded, but she let the subject drop. She had an irritating way of cutting to the heart of the matter. "Do you want to add Luke's house to the list of ones to silly string? Or maybe just drink more?"

Claire downed the rest of the wine in her glass. "Drink more," she said decisively. "Let's walk to that place a couple blocks over and go dancing. But I need to stop at the pet store first."

NINETY MINUTES LATER, CLAIRE PLASTERED HERSELF AGAINST the window of the Burger Boy down the street, startling a couple seated inside. She pressed her lips to the glass and blew, creating a mighty farting sound that rattled the glass.

A man paused mid-bite, laughing so hard that a pickle slipped out of his burger and plopped into his lap. His wife shot Claire a look and stood up from their table. The husband waved merrily at Claire, who broke into drunken giggles and ran away from the window.

"Oh my god." Nicole bent double with laughter. "That was the funniest thing I've ever seen." She lowered her phone, thumbs hovering over the screen.

"Lady Nicole," Claire slurred. The plastic monocle trembled in her left eye, threatening to fall out. "Thou shalt not send any more videos to Sir Kyle."

"Come on, he loves Old Timey Claire."

"Sir Kyle is with the one we don't speak of. I do not wish for that grumbletonian to know my whereabouts, nor my evening activities. It's none of his damn business."

"They probably have their thumbs glued to some video game controllers and haven't even checked their phones."

They paused under a streetlight in the parking lot to search the depths of Claire's purse for breath mints. The rank dumpster next to them churned Claire's stomach.

"Excuse me?" A voice called from the darkness.

They spun around. Claire struck a karate pose and clutched at her back, where a new fashion accessory now hung. A large, square-framed backpack with a mesh screen secured a happily panting Rosie resting against her back.

Nicole grabbed a large stick from the ground and held it aloft like a bat.

The woman from the restaurant approached, holding two bottles of water.

"Methinks the lady doth not be a panty-stealer," Claire whispered very loudly to Nicole.

"Are you girls okay?" The woman asked with genuine concern.

Nicole and Claire looked at each other and laughed.

"We're okay. Rough day," Nicole said, slurring slightly as she still shielded Claire.

"Drink these before you go to bed." The woman handed the waters over. "Can I call you a cab?"

"We have no need for a cab. We ride only upon the fabled horse, Nightshade. The finest steed in all the land." Claire attempted to whistle.

"We're okay. Thank you, though," Nicole said.

The woman nodded, smiled, and disappeared back inside the restaurant.

"Does this look like serial killer water?" Claire asked, inspecting the cap to see if the seal was still in place. Her monocle fell off her face and clattered to the ground. She squatted to pick it up, struggled to stand back up. "Screw it, I'm thirsty."

She guzzled the water and deposited the bottle in a recycling bin next to the dumpster. Nicole followed suit and poked her finger through a hole in the backpack to scratch Rosie's fluff.

"I can't believe the club bouncer believed you when you said Rosie was a celebrity dog."

Claire shrugged. "Who could tell from a distance? She looks just like Jack from *Stepwives of Seacaucus*."

They made their way slowly down the street to Claire's apartment. The alcohol helped take the edge off her anxiety, but she still probed the shadowy corners of every alleyway. The streets were quiet tonight. An occasional car passed, but they were the only two people on the sidewalk.

"We should take a different route," Claire said to Nicole and veered off down a side street.

"But this way is longer." Nicole pouted.

"You're supposed to vary your routine when someone is trying to murder you," Claire said as she stumbled into a trashcan. She knew she was vulnerable as she walked down the street drunk and in impractical footwear, but she just wanted to feel alive again.

Nicole sidled up to her and squeezed her biceps. They looped arms like they used to do in college, stumbling back to their dorm rooms after a rager. Maybe it was Claire's imagination, but Nicole seemed to be peering urgently into the darkness as well. Maybe this evening out had been a mistake.

Without a word, they both began to hustle, power-walking the last four blocks to the apartment.

"I have to pee the dog," Claire said in a loud whisper as she shrugged the backpack off and placed it gently on the ground.

"Why are you whispering?" Nicole whispered as Claire snapped the leash on.

"I have no idea," Claire said at a normal volume. Rosie barked at a squirrel and tried to sprint down the sidewalk, and Claire groaned as she gripped the leash for dear life.

They finally opened the glass-front doors of Claire's apartment building and took the creepy elevator up, too tired to worry about the mysterious stains and flickering light. They leaned against the wall until they made it to her floor. Claire unlocked the front door and kicked it open. Rosie hung heavily on her back. She wasn't going to give a murderer the chance to snatch her dog.

"Anybody in here?" she called, putting up her fists and stomping from room to room, turning on lights as she went. "I swear to god, I will fight you."

"I think it's safe," Nicole whispered as she kicked off her shoes and began wriggling out of her dress. Bold words for a girl who hadn't checked a single closet. But considering the lack of destroyed furniture and incriminating photos of loved ones, it probably was safe.

"Bed?" Claire asked as she let Rosie out of the mesh backpack. The corgi immediately rocketed from room to room as though she had never been here before.

"Bed."

Claire threw Nicole an oversized T-shirt and a pack of makeup remover wipes. Claire changed into a pair of pajama pants featuring small multi-colored corgis. She popped in their favorite romantic comedy from their college days, and they collapsed on the bed. Rosie, apparently exhausted from her bout of the zoomies, curled up at their feet.

Nicole was asleep within minutes, snoring quietly as her phone buzzed on the nightstand. A good night text from Kyle, no doubt.

Claire glanced at her phone, surprised to see that there wasn't a text from Jason. Or from Luke, for that matter. For someone who was so concerned about making sure she was safe, he didn't seem to care now. She plugged her phone in to charge and lay back, staring at the ceiling. The occasional siren sounded off in the distance, and somewhere down the hall, one of her neighbors played loud music.

She closed her eyes, but they snapped open at the smallest noise. Her nerves tingled, and her whole body was on high alert. She sat up and looked around, narrowing her eyes at each shadowy corner of her room.

Bed springs creaked as she eased her weight from the mattress and stepped lightly across the floor, turning lights on in the living room and kitchen. She peeked out the peephole in her front door. There wasn't anyone lurking in the blank stretch of scuffed beige hallway made yellow under the harsh fluorescent light.

She jiggled the handle, checking again that everything was still locked. Then she pulled on the doorknob, making sure the hinges didn't unscrew from the doorframe. Nothing budged.

Moving through each room, she checked that the windows were locked tight and thrust open closet doors like a child expecting to confront a monster.

Just as she turned to retreat back to the bedroom, a resounding boom came from the front door.

Claire jumped. Her adrenaline skyrocketed. She ran to her bedroom and pried up the loose floorboard.

Rosie jumped off the bed and ran to the front of the apartment, where she sat growling.

Nicole sat up in bed. "Wuzzgoinon?"

"Someone's at the front door."

Nicole's eyes flew wide, and she jumped out of bed.

Claire pulled the stun gun from her hiding spot and clutched it as they made their way back to the front door. She held it in front of her with a single shaking hand.

Another knock split the silence as Nicole darted into the kitchen and returned with a butcher knife.

"Who is it?" Claire called, trying to sound authoritative.

"It's Luke. Open up."

"He sounds mad," Nicole whispered.

Claire pressed her face to the peephole, confirming that the hulking shadow outside her door was actually Luke and not a murderer.

She pulled the door open slowly. Her heart leapt in her chest at the sight of him. "What are you doing here?"

He pushed the door open the rest of the way and stepped inside.

"What the hell were you thinking, running around drunk in the middle of the night?"

"Um...living my life?" she answered.

"Did you even stop to think about how vulnerable you were tonight? If this freak wanted to come after you, all he would have had to do is waggle a cheeseburger at you and you would have crawled right into the back of his rape van."

Her mouth dropped open. She slapped the stun gun on

the counter, balled her hands into fists. She wouldn't have been surprised if steam actually came out of her ears.

"Luke, just because one bad thing happens to you doesn't mean you stop living your life. Murderer or no murderer, I have to carry on. And yes, letting loose a little may not have been the safest idea in the world, but I wasn't alone. I had Nicole. I had Rosie in my backpack. I have the police on speed dial. I'm not going to let this person own me. They want me to be afraid."

"And you should be. Damn it, Claire." He raked a hand through his hair.

A knife clinked in the butcher block on the counter, and Nicole slowly inched her way back toward the bedroom.

He held up five fingers. "Five women have disappeared. Five. None of them have ever been found."

Claire raised her arms at her sides. "As you can see, I'm perfectly fine."

"Sure, this time. Claire, I don't want to do this, but you've left me with no choice."

She blinked and frowned. Was he going to handcuff himself to her? Restrain her and hide her in his attic? Did he have a sex dungeon of some sort?

"If you don't start being more careful—starting right now—I'm going to have to give her a call."

What the hell was he talking about? "Her, who? Don't call Mindy—she's very protective of her sleep schedule."

Luke pulled his phone from his pocket, scrolled for a moment, and showed her the screen. "Alice Alejo" was listed as a contact.

Her mouth dropped open. "How in the hell did you get my mother's phone number?"

He raised his eyebrows. "The internet."

"There's probably a hundred Alice Alejos in Miami."

"There aren't. There were six. And only one lived with a Roy."

"Wow, you are a massive stalker. Great, I have three now."

He frowned. His eyes flashed in the light of his screen. "I told you I was going to take your personal safety seriously. Someone has to. Be more careful, and I'll delete her phone number. But if you keep behaving like a college sophomore on spring break, I'm going to call her and tell her the truth."

"Get the fuck out of my apartment," she said, pointing so forcefully at the open door that her biceps cramped.

"One more thing." He reached behind him to pull at his backpack.

"No more things. Get out."

Luke unzipped a compartment and pulled out a white binder. He handed it to her. Her hands drooped at its weight.

"If you think you can get back in my good graces with a stop at Office Max, you are sorely mistaken."

Despite her words, Claire cracked the binder open and flipped through a couple pages. Luke had reprinted some of the same articles that she had in her original murder binder and added his research as well.

"I thought you could use a new one since the old one is now...evidence."

She closed the binder and put it on the bar.

"Out," she said simply.

He turned to go. He was almost in the hallway when he turned to face her. He grabbed her hand and looked deeply into her eyes. His brows were furrowed, and his gaze was troubled.

"Just be careful." He released her and left without another word.

She watched him the whole way down the hallway, but he never looked back. She closed and locked her door and leaned against it, dragging her hands over her tired eyes.

A headache was already brewing, so she went to the kitchen for a glass of water. She craned her neck. The bedroom door was closed. She flipped the cover of the binder open. All the pages were neatly enclosed in sheet protectors. The victims were separated by tabs, and the labels looked as though they had been created with a label maker.

She rolled her eyes and slammed the binder shut.

"Binders are *my* thing." She set her glass down a bit too heavily on the countertop and turned on her heel. She treaded wearily back to the bedroom, where Nicole was already asleep again. Claire collapsed into bed beside her and fell into a dreamless oblivion.

An hour later, she bolted upright in bed.

"The notebook." She threw the blankets off her legs.

"You want to watch a chick flick *now*?" Nicole sat up beside her.

"No! I just remembered something about Courtney." She slid out of the covers, flipped on a light, and fell to her knees beside the bed. "Remember all the guys she was sleeping with freshman year?"

"Sure." Nicole yawned. "I mean, I remember that there were some. I couldn't tell you any of their names. There were so many."

"Exactly. That's when I started keeping the notebook."

"Holy shit. I forgot about that thing."

Claire lay on her belly and shuffled things around under her bed. Finding nothing but dust bunnies and misplaced socks, she turned instead to her closet. There, at the bottom of a box full of Venor paraphernalia, she found the notebook.

"This is it!" She hoisted it triumphantly over her head.

She collapsed onto the bed and opened it up.

"Let's see. Six men in September. Eight in October. November was a bit of a dry spell, only four that month. Hmmm. I only got about half of them by name. Joe Simmons—couldn't be him. He moved to Tokyo. Brett Hassinger now lives in Minnesota with his wife and kids. Hector plays for the NFL. Let's hope he gave up the performance-enhancing drugs that she told me affected his package." She pointed to a note.

"Then there's Older Douchey Philosophy Major, who clogged our toilet afterwards."

"Oh, I remember him! You texted me at three a.m. to come over and pee."

"Brian the Art Major still lives around here," she said to herself as she put a star next to his name.

"He was so nice, though. Remember he painted that mural for The Bean for free?"

"You're right. Oh, this month she went on a Lacrosse spree. There are lacrosse jocks three through seven. Never bothered to get any of their names."

"What's the deal with 'Older Rich Guy'?" Nicole pointed at a paragraph.

"Hmm. Looks like he was chubby and nerdy, but Courtney supplied her services to him in exchange for alcohol. Classic Courtney. I don't really remember him too well, but I'm pretty sure I got a bottle of high-end vodka out of that particular fling." She groaned. "I forgot how many guys there were."

"Didn't she sleep with a professor, too?"

"Shit, I forgot about him. She never told me who it was.

He at least had the decency to hook up with her in his office instead of our dorm."

Claire yawned and closed the notebook. It was not quite the revealing bombshell she had hoped for. "I'm exhausted. How about we look at this tomorrow?"

Nicole nodded, and she set it on the bedside table. "Take some pictures before someone breaks in here and steals it." She yawned and turned on her side.

She was right. Things had a way of disappearing in this apartment.

CHAPTER EIGHTEEN

To Do:
- *Obstacle course meeting*
- *Meeting with M and K*
- *Don't think about binder-making idiot*

"I AM CAPABLE OF GOING TO MY OWN BATHROOM WITHOUT getting kidnapped," Claire said as she walked down her hallway.

Mindy, who had begun to follow her, paused at the row of chamber awards on the wall. "I just wanted to look at the awards again," she said, pulling down a tear-drop shaped glass award and shining it with the end of her T-shirt.

Claire rolled her eyes as she shut the bathroom door harder than necessary. Solitude at last. No one had left her alone for what felt like an eternity. This was getting absurd. In addition to her wedding dress and dirty underwear, the

Widowmaker had also claimed her independence. She wasn't going to stand for it.

Her eyes darted to the window every couple of seconds as she washed her hands. Fatigue settled on her like humidity, bogging her down after days of being on high alert. Everywhere she went, she felt eyes on her, real or imagined. Every dark alley contained the Widowmaker. Every arbitrary sound in her apartment was the prowler waiting to take her.

Back in the living room, Claire sat on the floor in lotus pose and picked up her pen. "Did you have any questions about the schedule before you leave?"

Kyle awkwardly uncrossed his long legs, jostling the coffee table as he stretched. "I think you covered it all." He slapped a hand on the mountain of paperwork in front of him.

"Great." She shuffled some loose papers into their designated binder. "I'll send the updated spreadsheet to your work email. Is something wrong?" she asked. A goofy grin on his face was so wide that it nearly pushed his glasses up.

"Nope. I'm just really excited to ask Nicole to be my wife. Everything you've come up with is perfect. I can't wait to see the look on her face." He reached over and slung an arm around Claire, giving her a quick side hug.

She smiled at the excitement sparking in his eyes. "I'm glad Nicole found someone like you. Do you have any single brothers I don't know about?" she teased.

Kyle shook his head. "Just my sister, Lauren. I doubt you're interested in her. Although I believe I distinctly remember that one time in college—"

"Nope. I remember that night. You had too many rum and Cokes and you imagined everything," Claire said quickly, but her cheeks were hot. "By the way, now that the professional portion of our meeting is over, there's something I've been meaning to ask you. Did you know that Luke was researching the West Haven Widowmaker case and believed I was the next victim? Because if you did, that's really shitty."

Kyle had just taken a swig from his water bottle, and he choked, sending a fine spray over the piles of binders and paperwork. Mindy reached over and pounded him on the back until he could speak again.

"Sorry, wrong pipe. No, Claire, I had no idea. He's fanatical about his work, as I'm sure you noticed. He won't tell anyone what he's working on, not even his best friend. I did think it was weird that he kept asking me who you were with and what you were doing, but I just assumed he was trying to find ways to casually run into you. I didn't know he was afraid for your safety." Kyle fiddled with a loose string on his cargo shorts. The day wasn't warm enough for shorts, but he wore them anyway.

Claire shook her head. Kyle had no reason to lie.

There was a knock on the door, and everyone froze. Claire's heart thudded into instant alarm mode. Was it the Widowmaker? Jason? Her mother? Each was more terrifying than the next.

Kyle grabbed her arm and forced her behind him. Mindy stood next to him, and they created a unified front as they crept over to the door. Keeping the chain on, Kyle opened the door a crack.

"Mancini's Pizza," droned a nasally male voice.

"I didn't order pizza," Claire whispered.

"What's in the box?" Kyle said, in a tone much deeper than usual.

"Pizza? It's already paid for," the voice said. The toe of a dirty pair of Reeboks was just visible through the narrow slit of the open door. "The note said to deliver it to this address."

"Just set it on the floor and back away," Kyle said.

"Uh, okay," the voice said slowly.

Something hit the carpeted floor outside. Footsteps retreated down the hallway.

"Stay here," Kyle instructed.

Mindy backed Claire into a corner of the living room and thrust her arms out to the sides. Claire peered over her friend's arm as Kyle brought a cardboard box inside and set it on the kitchen island. He retrieved a butcher knife from the block on the counter and extended his arm as far as it would go. He flipped the box lid open with the tip of the knife and jumped back as if expecting a family of rats to come scurrying out. When nothing happened, he peered over the lip of the box.

"Oh, no way," he said, enthusiastically tossing the knife on the counter. "Claire, come look at this."

She ducked under Mindy's arm and approached the island.

Inside the box was not a murderer or a family of rats, but a pizza. A complex network of pepperonis crisscrossed the cheese, forming the distinct shape of a corgi. Stubby little pepperoni legs stood under the long body, and tiny pepperoni triangles made up the corgi's pointy ears.

Kyle glanced at his phone. "Luke wanted you to know that the pizza is from him and not from the Widowmaker. It's safe to eat."

She bit her lip. Did he seriously think that sending a pizza was enough to make up for concealing the fact that she was the target of a serial killer?

"At least his guilt manifests in fine Italian cuisine." Mindy slid open Claire's cutlery drawer and withdrew a pizza cutter. Claire snagged a quick picture before Mindy attacked the pie.

Kyle took a piece for the road and waved goodbye. "Remember, call me if you need anything," he said as he left.

"I know. Thank you, Kyle. Drive safe," Claire said. As soon as the door closed, she slapped a piece of pizza on a paper plate and went back to the living room. There was no sense in wasting it. Mancini's Pizza was legendary in West Haven.

They ate in silence for several minutes. Claire set her empty plate down and rested her head in one hand.

"What's wrong?" Mindy inquired over a bite.

"Nothing, just tired."

"I've seen you tired. This is not tired. Now tell me what's wrong or your solo bathroom time privileges will be revoked."

Claire shot her a dirty look. "I *am* tired. But I guess it's more than that. I feel numb. And terrified. I'm terrified to close my eyes at night. I'm terrified to open my door when someone knocks. I'm afraid to take Rosie on our long walks through the park alone. She's going to get fat, and then that sexy veterinarian will think I'm a bad dog mom." She stifled a cry and glanced at Rosie, who was munching on her dinner in the kitchen.

"But most of all, I'm just mad. I'm mad at the Widowmaker for breaking in here and stealing my shit. I'm mad at myself for allowing someone to make me feel this way. I'm mad at Luke for keeping this huge secret from me. I'm mad at Jason for ruining my happily ever after and also for maybe being a murderer. I'm mad at the police because they won't even admit there's a serial killer, let alone come any closer to catching him. Why is everyone so incompetent?" she demanded, voice pitching in hysteria.

Mindy had paused with a bite halfway to her lips, eyes widening as Claire's tirade progressed. "Do you want to go to Sephora? Get some new lip gloss?"

"No. You know what I want to do?" Claire wiped her hands on a napkin and stood up. She pulled a backpack off her coat tree and sat it on the ground, dropped her new murder binder inside. "I want to figure out who this guy is and nail his ass to the wall. Get your purse."

Mindy threw down her paper plate and wiped the grease off her fingers with a napkin. "Where are we going?"

"To find an asshole. But first, we have to make a pit stop."

An hour later, Claire and Mindy struggled across Luke's front yard with a five-foot-tall whiteboard on wheels. As they stumbled onto the porch, the front door flew open.

Luke looked surprised. He wasn't wearing a shirt, and the late afternoon sun cast a golden glow over a chiseled six pack. "Claire, I—"

"No. You've done enough talking." She dragged the front wheels over the threshold. Luke stood by to let her enter. He took the whiteboard by the middle and hefted it inside.

"Thank you," she said reflexively before she could stop herself. Damn it. "We're here for one reason: to figure out who the Widowmaker is. We need to see everything you have."

"Deal. I'll take this to the office." He wheeled the whiteboard down the hallway. The gray sweatpants that hung low on his hips left little to the imagination. Not that she'd noticed.

Claire knelt to let Rosie out of her backpack. She immediately scampered after Luke.

"Okay, I know we hate him. But this house is *amazing*,"

Mindy whispered, running a hand over the granite countertop in the kitchen.

"I know. Come on." She half dragged the gawking Mindy to Luke's office.

Between the furniture, the whiteboard, and the fact that every usable flat surface was crammed with papers and pictures and theories, things were a little tight. Claire flattened herself against a wall as she wrote on the board. She nudged into something soft and glanced down. Rosie was lying on what appeared to be a brand new dog bed, gnawing on a bone.

"I didn't know you have a dog."

"I don't."

"Then why do you have a dog bed in your super-secret office?"

"I assumed you'd want Rosie on-premises during Kyle's proposal. I thought I'd make her a comfortable place to hang out where she would be safe."

When Luke turned around, Mindy raised her eyebrows so dramatically that Claire feared they would get stuck that way. Mindy took a seat in one of the leather chairs opposite Luke's desk and drew the binder to her lap.

"Ooh, I like what you've done with the murder binder." Mindy flipped the cover open and pointed at an infographic that Luke had apparently put together to summarize the case.

He smirked.

Claire glared. "The original was better. Oh, that reminds me." She reached into her purse and pulled out a manila folder. She stalked over to the whiteboard where the grainy, low-quality image of her hung next to the other victims. She ripped it off and taped a glossy, professional headshot in its place.

Luke raised his eyebrows.

"What? If you're going to sit in here brooding over the Widowmaker, you may as well have a decent picture of me. Okay, ages. Go!"

Mindy read off the ages of the victims, and Claire scribbled them underneath the correct person.

"Race?"

"All Caucasian. Except for Ariel."

They went through several more demographics, including hometown, location of their disappearance, college major, and estimated annual income.

"Ariel doesn't fit the bill," Claire said, frowning at her column. "She didn't even go to Venor. What would the Widowmaker want from her?"

"He probably grew up near her or went to high school with her. She was the first one." Mindy shrugged. "And it happened not long after she got married. Oh, question. Did the stalking at the restaurant start before or after she got married?"

"Before," Luke said. He typed at his computer, bringing up a document that Claire couldn't quite read.

"How do you know?" Mindy asked.

"I interviewed her mom."

"What? Let me see." Claire edged out from behind the board and came to stand at his shoulder. He had unfortunately put a shirt on.

Luke fast-forwarded through several minutes of B roll of a childhood bedroom. Rows of medals hung on the wall. A picture of a young Ariel was stuck to a bulletin board along with a dried flower and what looked to be a love note. He paused when a gray-haired woman in her sixties appeared on camera. "Loretta Smith–Mother of Ariel Pullizi" appeared in a banner at the bottom of the screen. Shivers ran down Claire's spine. Ariel and Loretta shared the same toffee brown eyes, the same porcelain skin.

"Ariel was a good girl," Loretta said. "Even when she left home and moved in with Tony, she came over every Sunday for dinner. She would bring me flowers from her garden. She could dance, too, you know. She waitressed to pay the bills, but her real dream was to be a dancer. We didn't have the money for her to go to college, and unfortunately there isn't much of a market for dancers in Wilkes-Barre."

Loretta paused onscreen, and wiped a finger underneath her eye. "I remember the last day I saw her. She came over for lunch. Something was bothering her, but she didn't want to talk about it. I assumed it was the stress of newlywed life. They had only been married for two weeks at that point, fresh from their honeymoon in the Poconos. Anyway, later that night was when she disappeared."

Claire gripped the back of Luke's chair. Her chest was tight, and it was hard to breathe. Had she already had her last lunch with her mother? Would Luke be interviewing her someday?

Mindy snaked an arm around Claire's waist and rested her chin on her shoulder. Her head drooped against Mindy's as they watched Loretta's tearful recollections.

"Did you ever find out why she was upset that day?" Luke's voice asked offscreen.

Loretta nodded. "Tony told me later that their apartment had been broken into. Someone left a big bouquet of flowers and took all kinds of things—mementos, I guess. Clothing, pictures. Now they didn't live in a very nice part of town, so crime was pretty common. He didn't take their TV or video game machines, though. He only took personal stuff. That's why I think the Widowmaker took her."

"Did Ariel ever mention that she was being watched?"

Loretta shook her head. "She didn't like to worry me. I didn't learn about the stalking until after she disappeared. Apparently, a black car with tinted windows would sit outside the diner for hours, usually on weekends. Tony swore he saw it outside their apartment a couple of times, too. The police were called once or twice, but it's almost like he knew. He would always be gone before they arrived."

Claire straightened, walked back to the whiteboard. She wasn't sure how much more she could take.

Luke paused the video. "I tried to interview Tony too, but he didn't want to be involved. All the stories are like that. The flowers, a break-in. Ariel was the only case where they happened the same day."

She wrote "flowers" and "break-in" on the board, then tapped the marker in her hand. "Do you think they're being ordered at the same florist?"

He shook his head. "I already checked into that angle. All four were from different shops."

Mindy excused herself to the bathroom, undoubtedly wanting to experience one of the Toilet King's legendary toilets.

The silence between Luke and Claire gaped.

He cleared his throat. "Could I just say something?"

"You don't deserve to say anything."

He leaned back in his office chair. His face was drawn, and it looked as though he hadn't slept well. "I get that. And you're right. But I just need you to understand."

She rubbed her temples. Another headache. "If it means we can concentrate on this—" she pointed at the murder wall, "—then you can have three minutes."

He took a deep breath. "I've been looking for a reason to move back here ever since I left for California. The Widow-maker story broke, and I decided then and there that I was coming back, and I was going to make my next documentary."

He stood and paced in the tiny patch of office that wasn't crammed with furniture and equipment.

"I wanted to catch the bastard, to figure out who was responsible before the police even admitted there is a Widowmaker. I wanted to bring some justice to the families of the victims, give them a chance to tell their stories. These women had lives, jobs, hobbies, family. They were real people. I needed to tell their story. And I was curious about you. I didn't think you were a target at first. I thought you could be a source. I knew you went to Venor. I knew Courtney was your roommate because of Kyle. Then I came over and just got this feeling."

He paused. "Two feelings, really. You fit most of the profile, and I was worried that you could be next. Especially after you got the flowers. And I also knew that I didn't want anything to happen to you."

Claire held her breath. Her heart beat uncomfortably fast in her chest. She bit back a thousand sassy remarks and let him continue.

"You have an incredibly annoying habit of putting yourself in danger. I probably should have told you what I suspected—"

"You think?" she said sarcastically.

He stepped closer to her, eyes burning with intensity. "I regret not telling you. But I don't regret getting close to you," he said, lifting a calloused hand to her cheek.

Not now, vagina. She cursed her nether region and its affinity for assholes.

"You are unlike anyone I have ever known. You are kind, creative, and almost suspiciously sweet when you think no one's watching. You'd rip the shirt off your back and knit it into an afghan if there was a dog on the street who was slightly cold. You ask long-winded shopkeepers about their wife's blood thinner medicine. I couldn't allow anything to happen to you. You mean...something to me."

He brushed his thumb over her cheek. The anger ebbed, just a bit. Her willpower slipped.

"I won't lie to you again. Can we make this work?"

The shame still burned inside her, stinging her like nettles. He had betrayed her, hidden unimaginable secrets. And yet, truth was in his eyes. And they had bigger problems.

She exhaled. "I forgive you. I will put my better judgment aside and try to trust you. But, Luke, if you lie to me again, we are done. I will not work with you. I will not hang out with you. I will literally never want to see you again for the rest of my life. If you can agree to those terms, then we can start fresh. But I mean what I say, so consider carefully."

He pulled her in, wrapping her in his arms. She resisted for a moment, pressed against the unyielding solidness of his chest, and then allowed herself to be engulfed in his scent.

After a moment, she pulled back. "We have to find him, Luke."

"I know."

Their gazes locked. There were bags under his eyes and a hefty amount of stubble dotted his strong jawline. The tension between them was palpable, like they were magnets fighting the distance between them. He took a step forward. Claire took a step forward.

What was she doing? He had betrayed her on a level usually reserved for soap operas or reality TV. She should be running in the opposite direction.

His comment about protecting the people you care

about echoed in her mind. What was he saying? That he cared about her? The marker tumbled out of her hand. They both bent down and reached for it. Their faces were inches apart. The minty tang of his toothpaste stirred something in her. Her breath hitched in her chest. In this room surrounded by the haunting smiles of the murdered women, she ached for human contact. A little closeness to chase the dread away.

The door crashed open. "Wow. Can I just say that I think my butthole is the cleanest it has ever been in my life? Who knew that a bidet could—" Mindy stopped. "What are you guys doing? Do I need to come back?"

"No," Claire said firmly. She stood, turned back to the board. "I dropped my marker. Did you have any epiphanies while cleaning your butthole?"

"Only that I am seriously in need of a toilet upgrade," Mindy said, collapsing into the chair again. "Where were we?"

"Where did Ariel go to school?" Claire asked the first question that popped into her head. Her craving for contact was gone. It was time to get back to business.

"Wyoming Valley," Luke answered. He rolled a pencil between his fingers.

"Mindy, do you think you could reach out to the school and get a copy of an alumni list? Or a yearbook?"

"So we can cross-reference the alum and see if any of them went to Venor?" Luke leaned forward in his chair. "Not bad, Hartley."

"I'll email them now." Mindy pulled her tablet out of her backpack. The screen illuminated.

"I have one other thought." Claire turned away from the board. She didn't like what she was about to say.

"What's that?" Mindy asked as she tapped away.

"What if we set a trap to catch him?"

"What kind of trap?" Mindy asked. Her eyes sparkled, brain probably already whirring with ideas.

Luke's eyes hardened. He crossed his arms.

"You know how sometimes I feel like someone's watching me when I take Rosie for a walk at that park on Fifth Street?"

Mindy nodded. Luke scribbled something on a sticky note.

"What if I pretended to be super drunk and alone and took Rosie for a walk in the middle of the night? He would be crazy not to try and catch me."

"Absolutely not." Luke slammed his pencil down on the table. "It's too dangerous."

"What if it wasn't you?" Mindy asked, lowering her tablet. The blue glow cast a mystical look over her.

"What do you mean?"

"What if I dressed up as you? All I need is a blond wig." She tugged at a strand of her raven-colored hair.

Claire shook her head. "I refuse to put you in the path of a serial killer. Not to mention you're like five inches taller than me."

"You're always wearing heels. I'll wear flats. He's a man. He won't notice from a distance."

"I hate to admit it, but she's probably right," Luke said. "He's going to see what he wants to see."

Claire folded her arms. She liked the plan a lot better when her loved ones weren't in danger. "Min, I can't put you in danger. I just can't."

"Claire, it'll be fine. If he even shows up and tries to take me, which I doubt, he'll notice that I'm not you. He's not going to take me. And if he does, I'll stab him right in his stupid serial killer face." Mindy dug in her purse for a moment. A four-inch hunting knife appeared from the depths.

"She won't be in danger." Luke sat up in his chair. "We'll have cars all over the place. Nicole and Kyle outside your apartment, you and me outside the park. You could even tip off Detective Smith and—but then an officer might patrol the scene and scare him away." He broke off, staring at the far wall again.

"We're doing this." Mindy gently shoved Claire out of the way and flipped the whiteboard over. She found a blank spot and began to write.

"Fine. But not until after Steve's proposal." Claire dropped to her knees and scratched Rosie behind the ears. She was practically comatose in her new orthopedic dog bed.

They sat for several more hours, planning their Widow-maker trap and pouring over data. Jason was looking less likely by the minute. He might be an asshole, but he wasn't crafty enough to pull off five murders.

Luke offered Claire and Mindy guest bedrooms for the night, but they refused. It was like the rubber band snap of tension between them in the office had never happened. Plus, Claire hadn't truly forgiven him yet.

She and Mindy drove back to the apartment and fell into bed utterly exhausted. Claire woke with a start in the middle of the night, struggling to pull herself out of a dream. She had been locked in a trunk with all the victims. They all screamed, but no one came to help them.

She sat up in bed and opened her nightstand drawer. The Taser was there, recently relocated from her floorboard hiding spot. Her doors were locked. She was as safe as she could be. But the West Haven Widowmaker was still out there, watching and waiting. And she would find him.

She slithered out of bed to check the windows one more time—just in case. A beat-up Ford was parked on the street below. She picked up her phone, aimed the camera at the truck, and zoomed. Luke was asleep behind the wheel, arms folded over his chest. Her heart leapt beneath her ribs.

She tiptoed across her bedroom. Mindy would never consent to an unsupervised walk down the stairwell. The floor creaked. Claire paused. She glanced at the Mindy-shaped lump under the cover, but it was still. She cracked the door open and slid out into the hallway. Grabbing a pair of shoes, she stepped out the front door and jogged down the hallway, half expecting her apartment door to crash open to reveal a swearing Mindy.

Claire made it down the stairs and onto the street. Freedom!

Shit, she should have brushed her teeth again. And fixed her hair. And double-checked that she applied enough deodorant. Oh well, too late for that.

She tapped lightly on Luke's window. He jumped as though she had shouted in his ear. She waved. He rubbed his eyes and opened his door.

"What are you doing out here?" he scolded.

"Me? I live here. What are you doing out here?"

"Just keeping an eye on things."

Her heart felt like a peanut butter cup someone had stored in their pocket—warm, squishy, and a little bit deformed. That must be why it was beating like this. What was wrong with her? He had hidden an unspeakable horror from her. This was not a time to get mooshy.

"You've met Mindy. I'm pretty sure she could single-handedly bring down the Widowmaker. You don't have to worry."

He crossed his arms. "I can't not worry about you. The

police aren't even coming around every hour anymore—every four at most."

"How long have you been sitting here?"

His ears turned red. "Tonight?"

"Luke," Claire said softly. For some reason she wanted to reach through the window and kiss his stupid, lying face. Instead, she crossed her arms. "That's so creepy."

He opened his mouth to say something, but she interrupted him. "Kidding. I appreciate the fact that you're trying to make up for irresponsibly hiding some incredibly important information from me. But seriously, we can handle it. Go home and get some real sleep. I better get back up there before Mindy wakes up and finds me gone. She might legitimately blow a hole in the side of the building."

———

THE NEXT THREE DAYS PASSED IN THE BLINK OF AN EYE. Although Claire still woke up nearly every night drenched in a cold sweat and reaching for her stun gun, she hadn't received any more creepy flowers. No one had tried to breach her brand-new door and deadbolt.

After changing all her passwords in case the Widowmaker had hacked her accounts, she started an email thread with her friends, planning to catch the killer. Just like her proposals, the trap was planned down to the minute. Assuming the Widowmaker followed her, it would be their best opportunity to catch him in the act.

When she wasn't planning vigilante justice or finalizing the details for the Jet Ski proposal, she was writing new blogs.

Wendy's disaster of a TV interview had sent a wave of traffic and inquiries to her website, and she was seriously considering hiring another assistant to keep up with the flood. Requests were coming in from all over the country, asking Claire if she would be willing to travel to help plan proposals. Comments also appeared across her blog, alternating between criticizing her for her lack of professionalism and providing condolences for her broken engagement.

On Friday afternoon, she sat behind her closed office door at the warehouse, answering emails and brainstorming. She stared at a request from a man in London who offered her a huge amount of compensation to travel to him, and she nervously twirled her hair. She had never imagined planning proposals anywhere but West Haven, where she knew her vendors, caterers, town officials, and just about anyone else who could help her cut through some red tape. She made a note to talk to Mindy and her mom about it, then put it aside.

An email from Nicole appeared in her inbox. Ten pictures from Barney's proposal were attached, and they were even more beautiful than she remembered. While the malfunctioning fountain had been an embarrassing setback, there was no denying that it made the pictures utterly spectacular. She especially loved one that captured Victoria's enthusiastic yes, a stream of droplets dripping over the edge of the umbrella.

"And done," she muttered, clicking "publish" on her latest blog post. She teased a water-based proposal with details to follow and closed her laptop. An alarm went off on her phone. It was nearly three o'clock. She changed into all black and headed down to the marina to make sure true love won again. Second on the list? Not getting kidnapped and murdered.

CHAPTER NINETEEN

To Do:
- Final rehearsal for S proposal—don't forget the cue cards!
- Work on "Sit" command with Rosie
- Send thank you card to River Authority

AFTER HOURS OF REHEARSAL, THREE TANKS OF GAS, AND ONE frantic recheck of her liability policy, Claire was satisfied that she had done all she could do to prepare for Steve's proposal. She eyed the sun as it crept lower in the sky. Emily, one of Claire's trusted helpers, walked Rosie along the edge of the river under strict orders to stay within eyesight at all times. Two photographers hid behind trees, clutching their cameras as they waited for Tara to arrive.

Steve straddled his Jet Ski as it bobbed gently at the river's edge. "Hey, Tara," he said casually into his phone. "What's the name of those purses you like so much? Yeah, those. I'm down at the marina, and they're doing one of those pop-up things down here. They're selling them for like fifty—oh, okay. Yeah, I think we'll have time before dinner. I'll see you in ten."

"She's coming?" Claire asked, trying to ignore the tight fist of anxiety in her chest. Getting the girl to come to the scene without professionally arranged transportation was something that Claire always tried to avoid, but Steve hadn't wanted to arouse any suspicion until the last possible moment.

"She's on her way. You were totally right. She barely even let me finish my sentence. I still think she's going to be disappointed that there aren't actually any purses, though."

"You mean like this one?" She pulled a coral-colored satchel out of a gift bag that she had hidden behind her projector table.

"You're the best," he said and tossed his phone to her. She tucked it into Tara's new purse.

Steve shoved his Jet Ski into the water and roared off to take his place in the river.

"Okay, places everyone!" Claire shouted, shooting another look at Rosie and Emily. Two of her usual videographers scurried to different corners of the marina parking lot and took refuge behind the bushes. Thank god she hadn't had to tag Luke in for this one. He probably would have changed the location, time of day, groomsmen, anything that wasn't nailed down.

Claire used a small remote to turn on a projector and hidden speakers that were set up in the parking lot. A still of Steve's crooked smile and slightly misshapen nose illuminated the screen. She glanced at the laptop to make sure the video was queued and took a final sweep of the area to confirm that everyone was in place. The future groomsmen were already out in the river, temporarily anchored and waiting for their musical cue.

When a white SUV turned onto the lane and wound its way down to the parking lot, everybody rushed to their positions.

Tara parked beside her boyfriend's truck and got out. She was sporting a scintillating amethyst gown that hugged her petite figure and flowed gracefully to the tops of her metallic gold heels.

"Steve? Where the hell is the pop-up store? We're going to be late for dinner." Her New Jersey accent was stronger in her displeasure. She picked up the train of her dress and called for Steve again. When no one answered, she took a full turn and examined the parking lot.

"What the hell?" Spotting the projection of Steve's face, she walked toward the screen.

As she approached, Claire reached over and hit the play button on her laptop.

Tara stopped dead in her tracks as Steve's voice boomed out of hidden speakers. One cameraman crouched behind her to get the shot of her watching the video unfold, and another hid behind the screen to capture her reaction. Nicole had a pre-arranged shoot in Scranton, so Claire had to put her trust in the hands of her backups.

"Hey, Tara. You're probably wondering why I'm hiding from you right now," Steve said in the recording. "The truth is, I wanted to ask you something really important tonight. We met for the very first time at this marina. It was the middle of July, and you were on a picnic with another guy. And I, being a complete douche, was trying to show off in front of you while I trained for *Engage Throttle*.

"You were pretending not to watch, but you were. And I know this because, being a young and stupid kid, I came off a new jump I was testing, and I botched the landing. The last thing I remember was the crushing blow of my ride landing on top of me and forcing me underwater. I had to have been almost a hundred yards out."

He looked into the camera with soft eyes. "And you saved my life. You swam the length of a football field in a cute little sundress and pulled me back to shore. You gave me mouth-to-mouth and didn't even get mad when I spit river water in your face. Although, I do seem to remember you calling me an idiot and shaking me when I regained consciousness. I wouldn't be here today if it wasn't for you," he said, holding his arms open wide at his side.

Tears had sprung into Tara's eyes. She wiped them away as she watched the video, still clutching her train. If she heard the camera shutters' soft clicking, she didn't say anything.

"With all that in mind," Steve's recording continued, "I have been saving for the past three years so I can ask a very important question to the girl who saved my life. But first, I wanted to ask someone else."

The video transitioned, showing a shaky hand-held shot of Steve in his car.

"I'm sitting outside of Tara's house right now. She's at work, and I'm about to ask for her dad's blessing."

The camera transitioned to a view of a living room. An older man sat in an armchair with a bag of Cheetos on his lap. Steve sat in the chair next to him. There wasn't any audio, but the older man embraced Steve, leaving an orange stain on his back.

As Claire flashed a green cue card, dozens of floating lights lit up, marking a path on the river.

Tara smiled through her tears. Suddenly, her favorite song, a heavy, seventies-era rock ballad, blared out of the hidden speakers. She jumped and nearly stumbled in her heels.

The Jet Skis gunned to life. Claire swept the scene. Everyone was accounted for. Several heads poked over the side of the bridge, watching the display below. The small fleet of Jet Skis began their intricate routine. She prayed that no one would be injured—Tara was hardly dressed to rescue Steve tonight.

Tara grasped her train and walked to the edge of the water as the group performed barrel rolls, sharp turns, and jumps over the expanse of river in front of them. As the song welled into the chorus for the last time, Claire held up the orange cue card. Steve zoomed away to the farthest reach of the allotted space, went around the bridge supports, and flew toward the final jump.

Wind whipped at his hair. His eyes narrowed in concentration. He approached the ramp at breakneck speed, sailed off the end, and performed a flawless backflip. He landed triumphantly on the other side. The crowd of people who had gathered on top of the bridge cheered wildly.

Weak with relief, Claire leaned heavily against the projector table. She sent up a silent prayer of thanks as Steve and the other men zoomed to shore, easing their machines onto the muddy bank of the river. Steve swung his leg over his Jet Ski and marched over to Tara. At his signal, Claire took the ring box out of her pocket and tossed it to him.

He nearly missed the box, but he managed to snatch it from the air with his fingertips. He laughed and got down on one knee in front of Tara, breathing heavily. He ran a hand through his damp hair.

He had barely gotten the words out when Tara leaped into his arms, apparently not caring that Steve's tuxedo wetsuit was, well, wet. She wrapped her legs around him and furiously kissed and hugged him, not even glancing into the ring box. Eventually, he set her down and slid the sizable emerald-cut diamond onto her ring finger.

As Tara cried and hugged him, Steve triumphantly pumped his fist to the sky. The shutters clicked rapidly. That picture would be perfect for the blog.

After his friends took turns hugging and congratulating the happy couple, Steve led Tara over to Claire.

"Tara, I want you to meet—well, actually, re-meet, the person who made all this possible." He extended a hand toward Claire.

Tara looked confused for a moment, and then a flash of realization lit up her eyes. "Oh my god, the floozy?"

"The one and the same. I'm so sorry we lied to you about the puppy." Claire smiled. "Steve really wanted this to be a surprise."

"You planned this whole thing?" Tara asked, eyes wide.

"With Steve's help, of course. I loved the story of how you met so much. I was really excited to plan your proposal."

Tara leaned in and hugged her tightly. "Thank you so much. This was beyond perfect. And I'm sorry for calling you a tramp that day."

Claire laughed. "Totally understandable. Now I figured you might get a little wet tonight," she said, reaching around behind her and pulling out a garment bag she had hung on a tree. "So you can put this one on, and I'll take the one you're wearing to be dry cleaned. You'll have it back tomorrow."

Tara unzipped the bag, revealing a rhinestone-studded, floor-length gown in an intense shade of hot pink.

"Oh shit! I love it." Tara ran a hand down the silky length of the dress.

Claire beamed. "The restrooms over there are unlocked." She indicated the public bathroom a few feet away. At least, they were when she last checked.

After the happy couple changed and posed for a few pictures, they drove off to celebrate their engagement over dinner. Claire began the tedious process of tearing down and collapsing the video equipment and corralling the floating disco lights with help from the groomsmen. Rosie snoozed in the green grass, completely exhausted from all the excitement.

Claire arrived home with an aching back after midnight. She waved as her helper, Emily, drove off. Nicole's lime green Fiat was parked on the street, slightly out of the lines. Claire thumped her head against the steering wheel. Would she never be alone again?

As she entered the stairwell with Rosie, a realization struck her. She hadn't thought about the Widowmaker for hours. As fatigued as she was, the realization energized her. She leapt up the stairs two at a time, half dragging Rosie up the remaining floors. She was taking her life back. She wouldn't live in fear. Tomorrow night, they were going to lure that son of a bitch in and catch him for good. There wouldn't be any more pictures on Luke's wall of victims.

CHAPTER TWENTY

To Do:
- Watch some self defense videos
- Send Roy birthday present
- Drop off Tara's dress

"YOU PACKED SNACKS?" LUKE DUG THROUGH THE REUSABLE shopping tote Claire had hefted onto the center console of the car he had rented for the occasion. His truck would have stuck out like a sore thumb in the sea of sleek sedans driven by most West Haven residents.

"We don't know how long we'll be here." She popped a gummy bear into her mouth and slouched low in the seat.

Darkness had settled over the park. It was lit only by the streetlamps that were spaced out every twenty yards. Technically, the park closed at sundown, but locals never listened.

Calling Buchanan Park a park was generous. During her

freshman year at Venor, it was an empty grass lot maybe one hundred yards by twenty yards. By her sophomore year, a company bought the lot and tried to turn it into a strip club. In order to keep the club from sullying the historical district, the town council claimed that President James Buchanan had addressed the town of West Haven from that very strip of land and declared it a historical landmark. Now, it was an unremarkable park with a handful of picnic tables and a short walking trail that was most frequently used as a toilet by drunk frat boys.

"Do you see anything?" She asked for the tenth time as she peered through the binoculars she had borrowed from Kyle. He was the only twenty-five-year-old she knew who was an avid bird-watcher.

"Not yet."

A chill ran down her spine. The Widowmaker was probably out there somewhere in the dark. Watching. Waiting. No telltale black sedans were parked in the long row of spots that ran parallel to the park. A few other vehicles had joined them in the lot, but their occupants had exited to the Italian restaurant and the beer garden one block west.

Two blocks away, Nicole's Fiat briefly flashed its headlights. "That's the signal. Here she comes."

Claire and Luke shrunk down in their seats. Her heart hammered at the sight of Rosie, clearly delighted at the prospect of a late-night walk with her favorite babysitter. Mindy stumbled behind her, wearing a curly blonde wig and carrying a wine bottle. Despite the difference in height, from this distance Mindy looked a lot like her. Should she be offended that Mindy's impression of her included a half-empty bottle of wine? Whatever. It would be worth it if they caught him.

Claire checked her crossbody purse for the millionth

time. Pepper spray, zip ties, and her stun gun were jumbled inside. That wouldn't look suspicious at all if she was stopped by the police for loitering.

As Mindy walked under the marquee of the historical art deco movie theater, a wave of panic engulfed Claire. She should never have allowed this. Her dog and her best friend were out in the open, exposed, while a serial killer roamed the streets. She paused with her hand on the door handle, ready to fling it open and demand that the whole ploy be stopped.

Luke reached out and caught her hand. Callouses rubbed rough against her skin. She tore her eyes away from Mindy for a moment. He shook his head.

Claire settled back in her seat, heart still beating uncomfortably fast. She pulled her hand away, lofting the binoculars with two hands. She should have insisted on being in Nicole's car. Luke was too much of a distraction. Somehow, Nicole and Kyle had managed to turn the stakeout into a date night complete with scavenger hunt and themed stakeout snacks.

Mindy took slow, lumbering steps. She drifted from one side of the paved walk to the other. Rosie tugged at the leash, glancing back every couple of seconds as if asking what the holdup was. Mindy was fifty yards away, about to round the corner of the walking path. Claire bristled. What if the Widowmaker came for her while she was this far away? Surely, they wouldn't catch him in time.

Nicole's Fiat passed slowly behind their rented Toyota. They were supposed to slink around the block and stop on the other side of the park.

Mindy began her second lap, shooting a glance at Claire as she uncorked the wine with her teeth and took a big sip.

"She's not actually supposed to drink the wine. Nothing's happening. Maybe he's not here." She pressed the binoculars so hard against her eyes that they were sure to leave a mark.

"Give it time, Miss Impatient. We already know he's a lurker. He's not going to just run in, guns blazing."

Even though their windows were closed, Mindy could still be heard humming loudly, still staggering around the trail as Rosie plodded on. The clock on the dashboard seemed to have stopped moving. How could time be passing so slowly?

Suddenly, a dark figure appeared at the far end of the park. The figure was clad in gray sweatpants and a gold Venor University sweatshirt.

"Luke!" Claire hissed. Would the Widowmaker be dumb enough to attack someone while wearing a sweatshirt with his alma mater? If it was him, he sure wasn't one for fashion.

"I see him." He pulled a metal baseball bat out of the back seat of the car. One hand paused on the door handle.

The man bent at the waist, stretching his fingertips toward his toes. Did the Widowmaker always do calisthenics before kidnapping someone?

"Maybe he's just a jogger. He doesn't seem to have even noticed Mindy."

"How could you not notice Mindy?" she spat. "She's wearing a leather miniskirt and walking the cutest dog in the world. Oh god, he's running. What do we do?"

A pair of red Nikes flashed as the figure jogged down the walking path, hood up. His face was obscured as he ran beneath the lights. He passed by their car, sneakers slamming into the concrete as he went. Medium build, not quite six feet tall. Caucasian? It was hard to tell in the dark. Who was he?

"Luke. He's gaining on her. What do we do?" Everything in her screamed for her to run to her friend.

Luke was silent. The figure rounded the corner of the trail. Less than fifty yards stood between him and Mindy.

She glanced at Luke once more. His hand was on the door handle, but his eyebrows were knit together.

"Fuck it." Claire flung the car door open, jumping out and not bothering to close it behind her. She took off like a rocket, sprinting across the grassy expanse. Was it her imagination, or had the stranger picked up his pace? Twenty yards separated him and Mindy. Now fifteen.

Her breath came in ragged gasps as she dug in her purse. What should she use? Pepper spray? She pulled it out, but she tripped over a tree root and it fell through her fingers, rolling onto the dirt. There was no time to go back. Ten yards now. Five.

"*Ahhhh!*" Claire screamed a battle cry as she slammed shoulder-first into the jogger. He wouldn't hurt Mindy. He wouldn't hurt anyone ever again.

"Claire, what the—" Mindy whirled around.

The jogger crashed to the ground. Claire fell on top of him. He lashed out, pushing her away, but she straddled him, keeping him on the ground through sheer will.

"Jesus Christ! What the hell, lady?"

"Bottle." Claire held one hand out.

Without missing a beat, Mindy tossed her the wine bottle. Propelled by adrenaline, she smashed it on the ground. The oaky smell of chardonnay oozed into the air. She held the jagged neck of the bottle toward the jogger.

"Who the fuck are you?"

Footsteps thudded from every direction. In seconds, Nicole, Kyle, and Luke stood in a menacing circle around them.

"Me? Who the fuck are you?" The voice was distinct, vaguely familiar.

She ripped the hood away from his face.

"Oh, god."

"Rick?" Luke gripped Claire's arm, pulled her off the man.

Shawna DeLong's widower lay on the ground, surrounded by splintered bits of broken glass. The last time Claire had seen him on TV, he was reciting a poem at a vigil for Shawna. She had steamrolled a grieving man into the ground and threatened him with a broken wine bottle. She was a monster.

"Luke?" Rick asked, still sounding dazed.

"How the hell do you know him?" Nicole asked.

"I interviewed him a couple of weeks ago. We are so sorry, man."

Luke and Kyle hoisted Rick up. He rubbed the side of his bald head.

"What the hell are you guys doing? Do you run an organized crime ring on the side?"

"We're looking for the Widowmaker," Claire blurted out. "He's after me."

Rick's brown eyes grew darker. "If you find him, let me know."

"I'm really sorry," she continued, reaching over to dust off the dirt that covered the left side of the gold sweatshirt.

"Don't be." Rick tugged his hood back up and popped his earbuds back in. "Do what the police won't. Find him." He took off down the path.

Claire slapped a hand to her forehead. "I can't believe I did that. I'm a monster." She bent down and began picking up the larger glass pieces. How much glass had she picked up in the past two weeks? She really should invest in some work gloves.

"At least he's not trying to press charges," Kyle said. He had a smudge of blue icing on his cheek.

A slow clap echoed across the park. The group turned in unison toward the source of the sound.

"Well done, Claire." It couldn't be. But a second later, a skeletally thin woman slid under the streetlamp. Wendy. "You've assaulted a widow."

"Widower," Claire corrected.

"Whatever. And I got it all on camera." Wendy shook her iPhone at the group. "I can't wait to see what Marnie thinks about this new footage."

"Do you seriously not have anything better to do than follow me around?" Claire's hands bunched into fists at her side. What she wouldn't give to slap that smug look right off Wendy's face. "Don't you have friends? Work to do? A date with Jason? Oh, wait. He's probably at Poker Night, right?" She laced her voice with fake sympathy.

"Oh boy." Kyle pulled his phone out and held it up in the direction of Claire and Wendy. "I am recording this conversation as evidence in the event of civil litigation," he announced in a loud voice. "By continuing to speak, all parties present are providing permission to record this interaction."

Wendy barely spared a glance toward Kyle. She pried her Louis Vuitton clutch open, deposited her phone, and crossed her arms. A blob of chewing gum rolled around her half-open mouth. "Please. Like you're so interesting. I was on my way to my car when I saw you charging some guy like a maniac."

Claire stepped forward. Mindy, still wearing the blond wig, took a step closer as well, eyes narrowed.

Wendy smelled like cinnamon and mediocrity.

Claire stared into Wendy's mucus-green eyes. "I don't believe you. Stop following me, or I will go to the police."

"Again," Wendy said, moving nearer. "I wasn't following you. Why were you attacking that guy, anyway?"

"It's none of your business." Claire inched even closer. They were practically boobs to boobs now. Wendy cocked one eyebrow, seemingly daring her to make a move.

Claire lunged forward as though she was about to hit her but stopped before making contact with the overgrown poisonous weed. Wendy screeched like a barn owl and jumped back. Her heel got caught in the soft ground and she tipped backward, splashing into a shallow mud puddle. A wave of muddy water cascaded around her, soaking her white cashmere sweater. She sputtered, bits of mud stuck to her cheek. Pitiful thing.

"You stupid bitch," Wendy roared, flailing her arms like she was drowning in the deep end of the West Haven Community Pool. She struggled to get up, fell in the mud again. "I will end you. I'm going to win the award this year, and then I'm going to marry Jason."

Oh no, she fucking *didn't*. A hand gripped her arm, but she shook it off.

"Let me make something very clear." Claire knelt at the edge of the mud puddle. "You're not going to win the award this year. In fact, you're not ever going to win it. It doesn't matter how many times you follow me, try to assassinate my character, or how many of my fiancés you sleep with. You're not good at what you do. You don't listen to your clients. You don't even really care about them. You care about how their proposals make you look."

"I care about them," Wendy whined like a teenager who wasn't allowed to go to the mall with her friends.

"Really? What were the names of the last couple you worked for?"

"Why should I tell you?" Wendy hissed.

"You don't know, do you?" Claire shook her head. She rose to her feet. "I'm sorry you're so unsatisfied with your life, Wendy. I hope you find what you're looking for."

Claire turned on her heel and strutted across the park with her head held high. A chorus of "daaaaaaamn" followed her.

CHAPTER TWENTY-ONE

To Do:
- *Try meditating*
- *Call dress shop about N's gown*
- *Scour internet for video of flattening an innocent widower*

NAUSEA GRIPPED CLAIRE'S STOMACH AS SHE DUMPED CREAMER in her mug the next morning. She had poked the bear. Well, technically she had startled the bear into flopping into a mud puddle and ruining her cashmere Christian Dior sweater. Either way, there was sure to be retaliation.

And worse, it had all been for nothing. They hadn't caught the Widowmaker. Not even a glimpse of him. Instead, she had just assaulted an innocent man and gotten caught on camera by her worst enemy. Would there be no end to the punishments this summer?

She didn't have time to dwell on what Wendy would do

next. There were bigger problems today. Like her 10:15 meeting with Luke. She had had ample opportunity to tell him about the choreographed dance for Nicole's proposal, but his betrayal still stood between them like a glass wall. Recording the dance with Claire and sending it out to the attendees was the least he could do.

Her phone pinged, and she glanced at the screen. Speak of the smarmy douchebag.

Don't be late.

She rolled her eyes and downed the dregs of her coffee. Only Luke would hide earth-shattering information from her, fail to catch her attempted murderer, and then pretend he still had the authority to boss her around.

Dread settled in her stomach like an anchor as she bustled around the kitchen, accidentally knocking over her cordless vacuum that still held the particles of glass from the park the night before. She wasn't about to let a dog get hurt because of her overzealous interrogation of Rick.

She gave herself a pep talk as she climbed into the shower.

"Keep things professional, Claire. Don't think about him lying to you and hiding life-threatening facts from you. Don't think about him with his shirt off. Just remember what a big, fat liar he is. Well, he's not fat. He's kind of ripped. But don't think about that either. All you have to do is get through Nicole's proposal, and then hopefully that asshat will hitch a ride back to California where he belongs. You need him only for his camera-wielding abilities and his treasure trove of knowledge about the person who's trying to kill you, not for anything else."

She opted for workout clothes, already rolling her eyes at the comments he would be sure to make. After nearly strangling herself with a sports bra, she slid on a tank top and a pair of yoga shorts. She grabbed Rosie, the leash, and the backpack and left her apartment in plenty of time. She was just a mile away from the house when she screeched to a halt behind a tractor.

Claire tilted her sunglasses down her nose and stared at the old man astride the giant machine in front of her. He putted down the country road, lifting a hand to wave at a car passing in the opposite direction.

Rosie stood on her hind legs and barked out the passenger side window, but the farmer took no notice.

Claire smacked one hand against her steering wheel and swore. She had two minutes to get to Luke's, but her speedometer was only registering fifteen miles an hour. She nudged the nose of her car into the other lane. A blind curve mocked her. Grumbling, she swung back into her lane.

She turned up her music, performed a quick round of alternate nostril breathing, and managed to stay calm until the tractor turned off down a dirt lane a short distance from Luke's. She stomped on her accelerator, flying the remaining distance. When she pulled up and parked her car, he was sitting smugly on his porch in an Adirondack chair, staring pointedly at his watch.

She clenched the steering wheel in a death grip. Before Luke came to town, she had never once been late to a meeting. What was it about him that tipped her world off its axis? Next meeting, she was leaving half an hour early. She would show up at dawn and drag him out of bed.

She slammed her door and trudged to the porch, waiting for the inevitable smart remark. Rosie dashed happily to Luke and licked his ankles.

"I got stuck behind a tractor. But I'm not apologizing

because I can't control agriculture, and frankly, you owe me."

Luke whistled and bent to pick up Rosie. He wore dark jeans and a checkered button-down over a T-shirt with a band name she didn't recognize. He scratched under Rosie's chin, and her tongue lolled out of her mouth. The band name—All Our Yesterdays—was soon obscured by a layer of corgi fur. "Fair enough. Shall we start?"

She narrowed her eyes. "What? You don't want to berate me for being late even though you specifically told me to be on time? I thought professionals respect the value of each other's time."

He put the dog on the porch, then stood and placed a hand on her shoulder. "Generally they do. Come with me. I have something to show you."

"Oh good. I was wondering when you would deign to let me know who else wants to kill me."

He tried to take her hand, but she snatched it back from him. Ignoring her comment, he led her inside. As they passed the doors of his office, her heart thumped and her stomach lurched. Her picture was in there, on the walls of horror. Surrounded by women who would never be seen again.

When he opened a set of doors, she nearly dropped her phone on the marble floor.

The shelves that lined the wall opposite the windows had been transformed from unappealing, empty dust-catchers to a library that would be the envy of any collector. Rows upon rows of books stretched the length of the room. It was straight out of a fairy tale.

"Oh my gosh." She ran a finger down the spine of one of her favorite books. "It looks just like the ballroom from *The Princess and the Arrow*. How did you do all this?"

He shrugged. "Well, I heard your suggestion about filling them with trimmed book spines. I tried it out, and it looked awful." He kicked at a group of glued-together book spines. It skittered across the floor.

Claire frowned. Her skin prickled. Five minutes in and she already wanted to kill him.

"These are real books. I had them shipped from my place in California. There's more room for them here, anyway."

"Well, if I had known you were a bibliophile, I would have suggested real books from the start."

"You thought I don't read?"

"I figured your full-time job of being a lying douche prevented many leisure activities." She ran a finger over one of the rows.

Luke's mouth hardened into a line. Maybe she was being too harsh. She did need his house for the biggest proposal of her career, after all.

"All of these are yours?" She traced a finger over another row.

He nodded. "I collected them over the years, inherited some. I can't pass a secondhand bookstore without picking something up."

Her enthusiasm for the proposal was quickly overwhelming her desire to be rude. It really was better than she had imagined. No more dusty, stuffy ballroom. She threw her arms out to her sides and spun in place. Her heart soared. "I love it. It's perfect. Absolutely perfect. Just wait until you see the rest of the decorations. It's going to be nothing short of magical."

"Nothing but the best for Kyle."

"Where's Rosie?" She scanned from one end of the room to the other.

"Oh, she's probably over here." Luke walked over to a small built-in bar on the far side of the room. She followed him.

"Is that...another dog bed? And seven chew toys? And a pet water fountain?"

"I just wanted her to be comfortable during the meeting."

Rosie was on her back, thrashing back and forth with a stuffed lobster in her mouth. Claire desperately wanted to take a picture, but she wouldn't give Luke the satisfaction.

He shoved his hands into his jean pockets. "So, what did you want to discuss today? You look pretty casual." He nodded at her ponytail and shorts.

She tucked a wayward strand of hair behind her ear and crossed her arms. She was going to be professional and aloof. There was no way she was going to pay any attention to the biceps that were threatening to rip right through his button-down. And the adorable guilt gifts for the dog were already forgotten.

"I am casually dressed today because it's conducive to the meeting agenda. This week, I hammered out all the details with the caterers, the decorators, the carriage company, and I nabbed the rest of the props I need. They're in my trunk. I'm going to keep them here at your house because I don't want Nicole to see them at my place or the warehouse." She raised her eyebrows, daring him to challenge her.

"I'll bring them in before you leave." He leaned against a bookcase. Maybe he sensed that this wasn't the end of her agenda.

Why was she nervous? She shouldn't be nervous to ask him for a favor. He owed her. "As you know, the date is set for two weeks from today. The last piece of the puzzle that

Kyle wanted was for everyone—all the family on both sides —to learn a simple dance. So, to save him some money, I told him I would figure something out, record it, and send it to everyone so they could learn it before the big day. And, since you owe me a lifetime of favors after the incident, you are now my dancing partner."

"A lifetime of favors." Luke whistled.

She raised her chin, stared him down. "Am I wrong?"

"No, you're not wrong. What's the song?"

"Nicole's favorite song. 'Scintillate' by Monochrome Monday."

"That's a long song."

"I know. I'm surprised you know it." She bent and untied her shoes, setting them neatly by the door.

"I like all kinds of music." He fiddled with his phone for a moment. "Show me what you've got so far." The song spilled out of nearby speakers, slow and soulful.

Claire rushed to the center of the room and held her arms in the air as though she had a partner. "Okay, so I've figured out about six eight counts," she said, beginning to sway to the song. "I figured even that was pushing it."

She continued to sway and move in small steps, now and then adding a dip or a twirl. Spinning on the toe of the white ankle socks she wore, she fought her natural clumsiness to glide over the smooth marble. She counted under her breath as she moved and frowned in concentration.

Luke smiled as he watched her. He was probably judging her form and plotting suggestions to make it better. Over her dead body.

"Okay, so that's all of them." She paused to catch her breath. "It just repeats from there until the end. What do you think?"

"Do it again." He started the song over. His eyes burned

her as she stepped and twirled, socks quickly gathering dirt. She really needed to get a cleaning crew in here before the proposal.

As she finished the dance a second time, Luke crossed the room and took her hand. The other found its way around her waist to the small of her back, and he pulled her closer. Even though he'd only seen her do it twice, he followed her seamlessly, allowing her to take the lead at first, but by their third time through the dance, he was twirling her out, bringing her back in, and dipping her to dizzying lows.

They sailed across the room, growing more confident and more daring with each step. Their bodies glided together in perfect rhythm.

A pool of sweat formed on her lower back, and her cheeks grew hot. Could he tell that her back was sweaty? He was holding her so tightly. She couldn't take her eyes off his as he led her across the dance floor. They were a serene green today, more lagoon than hurricane. She lost herself in the rhythm of the music, the sensation of his skin on hers.

Damn it. The eight count didn't end where she had envisioned it. "What if, at that instrumental break right before the last verse kicks in, we have the couples kind of disappear against the wall and have Kyle pull Nicole in for a solo dance at the end?" she asked.

"I like it." He stared down at her. She still clung to him, breathing heavily with the exertion. It was a good thing she wasn't interested in him, because out-of-breath pizza addict in spandex shorts probably wasn't an attractive look for her.

They ran through the entire dance several more times, until they nailed every dip and twirl.

"We'll have to make sure people don't drink too much before the dance. I don't want anyone careening through your windows." She nodded at the floor-to-ceiling windows that led to the patio.

He laughed. "Are we ready to film it?"

She took a step back and shook out her limbs. "I'm ready if you're ready."

He left to find a camera and tripod. Now was as good a time as any to stretch. By the time he came back, Claire was upside down.

"What the hell are you doing?" he asked, addressing her pointed toes, which were inches from his nose.

"Headstand. Shh," she said, her voice strained. Her linked hands cradled her neck as her forearms pressed into the floor.

Luke bent down to look at her.

She could barely see his face over the mound of her chest that obscured nearly everything from view.

"Are you sure you can breathe down there? You look a little smothered."

"Shh," she hissed at him. She breathed deeply for several more seconds, wobbling minutely, before dropping her legs down and righting herself.

Luke had stripped down to his T-shirt and set the camera up in front of the windows. He made some final adjustments and glanced over at her.

"You're crazy, you know that?"

"And you're a lying sneak. I guess we all have our thing." She twisted her entire body in an attempt to glare at him while she did cow face pose.

He tucked a remote in his pocket and held his hand out to her. She untwisted herself and hopped up from the floor without his help.

"Okay." She shook out her limbs. "I'll do a brief intro

and walk through the steps, then we'll run through the whole thing together."

"Sounds good," he said. He moved to stand behind the camera and pressed the record button. "When you're ready."

"Hi, everyone! I'm Claire, and today, with some help, I'm going to be teaching you a simple dance for the final stage of Kyle's proposal to Nicole. Remember, this is a huge secret, so please don't mention anything to Nicole. I'm also sending you all a link where you can download the song for free so you can practice. Okay, so now we're going to learn the first eight count." She went through the motions for each eight count, slowly once and then more quickly. Then she strung all of them together.

She paused and glanced at Luke behind the camera. "Was that okay?"

"Sounds good to me," he said, hitting the pause button. He walked over and pulled her close.

She tried not to focus on the ripple of his toned back muscles beneath the well-worn cotton of his T-shirt, or the sensation of her body pressed against his chest. For a second, they stared into each other's eyes.

She blinked. The sex embargo was in danger again. How had this happened? Was it the damn dog beds? "Ready?"

Luke took his hand from her back for a moment and hit the record button on his remote.

She turned to the camera again. "Okay, so now with my lovely partner, Luke, we'll demonstrate each eight count broken down, first without music, and then with the music. Ready, Luke?"

He nodded.

She verbally described the steps as they swayed, step-ball-changed, and twirled through the choreography. They were perfectly in sync, never missing a hand or stepping on each other's feet. For a moment, she just allowed herself to be held and steered around the room. There was no camera, no shadowy figure waiting in the darkness. What she wouldn't give to keep this moment forever, suspended in time.

As the song transitioned to an instrumental break before the last chorus, Luke dipped her breathtakingly low, catching her before she hit the ground. Her spine bent like a spoon yielding against hard ice cream. Butterflies fluttered in her stomach. She looked up at him, smiling at their success. They locked eyes as he gently pulled her back up. He didn't relax his tight grip on her. They should be breaking apart, clearing the dance floor. But for some reason, she couldn't leave.

As the song began to crescendo, he placed his hand on her flushed cheek. There was a question in his eyes. The bottom fell out of her stomach.

"Screw it," she said and crushed her mouth to his.

Her heart beat furiously as she reached around his neck, running her hands through his hair and arching her back to press herself closer to him.

His lips were simultaneously greedy and soft as he snaked his hands around to her back and gripped her by the ass, wrapping her legs around his waist.

Shit, he was groping her back sweat. It probably felt like caressing a wet seal.

Her worries about back sweat disappeared as his hand slid under her tank top, teasing her skin deliciously as it trailed over the small of her back. She moaned softly, skin tingling at his touch. He surged forward, bumping them into the bookcase.

The hem of Claire's yoga shorts caught the edge of a book and sent it tumbling to the marbled floor. Luke pressed her against the shelves, feasting ravenously on the stretch of her exposed neck. *Holy shit.* Her stomach clenched—was it nerves or molten desire? Every inch of her felt like it might explode, or maybe crumble. It had been months since she had been touched like this. Actually, she'd never been touched like this. Jason couldn't have found her erogenous zones if she had marked them with road flares and neon signs.

Gross. Don't think about Jason. Had she applied enough deodorant today?

Luke tugged the neckline of her shirt down, and all thoughts of Jason and deodorant dribbled from her mind like water through cupped fingers. His mouth began a tanta-lizing journey from her neck to her cleavage. He pinned her hands at her sides and pressed her against the shelves again.

She flexed her fingers helplessly, completely at the mercy of the sweet agony he was currently spreading from head to toe. *I hope he doesn't tell Kyle about this, and then they start calling me Back Sweat behind my sweaty back.*

But the inner monologue immediately shut up when he kissed her collarbone with an open mouth and blew lightly on the spot, sending a shiver cascading up her spine.

He yanked her shirt over her head and several things happened at once.

Kyle walked into the ballroom carrying a sixpack. Luke and Claire sprang apart. Kyle stopped dead in his tracks, a flush creeping over his cheeks. Claire bumped into the bookcase. Something metallic slid on the wooden slats above her head.

She had a split-second view of Luke and Kyle panicking, then the world went black.

CHAPTER TWENTY-TWO

To Do:
- *Research Botox injections for back sweat*
- *Buy a helmet*
- *Blog post on pros/cons of at-home manicures*

DARKNESS ENGULFED CLAIRE LIKE A DENSE FOG. WAS SHE floating? Why couldn't she open her eyes?

"Blunt trauma to the rear cranium." A very official-sounding voice floated in from the edge of her periphery. She craned her head—oh, her head—in the direction of the voice. Was there an icepick lodged in her skull? Did the Widowmaker finally get her? Did she fall asleep watching *Grey's Anatomy* again?

"She lost a lot of blood. The boyfriend said a bookend hit her in the head, but did you notice the bruising and discoloration around her eye?"

Claire mustered some strength and forced her eyes

open. She was in a hospital room. A monitor beeped at her bedside, and something was stuck to her finger. She tried to claw it off, but she could barely lift her other hand.

A man in a white coat turned around and noticed she was awake. The woman beside him looked at her with pity in her eyes.

"Miss Hartley, I'm Dr. Weaver, and you've been admitted to West Haven Hospital. Your boyfriend brought you in because of trauma to your head. Can you tell us what happened?" He pulled a small flashlight out of his pocket and shined it in Claire's eyes. She flinched and pinched her eyes shut.

Could heads actually split open? Because she could swear hers was in two separate pieces. She reached up with her unencumbered hand and felt the back of her head. There was a smooth, hairless spot that wasn't there this morning. A two-inch bandage covered the spot.

They shaved her fucking head.

"Oh my god," she said. The heart monitor beeped faster. A wave of panic welled up in her. She was going to have a bald spot for Nicole's engagement. Were hair plugs for twenty-five-year-olds a thing? Maybe she could clip in some extensions. She tried to sit up, but the doctor pressed her gently back into her pillows.

"Try to relax, Claire. You're safe here. We gave your emergency contact a call, and your mother said she was in Palm Springs but would try to catch the next flight."

"No," she half shouted, sitting up again. The world swam in front of her eyes, and pain split her skull like lightning. "I'm fine. She doesn't need to come back. And he's not my boyfriend."

"Did he hurt you, Miss Hartley?" A woman in a

burgundy suit walked to the bedside and laid a hand on her arm.

"What? No! Well, just my feelings. We were dancing, and I bumped into a bookcase. I must have knocked something off the shelf," she said, pressing a hand to her tender skull. The pain made her eyes water.

"Try not to touch your stitches," the doctor chimed in from the foot of the bed.

"Claire, this is a safe space. You can tell us what really happened," the woman encouraged.

Claire glared at her even as the lady's face swirled in front of her eyes until she resembled an Impressionist painting. "I just did."

"He's never laid a hand on you?"

"I wouldn't mind if he laid a hand on me, if you know what I mean." Claire tried to wiggle her eyebrows. Where the hell was Luke? Had he abandoned her at the hospital to drink a six-pack with Kyle? She had been so close to getting a front-row seat of a full unveiling of that six-pack. Did this mean her sex embargo was technically still intact? Did she want it to be?

The nurse at the foot of the bed rolled her eyes. "Head trauma," she said to the doctor.

"Miss Hartley? Did he hurt you?" The woman in the suit prompted.

"No. He did lie to me about the fact that I'm being targeted by a serial killer, but I'm not sure you can prosecute for that. Or for his massive ego. Or for those forearms." Was her internal monologue broken? Get it together, Claire.

"Sure he did, sweetie." The nurse patted her arm.

The doctor and nurse exchanged a curious look before the doctor went back to tapping on the laptop at his workstation. None of them reacted to the bombshell she had just dropped. Maybe being targeted by a serial killer wasn't considered a big deal in the medical field.

"How did you hurt your eye?" Suit woman asked.

"I fell asleep in the shower and hit my head against the wall."

The woman raised her eyebrows. "So, in the space of maybe two weeks, you've managed to give yourself a black eye, knock a bookend onto your head, and lose almost a pint of blood."

"I inherited my natural grace from my mother," Claire said, craning her neck. Her purse was on a chair on the other side of the room. Had any of her clients called?

"All right." The woman dug a card out of her purse. She left it on the edge of the bed. "If you change your mind and want to talk about what's really going on, please give me a call." The woman walked out of the room.

"You've suffered a grade three concussion." The doctor hung her chart back on the end of her bed. He walked over to the wall and dimmed the lights.

"Better?"

She nodded and relaxed her squinted eyes. "Thank you."

The doctor reached into his pocket and pulled out a red ball. He showed it to her and then hid it behind his back.

"What's in my hand?" he asked her quietly.

"A red ball," she said slowly. What the hell was this about? "Are you going to start juggling?"

"No. Who's our nation's current president?"

"President Vance," she said after a moderate pause. Did he think she was an imbecile?

"Good. And your name is?"

"Claire," she said, struggling to make her mental cogs work a little faster.

"Okay. Your memory seems to be fine, so we'll start getting your discharge forms ready. You'll probably experience some dizziness, disorientation, confusion, and sensitivity to light for a few days. You need to take it easy and try to avoid getting hit in the head in the near future."

"The far future is okay, though?"

The doctor ignored her. He rattled off a laundry list of discharge instructions that she barely understood. Where the hell was Luke? Was she going to crawl into an Uber in a hospital gown to get back to his house?

"Thank you, doctor," Claire said as he left, grabbing a hunk of hair from the back of her head and examining it for blood. It was a saturated, brown-red color. Great. Was her new bald spot permanent? How noticeable was it? She was going to have to completely change her haircare routine. As everyone exited the room, she reached over to the chair next to her bed and dug through her purse.

She dialed her mom's phone number. Her mom picked up on the first ring.

"Oh, Claire, honey. How are you?"

"I'm fine, Mom, just got bumped on the head."

"The doctor said you lost a lot of blood. I'm at the airport right now fighting with this attendant trying to get a flight home, but everything's booked."

"Mom. You don't need to come home. They're discharging me already. I'm perfectly fine. It's really not a big deal."

"My Clairebear is in the hospital. Of course it's a big deal! That's what I've been trying to explain to this idiot," her mom barked.

"Mom, I'm sure they're just doing their job—" she began again but stopped when she noticed a bouquet of blush-colored lilies sitting on her bedside table. She reached out with one hand and picked up the card that accompanied it, half listening to her mom jabbering away.

Claire ripped open the envelope and pulled out a plain white sheet of paper folded into quarters. Who was quick enough to have sent her flowers already? And what appeared to be a random homemade card? Nicole and Mindy weren't even here.

The outside of the card showed a clumsily drawn cartoon dog with a speech bubble stating, "Sorry to hear you're having a *ruff* day." The inside of the card was blank except for a single black pawprint. The pawprint was missing a toe. Just like Rosie.

She dropped the card. Her heart monitor went berserk. Her lungs seized. The blood in her veins ran cold with ice. An animalistic, blood-curdling scream escaped her lips.

Luke slammed the door open, looking frantic. "What? What's wrong? Are you okay?" he asked.

"Mom—I have to go. I'm fine. I just saw a spider, sorry. Please stay in Palm Springs. I'll call you later. Love you, bye." Claire pressed the end button and waved the card violently at Luke.

He read the message scrawled inside.

"Is that—?"

"Luke, who has Rosie?" The panic made her voice several octaves higher than usual.

"Kyle. I'm calling now."

As he went out into the hallway, Claire pinched the paper between two fingers and set it back on her bedside table. A small row of letters were printed at the bottom. What did they say? She squinted and fought to focus her vision. "From the Desk of Lucas Islestorm" was printed at the bottom. Her heart monitor beeped frantically. She upended her purse in a frantic search for Detective Smith's business card and dialed his number.

"Detective Smith? Hi, this is Claire Hartley. I have something you need to look at. I'm in West Haven Hospital, and someone sent me flowers and a card, and they added a paw print in ink at the bottom. And the paw print...it's missing a toe. Just like Rosie's right paw."

After Detective Smith confirmed that he would leave right away, Claire hung up the phone.

"Luke!" she shouted.

Luke ran into the room again, clutching his phone to his ear. "She's been in the ballroom the whole time? Oh, thank god. Kyle, I need you to check her paws. Yeah, it looks like one of them was stamped—Her right paw? Shit," he said, running his fingers through his hair. It stuck straight up as though he had been electrocuted.

"What do you mean the power was out?" He sat in the chair next to Claire's bed, head in his hands. "I never leave that door unlocked. Kyle, you need to get out of there now. Take Rosie and go. He could still be in the house."

After another minute, Luke hung up the phone.

"What the hell happened?" Claire asked, leaning forward.

"Kyle said the power went out, so he went into the basement to check the breakers. The basement door that leads to the side yard was hanging open, and the door to the closet where the fuse box is was locked. I never lock that door. Eventually, he found the key to unlock it, and when he cracked it open the main breaker was flipped. By the time he got upstairs, twenty minutes had gone by."

"Did you see the back of the card?" She pointed to the inscription.

He swore. "I can't believe this asshole was in my house. I

can't remember if I locked the office door. If I didn't, he'll have seen all the research. He probably destroyed everything."

Her heart was still beating chaotically. She breathed in ragged gasps, willing the tunnel vision to subside. "That fucker touched my dog."

"I'm so sorry." Luke reached out and took her hand.

"He's going to pay."

CHAPTER TWENTY-THREE

To Do:
- Figure out who the Widowmaker is once and for all
- Nail his ass to the wall
- Consider sending Rosie to Florida until all this
is over

HOURS LATER, CLAIRE SAT NUMBLY IN A WHEELCHAIR AS A nurse escorted her to the front doors of the hospital. Panel after panel of fluorescent light flashed by. A doctor scurried into a room with a harried look on her face. Dr. Weaver had been quite startled to learn that Claire was actually being targeted by a psychopath and wasn't just inventing a vibrant backstory due to head trauma. He and her nurse had apologized and brought her a cupcake from the cafeteria. Because that was how you apologized to someone for discounting their trauma as imagined. A hospital fucking cupcake.

The world outside the windows was pitch black as they

made their slow progress to the exit. The only bright spot in this hospital was Luke carrying her Kate Spade purse. He left her momentarily to bring his truck around, and the nurse stood protectively at her back.

Claire probed the dark corners of the parking lot. Was the Widowmaker here, even now? Standing in the darkness, waiting for his next move? What would be his next move? She shuddered and zipped the hoodie that Luke had fetched from his car.

The police had confiscated the note and flowers as evidence and grilled the security department about the camera on that floor. The flowers had been delivered to the nurses' station by a local florist. An officer had driven to the flower shop to question the owner. The police had also searched Luke's house from top to bottom and had found no sign of anyone.

Claire's stomach twinged at the thought of leaving the hospital. Her apartment wasn't safe. Luke's house wasn't safe. What was left? She sure as hell wasn't going to Florida. Not with Nicole's proposal imminent.

Luke pulled up in his beat-up black truck. Claire pushed herself up from the wheelchair. Why was the world tilting? Stupid planet couldn't get its shit together. When Luke reached her, he scooped her up into his arms.

"Hey. I'm not an invalid. I can walk," she said, struggling weakly to escape his arms.

"The last time you were upright, you knocked an expensive bookend onto your skull." He opened the passenger door with little difficulty and deposited her in her seat. He set her purse on the floor next to her feet. She snatched it up into her arms. Nobody put Kate on the floor.

"That was your fault," she muttered as he belted her in.

He closed her door, and she flinched. The sound was

like a thousand cymbals crashing next to her ear. When she leaned back, the seat poked her stitches. Groaning, she tilted forward so that her head didn't make contact with anything. It pounded. Did her heart somehow relocate to her skull? She could feel every heartbeat pulsing in her eyeballs.

Luke hadn't gotten into the truck. He was pacing outside the driver's side, talking on the phone. He glanced in at Claire, turned his back to her. His hushed tones emanated through the truck clear as day.

"Yeah. I don't know what to do. I think I can keep her safer at my house. The police said everything is clear, but I want to see for myself. I'll sit up all night if I have to. I don't want her to be alone anymore until they find this asshole."

He listened for a moment. "The power was cut, so there won't be much security camera footage to check. The asshole knew what he was doing. I knew I should have gotten a backup generator."

Luke slid his phone back into his pocket and climbed into the driver's seat. The truck stuttered as it started up, like it had been woken from a deep sleep.

"That was Kyle checking up. He said Nicole offered to keep you for the night, but I told him you're staying with me."

As annoyed as she was to have her friends offer to "keep" her, she couldn't face her empty apartment tonight. "That's probably for the best. It's probably Paint-Your-Own-Stained-Glass night in the Collins household," she said, closing her eyes and bracing her head against the cool glass of the window. "But we will be FaceTiming Rosie before bed, and I am picking her up tomorrow."

"Does anything sound good to you food-wise?"

She considered for a moment. "Sushi."

"Sushi it is." The truck shuddered as he pulled out of the hospital.

Claire dug in her purse and glanced at her phone. She groaned.

"Are you in pain? Do you want some ibuprofen until we get your prescription?" He glanced over at her and rubbed her leg.

She threw her phone back into her purse. "Thirty-seven texts, eleven missed calls, and four voicemails. Three of which are from my mother."

"Ouch." He grimaced. "I told Kyle to talk to Nicole, and she can talk to Mindy. That covers those bases. Do you want me to talk to your mom?"

"Oh god, no. Then she'd be asking me why there's a man in my life that I haven't told her about and—uh, not that you're a man in my life." She squirmed a bit in her seat. "I mean you are a man, and you're in my life, but you're...just... well, yeah. She wouldn't take that so well."

He frowned as they entered the pharmacy's parking lot. "Right. I'm going to pick up your prescription. Do you want anything from inside?"

"I think I'm set. Thanks, Luke." She squeezed his hand. Even though he was a bossy know-it-all who had hidden an unforgiveable secret from her, and he had almost killed her with a stupid, poorly secured bookend, and he put that goddamn tandem bike in her proposal at the last second... wait, what were they talking about again?

She shook her head, trying to clear the cotton that seemed to be lodged in it. "Take this." She pulled her wallet out and waved her credit card at him.

"Nice try." He completely ignored her offering.

Claire frowned. "Take my card, dammit," she called as he shut his door.

He ignored her and locked the doors. His head cocked, and he turned to look over his shoulder as if checking to make sure she hadn't suddenly bolted. He met her eyes and shot her a slow smile as he stepped inside and disappeared behind a tampon display.

The memory of the day's painful events evaporated. All that was left was the panty-searing sensation of Luke's hands on her body. And the kiss—hot damn, that kiss. Surely the medical emergency would have erased the back sweat from his memory, right?

The lights of the pharmacy burned into the car, punishing her retinas and stabbing a pickaxe into her brain. She fished a pair of sunglasses out of her purse and slid them on. Much better.

Luke came back ten minutes later with a bottle of birch beer and a paper bag. He handed both to Claire. "You can take one now, and then another one in four hours. Oh, and your pharmacist says hello and to feel better. He also said to tell you he and Martha are having a baby."

"*What?* Oh my gosh, this is so exciting. I planned the cutest proposal for them two years ago. They went kayaking in Saylor Lake and all these synchronized swimmers popped out of the lake and—let me just make a note to send a congratulations card after I get this stupid bottle open."

She groped weakly at the child-resistant bottle. He tried to take it from her, but she swatted his hand away and squeezed hard, eventually unscrewing the top.

"Isn't this a heavy-duty narcotic?" she asked, popping the oval tablet in her mouth and washing it down with a swig of birch beer. "And how did you know I liked this soda, anyway? Have you been stalking me, too? Wait, what am I saying? Of course you are. I found you outside my window in the middle of the night."

He laughed. "It's Pennsylvania, everyone likes birch beer. And secondly, yes. You're probably going to be feeling pretty great in about twenty minutes. I'll be watching you carefully to make sure you don't try to drive a forklift until you're off the medicine."

"I'll drive a forklift if I want to," she grumbled, staring out the window with a frown. Hmm, a forklift proposal. She should do some scouting to see if any warehouse workers were looking to get engaged. "Stupid bottle can't tell me what to do."

As they drove away from the pharmacy, Claire settled back in her seat and began replying to the flood of text messages and emails on her phone. After twenty frazzling minutes, she tossed her phone into her bag and leaned her head against the cool glass.

Luke laid a hand on her leg and rubbed her knee with his thumb. Her whole body tingled at his touch. "Sorry about the head wound."

She shrugged. "I was completely okay with what was going on before my awesomeness affected the gravitational pull of the earth and sent that bookend hurtling into my skull."

"You lost a lot of blood. You were so pale by the time I got you into the truck. I probably should have called an ambulance, but the only thing I could think of was getting you to the hospital as fast as possible." His grip on her knee tightened.

"Did I bleed in your truck?" She turned her head to look but stopped when a jolt of pain seared through her head.

"I put a towel down," he admitted sheepishly.

A rough terry cloth scratched her cheek. "You're lucky it was me who found out about your poorly secured decorative household item. If that would have fallen on Nicole during the proposal, I would have been forced to kill you."

"I would expect nothing else."

"Can I ask you something?" Her phone buzzed again, but she ignored it.

"I suppose." He crawled to a stop at a red light and turned toward her.

"You're a well-off guy."

"Was that a question?"

"I wasn't done. You clearly like nice things. Why do you drive a truck that's a million years old?"

Luke went silent. His mouth hardened into a thin line. Uh-oh. Note to self—do not ask about the truck.

"It was my dad's."

Was? Had he passed away? This was what she got for not doing an in-depth internet stalk on her contracted employees. "I'm sorry for insulting your truck. It's a good truck. I can tell." She slapped the dash and stared at her hand under the moonlight. She wiggled her fingers. There were still five, right? Something strange was happening in her body. Why couldn't she stop smiling? Luke was trying to open up about his possibly dead dad.

"You want to know something kind of funny?" Was he changing the subject?

"What's that?" Claire's head was fuzzy again, but this time it was more pleasant, like she was floating through cotton candy clouds. She put her hand out in front of her and just stared at it.

"I'm pretty sure I got everything that happened in the ballroom on camera."

"Everything? Even the—"

"Yep," he said, nodding as he turned into the town's

second-best sushi restaurant, which for some reason had a drive-thru.

She smiled. "You should edit that before sending it out. Promise me. I don't want to scar anyone for life."

"With your boobs or your blood?"

"Either. Both." She stared at her hand again. Swirls formed over her knuckles. Was her skin coming alive? What the hell was in that medicine? She flipped her hands over, studying her palms. No swirls. She was losing it.

Luke grinned at her as he ordered their food. She crawled over his lap to present a card to the cashier, demanding to pay.

"That's a gift card for Sephora, Claire." He shook his head and buckled her seatbelt again, then set the bags of shrimp tempura on her lap. As they drove away, he reached over and rested his hand on her knee again.

Knee-stroking, making-out-against-a-stack-of-books Luke was so much more tolerable than Luke the Filmmaker/Bike Sneaker.

When they reached a red light, he turned to look at her. "How's your head?"

She flashed him a goofy smile. "You know, it's actually great. I feel like I could run a marathon. Okay, maybe a half marathon. Do you think I should try? Oh, or maybe Steve would let me borrow his Jet Ski. Have you ever ridden one? Steve did a backflip on his. He looked like he was flying. Are we flying? We're flying. This truck is actually a magic carpet, isn't it? Tell the truth." She leaned over and poked him right in the face.

"Yes, you're right." He pressed a button. There was a *thunk* as all the doors in the truck locked. "This is actually a magic carpet. I borrowed it from the Middle East for Nicole's proposal."

"Oh, Nicole! I love her. Not in like a lesbian way, although there was this time in college where we...is that a *gorilla*?" She pressed her face to the glass as they passed by a car dealership with an enormous gorilla. It was probably inflated, right? Not real. Maybe... "Holy shit. Someone needs to tell the president that King Kong is in West Haven. You know the military. Do you have the National Guard on speed dial?"

Luke was laughing at something—her?—as he pulled into his driveway. He turned the truck off and got out.

Her cheek tingled, and she scratched at it but didn't feel anything. She poked at her nose. Nothing.

He opened her door. "So, you were saying about that time in college?"

"I can't feel this. Should I be able to feel this?" She jabbed her finger into her cheek.

"That's just the medicine, Claire." He took her hand and set it in her lap. "Now *please* stay here while I take this to the kitchen. I need to take a quick look around the house to make sure that everything is safe. But then I'm going to be right back to help you inside. Do not get out of your seat," he said sternly.

"Oh, right. 'Cause murderers. Carry on, constable." She held up her hands as proof of her innocence.

As soon as Luke disappeared inside, however, she fought wildly with her seatbelt until it came unbuckled. She escaped the vehicle and ran into the yard, hands flailing at her sides. What a beautiful night. The stars were out, the crickets were chirping. Her matted hair clung to her face as she spun around in circles before drunkenly jogging at a sideways tilt to the garage. She dodged a punching bag suspended on the rafters. Two sawhorses stood in the middle of the open space, supporting a thick wooden board marked with pencil.

"Nice horsey," she whispered, stroking the unfinished plank with one hand. "Don't be scared. I'm not here to hurt you."

She lifted her leg over the board and straddled it. Her toes barely brushed the ground. She hummed the *William Tell Overture* to herself, bouncing on the board. Luke's tools swam pleasantly in front of her eyes.

"Luke!" she exclaimed when he rushed around the corner of the garage. "There's something wrong with your horse. I think he's malnourished. And he's pooping sawdust." She leaned over and frowned at the piles on the floor.

She began to slide off the board, but Luke caught her before she hit the floor. Despite her protests, he scooped her up and carried her inside the house like a groom bringing his bride home.

"Hey," she pouted, stretching her arms back toward the outside. "We have to feed the horses. Hay. Hahaha." She laughed to herself. "Oh, excuse me, sir," she apologized to a coat rack and saluted.

"You have the neatest house," she said, reaching out to touch the granite countertop on the island as he carried her past the kitchen.

Luke shook his head and turned her sideways to carry her up the stairs.

"You know, I'm getting kind of sleepy." She rubbed her eyes, then looked at her hand and gasped. "What the hell is this black gash on my hand? Is this that flesh-eating bacteria? What kind of pills did they give me?"

"It's eyeliner," he promised as he placed her gently in the middle of the bed. He brought over a dinner tray, then set out her sushi, folding a napkin to the side and dumping a small amount of soy sauce into a dish. "Eat," he said.

She unwrapped her chopsticks and looked at them, utterly bewildered.

"Look, Luke, they gave us wood with our fish." She put one in each hand and attempted to pinch a slice of California roll between them. It toppled from the wooden instruments and plopped into her puddle of soy sauce. Shrugging, she used her hands instead and took intermittent bites between making her chopsticks dance. A generic sitcom filled the room with canned laughter.

Luke scarfed down his shrimp tempura from a chair in the corner of the room.

Claire startled awake to him pulling a clump of rice out of her hair. When did she fall asleep? She had to play it cool. He probably didn't even notice she was sleeping.

"Are we going shopping?" she asked, staring at him with one eye open.

"Yes, Claire. We're going shopping."

"'Kay. I have coupons."

A moment later, she frowned and sat up. "No."

"No what?" He crouched down.

"No pants." She shuffled her legs under the covers, kicking and wiggling until a pair of shorts fell out from under the covers and landed on the navy blue area rug.

Luke chuckled and shook his head. "Sweet dreams." He leaned over to press a gentle kiss to her forehead.

"Don't put the rabbits in there," she mumbled. "'S not Labor Day." Then she drifted into a very deep sleep.

CHAPTER TWENTY-FOUR

To Do:
- *Throw away damned medicine*
- *Pick up Rosie and never put her down again*
- *Send coffee and donuts to the hospital*

CLAIRE OPENED HER EYES. WHERE THE HELL WAS SHE? WHAT day was it?

She jolted upright, a lightning bolt of pain radiating from her scalp. Rosie wasn't here. Luke was asleep in a chair in the corner of the room. The metal baseball bat was next to him. Silky sheets rubbed against her bare legs. Where were her pants? She whipped the covers off and stared at her ostentatious choice of underwear—an electric blue thong. She slid out of bed and turned to face the windows, pulling on her yoga shorts.

"Morning," Luke said from behind her. He was shirtless,

painted with the gold light of the early morning like a Greek god.

She tugged the waistband of her shorts to cover the lacy underwear. Her face was hot. At least it wasn't granny panties this time. "Morning," she said, running her fingers through her hair. It was a hopeless mess, still matted with blood in some places. She might as well shave the rest of it off and start fresh.

"How do you feel?"

"Like hell." She gingerly touched the bandage that covered her stitches. Shit, had she bled onto Luke's pillows? She was going to have to buy him a whole new set of pillowcases.

"More meds?" he asked, getting out of the chair and stretching. Those damn gray sweatpants were back, clinging loosely to his hips.

She tried not to stare as she shook her head. "No way. That stuff made me so loopy yesterday. Did I ride your sawhorse?" She frowned.

"You did do that. And a myriad of other things. I wish I had gotten them on camera." He smirked.

She sat on the edge of the bed again, clutching her head. It wasn't funny. "Yes, I'm sure it would have been a thrilling addition to the documentary."

Luke put his hands up. "I didn't mean—"

"It's fine," she interrupted. "Did I imagine it, or did Kyle walk in on us yesterday?"

He walked behind her to check the gauze on her head. "Yep. We should be able to take this off now. Come with me." He pulled her into the bathroom.

Her shoulders hunched up around her ears. "Oh god. So, everyone probably already knows that we—"

"Probably." He washed his hands and then sat her on

the sink. So much for avoiding the drama. There were probably a thousand texts on her phone from Mindy and Nicole.

"We should really do a more thorough sweep of your house today. I don't have a lot of faith in the police these days." She picked up her phone and sent a video chat request to Kyle's number as Luke fussed with her scalp.

"I checked last night after you fell asleep. I didn't see much, but I'll show you the tapes that I gave to the police."

She shuddered. Did she really want to see it? Kyle answered the video call, still in bed and obviously only half awake.

"Morning," he said.

"Hey, Kyle. Sorry for calling so early. I just wanted to check on Rosie."

"What's Luke doing to you?" Kyle asked, clearly puzzled. The view changed as he climbed out of bed and went to his living room.

"Just checking my stitches from yesterday."

Luke peeled the gauze off. "Looks good," he said, tossing the material into the trashcan.

"Want some pain meds that aren't going to cause you to ride household objects?" he asked as Kyle went in search of Rosie.

"Please."

Rosie came into the frame. She was lying on a blanket in a pool of early morning sunshine and refused to wake up when Kyle stuck the phone in her furry little face.

"There's my little RoRo," Claire cooed. "She's just sleeping right? She's not in a coma or anything? She's been through a trauma."

Kyle picked up one of Rosie's paws and dropped it. It merely flopped back to its original position.

"She's tuckered out. Rosie, do you want some cheese?" Kyle called in an exaggerated happy voice.

Rosie sprang to her feet and wagged her stump of a tail so hard it nearly knocked her over.

"Thank you for letting me see her. I'll come get her after I talk my mom off the ledge. I'll text you."

"It's no problem." Kyle yawned into the camera. "Listen, I'm really sorry about yesterday. I had no idea that someone had broken in. I thought Luke was just an idiot and left the door open. I would never put Rosie in danger."

Claire's breath hitched. "It's not your fault. I'm sorry for putting you and Nicole and, well, everyone in danger just by associating with me. I'll see you soon."

After they hung up, the phone pinged, showing that her notifications had nearly doubled from the night before.

"Oh no. Do you mind if I make some calls? My mom is losing her shit," she said.

Luke laughed as he covered her wound with antibacterial ointment and fresh gauze then handed her some ibuprofen. "The balcony would be a great place for that." He pointed to the sliding doors next to his dresser.

"Thank you," she mouthed, dialing. Her mother picked up on the first ring.

She didn't emerge from the balcony for another hour. She sat on a padded chair, enjoying the warm breeze and the smell of grass as she spoke to her mom, two vendors for the upcoming proposal, Nicole, and Mindy. She glanced over her shoulder as she recounted some of the juicier details on a video chat to Nicole and Mindy. Luke appeared to have vacated the bedroom.

"I know." Claire propped her legs on the balcony railing for some much needed sun. "He's still the worst and I'm still mad at him, but holy shit is he an amazing kisser. Nothing like with being with Jason. It was so hot." Her skin tingled at the memory.

"To be clear, there was no stopwatch involved?" Mindy teased.

"Not that I could see."

"I knew this would happen. Does this mean you're considering giving up your sex embargo?" Mindy asked. She was in her bathroom, doing her makeup. Gavin's still-sleeping body was barely visible through a crack in the door behind her.

"No. Well, I don't know. He's so complicated. And I have bigger things to worry about right now."

Her stomach clenched. In her drug-addled state, she had nearly forgotten the Widowmaker had prowled around this very house less than twenty-four hours ago. What had Luke's security tapes shown?

"Oh my god, I almost forgot after all the sexy talk. What did the police say?" Nicole asked.

"They took the note and flowers and are going to test for DNA and fingerprints and whatever else they can, I guess. But it won't amount to anything. The florist said a nine-year-old boy came into the store with a hand-drawn card. He kept looking out the window, and he had a roll of cash in his pocket and a piece of paper with instructions. Creep must have paid him off to come inside and order them. They already went through Luke's place but didn't find a thing besides the door hanging open in the basement."

"Oh, Claire. I'm so sorry. They're going to catch this guy. Or girl. This creeper," Mindy corrected.

"That's the thing, Min. I'm not even sure that the police care. It's blatantly obvious to me and everyone else that all these disappearances are connected, but they just keep denying it. I just want this creep out of my life before he hurts my mom. Or Rosie. Or you guys."

Suddenly, the sun-drenched balcony didn't feel as safe. She stood, surveying the land. Nothing looked out of the ordinary, but she lowered her voice nonetheless and sat with her back pressed against the wall. She flipped off the backyard for good measure.

"Crap, guys, I have to go. Rosie just took an entire block of cheese from the countertop." Nicole disconnected, and her video disappeared.

"Can we meet at ten tomorrow at the office and go over everything we still need for Nicole's proposal?" Claire asked Mindy. "I'm planning to play the guilt card this week to get Luke to let me store the rest of the decorations at his place. He did almost kill me with a bookend."

"Sounds good. Be careful. And text me if you want to stay with me tonight."

"Thanks, Min." Claire ended the call. She opened the sliding glass door and crept back into Luke's bedroom. He wasn't there, but the amazing aroma of bacon wound its way seductively into the room.

She took a few minutes to brush her teeth, wash her face, and gingerly French braid her hair before walking downstairs. On the bright side, she could hardly see the gauze through the plait. Apparently, she was going to be Frenching it for a while.

Luke, still shirtless, was just setting what appeared to be stuffed and rolled French toast onto plates with bacon. It took a bold person to cook bacon shirtless. He smiled when she came in. "How did it go?"

Claire shook her head. "My mother actually cried, but she's stopped trying to leave Palm Springs. Nicole and Mindy were just glad that I'm not dead."

He set a plate in front of her and sifted some powdered sugar over the toast.

"I'm pretty glad you aren't dead too. Just think of what it would do to my insurance." A bottle of maple syrup slid down the length of the island where it stopped next to her plate.

"Don't tell me. In addition to serving your country and creating documentaries, you also secretly bartend?"

"You bet. That's how you meet important people in California."

"Seriously?"

"Yep. It's how I met the guy who funded my first project."

"Wow," she said. "Is there anything you can't do?"

"For some infuriating reason, I can't seem to get you out of my head." He tossed a dishtowel over his shoulder as he transferred the rest of the bacon onto some paper towels. "But that's about it."

Her stomach clenched, and a warmth spread between her legs. Oh, no. Do something. Talk about the food. "This looks amazing. Is that stuffed French toast?"

"With cream cheese and strawberries," he said, setting the pan in the sink.

She clutched at her heart. "I needed this," she said. "Thank you."

He dug some silverware out and sat next to her.

Claire smiled as they ate in comfortable silence. The powdered sugar melted on her tongue.

"You look exhausted." She brushed her thumb over a dark circle under his eye. Her skin tingled, and she pulled her hand back. "Do you ever sleep?"

"I stayed up most of the night editing the video for the dance. I sent it out to the contact list you gave me."

"But I didn't even get to look at it," she protested.

"It's fine, trust me. Control freak," he teased, booping her on the nose with one finger. "Besides, I had to make sure you didn't wake up in the middle of the night and climb up to the roof to catch a star or whatever whim your drug-addled brain would be chasing."

She sighed. "Fine." She stood and collected their plates. She deposited them in the dishwasher, and then glanced around the room. "Is it awful? Knowing he was in here?"

Luke's eyes narrowed. "It feels dirty."

If her mom were here, she would find the world's largest bundle of sage. "I know what you mean. My apartment felt the same way. Did you check your office last night?"

"It was still locked. It doesn't look like anything was missing or moved. I keep that stationery all over the house, so he could have gotten it from anywhere."

She shivered. "Can we do some more murder brainstorming? I feel like I need to do something, to take control of this situation. I have an hour or so before I need to leave."

"Yes. Definitely." He stood and took her hand. "Let's go to my office."

Luke settled into his desk chair and swiveled toward her. "Any new thoughts since we last discussed?"

"No, and it's killing me. I can't think of anyone who would have the motivation to do this. Jason's the only person I can think of who would have enough reason to want to kill me. Or Wendy, I guess. Maybe they're working together. I put together a little chart." She hefted the new murder binder out of her purse and thunked it onto his desk. She flipped to a new section of notes bound in sheet protectors. "This is the general breakdown of my theory, including motive, means, and opportunity."

Luke raised his eyebrows.

"What? I watched a couple of episodes of *Mysterious*

Murders. Anyway, I have to admit, motive is a tough sell here. It kind of makes sense for him to want to kill me, but I don't understand what he would want with the other girls. I don't remember him ever mentioning even one of them."

She jabbed at another part of the page. "We don't know how, or even if, the girls were killed, so means is also hard to prove, though Jason's large size and history of participation in football make it likely that he would be capable of overpowering another, smaller person."

"You're talking like a cop."

She took a breath and pointed to the last section. "Whatever. As for opportunity, he was unemployed for most of our relationship."

"He had all the time in the world," Luke observed, pulling her notes out of the binder and photocopying them. He tacked the new sheets under the suspects section. "And the rest of the pages?"

"Handwriting samples from some cards I forgot to burn, and pictures I took of the notes before the police confiscated them."

"Not bad," he said. Was it her imagination, or did he actually look impressed?

"Like I said, I'm not convinced that Jason is the Widowmaker. Frankly, he's too lazy to murder five people, and he's not clever enough to hide the bodies. I do think the Widowmaker went to Venor, though. Did you manage to get the alumni lists?"

"Yes." Luke pointed at a binder on his shelf. "But there are thousands of names. I don't know how to narrow it down until Mindy gets that yearbook from Wyoming Valley. I'm fairly certain that we're looking for a man, but what if it's not?" He stood behind the desk, his hands clasped behind his head, and stared at the walls covered in pictures.

"I've seen crazier shit from Wendy than any human male," Claire conceded. "She for sure would love for me to die. She's too posh to be a murderer, but that doesn't mean she wouldn't pay someone to do it or enlist Jason's help. She didn't go to Venor, though, and I don't think she knows the other girls. There's no motivation there. What was that big break you mentioned you had with a witness a few weeks ago?"

"I spoke with some of Courtney's neighbors. A near-sighted old lady down the street told me that every few days for two months a black sedan with tinted windows would park in front of her house, right around the time that Courtney would go for her runs. She told me that every time Courtney went back inside after her run, the car would drive away. Like it was just waiting for her, watching. So that confirms that Courtney didn't run away."

"Her husband said she was really excited about a promotion at work," Claire muttered to herself. "It wouldn't have made sense for her to run away with that on the horizon."

Luke's eyes snapped up. "Wait, you talked to her husband?"

"I ran into him." In his driveway, but he didn't need to know that. "We're acquaintances."

"Why didn't you tell me?"

Claire shot him a dirty look. "You seriously want to use my connections to interrogate a grieving widower?"

"That's not what I meant" Luke held his hands up defensively. "I'm not that much of an asshole, geeze. It's relevant to the motivation."

"Mmhmm. So why didn't the nosey neighbor call the cops about this mysterious black sedan?"

"She did. She called the police about the car about a

week before Courtney disappeared, but the car took off before they made it there. She even had the license plate number of the car. The police ran the plates, but I guess they were fake."

"Wow. So, we're dealing with someone smart and creepy with a lot of time on their hands."

"It seems that way. There have been studies done on serial killers. Dozens of them." He started to pace. "Most of them suggest a certain degree of similarity between serial killers in their motives and characteristics. They're usually young—in their twenties or thirties when they start. They usually look for victims locally. They often know their victims. That fits our profile. They're smart. They sometimes have a period of religious fanaticism, so I was looking into the member lists for campus clubs that fit the bill. That was a dead end. A lot of serial killers are found to have tumultuous family problems, like no father figure, but in today's day and age that's commonplace."

"Plus, there are always people who break the mold." She leaned against the wall.

"Exactly. There are too many variables. And since they've never found any bodies, we don't know how he killed them or whether he abused them before death. We don't know if it was sexually motivated. We don't know anything." He pounded his fist on his desk.

She covered his hand with hers. He was arguably more upset about this than her, and she was the one being targeted by the psycho. "I mean, he took my underwear. That sounds like a sexual motivation. We'll figure it out. Someone has to." A plan was forming in her mind. But there was no way she was going to tell Luke about it.

"I think you should tell the police about Jason."

"It's just a hunch. There's probably nothing concrete there."

"Either way, it could give them a new angle."

Claire glanced at her watch. "You're probably right. I'll call Detective Smith on my way home. I should get going. I have a ton of stuff to prepare for a meeting with Mindy tomorrow. But I'll keep you posted on anything else I come up with."

Luke stood. "Claire, you can't drive. You have a concussion."

Would the inconveniences never end? Her hands balled into fists. She loathed having to rely on other people. "Do you have time to take me home?"

"Of course. We'll take your car and I'll have Kyle pick me up."

"Just try not to make out with me again when he shows up. My skull can't take it."

"No guarantees."

"FINALLY," CLAIRE MUTTERED HOURS LATER. NICOLE SNORED lightly on the pillow next to her.

She glanced at her watch. It was just after midnight. Go time.

Claire put one foot on the floor and then slithered out of bed. Her Taser sat on the bedside table. She took it with her and crawled on her hands and knees over to the bedroom door. The knob clicked loudly as she turned, but Nicole was a deep sleeper.

She took a step into the hallway and turned. Rosie was sprawled on her back like a furry, twisted pretzel. Moonlight streamed down on Nicole's sleeping form. She hesitated at the sight of her best friend, unconscious and unaware. Nicole was getting engaged at the end of next week. What if getting engaged put her in the Widowmaker's crosshairs? She went to Venor, she knew Claire. If the Widowmaker really was Jason, hurting her best friends would be one of the most savage ways to get to her.

Her heart thumped in her chest. The Widowmaker had taken enough from her. There were too many people she loved in this world, too much at stake. Tonight, she was going to fight back. She was going to hunt a killer.

She slid open the doors of her hallway closet. There it was—her hoarder trench coat. Underneath its khaki exterior it concealed seventeen pockets. Half of them were filled with stale dog treats and rolls of poo bags. She really needed to take it to the dry cleaner. Later. For now, it went with her to the kitchen and was hung on a drawer pull.

"Okay, what do we have here?" She opened several drawers and pulled out a paring knife, a butcher knife, a corkscrew, and an egg slicer. She tucked them into the pockets of the trench coat along with the Taser and some zip ties left over from the stakeout. Another drawer held pepper spray.

"Damn it."

Jason, after drinking a fifth of whiskey on a dare, had sprayed it in her apartment the previous spring, sending everyone in the room choking and sputtering into the hallway. She had never replaced it.

She tucked her phone in her bra in case she was abducted during her mission and shrugged into the coat. Hopefully, the butcher knife wouldn't stab through the pocket and chop her toe off. That would be hard to explain.

The last thing she grabbed was a heavy-duty flashlight that could do some serious damage if used as a weapon. She slid on a pair of tennis shoes and a floppy black hat she hadn't used since her last trip to the beach. She snuck out the front door and locked it behind her. The egg slicer rattled as she box-stepped down the hallway and pirouetted for good measure.

Outside, West Haven was suspiciously calm. A handful of vehicles passed by on Beaumont Street. It was time to revisit Buchanan Park. She slunk down the sidewalk, sticking to the shadows. The flashlight was heavy in her hand.

The common threads between all the victims stories were the flowers, the break-ins, and the black sedan with tinted windows. She couldn't stake out every florist in the entire city indefinitely. She couldn't do anything to stop the break-ins. But she could go find the black sedan. She had told Detective Smith about the sedan theory, but he hadn't seemed impressed.

She probed the cars parked along Beaumont. White Ford. Red Saturn. Silver Honda. No black sedans in sight.

Jason drove a green Acura, so at least she didn't have to worry about him. Though maybe she should do some surveillance on him just in case. Maybe Wendy had a black car that he periodically borrowed for creeping.

Was that footsteps behind her? She stopped abruptly in the middle of the sidewalk. She couldn't be sure, but it sounded like there was an extra footstep after she stopped. Should she bend down and tie her shoe and let them pass? Maybe there wasn't anyone there. She kept walking. There were storefronts ahead.

She paused in front of a store and pretended to browse the steel-toed boots in the window. There were definitely footsteps coming from down the sidewalk. She reached into one of her pockets and pulled out the paring knife. The footsteps stopped and changed direction as the pedestrian behind her turned off down a side street. Claire relaxed her grip on the knife and resumed her search.

The cars parked on Beaumont Street ranged from mini-vans to sports cars to SUVs. Some of them were black, but none of them had tinted windows. Maybe the Widowmaker lived near the park? She should check the residential blocks to the north.

She rounded the walking path at Buchanan Park and cut through the grass where she had tackled Rick days before. She didn't feel eyes on her this time. Maybe the Widow-maker was binge watching something on Netflix. Even murderers needed a source of entertainment besides murdering, right?

Bramble Drive was lined with modest ranch houses and cracked asphalt driveways. The cars were a little older, a bit more beat-up than the ones on Beaumont Street. She shined her flashlight up the dark driveways and decided to cut down an alley. One of the houses had a backyard that over-looked part of the park. The windows were dark. Was that a black sedan next to that overflowing trash can? Were the windows tinted? She squinted. A six foot chain-link fence blocked her path. Very large, partially destroyed dog toys were scattered in the yard. Maybe she could just get a bit closer.

She scanned the front of the property, but the entire lot was contained by the fence. How the hell did they get the car out? There must be a gate somewhere, but she didn't have time to dilly-dally. The flashlight's beam couldn't quite reach the license plate or give her a good look at the windows. She stuck her hand through the fence and fed the flashlight through. Still not close enough. She looked at the top of the fence. This was a bad idea. But what if this was his house? What if the only thing standing between her and the safety of her friends and family—not to mention justice for five missing women—was this stupid fence?

Claire clamped the flashlight in her mouth and put her fingers on the fence. She shook it. It was sturdy enough to hold her weight. She attempted to cram the toe of her Keds into a link a foot off the ground. Damn it. If she had worn her pointed-toe stilettos, she'd have been over this stupid thing already. That's what she got for choosing sensible footwear. She wiggled her toe until she could gain enough purchase to take a step. She repeated the toe-cramming process until she hit the top of the fence. The links wobbled back and forth as she considered her next move.

Maybe this was close enough? She grasped the fence with one hand and pulled the flashlight out of her mouth. She leaned over the top rail and extended her arm as far as it would go. The beam still didn't reach. Damn it! She climbed a bit higher and swung one leg over. The top of the fence had jagged links. If she took a wrong step, she would almost certainly rip her pants...or something worse.

At that moment, a siren woop-wooped behind her. She screamed. Red and blue lights illuminated her and flashed off the neighboring walls and fences. Well, shit. Wendy was going to love this. Wait, should she put her hands up? She was technically trespassing. She wasn't about to get shot.

Her hands flew in the air. The flashlight tumbled to the ground and hit hard. It broke apart and sent the batteries rolling into the weeds on the side of the alley. She was trapped, straddling the fence. But she would need her hands to climb down. Maybe if she just did it slowly. Why wasn't the officer getting out of the car? Were they calling for backup?

She lowered one hand and held the top of the fence. She

would just swing her leg back over. Nice and easy. No harm, no foul. She raised her right leg, but she was stuck on something. The fence had grabbed hold of her trench coat. Oh, no. This was not good.

The door of the cruiser slammed. Claire screamed and lurched. Her leg moved free of the fence, and she tumbled down the other side. *Riiiiiiip*. Her coat remained suspended as she collapsed to the ground. Seconds later, her Taser and the butcher knife landed around her.

"Miss Hartley?" Detective Smith stepped into the lights and knelt down next to her.

"Oh! Detective! I was—ouch." She clutched the back of her head. The fall had brought a whole new stabbing wave of pain.

"I know what you were doing. I wish you wouldn't." He extended a hand to her, helped her up. He glanced into the yard and nodded at the car. "That's not the one."

"How do you know?" Her trench hung from the fence in tatters. Did this mean he was taking her seriously? Was he going to arrest her? Would Kyle wake up if she called him for legal counsel?

"I've been looking into the angle. I realize you don't have a lot of faith in the police, but please know we are taking the threat against you very seriously. You don't need to investigate this yourself."

He knelt down and handed her the Taser. There was a clatter, and the egg slicer fell from the coat. He picked it up and held it out to her. "What exactly were you planning to do with this?"

She shrugged. "I ran out of pepper spray, so I had to have options."

Detective Smith chuckled and pulled a plastic evidence bag out of his coat. He piled the contents of her pockets inside. "You're spunky. Why don't I give you a ride home?"

"You're not going to arrest me?"

He pulled her coat—or what was left of it—from the fence and handed it to her. "You've been through a lot. I think we can let this one slide. But if I catch you investigating on your own again, I'm not going to be as lenient."

"Don't worry. I'll leave it to the professionals," she said as she climbed into the passenger seat of the cop car. And maybe she would. That was her only trench coat.

CHAPTER TWENTY-FIVE

To Do:
- Consider spying on J but don't get caught
- Cost comparison renting/owning fairy lights
- Pick up scrolls

"Okay," Claire said, pacing across the warehouse. "Let me run through the list one more time."

Pacing was the only way she could stay awake. After Detective Smith had dropped her off at the apartment, she had woken up every twenty minutes to check that the windows and door were still locked and to do a Google search for her name. So far, Wendy hadn't released the footage of Claire attacking Rick. It was only a matter of time. Maybe she could convince Jason to delete it.

On her way to the warehouse for her meeting with Mindy, she had taken the most roundabout, out of the way route to be sure she wasn't followed. At least it was a beautiful day. Aside from the sudden influx of pollen, the spring morning seemed at odds with her life circumstances. How could a serial killer prowl these streets with fresh flowers spilling out of window boxes? Did he stop at the walk-up window at Cheryl's Coffee House? Was he a macchiato man or a black coffee guy? Hiding from the Widowmaker was wearing on her soul. She absentmindedly touched her gauze, then snatched her fingers away. Luke had scolded her for doing this approximately thirty times since the accident.

She took a moment to breathe, bring herself back to the moment. "We have a crapton of boxes and packaging tape to give to the moving guys so we can avoid their materials fee." She pointed at a mountain of cardboard that stretched halfway up the wall. "And I'm meeting them at seven to direct as soon as she leaves for work."

Mindy made a check on a large whiteboard that detailed the individual tasks for Nicole's proposal. "And I called Sharice for hair and Judy for makeup, and they're going to meet us at the gym at four. They'll hide in the manager's office until Nicole comes out of the locker room. The seamstress is finishing up the alterations on the dress and said we can pick it up this Friday. They're going to steam it too."

"Awesome." Claire continued to pace. "And the shoes?"

Mindy walked over to a shelf along the wall marked N. She picked up a shoebox and brought it over to Claire, lifting the lid.

A pair of high heels covered entirely in rhinestones glittered under the overhead lights. "Is it weird that I'm kind of crazy jealous of these shoes?" Claire lifted one out of the box and turned it in her hand.

"No way. I was thinking about asking the manufacturer for two more pairs," Mindy said with a mischievous smile.

"Do it." They fist-bumped. "I can't believe we're four

days out." Claire shook her hands at her side. There was still so much to do.

"We're going to be fine," Mindy said. She was rarely rattled. "Everything's set up. We just need to move the rest of the decorations and candles to Luke's, check on the landscaping, check in with the family to make sure they're all learning the dance—which, by the way, that video was super-hot. The chemistry was so intense that I half expected my laptop to burst into flames."

Claire smiled. "He picked it up after only seeing me run through it twice. I was impressed and a little annoyed." She stared off into a corner of the warehouse for a moment and smiled to herself. "But anyway." She snapped back to attention. "What else is left? I'm leaving in twenty minutes to pick up the scavenger hunt clues on the scrolls from that artist on Fourth Street. Is the string quartet booked?"

Claire dug through her purse. Where the hell was that aspirin? She tossed a pack of breath mints, a stress ball, and her Taser on the conference table before successfully finding the bottle.

Mindy pushed back from the conference table. "Actually, there's been a bit of a change with the quartet."

A lead fist of dread sunk in Claire's stomach. "Oh god, what?"

"I cancelled them."

Claire stared at her. "Mindy. For the love of Chanel and all that is holy, what do you mean you cancelled them?"

"Don't freak out." Mindy held her hands out in front of her. "I cancelled them because something incredible happened."

Claire crossed her arms. "It better be a freakin' miracle. What?"

"Okay," Mindy said, pulling out a sheet of paper on

which she had scribbled a bunch of numbers. For someone who leaned toward the ditzy side of the spectrum, she was remarkably good with numbers. She handed them to Claire.

"If we go with our second-choice caterer instead, we can afford to have Monochrome Monday make a personal appearance and play the song live. And still come in just under budget."

Claire's mouth gaped. "He's going to be in town?"

"He just announced a special show at the Susquehanna Center the day before the proposal."

"Shut up," Claire said. She collapsed into a chair. "We got Monochrome Monday."

"We got Monochrome Monday."

Claire quickly recovered from her shock and grabbed Mindy's hands. They hopped in unison, dancing in a circle. Rosie abandoned her bone and ran over to nip at their heels. She didn't tolerate nonsense like jumping. Claire came to a halt and gently put the dog back on all fours. As she stood, her head ached like someone was squashing it into a meat grinder. This concussion shit had better clear up by proposal day.

"Stupid head wound. Did you tell Kyle?" she asked Mindy.

"This morning. He freaked out."

"I can't believe you waited so long to tell me!" She gripped Mindy's shoulders and shook her. Her glasses slid down her nose. "This is the best news I've heard since that deli with the bagels started delivering. Mindy, you are a goddess."

"I learned from the best," she said and flipped her clipboard back to the front page. "I'm going to move the tables and linens into the van as soon as you leave. Did Luke still say it's okay to come over this afternoon to start setting things up?"

"I think so. I'll text him." She pulled out her phone. "Oh, I have to tell him about Monochrome Monday."

"So." Mindy leaned oh-so-casually against their whiteboard. "If he's not around today, you have to tell me everything."

Claire glanced up. "I already told you everything."

"I know, but I want a reenactment."

Claire laughed. "You're weird."

Mindy slid her glasses down the bridge of her nose. "Did you make a formal decision? About the embargo?"

Claire groaned. She had been dreading this question. "I don't know. He's infuriating and egotistical and he lied to me. But he apologized in his own douche way and has really gone to great lengths to make it up to me. And he bought Rosie two dog beds. He's so smart and talented and stupidly hot. Do not tell him I said that." She pointed sternly at Mindy. "It's complicated. I'm going to table thinking about it until after Nicole's proposal."

Mindy smiled. "For the record, I think you balance each other out. You work well together. You're a romantic, he's a cynic. You're a planner, he's a 'visionary.'"

"Thank you for reminding me to add those unredeeming qualities to my list of reasons not to get involved."

"He's miles beyond Jason. No offense."

Claire glared at her. "We don't say his name. But you don't think it's too soon to be... considering moving on? He was going to be my husband."

Mindy rolled her eyes. "It's been what, nine months? Longer? Jason had the personality of a sack of potatoes. He could never keep up with you. That relationship was over for a long time before you actually called it quits. Plus, Luke's not on your list of Widowmaker suspects."

"I guess that's true." Her hackles raised at the memory of the last few months with Jason. He spent all his time sitting on the couch in his boxers, playing video games. He didn't help with dinner and claimed a mysterious dust allergy that precluded him from cleaning.

"I think he was depressed, though, you know? It's really hard when you graduate and can't find a job. And then there's the whole living with your girlfriend who's making more money than you thing."

Mindy snapped her tablet lid shut and folded her hands on the table. Her steady eye contact was almost unnerving. "Claire, it wasn't your fault. Jason had free will. He could have worked a part-time job to help out. He knew what he was doing when Wendy dragged him into the men's room. He was spiteful and conceited. And that one time at Joey's Christmas party he called you the C word when you told him he'd had enough to drink. This isn't Scotland, you can't throw around the C word like any other noun. That's unforgivable. It just wasn't meant to be. In fact, maybe that's why things fell apart with him when they did—so you had time to meet someone better. Deep down, you knew you deserved better."

Claire narrowed her eyes. "Why do I feel like you've been waiting for a long time to say all these things?"

"I plead the fifth." Mindy slid her tablet into her purse.

Enough talk about boys. "Do you need help loading the tables? I remember from the Donner proposal those things are freaking heavy."

Mindy shook her head. "Gavin's meeting me here to help after his last final."

"Nice, free labor. Try not to have sex on all the tables, okay?"

"Hey," Mindy said, throwing the whiteboard eraser at Claire. "It was one time. Okay, it was four times."

Claire laughed and gave her a hug. "I'm going to pick up the scrolls. I'll meet you back here, and then we can go to Luke's to unload those and check on the landscaping."

"Claire?"

She paused with her hand on the door and turned to face Mindy.

"Do you want to talk about it? I mean, about what happened at the hospital."

Tingles shot up and down Claire's spine.

"Not yet."

Mindy nodded and bit her lip. "Are you sure you want to go alone? I can come with you."

Claire shook her head. "Stay. It's just a few miles. I'll be perfectly fine."

Ten minutes alone in her car without sympathetic glances or probing questions sounded like heaven. She pushed open the heavy warehouse door and exited. The sun had encouraged tiny green weeds to pop up in her flowerbeds again, but there was no time to weed. She lifted her face to soak in the Vitamin D as she strode across the parking lot and got into her car. The warmth banished the darkness that haunted her and allowed her to focus on the task at hand. She threw her car in reverse and zoomed out of the parking lot, singing along to a metal song as she made her way to Fourth Street.

She made a couple of extra turns and glanced frequently in the rearview mirror, but West Haven was free of black sedans once again.

She swung her car into an open spot on Market Street

and decided to walk the rest of the way. Rosie climbed obediently into her doggy backpack, and she slung it gently over her shoulders. Rosie panted happily from inside the pack and curled up against the small of Claire's back.

Casting a glance in both directions, Claire locked her car and headed toward the artist's shop. The sun beat down overhead, but a cool breeze lifted the ends of her hair.

Rosie let out a low growl from inside the mesh pack. Claire turned, expecting to see a passing squirrel or another dog. Instead, an unremarkable-looking man stepped onto the curb behind her. They made eye contact briefly, and he stooped to tie his shoe. The fist of fear that gripped her stomach tightened. The porkpie hat perched on his head nearly blew away as he bent down. Surely, the Widowmaker wasn't a porkpie hat kind of guy.

She turned on her heel, determined not to let Porkpie Guy bother her. He was just another pedestrian, using the sidewalk like any normal human being. Her pace quickened as she passed a used bookstore. She glanced in the long shop window. The man was now trailing behind her by about twenty feet. His hands were in his pockets, and he seemed nonchalant, but the back of her neck prickled. She needed to stay calm. Maybe he was just headed to the nearest haberdashery to get another stupid hat.

At the next intersection, Claire jogged across the crosswalk, putting four lanes of traffic between her and the man. He ducked into a shop on the other side of the street. Her heart rate slowed.

"Mommy's being paranoid," she muttered to Rosie as she approached her favorite flower shop—fortunately not the same shop that the Widowmaker seemed to frequent. As she leaned in to smell some tulips, she accidentally bumped into a blue-eyed man in a Red Sox baseball cap.

"Sorry." She side-stepped to give him some space.

"No worries." He smiled at her as he entered the store.

Claire waved merrily at the florist inside, who was trimming thorns from the roses. She was still several minutes early, so she wandered into a café two blocks down and ordered a cup of coffee to go.

The scent of hazelnuts sparked a memory of Sunday mornings at her mom's house. Roy got up at dawn and brewed a pot of hazelnut coffee every Sunday before he went out to tinker on the '63 Corvette Stingray he was hellbent on restoring. Her mom, like Claire, tended to sleep in. When they were both up for the day, they would get dressed up and go shopping. They always tried to find a trinket for Roy when they went—a new multitool, a vinyl album. The memory and the coffee warmed her as she stepped into the artist's gallery.

"Stacey, these are gorgeous!" Claire exclaimed as she unrolled a scroll in one hand. Calligraphy looped and scrolled down the length of the paper, every bit as regal as she had imagined.

Stacey grinned. "This was a fun project. I'd love to see pictures after the proposal."

"I'll send you some," Claire said as she put the scrolls back in their box and tucked it under her arm.

She walked back out into the sunshine and decided to pick up a salad for dinner at the bistro across the street. As she crossed over, her stride faltered. The man in the porkpie hat was sitting on a bench outside the restaurant, reading a newspaper.

"It's just a coincidence," she assured herself as she hurried to reach the curb before the light changed. She stood tall as she walked past the gentleman. His eyes burned into the back of her head as she walked straight inside the restaurant.

While she waited for her take-out order, Claire pulled Detective Smith's card out of her wallet and hesitated. She really couldn't afford to get murdered the week of the biggest proposal of her life. She dialed his number, holding her breath as it rang.

"This is Detective Smith."

"Detective Smith? This is Claire Hartley."

"Are you all right?" His tone was urgent.

"Yes. Well, I think so. I might be being followed."

"Where are you?"

"The Willow Tree at Market and Seventh."

"What does the person look like?"

"He's a white male, probably late forties or early fifties. He followed me down the street earlier and he was waiting outside a restaurant when I came out of a shop."

"Is he wearing a ridiculous hat?"

"Yes," she answered, genuinely surprised.

"Does he have a mustache that looks like a wooly worm?"

"He does."

"That's Officer Shiccitano. He's been keeping an eye on you for us. And apparently dressing like a hipster."

"Oh, thank god. I'm sorry for overreacting."

"No need to be sorry. Stay out of trouble, now."

"Thank you," Claire said and hung up. "Would have been helpful if they'd let me know ahead of time that they're assigning me a full-time creep," she muttered as she picked up her salad and edged back out the door.

"Officer Shiccitano." She nodded at the man as she passed him.

"Miss Hartley," he said, looking surprised as he tipped his hat to her.

She sensed him get up to follow her at a leisurely distance. It would be much harder for the Widowmaker to take her when she was being followed by a '70s porn star. As she rounded a corner, she glanced behind her. He was half a block behind her, bent over to examine a row of shoes outside a variety store. But who was that behind him?

Her stomach dropped. Lurking a few paces behind Officer Shiccitano was the blue-eyed man in the baseball cap she had bumped into at the flower store. Was it her imagination, or was he staring at her as he turned around?

"It's just a pedestrian, Claire," she said quietly. Despite her assertions, she jaywalked in the middle of the street on the next block. After several hurried steps, she glanced back and saw the man in the baseball cap pressing the button to cross the street at the intersection across from her. Officer Shiccitano had paused at the same light and was now staring suspiciously at the Red Sox fan.

She veered off of Market Street and took a right, heading for the park where she planned Barney's proposal. She would make a complete loop. Surely the Red Sox fan would have no reason to take the same route. A bass-heavy song thudded out of a music store as she passed by. She ducked into an alley and glanced back. The officer was still following her. He seemed to notice her gaze and looked over his shoulder. The man in the baseball cap had fallen just behind him. If this blue-eyed dingus was the Widowmaker, it was a miracle he hadn't been caught yet.

The officer's eyes narrowed. His hand snaked to his hip. Though his presence was comforting, her heart still thumped in her ears. Claire took a left at the next intersection and wandered down a narrow alley behind the Market

Street shops. Both men followed. Her steps echoed in the narrow space. This was a mistake. The safety and bustle of the street was gone. What good was one cop against a serial killer? A cat sat on top of a dumpster, staring judgementally at her. She sped up, half jogging as she reached the end of the alleyway. She turned back toward Market Street but stopped when Officer Shiccitano's voice rang out.

"Excuse me, sir. I'm going to need to see a form of identification." He flashed his badge at the pedestrian.

The man in the baseball cap reddened. "Hey, listen, I'm not looking for any trouble—" he began, but stopped when an ear-shattering shriek split the air.

"LEAVE HER ALONE!" A dark-haired girl in a trench coat flitted around the corner and charged full force at the man in the baseball cap. She hit him right in the abdomen and tackled him to the ground.

"*Mindy?*" Claire asked.

Mindy ignored her and instead focused her energy on kicking and swearing as Officer Shiccitano dragged her off the man in the baseball cap.

"Ouch! Damn it, woman. I'm a private investigator." Red Sox guy grunted as a final flailing kick nailed him in the shin. "Claire's mom hired me to watch out for her."

Mindy stopped struggling. "Oh."

Officer Shiccitano stepped between Mindy and the man on the ground. "I really am going to need some form of ID."

The man handed over his license and stepped closer to Claire, who was still several feet away. She took a step back.

"Claire, I'm Brian. Your mom hired me. Call her. She didn't want me to tell you I was following you because she knew you would be mad."

"Well, she's not wrong," Claire said. She dialed her

mom's phone number. Her mom picked up almost immediately.

"Hi, sweetheart! How's my Clairebear?"

"Mother, did you hire a private investigator to follow me around?"

"Sweetie, you know I worry. I have a terrible premonition that something awful is going to happen. Brian's just looking after you for me because you refuse to move home. And I wish you would let me read your cards—"

"What's his full name?"

"Brian B. Wilson."

"We'll discuss this later." Claire hung up and turned to address the policeman.

"According to my mother, the PI's name is Brian B. Wilson."

"Checks out," Officer Shiccitano said, returning the man's wallet.

"Take my card in case you need to contact the West Haven PD." He produced a card and handed it to the PI.

"Thank you, officer. And sorry again, Claire," Brian said. "I'll see you to your car, if you don't mind."

Claire suppressed a sigh. "If you must."

She hustled down the street, teeming with rage. Mindy caught up to her.

"Want to tell me why you're part of this ridiculous parade instead of moving the tables?"

Mindy blushed. "I told you I didn't want you to go by yourself."

Claire smiled. "You tackled a fully grown man who could have been a murderer for me."

"I wasn't about to let you get kidnapped by a Red Sox fan." She slung her arm over Claire's shoulders and planted a kiss on her cheek.

CHAPTER TWENTY-SIX

To Do:
- *Pick up boxes from liquor store*
- *Have a serious conversation with Mom about boundaries*
- *Confirm menu*

"OH, GOD. WHO'S DEAD?" CLAIRE GROANED INTO THE PHONE, blinking sleep from her eyes. It was five a.m. and her head pounded.

Mindy sat up in bed next to her and flicked the bedside light on. "Is it me? Am I dead?" she slurred.

"What's your ex's name again? The one who's dating the crazy girl?" Luke's voice was urgent in her ear.

Claire yawned. "Jason. Jason Goldman." Why the hell was he calling her at the butt crack of dawn to ask about the worst mistake of her life?

"Turn on the local news," Luke ordered. "He just got arrested."

"*Arrested?* For what?"

Mindy threw the covers off and sprinted for the TV. She slipped on the area rug and almost fell but managed to smash the power button. The TV flickered to life.

A reporter gazed seriously into the camera. "Stevens, who had left her home on Firestone Lane to go for a morning run last Saturday, has not been seen since. Security footage from a nearby home revealed Stevens getting into a car with Goldman the morning of her disappearance. Police entered Goldman's residence last evening and were seen removing several evidence boxes from the home."

The phone fell from her hand as her blood ran ice cold. Sure, she had entertained the idea that Jason could have been the Widowmaker. Could he really be the Widow-maker? Had she been engaged to a serial killer? Had she served a murderer breakfast in bed on his birthday five years in a row? How could she have missed the signs?

A mug shot appeared. Jason's pale blue eyes were wide and wild, like a cornered animal. Footage rolled of police marching out of a ground-floor apartment with a half dozen cardboard boxes. Wendy stood in the parking lot wearing nothing but one of Jason's T-shirts, crying and screaming at the officers.

"The police have declined to comment on the allegations that Jason Goldman is the West Haven Widowmaker, who the community believes is responsible for the deaths of up to five women," the reporter continued.

Claire's stomach heaved. She stumbled out of bed and ran to the bathroom, falling to her knees in front of the toilet. She vomited what little there was in her stomach and collapsed to the cool tile floor, hugging her knees to her chest. Her heart pounded. Her head throbbed. This couldn't be. It wasn't possible.

Mindy dropped down next to her and cradled her head in her lap. She didn't speak, but ran her fingers through Claire's hair. Rosie tippy-tapped her way into the bathroom and collapsed on the floor next to Claire. She laid her muzzle on Claire's leg and whined.

"I can't believe it," Claire whispered. The bile burned her mouth. "Jason is the Widowmaker."

Mindy stared blankly. "The man can't even pick out two matching shoes. How did he commit and cover up five murders?"

"I don't get it. He barely knew Courtney. Why would she get in his car?"

"Who knows? It's Courtney. Maybe they were sleeping together."

Something rattled against the hardwood floor in the bedroom.

"I'll get it." Mindy slipped out from under Claire and disappeared. She reappeared a moment later and held out Claire's phone. "It's Detective Smith."

Claire took it. "Hello?"

"Miss Hartley, it's Detective Smith. Could you come down to the station today? We have some property that we'd like you to identify."

"What kind of property?"

"Just a few things that we believe Jason Goldman may have taken from you. You may not have seen the news. He's been taken into custody for the disappearance of Courtney Stevens. Can you come today?"

"I'll be there in an hour." She ended the call. "They said they have some of my property," she said to Mindy, who was perched on the edge of the tub. "Do you think it's my wedding dress?"

"I hope so. That dress was a masterpiece."

Claire climbed shakily to her feet, clutching the vanity for support.

"I'm coming with you. And don't forget to brush your teeth—you smell like vomit. Come on, Rosie," Mindy yawned and stretched. She led the dog out of the bathroom.

Forty-five minutes later, Claire, Mindy, and Rosie pulled into the police station. When Mindy cut the engine, the silence was deafening.

"I can't believe this is really happening." The front door of the station loomed in front of her.

How could this be? Had she really spent five years of her life with a murderer? And how had she never noticed? What signs had she missed?

There had been one night the previous spring when Jason had stumbled into the apartment after one a.m., covered in what looked like bright red blood. When she had asked him about it, he said he was helping a friend paint his living room. He had thrown the shirt in the trash, and she had scrubbed the bathroom sink until it was free of the red smudges he had left everywhere. Had she inadvertently covered up evidence? Her stomach twisted. She made a mental note to check the date of Jennifer's disappearance.

"It makes sense if you think about it." Mindy's hands were still on the wheel, and she, too, stared at the station. "Since you kicked him out, he's been completely obsessed with you. He knew that Rosie was the best way to threaten you. He knows where you live and work, what your schedule's like."

Claire shook her head. "Something just doesn't feel right. He never once mentioned any of the other girls."

"Serial killers can be incredibly sneaky. They fool everyone—their parents, spouses. Look at the Keystone Killer. It took forty years to catch him and that only happened because his third cousin submitted her DNA to a database."

Her phone buzzed. Her mother. She ignored the call. Surely, she hadn't heard the news yet. Did she have Google alerts out on everyone Claire knew?

"Come on. Let's get this over with," Mindy said, patting Claire's leg. "And then we celebrate with brunch."

"Celebrate?" She shot Mindy a look. Celebrate spending the majority of her adult life with a serial killer under her roof?

"It's over, Claire. You're not in danger anymore."

Claire released her vice-like grip on the passenger-side grab handle. "Does this mean I get to go to the bathroom by myself now?"

Mindy laughed and shoved her. "Come on."

Mindy half-forced her up the steps to the front desk at the station. Detective Smith appeared seconds after their arrival.

"Miss Hartley, would you follow me, please? Just Miss Hartley, thank you," he said to Mindy, who had linked arms with Claire. Mindy slunk down into a chair, visibly disappointed. Claire handed her Rosie's leash and followed the detective.

"Thank you for coming in so soon," the detective said as he guided Claire through a set of double doors and down a long, beige hallway. He opened the door to an interview room and gestured for her to sit down at the stainless-steel table in the center of the room. She sat facing the long mirror on the opposite wall.

A number of evidence bags were spread out on the table.

"Can you tell me if you recognize any of these articles of clothing?" He tapped one hand on the table.

She leaned forward. A pair of polka-dot, bikini-cut underwear was in one bag. Her stomach clenched.

"Those are mine." She pointed to the bag. Next to that one was a pair of boy shorts with corgis on them. "Those are mine also. Were these at Jason's?"

The detective nodded. "Can you confirm that these were in the dirty laundry basket on the evening of the break-in at your apartment?"

She paused. "I— Probably. They were some of my favorites." And now they were in police custody. Why had Jason broken in just to steal her underwear? And where the hell was her one-of-a-kind wedding dress?

He leaned forward. "Can you at least confirm that these articles of clothing were in your possession after Mr. Goldberg vacated your residence last year? He didn't take them with him when he left?"

"No, I definitely had them after he moved out. I remember wearing these when—well, never mind." Her almost-hookup with that guy from Pilates class was not something she wanted scribbled in a police case file. Was she ever going to get her underwear back, or did they live at the police station now?

"Thank you, Miss Hartley. And for the record, the remainder of these items do not belong to you?"

Claire glanced at the bags again. A silver-plated hand mirror was in another bag. The other held a pair of underwear she didn't recognize.

"I've never seen them before." Who did they belong to? Courtney? "Did you find my wedding dress?"

"No, we didn't recover any wedding dresses from the residence. I have one other question for you. During your relationship, did Mr. Goldberg ever mention any of these women?"

He slid a list of names across the table. The Widow-maker victims, which she could have quoted from memory, stared back at her. They were finally taking the Widow-maker theory seriously. It only took five dead women.

"He did kind of know Courtney. I think the three of us were at a few of the same parties in college. But he never talked about her, or about any of the other girls. Does this mean the police are finally admitting there's a serial killer at large?"

Detective Smith took the list back. "The official position of the police is that the Widowmaker does not exist. But the other missing person cases are still considered open and active investigations. We would be remiss not to investigate every possible angle."

She leaned forward. "Do you know why she got in his car that morning?"

"I can't discuss any of the details in an ongoing investigation."

Figured. "I understand. It just seems weird. And I don't understand why he would break into my apartment. I hadn't had a chance to change the locks since he moved out. He could have just used his key."

"Sometimes perpetrators disguise crime scenes as break-ins to throw people off." Detective Smith tucked his notebook in the pocket of his suit jacket. "You'll likely be hearing from us again, Miss Hartley. You may be called to testify at the trial. Thank you for your assistance this morning." He offered her another firm handshake and held the door open.

Her stomach clenched. She trembled as she rose. A trial? How could she face Jason again knowing what he had done? Her fingers and toes felt numb as Detective Smith led her back to the lobby. The lobby where Jason had probably been brought in just hours ago. Was he in jail now, or in an interrogation room somewhere in the precinct?

Mindy jumped up. "Tell me everything," she insisted as they pushed open the doors.

The sun was just beginning to creep over the horizon. Everything was a startling shade of pink. The air was warm, and the smell of freshly baked bread drifted over from the bakery next to the station. It was a night and day difference from the stuffy, closed atmosphere of the station. The adrenaline had started to subside, and her headache came back full force.

Claire relayed the underwear situation.

"What a freakin' creep." Mindy shuddered as she got into the driver's seat. "Who steals underwear? You must have a magic vag."

"Please don't ever say those words again. Can we go home? And stop for coffee?" If she was being honest, now that her life was no longer in danger, she desperately craved solitude. She could run a nice bath at home, maybe even read a couple of chapters of that book she had picked up weeks ago. No one would bang on the door to complain about her spotty Wi-Fi or ask where she kept her nail clippers. She dug some ibuprofen out of her purse and popped them in her mouth.

"I have a better idea. I just have to make a couple of stops." Mindy pulled out of the parking lot and turned in the opposite direction of the apartment.

"Mindy, come on. I can't waste time today. The proposal is five days away. I still have to phone in the final menu for Nicole's proposal and see if the dress is ready for pickup and—"

"You can do all that from the car." Mindy handed her the

phone charging cord. "You have a good hour until we get there."

Claire groaned, but she immediately went to work. When Mindy had an idea, she was like a dog with a bone. There was no use arguing with her. While Claire left messages and confirmed a dozen different details with vendors whose doors had barely opened, Mindy stopped at the liquor store and the grocery store before driving off to the edge of town. Where were they going? And why was she buying booze at eight a.m. on a Sunday? They exited the town limits and traveled south on the highway.

As Mindy drove into a thick patch of forest, the reception cut out.

"I guess this means I can't call my mom back." Claire tossed her phone into her purse. Oh well.

"That was part of the appeal," Mindy said as she got off on an exit. They traveled down several miles of a rural two-lane highway, passing a run-down looking car dealership and a general store. She turned at a sign that said Stone Valley State Park.

"Min," Claire said, reaching over to touch her friend's arm. "Stone Valley?"

"It is your favorite." Mindy followed a narrow, winding road. A dense growth of evergreens surrounded them. "I know you haven't been here in a while."

Claire nodded. "Officer Shiccitano not-so-subtly suggested that I shouldn't go anywhere without cell phone service. But now..."

"Things are different. You're safe now. Which is why we're celebrating." Mindy swung the car into a parking spot next to a bear-proof dumpster.

Dappled sunlight streamed onto the needle-strewn path in front of them. Twenty yards away, two people stood on a picnic table. A banner was stretched between them, and they seemed to be trying to secure the ends to the front of a rustic pavilion.

"Is that Kyle and Nicole? How did you get them out of bed before eight?" Claire stepped out of the car and slammed the door. The pair looked around.

"Surprise!" Nicole threw her arms up in the air.

The banner sagged on one side, but the words "Freedom Brunch" were visible.

"What are you guys doing here?" Claire laughed and held her arms out. Nicole and Kyle descended on her in a group hug.

"We're celebrating your emancipation from...uh..." Kyle trailed off and adjusted his horn-rimmed glasses.

"Being targeted by a serial killer that I used to be engaged to?" Claire opened the back seat. Rosie popped out and immediately lunged for Nicole and Kyle. Nicole took her leash and led her to the pavilion.

She had only been awake for a few hours, but this already felt like the longest day of her entire life. Jason was the Widowmaker. A murderer. The words still sounded wrong. Shouldn't she be happy? Justice had just been served for five missing women. A dangerous killer (not to mention a lying, cheating ex who had evaded karma for too long) was behind bars. But something didn't feel right.

"Yes, exactly. Have a seat." Kyle nodded at the picnic table. A checkered tablecloth covered the rough wood. Candles littered the table.

"Guys," Claire said as she took a seat. "You didn't have to do this. Doesn't it seem weird to celebrate my ex going to prison?"

"After everything that asshole did to you and those other girls? No, this seems pretty appropriate. If you still had any of his stuff at your apartment, we would have brought it for a bonfire." Nicole folded a paper napkin and slid it underneath some plastic silverware.

Kyle dumped charcoal bricks into the grill and set a cast-iron skillet on it. Mindy popped a bottle of champagne. It foamed as she poured it into five glasses almost to the rim before adding a tiny bit of orange juice. A classic Mindy Mimosa.

She presented the drinks to the crew and sat down next to Claire. "We just wanted to celebrate because it's over, and you're safe. And we don't have to fight you for time in the bathroom in the morning anymore."

"And you don't have to talk about any of it if you don't want to," Nicole said, sitting down on her other side. They both leaned in for another hug, surrounding Claire in a perfumey cocoon.

"Sorry I'm late. I wasn't sure what kind of muffin was her favorite, so I just bought them all." The voice came from behind them. Claire turned around.

"Oh, hi," she said in surprise.

Luke stood in the early morning light. She had been so preoccupied with the morning's events that she had forgotten he was the one who called her first. The blue checkered button-down shirt he was wearing was rolled up to his elbows. He wore shorts even though there was still a chill in the air. He dropped a large bakery bag onto the table.

"I thought you'd be hard at work on your documentary now that the Widowmaker's been revealed." Claire stared at him. The case had just broken wide open. Why was he here?

Luke stepped inside the pavilion, stopped at the picnic table. He bent down and put his arms around her, lifting her off the bench, mimosa and all. When she was standing, he wrapped her in a bear hug. Mindy and Nicole sauntered off to the other side of the pavilion and began a loud conversation.

Her shoulders tensed. The lie still hung between them like a spiderweb. But he was trying, and she couldn't hold it against him forever. She relaxed and snaked her arms around him. He really did give a great hug.

"You okay?" He pulled back and held her at arm's length. His eyebrows knit together.

"Relatively speaking, yes," she said.

"You dropped the phone. I thought I heard vomiting."

Great. Her cheeks grew hot. "I had a pretty visceral reaction to the news." She stared out into the distance, down the path that was carpeted with dead evergreen needles. "Something doesn't seem right."

Luke cocked his head. "What do you mean? Jason was your number-one suspect."

"He was my only suspect. And he never once mentioned any of those other girls."

"Seems like he was pretty good at hiding things." He reached over and stroked her cheek.

"Maybe." She took a small step closer to Luke. He was like gravity, pulling her in even when she had a thousand other things on her mind.

"Order up." Kyle dropped a couple of plates onto the table. Bacon and eggs sizzled. He also set a small plate on the ground for Rosie. She wolfed her scrambled egg in seconds.

The five of them sat and ate together. They told stories about college and laughed. Even though her ex-fiancé had just been arrested and the biggest project of her career was staring down the barrel at her, a calm washed over Claire. Maybe it was the beautiful scenery or the sense of security that had been missing for the past month slowly returning. Maybe this would be the first day that she truly started to rebuild her life after the devastation that Jason had caused.

"A toast!" Mindy called out, standing up and lofting her champagne glass. "To Claire. You've been through more in one month than most people will go through in their entire lives. Throughout everything, you somehow managed to stay focused on our business and never let the fear stop you from chasing your dreams. You never quit. I'm so honored to call you my friend. And my boss."

"To Claire!" everyone cried.

Claire's heart grew in her chest. What a strange day. Horror and joy in equal measure. And it wasn't even noon.

"I do have some bad news, though." Mindy said as she sat back down.

That happy bubble deflated like a balloon. "What else could have possibly happened?"

"Wendy released the video."

Claire's stomach dropped into her butt. "How bad is it?"

"It's not great, I'm not going to lie. You do smash a wine bottle and threaten an innocent man. But, fortunately for us, the dumbass released the video the night before the Widowmaker case broke. No one will even hear about it."

Thank god. Surely, Wendy would be distracted from trying to ruin her life for a while with Jason behind bars. She fully intended to do a deep dive on the internet as soon as they made it back to civilization, but for the moment there was nothing she could do.

"Do you want to take a walk?" Luke asked as Claire threw away her paper plate.

Behind him, Mindy nodded fervently and made a thrusting motion with her hips. "Maybe Luke can take you home too," she called. "Then I can go pick up that dress for the Winter's proposal."

"I'd be happy to take you home."

"Okay." Claire looped her hand through Rosie's leash. "Thanks." She glared at Mindy over her shoulder.

The three of them set off together down the path. The pine branches waved lazily in the breeze as they walked. The park was still empty except for a handful of dog walkers and hikers. There was something comforting about being in the middle of this beautiful forest, an accused abductor and probable murderer behind bars and an obnoxiously handsome veteran holding her hand.

"So," Luke said, taking the leash from Claire after Rosie nearly ripped her arm off chasing a chipmunk. "Mindy said this is your favorite park. Why's that?"

"Lots of reasons," she said. "You'll see." They rounded a bend in the path and emerged from the woods. A serene lake glistened in the sunshine, joined on one side by a sandy beach. A fisherman bobbed in a rowboat thirty yards out.

"Wow," Luke said. "This is beautiful. I've never been out here."

"I used to come a lot with my mom. It's halfway between my hometown and West Haven. This lake has the coldest water you'll ever feel." She broke his grasp to step across the sand. She bent and put her hand in the water. The cold bit at her fingers, and she snatched them back. Rosie crept up next to her and touched the water with her snoot. She lapped noisily for a second before growling at a family of minnows.

Luke dipped his own fingers in and withdrew them. "Not as cold as the Pacific, but I see what you're saying."

She shoved him, but a smile crept across her face. "You always have to one-up me. The lake's not even the best part."

"Oh?"

She turned away from the lake and pointed at the small mountain behind them. "See that overlook?"

He squinted and shielded his eyes from the sun. "I think so."

"You can see the drive-in movie theater across the highway from the overlook. We didn't have much money growing up, so my mom and I would hike up to the outlook with our camping chairs and a radio and we'd watch the movies through a pair of binoculars."

Luke turned to her. His eyes were soft. He cupped her head in his hand and drew her to him. They crashed together like a wave meeting the shore. His lips met hers, tenderly at first, then urgently. She wrapped her arms around his neck. His shoulders were solid mountains underneath the cotton button-down. She pressed herself against him, intoxicated by his scent—fresh cut grass and clean linen. Did he just perpetually mow his grass? Why did he smell so good all the time?

Her heart thumped in her ears. Could he hear it? It was deafening. At least this time he shouldn't be able to feel her back sweat through her t-shirt.

He explored with his lips and tongue and held her so tightly she wasn't sure she could breathe. Something swelled inside her. The wall she had put up around her heart cracked and crumbled. She opened, petal by petal like the roses on the bush behind them. It was dangerous to let him in, but for once she didn't care.

CHAPTER TWENTY-SEVEN

To Do:
- *Give Mindy a raise*
- *Pack extra packaging tape*
- *Give N the best day of her life!*

THE NEXT FIVE DAYS PASSED IN A WHIRLWIND OF appointments, strategy meetings, and tastings. The hors d'oeuvres and wine had been selected, the horse-drawn carriage was booked, and Nicole's flawless princess gown was hanging in Claire's closet.

She wasn't sure if the pounding headaches that haunted her were a product of her concussion or from the crushing mountain of pressure from the biggest proposal she had ever undertaken. She had been given permission to remove her gauze and attempt to cover up her Frankenstein's-monster-style stitches and bald spot. Maybe she wouldn't look like a partially bald, drug-addled maniac for Nicole's proposal after all.

With Jason unable to post bail and still behind bars, she had settled back into her old routines. Rosie was allowed to stay home by herself. Her friends let her stay at her apartment alone. She no longer took nonsensical, roundabout ways to her destinations. She didn't whirl around in the grocery store, ready to assault whoever was behind her with a baby carrot. Even though she couldn't quite get rid of the niggling fear that something was wrong, life had returned to normal.

She peered groggily at her alarm clock when it went off at five thirty in the morning on the big day. She threw the covers off and did a long, luxurious stretch. Today, all of her hard work would finally pay off. Assuming everything went perfectly, Nicole would have the most romantic day of her entire life. Two of the people she loved most in the world would start their happily ever after off with a hell of a bang. The proposal would also virtually guarantee her the Planner of the Year Award. Not that it mattered in comparison to the joy of eternal love.

She checked her phone and saw a message from Luke. Always an early riser.

Luke: *Today's the big day. You've got this. See you tonight.*

Were those butterflies in her stomach from Proposal Day or from three simple sentences from the super-hot filmmaker? It didn't matter. She needed to focus.

She hopped out of bed and performed a five-minute yoga flow, trying to calm her nerves. After a quick shower, Claire threw her makeup and clothes for later that evening into a weekender bag and tossed the lot into her car. She pulled into the parking lot at the warehouse seconds before the moving van arrived. After showing them where the boxes were, she instructed them to wait behind her in front of the apartment until Nicole's car was gone. It would be hard to explain to Nicole why she was breaking into her apartment with three burly men in tow.

When the moving supplies were packed and ready to go, Claire led the way to Nicole's little apartment on the outside of town with Rosie riding shotgun. When Claire parked on the street, she checked the lot for Nicole's car and breathed a sigh of relief when she saw it wasn't there.

"All right, boys." She put her hands out at her side and wiggled her fingers. "It's showtime."

"You're sure this is okay?" the shorter one of the movers asked nervously as Claire let herself into Nicole's apartment.

"Trust me, it's fine." She headed to the living room and dumped a pile of boxes. Mercifully, Nicole was a minimalist at heart and had very little furniture.

"I mean, are you sure this is technically legal? To move someone out of their apartment without them knowing?"

She rolled her eyes. "I talked to the landlord, and I have a key. It's fine. I'll take the bedroom. You guys handle the big furniture out here and in the kitchen first." She indicated the sofa and TV stand.

The movers shrugged and began picking up furniture.

Hours later, panic was starting to set in. Nicole had more stuff than she thought. Who needed thirty ceramic chickens? The end was near, but she was perilously close to going over her prescribed amount of time for the moving portion of the day. She was also sweating like she had eaten four pounds of steak.

She took Rosie out for a pee break and pulled out her phone. "Min, I might have been a little overzealous in thinking I could get her entire apartment packed up in three hours. Is there any way you can meet the caterer at Luke's? I have to check on things at the pool and the archery range to make sure everything is set up."

"I'm at the archery range right now," Mindy said. "I just talked to the owner, and they're shutting the doors at five to make sure everyone is out by the time Nicole gets here."

"You are a lifesaver." Claire fist pumped the air as she and Rosie jogged back up the steps to Nicole's apartment. "I love you. Really. You're fantastic. I'll finish up here, check in to make sure everything is set up at the pool, and then I'll meet you at Luke's no later than noon. I'll bring lunch."

"Awesome. See you soon. And Claire?"

"Yeah?" Claire asked. Back inside, she spun the tape gun, trying to find the end.

"Remember to breathe. Everything is going to be great."

"Okay," she said, sticking the tape to one side of the box and noisily stretching the tape down the length. "Shit! Did you text Nicole and ask her about girl's night?"

"Yeah, I did that at eight. She said she's up for it, so she hasn't made any other plans."

"Good. Then we don't need to kidnap her. I'll see you soon." Claire hung up. Half an hour later, she pushed the last of the boxes out into the hallway and took a final survey of every room. There wasn't a fork, blanket, or framed picture left in the place. Bare spots where Nicole had hung her most-loved portraits shone on the wall, brighter than the surrounding paint.

There was still a slight stain on the carpet where Mindy had knocked over a container of hot pink nail polish during a rom-com marathon. A small hole in the wall marked where Claire had slammed into it by accident during a game of beer pong. They had shared countless laughs, stories, and bottles of wine in this tiny apartment. And now it would be someone else's.

She smiled. It was time for the next chapter of their lives.

When she turned onto Luke's driveway an hour later, a task force of landscapers on ladders were hanging fairy lights in the trees that lined the driveway. Near the house, Brian the PI fed a strand of lights up a ladder to a landscaper. Her mother had refused to call him off, even though Jason was in prison. She waved at them. She couldn't control her mother. Today was the only thing she could control, the one thing she could practically guarantee the outcome of. It was going to be perfect. It had to be.

She had to park fifty yards from the house because of the volume of traffic coming in and out. Vans belonging to the caterers and landscapers parked haphazardly along the driveway. Mindy's Miata took shelter under a tree and already showed signs of a bird poop attack.

Claire carried several bags of sandwiches and cups of soup into the house and into semi-organized chaos.

Yuffie, the chef from the second-choice catering company, waved at Claire with a hand covered in flour as she shouted at one of her assistants to bring her a pastry cutter.

"How's everything coming?" Claire asked, admiring the citrusy tang of fruit in the air.

"This kitchen's too small and it stinks of man in here, but I make it work," the squat woman said in a thick Russian accent. She wore a net over jet-black hair that was peppered with gray strands and sported a small mustache over her upper lip.

Yuffie's pastries were the best in the business, but her manners left much to be desired.

"I brought lunch if you ladies are hungry." She deposited one of the bags on the breakfast nook. "I'll leave it out here."

She found Luke in the ballroom, wearing a tool belt and jotting down some notes in his tiny notebook. She let Rosie out of her backpack to run around the ballroom. The dog ran straight for Luke and put her front paws on his legs, tail wagging like crazy.

Something stirred in Claire at the sight of him. A sense of peace crept up despite the army of people bustling in and out of the room and the biggest project of her entire career looming. Her feet seemed to propel themselves in his direction. She came up behind him, wrapped a hand around one glorious biceps. "Hello Mr. Fix-It," she whispered seductively in his ear.

Luke spun around and smiled. "There you are." He engulfed her in his arms and pressed a kiss to her cheek. Today, he smelled like sawdust. "You're on time." He stared at his watch with wide eyes.

She wriggled out of his arms even though they felt like home. "Shut up. I brought lunch." The bags rustled as she dropped them onto one of the long banquet tables that lined the wall. She waved at Mindy, who was spreading a white linen cloth over the chocolate fountain table.

"Have you talked to Kyle?" Claire asked.

He nodded. "He's at his place trying to unpack some of Nicole's boxes so she feels more at home when they get back tonight. He's nervous, and he said he's going to come early to make sure the band doesn't need anything before Nicole gets here."

"Good! He's going to do great. Could I see you outside for a minute? I just wanted to discuss logistics for the carriage." She tipped her head toward the backyard. There was time for a small detour from the schedule.

Luke slung his hammer back into its holster and obliged, following her out onto the patio.

She glanced around surreptitiously before grabbing onto his tool belt and tugging him roughly toward her.

He pivoted, pushing her up against the house, catching the back of her head before it hit the stone. He kissed her deeply, exploring the inside of her mouth with his tongue. She wrapped her arms around his neck. The stress melted away from her shoulders. She stood on her tippy toes, desperate to be closer to him. Had she ever been kissed like this before? For a moment, everything faded away. There was no proposal, no ex-fiancé-turned-murderer. There was only Luke.

He eventually drew back, kissed her just below her right ear. Tingles ran the length of her body as if she had jammed a fork into an electrical outlet.

"I've been thinking about you." He brushed a strand of hair away from her forehead. He cupped her cheek with a warm, rough hand and brushed his thumb over her bottom lip.

Claire couldn't help but smile. "I thought about you once or twice," she said. She laid a hand on his tool belt, directly above his zipper. "I like this," she said, tracing a finger over a tape measure.

He raised his eyebrows. "Oh yeah? Maybe if you're lucky later, I'll show you what's under the belt." He leaned in to kiss her neck.

A sigh escaped her lips. Sex embargo be damned. A shiver ran up her spine as he drew away, leaning one hand on the stone above her.

He pulled back, looking her in the eyes. "I want to take you on a date tomorrow."

"What?" she asked, head snapping up.

"A date. Surely, you've heard of them. Dinner, a movie. You wear a nice dress, and I'll wear this tool belt." He leaned forward and gently pressed the cool steel of his tape measure into her stomach.

She looked up at him, fighting to hide a smile. "Let's get through tonight, and then we'll talk about this date." Her heart grew in her chest as she kissed him softly and ducked out from under his arm. "I've got work to do." On her way inside, she grabbed his rear. It was as delightfully firm as it looked.

She spent most of the early afternoon handing out food to everyone working and hanging pictures of Kyle and Nicole in chronological order throughout the house, starting in the foyer and leading back to the ballroom. Dozens of pictures suspended on fishing line twirled in the breeze from the open windows. She lined the hallway with multitudes of candles and checked to make sure there was a fire extinguisher hidden inside the doorway of each room. The candles might be a bit of a fire hazard, but it was going to look incredible. Even Luke the perfectionist had agreed.

Her gaze drifted back to the corner of the ballroom, where Luke was setting a level on the stage. What did he mean, a date? As in, he wanted to date her? Would that make them an official couple? Despite the cocktail of hormones surging through her body demanding to find out what was under that stupid tool belt, she wasn't sure she was ready to date someone. Could someone ever really fully heal from a betrayal like Jason's? But her body demanded to feel those rough hands on every inch of her, and Luke was already too important to her to be a one-night stand. Damn it to hell.

Not to mention, Luke didn't exactly have a shining track record for honesty and commitment. A niggling voice in her mind reminded her what Kyle had said—Luke was a ladies' man. He hadn't said he wanted to date exclusively. A man with his jawline probably had fifty interested women at his beck and call. She needed to protect her heart. And yet...

Luke returned her butt grab as he strolled by, a sandwich in his other hand. She could appreciate a man with the ability to multitask. She swatted at him from her position on the ladder but missed. After she secured the last picture, she glanced at her watch.

"Hey, mind if I use your shower? I have to get ready to meet Nicole."

"Go ahead. I'll try not to think too hard about what's going on up there while I finish reinforcing the stage," he said, picking up a drill.

"Good luck," Claire said as she climbed down. He gripped her hips and lifted her down the last couple of steps. Warmth crept into her cheeks. Damn it. "It'll just be me. Naked and wet, sudsing all sorts of things you couldn't imagine in your wildest dreams." She got within a hair's breadth of his lips before turning for the stairs. "Bye."

Luke shook his head.

Claire emerged an hour later, wearing a short black cocktail dress. She was more dressed up than she normally would be for a proposal, but in addition to being the secret coordinator, she was also Nicole's guide for the evening. The slimming black dress added a formal feel to her look without drawing attention away from the glorious splendor of Nicole's princess dress. Today, everything was about Nicole.

Claire picked up her clutch, stuffed to the brim with cash for tips and emergency supplies, and took a walk around the kitchen. All the desserts were done, and the chefs were just starting to prepare the ingredients for the hot appetizers. She walked back down the hallway to where most of the crew was gathered.

A chocolate fountain now sat on one table, gushing slowly as it warmed up. Rich tapestries adorned the walls, and linens hung in sweeping arches. Fresh flowers in vases on the small tables perfumed the air. Claire's second-best photographer, Candace, bustled around, taking pictures of everyone working. Nobody matched Nicole's natural eye for photography, but Candace was a close contender.

Luke hustled around the ballroom with his camera on a tripod, stopping every few feet to peer through the lens. When he saw her, he picked up his backpack and slung it over his shoulder.

"Okay, everyone," Claire announced. "Luke is headed to the gym. I'm going to pick up Nicole at her apartment. Mindy, can you call the driver and make sure Monochrome Monday is on his way? I need a full test of the lights and speakers, and family members should be arriving in about an hour. Oh, and can you also run them through the dance a couple times with the recording? You're in charge."

Mindy nodded, scribbling furiously on her ever-present clipboard. "Got it!"

"Thank you, everyone! I'll be texting regular updates to Mindy, so she'll keep you posted on the timeframe. All the locations are fairly close, so with any luck the horse-drawn carriage won't impede our progress. Mindy can answer any questions you have. Oh, and don't let Rosie outside unsupervised or she'll roll in squirrel poop. I'll see you all later!"

Claire waved and strutted out into the late afternoon, mentally preparing for the biggest evening of her life.

Twenty minutes later, she stood in the middle of Nicole's now-empty apartment. Candace crouched in the corner of the kitchen, inspecting her lens for dust. Jerry, newly healed from his ruptured appendix, adjusted his tripod. A gift wrapped in shiny pink paper sat next to Claire on the floor.

She checked her watch for what felt like the thousandth time that day when she heard the jingle of the key in the lock. "Showtime," she whispered, situating herself in front of the door.

The front door opened, and a manicured hand reached inside and flicked the light switch. Nicole's brown eyes widened when she saw Claire.

"Claire! You're early for girls' night. Wait, where's my stuff?" Her mouth gaped. "I've been robbed! What the hell, Claire? I know you were always jealous of my sofa, but this is ridiculous."

"You haven't been robbed," Claire said, coming to put her arm around Nicole. "Your stuff has just moved."

"Moved?" Nicole's eyes were still wide. "Where?" She turned when she heard a camera shutter clicking, noticing for the first time that two other people were in the room with them. "Why are Candace and Jerry here?"

Claire held up her phone to Nicole, showing a picture Kyle had sent her earlier. Nicole's outrageous lime green sofa now stood in Kyle's living room next to his life-size Darth Vader figure. A framed portrait Nicole had taken of her family was mounted next to the sofa.

Nicole clapped a hand to her mouth. "Kyle moved my stuff to his place?"

Claire nodded. "He said he couldn't stand to spend even one more day not waking up to you." She gave Nicole a squeeze. "Coli, today is a very big day. Will you come with me?"

Realization seemed to dawn, and Nicole burst into tears. "Is this really happening?"

Claire laughed and hugged her. "Let's get you ready." The pink present landed in her friend's hands. "Open it."

Nicole tore the paper off and held up a brand-new swimsuit. Claire had opted for a one piece—no sense in risking a nip slip on the biggest day of Nicole's life.

"Well, this is... not what I expected. What do you have up your sleeve, Claire?" The tears were gone. Her eyes sparkled.

"Go put it on and you'll find out."

———

CLAIRE USHERED NICOLE INTO THE WOMEN'S LOCKER ROOM. Nicole had pelted her with questions during the entire drive, but Claire had carefully evaded all of them.

When she pushed open the double doors, a massive multi-colored inflatable obstacle course took up almost the entirety of the indoor pool. The air smelled of chlorine and plastic. The fluorescent lights above were off, and Luke had placed free-standing lights around the concrete edge. Ignoring a vivid mental picture of lights falling into the pool and electrocuting her best friend, Claire poked the edge of the course to make sure it was tethered correctly.

"All set in here?" Claire asked Luke when he exited the locker room.

He was wearing a very tight wet suit. Would there be no end to the distractions today?

"I think so." He smoothed his hair back. "Joe's ready to handle the above-water filming, and I'll be in the pool waiting for the underwater portion."

He held up his camera, which was now covered in waterproof housing. He strapped on a mask, a buoyancy compensator, and a re-breather and walked to the edge of the pool.

"The PI didn't follow you here?" he asked, turning as he fixed his mask.

"I forced my mother to give him the night off. I don't want his dumb baseball hat in the background of the pictures. He never takes it off. No one will be wrecking my vision for tonight. You look ridiculous, by the way," Claire called as he plunged into the water to test the gear. He didn't —he actually looked like a Navy SEAL about to undertake a covert operation, but that was beside the point.

She glanced at her clipboard even though she could have recited the timeline in her sleep. She had five minutes until Nicole needed to start the course. Every piece was in place. The princess dress, hairstylist, and makeup artist were waiting in the manager's office down the hall. As soon as Nicole finished up in the dressing room, they would take over the entire space to get her ready. The scrolls were tucked safely into a locker along with Claire's clutch. Photographer Candace had arrived and was deep in discussion with Joe, the third videographer. A lifesaving dummy wearing a pirate hat and billowy white shirt was sinking into the deep end of the pool.

"We're ready to roll. Everyone take your positions, please," Claire ordered.

She opened the locker room door a crack and squeezed inside.

"You're probably wondering why I brought you to a public pool." She smiled at Nicole.

"Kind of," Nicole agreed. "But I figured I'd just go with it."

"Before we take you to see Kyle tonight, there are some tasks you have to complete."

"What kind of tasks?" Nicole clapped her hands together.

"I'm glad you asked. Come on." Claire led Nicole out into the pool area and hit a button on the remote she had pocketed. The lighting scheme shifted. A rented rain machine suspended from the ceiling kicked on, sending a curtain of droplets into the pool. A recording of a thunderstorm played in the background.

"Nicole, tonight you are a fisherman's daughter on a ship at sea. Your father's apprentice has fallen overboard, and he is in desperate need of a rescue. Your mission is to run down the perilous length of this fishing boat and save him from the deep waters," Claire said, sweeping a hand at the obstacle course.

Nicole laughed, and a wide smile grew. "*The Princess and the Arrow?*"

"Of course."

Nicole hugged her tight. "Thank you," she whispered. When she drew back, there were tears in her eyes. She quickly wiped them away and covered them with her goggles.

"Ready?" Claire asked.

Nicole nodded as she made her way to the edge of the pool and stretched out her arms.

"Great. On your mark...get set...*go!*"

Nicole tiptoed across a slender tube wet with fake rain and leaped onto the first platform. She threw her hands out to steady herself as the entire unit drifted. The tethers held, and she quickly regained her balance. She skirted around a giant foam sledgehammer blocking her path and darted between two swinging balls. She hustled through an inflatable arch and crawled across a section of the float that looked like a ladder. Still mostly dry, she clutched at the hand grips as she climbed up a seven foot wall. She reached the top and fist-pumped before sliding down the other side on her belly and diving to the bottom of the pool where the dummy waited.

Nicole emerged from the water less than a minute later. She climbed out of the pool and hoisted the dummy in triumph. Claire clapped and cheered. Hopefully, Luke got the shot. Nicole probably wouldn't mind running the course again, but it wouldn't be authentic. Every moment of the day needed to be as authentic as Kyle's love for Nicole.

"Amazing job, Coli. You have the bravery and heart of a warrior and the grace and kindness of a princess. Will you come with me? Your kingdom awaits." Claire swept a hand toward the locker room.

"Hell yes!" Nicole nodded, pulling off her swim cap and shaking out her hair.

"Go change," Claire said and handed Nicole a box containing a silky robe and new strapless bra and panties. She pointed her friend in the direction of the showers.

Once dry, Nicole sat down on a chair in front of the long mirror that spanned the locker room vanity. The hair and makeup team got to work. Candace snapped photos of Nicole in the chair as Joe captured some B roll.

"Don't you dare cry again," the makeup artist scolded Nicole. "Just because I'm using waterproof mascara doesn't mean the rest of your face won't suffer."

Nicole laughed, casting her eyes down as Judy wiggled the mascara brush against her lashes.

The hair and makeup were finished right on schedule. As the hairstylist fixed one last curl, Claire pulled out a wrapped box and gave it to Nicole. "You should open this," she said.

Nicole took it and tore the paper off, revealing a decorative box. She lifted the lid. A small tiara was nestled within.

"Oh my gosh," she said. It shone under the overhead lighting, casting sparkles on the wall.

"Kyle's grandmother and mother both wore this at their weddings," Claire said. "But before you can put that on, we need you to put something else on."

Judy and Sharice backed out of the room to give them some privacy. Claire unzipped the garment bag she'd hung on a shower rod and removed the dress inside. Caribbean blue fabric cascaded to the floor, the full skirt shimmering with sparkles. Beads wove in an intricate pattern up and down the fitted bodice.

"Is that for me?"

"Why don't we find out?" Claire loosened the corset and held it open.

Nicole shed her robe, puddling the silk onto the floor as she stepped into the dress, using Claire's shoulder for support. Claire slid the dress up and pulled the strings of the corset back tight. The photographer's shutter clicked furiously as Claire secured the bow and turned Nicole around.

With her shining chestnut hair, fairytale dress, and glittering tiara, Nicole looked exactly like a princess. She glowed as she twirled in front of the mirror.

"You're gorgeous. Now, let's get this party started." She guided Nicole out of the locker room with Rosie and waved her thanks to the manager in his office.

"Are you ready for this?" she grinned and pushed the front door open.

Nicole gasped. A white carriage shimmered under the fading afternoon light. The pair of horses tethered to the front snorted and pawed at the ground. A small crowd of people had gathered. They all turned as Nicole walked out of the building, resplendent in her evening gown. The crowd parted, all smiles at Nicole as she descended the stairs.

Candace stood on the sidewalk, capturing image after image of Nicole making her way to the carriage.

The driver hopped down to greet her, bending and kissing her hand. "Your highness, your prince has asked that I deliver this message," he said, handing over one of the bound scrolls that Claire had picked up.

Nicole untied the ribbon and opened the scroll.

"Nicole," she read aloud, "Please forgive me for not meeting you here tonight. I've been making preparations for what I hope will be one of the best nights of our life. As you may have heard, I've moved everything you own to my apartment. I hope you don't mind. I couldn't stand to spend one more night without you next to me. You are my light, my love, my everything. Tonight, I'm going to attempt to pay back a little of the overwhelming joy you bring into my life." Nicole's voice cracked. "To begin, ask the driver to take you to the place where we had our first date. Love always, Kyle."

She looked at Claire, eyes shining with tears.

"Don't you dare," Claire warned her.

Nicole blinked back tears and turned to the driver. "Could you take me to the archery range on Sunset Drive, please?"

The driver bowed to her. "Certainly. Your prince also asked that I give you this." He drew a small square box out of his pocket.

Nicole opened it and revealed the shining silver charm bracelet. "Oh my gosh." She ran a finger over a sterling silver camera and a globe. "You two thought of everything."

The bottom of Nicole's silky dress brushed the foothold as the driver helped her into the carriage. Claire followed, sitting across from Nicole so that she wouldn't be in the pictures. After a moment's pause, they were out on the street, clopping at a reasonable pace through the suburbs.

Every street they turned onto, people stopped when they heard the clip-clop of approaching horses.

"Look, mommy, a princess!" a little girl called from the sidewalk.

Nicole flushed and waved before reaching over and gripping Claire's hands. "You planned all this without me knowing?"

Claire smiled. "Kyle and I have been planning for months. It was so hard not to tell you."

"I thought he was being all moody because he was getting ready to break up with me," Nicole said. She laughed and threw her head back.

"No, it was definitely because I bothered him every five minutes, making sure everything would be perfect today."

They spent a few moments in silence, listening to the rhythmic sound of hooves and admiring the perfectly cloudless sky through the open bars of the carriage. The route to the archery range was a rural one. The traffic was sparse. The sun hung low, exaggerating the shadow of the carriage.

"Oh look, we're almost there." A sign that said Weaver's Archery rolled into view.

Nicole clapped her hands together excitedly. "Please tell me I get to shoot something."

"You might," Claire said, smiling mysteriously.

"Yes!" Nicole's fist shot into the air.

When the carriage rolled to a stop outside the store, Claire stepped out and helped Nicole down. She led her through the building and out to the back, where a lone bow hung on a strap. Nicole pulled a scroll from the bow and unrolled it.

Nicole, you thought I was crazy when I suggested going to an archery range for our first date. I was so nervous trying to show off in front of you that I almost shot the instructor instead of the target, but you took to the bow like a bird takes to flight.

I'll never forget how amazing it was to watch you hit the target on the first try. You have amazed me every single day since. Brush up on your archery skills and hit the target for a special invitation.

Love, Kyle.

Nicole smiled and clutched the scroll to her chest, as though she could feel Kyle through the paper. She handed the scroll over to Claire, who sealed it in a plastic bag with the other one. Every prop from today would be carefully preserved and artfully arranged in a commemorative shadow box and presented at the engagement party.

Nicole strode up to the line, lifted the bow, nocked an arrow, and pulled the string back with her right hand. She stared down the target and released the arrow with fierce precision. It slammed into the center of the target and buried itself deep, quivering with the impact.

Nicole twirled around in a victory dance, and Claire applauded before handing over another scroll and a small package.

"Good thing I didn't miss. That would have been embarrassing." Nicole undid the bow on the package and revealed two more charms—a shiny silver arrow and a crystal heart.

"Oh, they're gorgeous," she said.

Claire bent over to fasten them onto her bracelet, and Nicole pulled her in for a tight hug.

"I love this," she whispered.

Claire hugged her back and smiled. "Open the next scroll!"

Nicole unfurled it and read aloud. "Your prince cordially requests your presence at the home of Sir Lucas Islestorm for a formal ball. Please bring your dancing shoes."

Nicole looked down at the black flip-flops she wore underneath her dress. She turned to look at Claire. "Do these count as dancing shoes?"

Claire shook her head. "Come on. I think we have what we need in the carriage."

The pair walked back through the archery store, Nicole excitedly brandishing her new bow. The quiver from Marco's shop was still slung over her shoulder.

Claire pulled a box from under the carriage seat and handed it to Nicole. "I think these will help."

Nicole removed the lid and gaped at the shoes that sparkled in the tissue paper. She lifted one out and turned it. Wordlessly, she kicked off her flip-flops and slid on the heels. She buckled the straps and stood, taking a few test steps.

"Give me a spin." Claire twirled a finger.

Nicole lifted the train of her dress and spun clockwise. She came to a stop and smiled, hugging Claire for the fifth time that night. "I love them. I love everything. So, we're going to a ball? Like a real-life, fancy-pants ball?" She clapped her hands excitedly. "Kyle's actually going to be there, right?"

"You'll see."

CHAPTER TWENTY-EIGHT

To Do:
- *Send thank you note to archery range*
- *Leave Yelp review for carriage rental company*
- *Send donuts to police station*

CLAIRE AND NICOLE TOOK THEIR SEATS IN THE CARRIAGE again, enjoying glimpses of the technicolor sky as the sun set over the row of one-story buildings. Nicole took Claire's hand as the horses clopped down the street, excitedly chattering about how amazing the evening was and how much she just wanted to see Kyle.

The energy radiating from Nicole was palpable. She couldn't stop smiling, touching her dress, examining her shoes. And every few feet she looked up, leaned to the side. It was clear that she was dying to get to the ball to see Kyle.

This was why Claire planned for months, worked all hours of the night and day. This day would be completely free of beer bottle caps and projectile vomit. And serial killers, for that matter. Every moment would be perfect, a microcosm of Kyle's love for Nicole. A familiar house edged into view as they turned onto Luke's road. Less than a mile to go. She pulled her phone out to text Mindy.

Suddenly, a loud crack split the silence. The horses jolted in alarm. The world tilted as the back right corner of the carriage collapsed. Claire tumbled out the open side onto the street below, followed a second later by Nicole, who landed squarely on top of her.

Claire gasped, the wind knocked out of her. Her elbow was bleeding, and her tailbone stung where it had struck the pavement. Candace and the carriage driver jumped down to help both of them.

"Are you all right? I'm so sorry. I don't know what happened." The carriage driver lifted Nicole to her feet before pulling Claire up.

"Coli? Are you okay?" Clutching her side and struggling to catch her breath, Claire circled around her best friend. She brushed a small smudge of dirt off the hem of Nicole's dress.

Nicole shot her a thumbs up.

"We're good," Claire said. "Are you okay? How are the horses?"

"Everyone's okay," the driver reported.

"What happened?" she asked. "Was it the axle?" Months of planning and hard work brought to a screeching halt by gravity and shoddy carriage equipment.

"No," the driver replied, bending down to take a look at the wheel. "It seems to be an issue with the wheel—maybe the hub. It almost looks as though it's been tampered with, but that would be crazy. I swear it wasn't like this when we left the shop."

Hot, white rage bubbled up inside Claire. This wasn't a coincidence. This reeked of Wendy. Was she seeking her revenge against Claire for getting Jason put in jail?

"I'm so sorry. Let me call you a car." The driver pulled a phone out of his pocket.

Her stomach clenched. They were fifteen minutes outside the city limits. They didn't have time to wait for a car. And there was no way Nicole could hop out of a taxi instead of a fairytale carriage—her entire arrival would be utterly ruined.

"Wait," Claire said. "Could we borrow one of the horses? We're on a bit of a schedule, and I would really appreciate it."

"Of course," he said, removing the restraints from his horse and leading him closer. "I'm so sorry about this, miss," he said. "I'll get my boss to write this trip off for free."

She laid a hand on his arm. "This wasn't your fault. It was just an accident. We'll keep the horse safe up at the house until it's convenient for your company to collect him."

Claire approached the horse again. She reached into her clutch and pulled out a baby carrot. It was meant for Rosie, but she probably wouldn't mind sharing. "Well, hello there, you big, handsome steed. Would you mind if my friend rode you for just a little while?" she cooed, patting him softly between the eyes. She stroked the length of his body. The horse turned its head and dipped its nose to her. He accepted the carrot.

"Are you sure you're okay?" Claire asked, turning to Nicole.

"I'm fine."

"And the dress is good?"

"All good. You cushioned my fall." Her tiara still sparkled under the fading light.

Claire stepped close and took her arm. "I'm so sorry about this," she said. "I'm ruining your night. It was supposed to be perfect." Tears of frustration welled in her eyes, but she refused to let them escape.

Nicole took both her arms and stared at her. "Are you kidding me? This is the best night ever," she said earnestly. "I'm moved in with my boyfriend, I get to be a freaking princess for a day, and my best friend drove me around town in a horse-drawn carriage. And now we're going to a *ball,* where I'm presuming Kyle will finally put a ring on it." She waved her left hand around.

"Oh, is that what you thought was happening? This is all just for fun. He doesn't want to get married for another ten years."

Nicole glared at her. "Shut up."

They both laughed, and the driver and Claire helped Nicole onto the horse. There was no saddle. Claire prayed that the horse was docile and wouldn't go sprinting off into traffic, or worse.

"Since you don't have a saddle, try to keep your feet flexed so that you're not squeezing the horse with your heels," the driver said as he placed the reins in Nicole's hands. "He might interpret it as an encouragement to go faster. You'll want to go nice and slow."

She attempted to scoot up even farther to make room for Claire on the back of the horse, but the fluff from her dress covered the entire back end of the horse.

"Oh, no." Nicole tried to gather the fluff around her.

"Don't worry." Claire picked up the lead rope. She gave the horse a gentle tug, and they set off down the road. "We're maybe half a mile from Luke's. We'll be there in no time." It was closer to a mile, but Nicole didn't need to know that.

"But your shoes—you'll never be able to walk that far in those." Nicole frowned at Claire's stilettos. "Why don't you just take the other horse?"

"Don't worry about me." Claire brushed off the back of her dress as she gently tugged the horse along. There was no time to tend to her bloody elbow. "I was born to walk in stilettos. Besides, I want to leave the driver with the other horse in case he needs it."

After the first quarter mile, Claire's ankles began to wobble as she walked over the uneven asphalt. Warehouse floors and sidewalks were one thing, but the pothole-ridden streets of West Haven were something else entirely. She nearly tripped several times as she guided the horse around potholes. By the time they reached the bottom of Luke's driveway, her feet were two giant blisters. Her arches ached and her skin was rubbed raw, but still she stood straight and tall as she guided the horse up the final stretch of driveway. Why the hell did this driveway have to be so long?

Photographers hid behind the trees and bushes strung with fairy lights. She could only imagine their confusion at the absence of the carriage.

Nicole stared up at the trees, face softly illuminated by the warm glow of the lights. Curls spilled onto her bare shoulders and down her back, and her tiara sparkled. Despite her tumble from the carriage, she looked royal.

When they finally reached the house, Luke rushed out to help Nicole down from the horse. He had exchanged his work clothes for a well-tailored suit, and his hair was attractively mussed.

"What the hell happened?" he whispered to Claire. "You guys are twenty minutes late."

"Our carriage broke."

He steadied Nicole as she stepped carefully onto the

path, rhinestone shoes glittering against the stone. "Is everyone okay?"

Nicole laughed. "I'm fine. Claire fell out first and then got flattened by me."

He shook his head at Claire. "That sounds about right." He swiftly inspected both of them, glancing for an extra-long minute at the scrape on Claire's elbow. "I'll fix that later."

"Handle this, will you?" Claire asked, handing the horse's reins to her helper, Emily, who led the horse to a nearby tree. Good enough.

"My lady," Luke said, taking Nicole's arm and guiding her toward the house.

"Oh, Luke. Your house is amazing. I can't believe I haven't been here before." She clung to his arm as her heels sunk into the damp ground. "Wait, do you really have a brother named Johnny Liam?"

He laughed as they approached the doorway. "You got me. I don't have a brother. Claire came up with the cover story." He shot a glance over his shoulder. "Not her best work."

"I wondered why nobody seemed to know his name."

When Luke opened the front door, he revealed a hallway lined with photographs and the soft light of hundreds of candles. He released Nicole, and she walked slowly down the hall, eyes brimming with tears. Her skirt billowed out, but thankfully didn't get too close to the open flames. A flaming bride-to-be was not on the agenda.

Candace walked backward in front of her with her camera, capturing her inspecting pictures of their first date, parties, and vacations they had taken throughout the years. A soft hum emanated from the ballroom.

Reaching the ballroom doors, she turned the handles

and pushed them open, revealing her entire family lining the room in a great circle. Each family member held a candle. Flames flickered as they began singing the timeless fairytale song from *The Princess and the Arrow*. The chorus filled the room with warmth.

Nicole nearly collapsed to the floor. She dabbed at her eyes, turning to look at each person. The family members smiled back at her. Nicole's parents waved, smiling through their tears. There was still no sign of Kyle.

The song came to an end, and spotlights flooded the back of the room. The light revealed a heavily bearded man in his early thirties with an acoustic guitar, looking out into the audience with sleepy, soulful eyes.

"Nicole, this one's for you," he said. The opening chords of *Scintillate* filled the room.

Nicole collapsed into a chair in the front of the room. Claire gave her a squeeze as she and Luke glided by, assuming their position in the crowd.

Claire nodded at the family members and waited for a moment. When the song broke into the first chorus, everyone grabbed their partners and spread out across the dance floor. Almost everyone remembered the choreographed moves, and some even added a few personal touches. Nicole's grandpa exuberantly spun her grandma out, nearly sending her crashing into the punch bowl. Mindy twirled by with her British stud, giggling at something he said.

Nicole watched as everyone she loved danced past.

"Monochrome Monday?" she mouthed at Claire, who was clutching Luke for support.

Claire smiled and nodded, pulling a packet of tissues from her cleavage and tossing it to Nicole as she and Luke went spinning past.

Luke pulled Claire closer. "You're wincing with every single step."

"I walked a mile in stilettos. You try it and see if you still have feet afterwards."

"I'll take a look at what's left of your feet after we're done here," he promised.

As magical as this moment was—better than she had even imagined in spite of the circumstances—she hoped the song would end soon.

Finally, as the soft melody swung up into the last chorus, Luke and Claire stepped quickly off the dance floor. Everyone else followed their lead, revealing Kyle, standing with his hands clasped in front of him and grinning at his soon-to-be fiancée.

Nicole leapt up from her seat and ran to him, flinging her arms around him. He laughed and buried his face in her hair. He took both of her arms and led her to the center of the room.

They danced for a few moments. Kyle twirled her out, filling the room with sparkles from her crystal speckled skirt. They came back together for a dramatic dip as the last verse faded out. He set Nicole upright, then kneeled on the floor and drew a small black box from his pocket. He opened it and revealed her dream ring—a sparkling princess-cut.

Her hands flew to her mouth and tears sprung in her eyes for the thousandth time that evening.

Monochrome Monday played his guitar softly in the background, and Kyle took a deep breath.

"Nicole," he said, clutching her small hand in his. "My princess, my soulmate. I knew from our very first date that my life would never be the same again. Before you kicked my ass in that archery range, I hadn't really given a lot of thought to my future. But when I met you, you changed everything. You convinced me that I could go to law school and follow the dream that I hadn't ever admitted to anyone. You challenge and encourage me every day. I am continually overwhelmed by your kindness and strength. When I look into your eyes, I see my forever. Life won't always be easy, but with you by my side I know we'll be unstoppable. Would you do me the greatest honor of being my wife?"

"Yes!" she exclaimed. She didn't even wait for Kyle to put the ring on before flinging her arms around him again. She knocked the ring from his fingers, and it soared high.

Claire leaped forward and snatched it from the air. She crouched and handed it to Kyle, who was laughing and blinking tears out of his eyes. Then she scuttled away like a crab. The moment was almost perfect. And maybe that was okay.

The audience applauded and converged on the happy couple. There wasn't a dry eye in the house.

Claire sent up a silent prayer of thanks and immediately retreated to the back corner of the room, where Luke had packed up his camera and scored a chair and a plate of chocolate-covered fruit.

She stole one of his strawberries and sat on his lap. "We did it." She smiled at him as she popped the fruit in her mouth. "Wait—are you?"

"No, I am not," he said as he swiped his napkin underneath his eye. "I got some dust in my eye from all these books."

"Lucas Islestorm. You are a romantic at heart. I knew it." Was it her imagination, or was her heart actually growing?

"I wouldn't say that. But I would say that maybe what you do for a living isn't entirely stupid. It might have a tiny bit of emotional significance."

"Uh-huh," she said as she selected a blueberry. She couldn't stop smiling. "Thank you for everything. And for being willing to compromise on some things." She laid a hand on his chest.

"You had some okay ideas." He pressed his hand over hers.

She felt his heart beat strong and steady under her palm. It seemed a bit fast.

He reached over and unbuckled her shoes with one hand, allowing them to drop to the ballroom floor.

She moaned in pleasure and nuzzled into his neck. All the challenges of the biggest night of her career had passed, and now she just had to enjoy the party.

CHAPTER TWENTY-NINE

To Do:
- Celebrate the best night ever
- SLEEP
- Get to work on Tyler's proposal

HOURS LATER, CLAIRE WAVED FROM THE PORCH AS THE caterers loaded the last of their equipment into the van and drove away. She shut the front door and leaned against it, reveling in the quiet. Then she collapsed to the floor in a heap and yelped when her sore tailbone rammed the Italian tile. Rosie zoomed down the hallway, a halo of dust covering her face. She assisted Claire by furiously licking her feet.

Claire's eyelids snapped open. Luke crouched in front of her. How did he move so quietly?

"How does it feel to have the biggest night of your career under your belt?" he asked, reaching over to stroke her cheek. His shirt was half unbuttoned, and a long strip of toned chest showed.

"Exhausting."

He leaned over, picked her up, and tossed her over one shoulder.

"Hey. I can walk," she said, but didn't fight as he carried her upstairs. He whistled for Rosie. She sprinted up the steps past them and shoved the door to the master bedroom open with her snoot. She rocketed onto the king-sized bed and rolled onto her back as Luke carried Claire to the far side of the room.

He opened the door to the bathroom and revealed a whirlpool bathtub, filled to the rim with hot water and bubbles. He set her down gently on the floor and gave her a slow kiss.

"Don't be too long." He stroked Claire's cheek with his thumb before pulling away.

She smiled gratefully at him as he shut the door. She stripped and lowered herself into the tub. Her elbow knocked into something as she got in, and she turned to find a glass of chilled white wine waiting for her. Wow, he really did feel guilty. Sinking up to her neck into the warm depths, she closed her eyes with a smile and sipped the wine, letting the flavor roll over her tongue.

It was over. The biggest night of her career, a triumph of true love. Apart from the carriage incident, everything had gone as planned. The band was amazing, the food and drink had rave reviews from all attendees, and, most importantly, Nicole said she had the best night of her entire life. She had gone home with Kyle to spend their first night as an engaged couple in their own apartment. Was it too soon to start working on the blog post? Or maybe she should get a head start on the patriotic proposal.

The jets in the tub pummeled the aches of the day away. Maybe, just this once, she should stop and enjoy the moment. She closed her eyes.

They snapped open a second later. Would fireworks be too tacky for Tyler's proposal? Maybe veterans didn't like them. Maybe they felt disingenuous. Luke would know.

It was no use. There was no way she could turn her brain off. She poked the stopper with her toe, allowing the water to recede.

Climbing out of the tub, she covered herself with a fluffy towel. She pulled a clean, heather gray V-neck from a laundry basket in the corner of the attached walk-in closet and tugged it on. It fell halfway down her thighs and skimmed just below the lacy hem of her underwear. Good enough.

She stepped into the bedroom and stopped dead in her tracks. Luke sat on his bed shirtless, a pillow on his lap. He had one hand behind his head, and the other was holding the remote for the TV.

"How was your bath?" He smiled even wider when he saw her outfit, then set the remote down and opened his arms wide in welcome.

"Amazing," she said, limping as she came over to him. She sat next to him on the bed and brought her knees up to her chest. "Thank you. And I kind of borrowed your shirt. Listen, do you think—"

He shrugged and shushed her. "It looks better on you. Now come here." He caught her ankle with one hand and tugged her toward him.

Claire shrieked, trying to wiggle the hem of the shirt downward as it slid up, exposing the black lace of her underwear. She tucked the shirt between her legs, and he lifted both her feet onto the pillow and pulled out a bottle of cocoa butter. Her concerns about the fireworks were on the tip of her tongue, but then he picked up her left foot, rubbing firmly but avoiding the blisters.

She moaned in pleasure and went completely limp. "Oh my god. Please don't ever stop."

"That's what she said."

She held up one hand listlessly and gave him a weak, moisturized high-five before he returned to rubbing her feet. He moved on to the other aching foot, rubbing it into bliss.

"You are incredible." Another moan escaped her lips. What had she been so worried about? Right, fireworks.

"You haven't seen anything yet," he said softly. He put her right foot on his shoulder and began to plant tender kisses on her ankle, then her calf, and up to her knee. He glided both hands up the length of her thigh.

She trembled beneath his touch as his hands gently pushed the hem of her shirt up. Her leg fell limply to the side as he climbed over her, skimming his hands over her stomach and tugging the waistline of her panties down just a centimeter.

He tenderly kissed the newly exposed skin. She was going to explode in a cloud of glitter. Her body was relaxed yet rigid, straining toward those lips. Oh, those lips.

An involuntary moan escaped her, and Luke must have taken it for encouragement, because he tugged her panties down another centimeter and kissed her again.

Her body opened, yearned. His touch sent tingles shooting everywhere. Her toes curled. Her hands fisted at her side. Involuntarily, she flashed back to the day Luke had opened his office door and shown her his four walls of horror. She had unknowingly been a part of it for weeks, almost the entire time he knew her. And he had never said a word until the evidence was undeniable.

And what would this do to their friendship? He lived here now. He was Kyle's best friend. What if they started dating, and it ended terribly? What if she spent every Friendsgiving for the next decade bristling when Luke walked another floozy through the front door? She was jeopardizing everything.

One finger slipped underneath the hem and was only centimeters from exploring deeper when Claire pushed up onto her elbows.

"Luke," she said softly.

"Hmm?" he asked, still planting a trail of kisses over her bikini line.

She shuddered and her back arched involuntarily. She burned. She ached. It nearly killed her to ask him to stop. "I can't," she pleaded.

He looked up at her from his position in between her legs. "What's wrong?"

She bit her lip. How could she even begin to articulate the jumble of emotions balled up in her stomach? Maybe it was best to just be honest. "You make me feel a way I haven't felt in a long time. Maybe even a way I've never felt. It's a lot, and to be honest, it scares me. We haven't even been on a date yet. We don't really know each other that well. And there is the matter of your reputation."

"My reputation?" His eyebrows arched and he sat up too. The softness in his eyes was gone. They were hard now, like glacier ice.

"There have been rumors of you being somewhat of a... ladies' man." The words tumbled out quickly, shamefully. She pulled her knees back and wrapped her arms around them. "And I've had my fill of ladies' men. I can't do casual dating. I get too attached. I'm a serial monogamist. An occupational hazard, I guess you could say." She couldn't bring herself to meet his eyes.

"There aren't any other women, if that's what you're worried about."

"That's good to know, but it's not entirely the whole problem. I'm a girl with baggage. The last man I let between my legs fucked my nemesis in a bathroom during my awards ceremony. And probably murdered half a dozen people. After Jason, I've come to realize how important trust really is. I can't go through something like that again. And after what happened with the whole Widowmaker ordeal, I'm having a difficult time fully trusting you."

Luke withdrew. "You really don't think you can trust me?"

"I just need some time, I think." She cast her eyes down and willed the blood to flow back to her head where it belonged. "And what if we did this—started something—and it all went horribly wrong? You live here now. We have the same friends. We would still see each other."

He shrugged. "Eh, I'd just move back to California."

She hit him. "I'm serious."

"Claire," he said, reaching out to stroke her cheek. "You are the most beautiful, infuriating, fascinating woman I have ever met. I get it. I messed up. Thank you for being honest with me. I'll wait. I can't promise that I won't try to persuade you, but I'll wait."

"How about we consider revisiting this—" she trailed a finger down his abs—"after we go on that date you mentioned."

"Fine." He sighed and kissed the top of her head. "You like Italian?"

"Of course. Who doesn't like Italian?"

"Good. Then I'm taking you out for Indian."

"Shut up." She dug her elbow into his side. "And I'm paying for the date."

"Ouch. No, you're not. Good night." He kissed the spot behind her right earlobe and sent another cascade of tingles coursing through her body. He threw off the covers and stood.

A weight had been lifted from her. Though her lady parts still veritably hummed for his affections, she had said her piece. He hadn't thrown her out, even though she had called him a ladies' man.

"Luke?"

"You change your mind?" he asked, turning back to the bed.

She laughed. "No. But you could stay, you know. Or I can go to the guest room if you're uncomfortable."

"I think we're past that point, don't you?" He climbed into bed and gathered her into his arms.

She smiled. There was a beat of silence. "Do you think fireworks are tacky? As a veteran?"

He unwrapped his arms and sat up. "What are you talking about?"

"For my next proposal. Mindy was thinking fireworks because two super cute veterans are getting engaged, but I wonder about PTSD and—"

"Claire."

"What?"

"You just finished the biggest proposal you've ever done. Can't you just enjoy the moment?"

"Right, because I'm sure after *The Suburban Hustle* came out you took a two-week vacation to Cabo and didn't pick up a camera the entire time."

Luke shrugged. "Point taken. Fireworks are fine, but definitely check with the groom-to-be. Night." He rolled over and turned off the light, then dragged her into the tangle of sheets with him.

The skin of his bare chest was hot beneath her cheek. Her nether regions still screamed at her. The memory of Luke between her legs seared into her brain like a brand. Maybe stopping the train to pound town had been a mistake. Maybe she should have relaxed and jumped in headfirst instead of overthinking like she always did. But something about being with Luke was different. She had been honest with him—maybe even to a fault—and that's what counted.

CHAPTER THIRTY

To Do:
- *Outline acceptance speech for POY Award*
- *Engagement gift for N & K*
- *Caterer for engagement party—not Yuffie!*

THE NEXT WEEK PASSED IN A BUSTLE OF APPOINTMENTS AND new client requests. Nicole furnished Claire with the edited pictures from Barney's proposal, and they were absolutely gorgeous. Claire presented them to the happy couple, who were already planning their honeymoon in Hawaii. Claire had been charged with planning Nicole and Kyle's engagement party. Nicole, who had waited for so long to get engaged that she apparently was hellbent on cramming as many events as she could into the shortest timeframe possible, decided that the upcoming weekend would be the perfect opportunity. Claire flew into a planning frenzy. Finding a venue and a caterer in less than a week was going to take a miracle. Hopefully, this wasn't a sign of impending Bridezilla behavior from her best friend.

Fortunately, things had largely fallen into place. Barney was so thrilled with the pictures that he rented the ballroom in his nearby hotel to her at a discount. One of their favorite caterers had a cancellation and squeezed them in. Nicole asked Claire to be her maid of honor, and Claire happily accepted. Between new clients and planning the last-minute engagement party, she barely had time for anything else. In light of the party, she had postponed her date with Luke. They had rescheduled it for the day after the party, when things would slow down a bit for both of them. He wouldn't tell her where he planned to take her, which both infuriated and intrigued her.

She posted a teaser blog featuring Nicole's proposal on Monday with the scant photos and B roll she had access to. By Tuesday, her website traffic had quadrupled. She scrolled over the post again, checking the current comment count— over two hundred. The pictures were flawless, and Nicole looked like a true princess despite the carriage incident. The Planner of the Year award was almost guaranteed.

She had reported the broken carriage to the police the night after the engagement. The driver of the carriage had been questioned, and they also checked the security footage from the camera outside the archery range where the carriage had parked. They had called Claire in to review the footage. At one point, a figure dressed in black had approached the carriage. A tool poked out of their sleeve, and the figure had loosened the bolt. She strongly suspected that the hooded figure was Wendy, but she had no real proof.

CLAIRE SPENT THE DAY OF NICOLE'S ENGAGEMENT PARTY careening from one task to another. Despite the stress, her heart was happy. By some miracle, she had managed to throw together a tasteful and sure-to-be joyous occasion to celebrate her best friend. Love always wins.

Wearing a floor-length red dress and matching strappy heels, she walked into the hotel an hour early. One of Nicole's aunts was lurking in the hallway. It was definitely the one with the peanut allergy and the surprisingly young boyfriend. What was her name again? Rhonda? Rachel? *Hmmm.* Claire opted for a cheerful wave and slipped into the bathroom. One final makeup check. Her falsies were in place, and her hair was as good as it was going to get. Luke was coming tonight, and it couldn't hurt to give him a little preview of Date Night Claire.

She walked into the ballroom and deposited her gift— the proposal shadowbox, a set of monogrammed towels, and Mr. and Mrs. Mugs—on the gift table. Ray, Nicole's father, appeared at her elbow. His salt and pepper hair was smoothed back with pomade. He looked like an aged James Bond.

"Did you hear Nicole lost her engagement ring?"

Claire's mouth dropped open. Not the beautiful princess-cut diamond Kyle had saved months to afford.

"Are you serious?" She racked her brain. She was almost certain Kyle had confirmed the ring was insured. But that wouldn't replace the sentimental memory. This party was already a disaster.

"Yeah, she lost it in the grass while they were golfing." He took a sip of his martini.

Claire stared at him blankly. Nicole hated golf. She said it was a sport designed by sexists. "You try swinging a club past anything bigger than an A cup," she had said the last time it had come up in conversation.

"Oh, stop it, Ray," Nicole's mom, Molly, said. She squeezed between him and Claire and gave her a big hug.

"You might say it was a...diamond in the rough." Ray wiggled his comically bushy eyebrows.

"You almost gave me a heart attack." Claire swore inwardly and leaned in to accept a hug from Ray. Bamboozled again by one of his magnificently ill-timed dad jokes.

"Anyway, should we go over the schedule? Dinner is at seven. There is a vegetarian option available for Aunt Linda. I had them remove the mango from the chocolate fountain arrangement because of Kyle's allergy. The champagne toast is scheduled for eight o'clock sharp." She handed over a schedule printed on premium cardstock.

"Thank you, Claire. Say, how long till we get invited to your engagement party, huh?" Ray inquired. He shoved the schedule into the inside pocket of his suit jacket without looking at it. Molly elbowed him in the ribs.

"Approximately forever," Claire said with a smile and started to walk away. "Oh, and Ray, please don't mention anything about a shotgun in your toast."

He chuckled.

Someone tapped Claire on the shoulder, and she turned.

"Barney! I didn't know you'd be here. It's so good to see you. Thank you so much for renting the ballroom at such short notice. We would have been in serious trouble without you."

"It was no trouble," he said and shook her hand. A watch that cost more than Claire's car glinted under the overhead light. "The pictures your photographer got are worth more than a few favors from me."

"She's so talented, isn't she? Is Victoria with you?"

Barney shook his head. "Parent/teacher conferences tonight."

"On a Friday? That sounds like cruel and unusual punishment."

He laughed. "You have no idea. Last semester, a parent found out which car Victoria drove and egged it because they didn't like their kid's evaluation."

"Oh my gosh. That's awful," she said. "Teachers don't get paid enough. Oh, Barney, you'll have to excuse me. The videographer just came in. Thank you so much again."

"Good to see you, Claire," he said as she sped off toward the door.

Luke had just crossed the threshold. He was dressed to kill in a black designer suit and tie. His normally unruly hair was shorter and parted smartly to one side. It looked like he had just walked off a shoot for a magazine. He waved at Claire and headed toward her. Her heart lifted.

"Barney looked happy," he told her as soon as he was within earshot. God, he smelled amazing. "Guess the fountain didn't ruin everything after all."

"He was really pleased with the pictures. Once again, Nicole saved the day."

"You don't look half bad." He took her hand and planted a tender kiss on it.

"And you look exhausted," she said as she traced her thumb over the bags beneath his eyes. "How are things going with the documentary?"

He frowned. "You know, I'm trying to plug Jason into what I have, and something's just not quite right. Can we talk about it later? After the party?"

A tingle of fear ran up Claire's spine. Curiosity burned. "Sure. It's a date. I better go find the bride-to-be." She stepped in to kiss him but thought better of it. Nicole's notoriously gossipy cousins were here. There was no reason to fire up the rumor mill before the hors d'oeuvres were even served.

Claire met Nicole as she was coming through the door with Kyle. Nicole was stunning in a midnight-blue lace gown. Kyle, in a three-piece suit, took off to greet his parents. She helped herself to a glass of champagne from a tray proffered by a passing waiter. Normally, she didn't drink at events that she planned, but this time she was part of the celebration.

Nicole's parents waved at them, and they both started to head over to the table where they stood.

"Where's Mindy?" Nicole asked as they passed by the bar.

"Mindy should be here in about an hour. She's on a video conference with our next client and—"

They both stopped dead.

"Is that—"

"You have got to be freaking kidding me."

Jason, wearing a charcoal gray suit, was standing by the bar with Wendy next to him, grasping a martini in her skeletal hand.

"But he's supposed to be in jail." Claire's heart was pounding so hard she could feel her pulse in her eyes. She gripped the back of a chair, suddenly lightheaded. Should she run?

"He must have finally posted bail. Hold my drink. I'm going to kill him." Nicole shoved her champagne flute in Claire's direction.

"Nicole, don't. It's not safe."

Nicole ignored her and marched straight across the ballroom. Claire followed a few paces behind. Jason wasn't going to add another victim to the list tonight. She tossed back the rest of her champagne and slammed the empty glass down on a nearby table.

They made a beeline for Jason, nearly knocking down Kyle's grandmother on the way.

"Oh hey, Nicole. I've been meaning to say congratulations on your engagement. What's up?" Jason tipped his beer bottle in her direction and gave Wendy a swift squeeze on her bony ass.

Wendy giggled and wiggled closer to him. She didn't seem to notice when a bit of beer dribbled down onto her dress.

"What's up? What's up? Oh, you know, I was just wondering what the hell my best friend's lying and cheating asshole of an ex and her stalker are doing at my engagement party. I'm surprised you were able to take a night off of your busy schedule of murdering people and spying on Claire for a social event you weren't invited to."

Luke looked up, narrowing his eyes at Jason. He came to stand in front of Claire.

Jason held up his hands in defense. "First of all, I'm not a murderer. And second, we just came here to get a message to Claire."

Nicole marched up to Jason, nearly nose to nose with him thanks to the extra four inches she gained from her Louboutins—an engagement gift from her mother. "Jason, murderers are not welcome here. You need to leave." She whirled around, eyes scanning the room. When she spotted her fiancé, she waved to get his attention and crooked her finger at him.

Kyle took a step forward and was midway through a sip of beer when he realized who Nicole was standing next to. He spluttered and set his drink on the bar. He strode over quickly and placed one arm protectively around Nicole and put a reassuring hand on Claire's shoulder.

"What are you doing here, Jason?" Kyle demanded.

"We need to talk to Claire." Jason rolled his eyes and took a sloppy sip of beer, dripping some onto his stone gray shirt. Some landed in Wendy's hair, and she pushed him away.

"Ew, babe. Now I'm going to smell like a bar bathroom all night and—"

"That's not going to happen," Kyle interrupted. "If Claire wants to talk to you, she'll call you."

Jason slammed his beer down on the table and drunkenly stumbled toward Kyle. Kyle and Luke stiffened. Claire swore she heard the audible crack of knuckles.

"Claire," Jason said, attempting to peer over Luke's shoulder. "I need you to call off the cops. I know you're the one who gave them my name. I'm not the freaking West Haven Widowmaker, and Wendy had nothing to do with your carriage problem."

Wendy gasped and dug her elbow into his side.

"I never mentioned a carriage problem," Claire said icily. She fucking knew it.

Jason stammered. "Uh, right. We heard about it. On your blog."

"I didn't advertise the carriage problem on my blog." She crossed her arms in front of her chest.

A small crowd of people began to grow around the group.

"Listen, Jason has a really good alibi for the break-in. We were at home. In the bedroom." She placed a territorial hand around Jason's shoulder.

Claire rolled her eyes. "As if anyone would believe the bullshit that spews from your mouth."

"I have a security camera outside my house, and I shared the footage with the police. The timestamp shows that we were there when the break-in happened."

"Really? How about the timestamp from the footage of Courtney Stevens climbing into Jason's car the morning she disappeared?"

Silence fell over the room.

"Jason didn't fucking do it," Wendy spat, but she didn't offer any alternative explanations. "And you got him arrested. Now I suggest you get my boyfriend's name out of your goddamn mouth. Oh, and I released that footage of you tackling a widow to the press."

"Widower. And he has a name." Claire started to take a step forward, but Luke grabbed her hand. "What were you doing, Jason? What did you do to that poor girl?"

"Listen." He shoved his hands in his pocket. "She did get in my car that morning. But it's only because I was selling her something."

"What, did she have a desperate need for one of your old football jerseys?"

"No. I was, you know." He mimed rolling up a joint. Great, her ex-fiancé was now a drug dealer. So that was why Wendy often smelled faintly of weed.

Kyle stepped in front of the pair. His cheeks were flushed. "Listen, you've said what you came here to say. This is a private party for invited guests only. Not cheaters and murderers and stalkers. Now get the hell out."

Jason burped loudly. "Fine. I'm going to take this little lady home and do unspeakable things to her." He gave Wendy another squeeze and shot a drunken look at Claire.

Claire rolled her eyes to cover the overwhelming sense of dread that was growing in her stomach with each second.

Jason grabbed his date's rear again. Was he being overly

affectionate with her or just losing his balance? How did this drunk and/or high idiot get away with five murders?

"Let's get out of here," Jason slurred. "I have a pair of handcuffs and a blindfold with your name on them, Clai—Wendy." He faltered and glanced down at his date. She was checking a message on her pink rhinestone-bedazzled cell phone and hadn't seemed to notice the near slip-up.

"So nice to see you again," Wendy called, her voice sickly sweet. She shot a deadly look at Claire before tugging Jason toward the door.

Still in earshot, Wendy began complaining loudly. "Thank god we're leaving. This was the lamest party I've been to since my Nana's funeral. And how is that girl engaged and I'm not? Did you see the gallery of her photos on the way in? They look like they were taken by a toddler with a Fisher-Price camera."

"All right, that's it." Claire tossed her clutch to Kyle and stormed toward the departing couple. Every cruel thing Wendy had ever done burned fresh in Claire's mind as she grabbed her by the hair and whipped her around.

A sudden hush fell over the room.

"What the hell did you just say?" Something was loose in her hand. She glanced down and opened her fist. A hunk of fake hair dropped to the ground.

"Ow! What the hell, whore?" Wendy glared at Claire and pressed a hand to her skull.

"I said, what the hell did you just say?" Claire was shouting now.

It wasn't fair. A probable murderer was out on bail. Her nemesis had tampered with her perfect proposal and then had the audacity to show up to the engagement party. No one insulted her friends' professions. *No one.*

Wendy took two steps forward and got right up in

Claire's face. Minty gum and the suffocating stink of her rich girl perfume filled her nostrils.

"I said your friend is an untalented hack," Wendy enunciated clearly despite the amount of alcohol she seemed to have consumed. "I can't believe anyone would want to marry her." She gave Claire a shove, making her bump into the buffet table. Several dishes rattled.

The sound of Claire's fist smashing into Wendy's nose halted all conversation.

An ear-piercing scream escaped Wendy's throat. "My nose! You bitch!"

Claire flexed her fist. There was almost certainly a startling amount of rhinoplasty compromised in that one hit.

Wendy launched herself at Claire in a whirlwind of stifling perfume and acrylic nails. She managed to grab hold of a hunk of Claire's hair. Her scalp smarted where her stitches had yet to dissolve. Wendy raised her knee and tried to hit Claire in the abdomen, probably flashing her vagina to the entire party.

"Nice try, but mine is real, bitch." Claire slithered into a better position and steamrolled Wendy in the opposite direction. Directly into the buffet table.

A warmer overturned, sending mashed potatoes and green beans oozing to the floor. Gravy splashed onto Wendy's tight mini dress. Oh, hell. Ray and Molly were definitely not getting their security deposit back.

Wendy roared and dove at Claire. "You're just mad because Jason picked me." She grunted as she tried to ram her head into Claire's midsection.

"You and Jason deserve each other," Claire said as she swept Wendy's legs out from under her and sent her crashing to the floor. Her head landed in a plop of mashed potatoes. Claire climbed on top of her and straddled her waist, pinning her arms to the side. "And for the record, he's been sending me apology flowers and love notes for the length of your entire relationship."

"I don't know what she's talking about," Jason chimed in, utterly drunk and unconvincing.

Wendy wrestled her right arm out from under Claire and slashed her across the face, breaking two of her fake fingernails off. Her cheek smarted. Claire slapped her right back, sending a spray of mashed potatoes across the carpet.

As Wendy moaned, Claire wiped the back of her arm across her face. Bright red blood appeared on the back of her hand. If those scratches left permanent scars, there would be hell to pay. She picked up a fistful of Wendy's hair extensions, smeared them in the mashed potatoes, sopped up some gravy, and stuffed them down Wendy's dress.

"Never—" Claire gave an opened-handed smack to the right side of Wendy's face. Wendy squirmed underneath her, unable to escape the hold that Claire had on her.

"Speak poorly—" She slapped Wendy on the other side of the face. One of her false eyelashes had partially come off and was hung off her eyelid like an escaping spider.

"Of my friend—" Slap.

Wendy's hands flapped uselessly, pinned to the floor by Claire's knees.

"Again!" After one final slap and a knee to her ribs, Luke and Kyle dragged Claire off Wendy.

Wendy pulled herself off the floor by clawing her way up Jason's pant leg. She had a glob of mashed potatoes stuck to the crown of her head, and green beans were falling out the bottom of her dress.

"Get the hell out!" Kyle roared at Wendy and Jason.

Wendy screamed in fury, grabbed Jason's arm, and started marching him to the door.

Claire reached down, picked up a gloppy mass of potatoes, and nailed Jason directly in the back of the head. He turned and glared at her but didn't say another word.

Somewhere in the corner of the room, a partygoer started a slow clap as the disheveled couple finally left the party. No one joined in, however, and the clapping soon ceased.

"So," Ray said, sidling up next to the group. He took a sip of his dirty martini. "Who are our new friends? Where do I know him from?"

"That's Claire's ex, Jason. He was arrested under suspicion of being the West Haven Widowmaker."

"Huh." Ray swirled his martini. "Doesn't seem like the type."

Nicole picked a green bean out of Claire's hair.

Claire surveyed the destruction. She had all but destroyed a five-square-foot area of carpet. That was going to be a tough one to explain to Barney. She was going to have to call in the big guns for the cleaning.

Molly appeared at Claire's side and started dabbing at her dress with a cloth napkin.

Every eye in the ballroom was still turned toward her. The gossipy cousins were standing in a circle in the corner of the room, whispering. Nicole's grandmother had collapsed into a chair. Great, now she was sending her best friend's family members into cardiac arrest. She was hot with shame and rage. Her stomach contorted. The cut on her cheek burned, and the palm of her hand stung. Without a doubt, she had ruined the party. How was she ever going to live this one down? Or even begin to make it up to Nicole and Kyle?

"Sorry, everyone," she said sheepishly, cheeks burning with embarrassment. She mumbled a quick "excuse me" to

Nicole, took her clutch back from Kyle, and ran out into the hall.

Was that Luke calling her name? She ignored it and ran until she pushed through the door of the ladies' room. She took a deep breath and stared at her reflection. Tears were threatening to slide down her cheeks, but she wouldn't allow that. She wasn't seventeen anymore, pining over a cross-country runner who didn't know she was alive. She was Claire Freakin' Hartley, engagement planner extraordinaire and fulfiller of dreams. She would not cry over a guy, especially a prematurely balding potato who was stupid enough to date a toxic woman like Wendy and who may have murdered five people. She pulled out endless sheets of paper towels and attempted to undo the damage.

A few moments later, Nicole pushed the door open a crack. "Claire?"

Claire turned to face her, tears running hot down her cheeks. So much for not crying. "I'm so sorry I've ruined your party. I don't know what came over me. I think the stress from the past month finally got to me, and I just snapped."

Nicole crossed the room and pulled her into a hug, ignoring the blobs of food that threatened her own dress. "Are you kidding me? People are going to be talking about this party until the end of the century. You got rid of two horrible, uninvited party guests. You should consider a career as a bouncer."

Claire gave her a watery smile. "I've made such a mess of everything. That was so incredibly unprofessional. And now Luke saw me go nuts, so he knows I'm a crazy person." She plopped down onto the pinstriped couch by the sink. "God, what is wrong with me?"

"Absolutely nothing. You literally just chased a murderer

away from my party. Besides, after that girl-on-girl action, I wouldn't be surprised if Luke's just more impressed with you than ever." Nicole squeezed her hand. "Let's get you cleaned up."

"No, no. You need to be enjoying your party, not carrying around my emotional baggage. I've already made you miss too much. Go talk to your family. Tell them I had a mental breakdown. I'm going to try my best to make myself look like a person and not a four-course meal, and then I'm going to help clean up the mess I made."

"Are you sure?"

"Yes. I'll be out in a few minutes."

"Okay. We'll get drunk and dance when you come back. Mindy's going to be so pissed that she missed this." Nicole chuckled as she left.

As soon as the door had shut again, Claire shoved a chair in front of it and sat again on the couch, closing her eyes and resorting to her old trick of alternate nostril breathing. Eventually her heart rate slowed to a normal pace, and the dread that had settled into her stomach began to dissipate. There was nothing she could do. She couldn't turn back time. She couldn't erase the memory of her pummeling Wendy from everyone's mind. All she could try to do was make up for it. She straightened up and set to the daunting task of cleaning herself up.

Flecks of potatoes and gravy covered the sink, counter-top, and floor by the time she managed to get the worst of it off. She scraped as much as she could out of her hair and then twisted it up into a knot. Her dress still showed wet spots all the way down its satin length. She opened her clutch and took out her spot-cleaning pen. But there was no point.

She resigned herself to a visit to the dry cleaner and

quickly touched up her eye makeup. Twirling in the mirror to examine the back of her dress—which escaped largely unscathed because Claire spent most of the fight on top of the dog pile—she deemed herself as good as she was going to get. She went to snap her clutch shut when her phone lit up with a message from Nicole.

DJ's playing our song next. Get those dancing shoes cleaned off.

The doorknob that she'd blocked with a chair wiggled. She couldn't very well hold the bathroom hostage all night. She did one final check of her damage control and thrust the bathroom door open, making a mental note to send apology gift cards to the caterer and the cleaning staff at the Heirloom Hotel. The handle rattler wasn't outside, so they must have gone off to find a different bathroom.

As she exited, she paused. When she had entered the bathroom minutes ago, hadn't all the lights in the hallway been on? Now, everything was dark, and she could only make out a glowing red exit sign way down at the end of the hall. Maybe the hotel was trying to save money. She shrugged and kept walking.

The soft lighting of the ballroom spilled out into the hall. Faint strains drifted out of a song Claire and Nicole had danced to on her twin bed in college while housing a community-sized tub of cheese balls. Everything still smelled strongly of banquet food. Hopefully, the caterer had been able to replace what she destroyed. If not, she'd order a crapload of pizzas.

She straightened her spine and stood taller, drawing her shoulders away from her ears and trying to adopt a serene expression. There was no way she'd let anyone see her like that again. Despite the nearly insurmountable evidence to the contrary, she was a professional, sane human being.

When she was less than ten yards from the double doors, a hand holding a napkin came out of nowhere and clamped over her nose and mouth. Her eyes flew wide in shock. Another arm wrapped around her waist and dragged her backward, away from the light and warmth of the ballroom.

Claire sucked in a breath to scream and clawed at the hand. Was it Jason? He hadn't left after all. She jammed her elbows backwards and made contact, but the edges of her vision were already going blurry. Her head was painfully fuzzy, like static on a TV. She fought, kicking wildly and trying to scream. Her shoe dangled precariously from her toe and dropped to the floor, and then everything went dark.

CHAPTER THIRTY-ONE

To Do:
- Apologize to mom
- From now on, carry Taser in bra

CLAIRE AWOKE NAUSEATED AND GROGGY. HAD HER EYES BEEN glued shut? Her lids had never been this heavy. Maybe her falsies had fused to her lower eyelids. She gingerly pried her eyes open and stared out at an underground parking garage. Floodlights shone every ten yards or so, but much of the garage was cast entirely in shadow. Massive concrete pillars emerged from the ground. The smell of dirt and gasoline was heavy in the air. Everything was silent except for the soft buzz of electricity.

Pain radiated from her scalp like someone had taken an ice pick to her head. For all she knew, Jason may have done exactly that. But where was he?

Her hands were bound to the pillar behind her back, and her arms were stretched back so severely that her muscles burned. There was a strange weight around her legs. She glanced down. That son of a bitch. Her missing wedding dress draped over her.

She tried to scream, but layers of duct tape covered her lips. Her bare feet were bound together by some rope, and they rested on the concrete floor of the basement. She fought furiously against the bonds that held her. They bit into her wrists. Adrenaline surged through her. She began to hyperventilate, struggling to control her breathing.

She wrenched herself back and forth, trying to loosen her bonds.

"I wouldn't do that if I were you," a quiet voice said from somewhere in the shadows. What the hell? That didn't sound like Jason.

Footsteps approached in the darkness. She fought even harder, heart slamming against her ribcage.

A dark figure emerged and strode toward her. When he stepped into the light, her thrashing stilled in confused recognition.

Barney Windsor. What the hell?

The hotel tycoon and flash mob proposer stalked up to Claire and stared into her eyes.

Ah, fuck. Could planning a proposal for a serial killer disqualify her from the Planner of the Year award? She owed Jason an apology.

"Those knots will just get tighter, you see. I was a Boy Scout." Barney pulled a knife out of his pocket and turned it in the light. He reached out and rubbed the tip of it against her face. He stared at her for a moment, then slapped her across the face with his other hand.

She gasped underneath the duct tape. Her face stung. Tears sprung into her eyes, but she was not going to give this psycho the satisfaction of seeing her cry.

He leaned in, inches from her face. "I'm going to take the gag off now. You can scream if you want, but no one will hear you." He slit the tape covering her mouth with his knife, catching the edge of her lip with the tip and sending a warm trickle of blood to her chin.

Claire immediately screamed.

"PLATYPUS! PLATYPUS!"

He took a step back. "Huh?"

Damn. Despite having a psychic for a mother, simply yelling the safe word they had agreed upon was probably not going to cut it without a phone. She switched to expletives instead.

"You sneaky, stalking piece of shit! How dare you! You've ruined everything! My business," she cried, already anticipating the headlines naming her as a proposal planner for serial killers. Her voice echoed off the walls and bounced back to her, a cacophonous symphony of rage and panic.

Barney waited, running his thumb over his knife as she continued to scream. After several straight minutes of shouting every swear word she had ever heard, Claire sagged against her bonds, gasping for breath and sobbing.

"Why are you doing this to me?" she asked, her voice raw. Was he really that mad about the fountain? If she didn't make it out of here alive, her best friend's last memory of her would be beating the shit out of Wendy in a pile of mashed potatoes.

He stepped closer again, looking her directly in the eyes. "You really don't remember me, do you?"

"Of course I remember you, Barney. I don't have the short-term memory of a goldfish." Her mind was sprinting a mile a minute. She couldn't move. There were no weapons, no one to hear her scream. She didn't even know where she was. He had all the control.

He held up a hand to stop her and brandished the knife with the other. "Not from the proposal. From before." The tip of the knife pressed into her exposed collarbone. It burned, but she didn't give him the satisfaction of a response.

"Before?" Her fingers clawed at the ropes binding her hands. What was he talking about?

"In college. You were a freshman. I was a junior. We dated."

"W-what?" Impossible. She twisted and stretched her ankles, trying to loosen the bonds. If she could keep him talking, maybe she could buy enough time to get them off.

"I dated your roommate too. We were all in the same business class. I'm not surprised you don't remember. You were as conceited then as you are now," he said. His nostrils flared, and the tip of the knife pressed harder. "I asked you on a date, and you went out with me out of pity," he spat the words out.

He used his free hand to smooth his hair. "I used to be a fat nobody who lived for homework and video games. No one respected me, no one took me seriously. I was friend-zoned by just about every girl in the school. Courtney only went out with me because I agreed to buy her alcohol. Every other girl shut me down. Except for you, Claire. You said yes."

A thunderbolt struck her. Older Rich Guy from her Courtney hookup notebook. It was Barney. She had forgotten the shapeless, pudgy kid who used to sit behind her in a business class. One day after class, he had cornered her and asked her on a date. He looked so nervous that she thought he might pass out, so she had said yes.

He seemed to notice the recognition in her eyes. "Ah, yes. Now you remember Bernard the loser," he spat. His knife pierced her skin, but she didn't want to look away from his face. A warm line of blood slipped down her chest, likely staining the sweetheart neckline of her gown. She had gone to twelve different bridal stores before she found this dress. How. Fucking. Dare. He.

She continued to wiggle her limbs, trying to remember her mom's lecture on escaping from bondage. She shouldn't have given Brian the PI the night off.

"I took you to a nice restaurant, brought you flowers, and complimented your dress. Do you remember what you said to me at the end of our date?"

A terrible realization dawned on her. "That you were a great friend," she whispered hoarsely.

"Yes, there it is. The F word that seemed to follow me my entire life," Barney spat. His eyes were wide and desperate like those of a caged animal. "Poor, fat Bernard Twigg who couldn't get a girlfriend. But you know something, Claire? After you shot me down, I started working out. I got better grades, and I took over my dad's company after I killed him."

He took a step toward her, and she jerked away from him, painfully thumping her head on the pillar at her back. She worked frantically at a knot with one hand. Had it loosened just a little? She needed to keep him talking so she could find out. "Wait a minute. Twigg? Your last name is Windsor."

"It was Twigg until my stupid whore of a mother told me who my father was. Clayton Montgomery Windsor II. He was married when he had an affair with my mother. He'd offered her money to get rid of me, but she decided to raise me herself. She didn't tell me who my father was until I was a sophomore at Venor. I wasted no time making my existence known to him. A little blackmail went a long way. He was long divorced by then and never had children. He groomed me for a pathetic management position at one of his hotels to keep me quiet, but he didn't know I planned to have it all."

"So, you killed him." She made a mental note to spring for the premium background checks for new clients.

He shrugged. "I was his next of kin. And I got everything that was due to me. I took his name and his hotels. His summer home in the Hamptons. I even took a few suits from his closet."

He backed away and did a full turn. "Not so much of a loser anymore, am I?" He held his hands at his sides, giving her ample time to observe his sharp outfit and slender waistline. "Now when I walk into a room, people take me seriously." His gray eyes were wild as he came back and ran a finger along the shallow cut above Claire's collarbone. He examined her blood on his finger for a moment and slid it into his mouth.

"Did you break into my apartment?"

"I did. Right before my own engagement. I knew you would never suspect me because you probably thought I was practicing those ridiculous dance moves in my office, cowering like a scared little boy who's nervous about asking a stupid question," he continued, growing more agitated with each step.

She bristled. How dare he make a mockery of his proposal?

"I had breakfast that morning, picked up my dry cleaning, watched until you left your apartment, and then broke in and wrecked your place. Afterwards, I took the long way

467

around to pick up Victoria." He smiled to himself. "Your binder was pathetic, by the way. Did you really think you could catch me?"

"But the police found my underwear from the break-in at Jason's house."

Barney clapped his hands and laughed. "That's the best part. I broke into his house and planted them there. You'd be amazed what you can do with a lock pick and some wire cutters. He's going to take the fall for everything. Even tonight."

A jolt of fear clenched her stomach. These were her last moments on earth. He was going to kill her. Rosie would be an orphan.

"You're the West Haven Widowmaker?"

"In the flesh," he said, raising his arms to the side and turning so that she could take it all in.

"Did you kill those other girls?" she whispered. "Ariel? Kayley?" The ropes that had bound her hands behind the pillar dropped lightly to the ground. She held her breath, but he didn't seem to notice.

He stopped in his tracks. A maniacal laugh suddenly burst forth from him. "They were all like you. They all turned down poor, fat Bernard. But I showed them. I showed them all." He leaned in and sniffed a fistful of Claire's hair. He nuzzled her neck and bit her earlobe, sucking on the earring that dangled from her left ear. His cologne was musky and stifling. A wave of nausea rolled over her.

"Why Ariel? She didn't go to Venor. She doesn't fit your type."

"Sure she does. Bitches are my type, apparently. I was in love with Ariel in high school. She turned me down to date some jock, and they got married after graduation. But I couldn't get her out of my head."

"So, you stalked her?" The longer she could keep him talking, the better chance she had of escaping her ankle bonds. The ropes bit into her skin, but she continued to point and flex her feet, loosening them millimeter by millimeter. Her hands were free. If she could get his knife, she stood a chance. This didn't have to be the end.

"I watched her. On weekends, I used to get in my mom's car and sit outside the diner, watching her work. I broke into her apartment once when I knew she and that imbecile were at work. And when I saw the little life she had made for herself there with him, I knew I had to have her. When I came home for Christmas break my freshman year of college, I took her after she closed up on Christmas Eve. She was so surprised to see me at first. She didn't know what was going on." He chuckled to himself.

"You know she was pregnant when you killed her." Did he really have no remorse?

Barney's eyes darkened, and he stood uncomfortably close to Claire.

"That's what I call a two-for-one special." He laughed at his joke before continuing. "Ariel had to be taught a lesson. She pleaded with me, told me about the baby as if that would stop me. After Ariel, I felt better for a while. It was a long time before I killed again." He waved the knife as he ranted, pacing across the floor.

"Why Jennifer?" She'd been the second victim.

"Jennifer." He rolled her name in his mouth like a piece of hard candy. "She was a real firecracker. She was in my English class. You could tell she was going to be something special. I sent her flowers, treated her like a lady. But once again, she only saw me as a friend. Naturally, I had to kill her, but I was patient. I waited until she got married, until she found the perfect house and perfect job. She thought she had everything. Then I took it all away from her." He laughed maniacally. "She barely even put up a fight."

"Is that why you wait to kill them until they're married?"

"Yep." Barney flicked a speck of dust off the sleeve of his suit. "I like to wait until they have everything they always dreamed of since they were six-year-old idiots in their pink canopy beds."

She shivered. That was a suspiciously specific statement.

"And then I rip it away from them the same way they ripped my heart away from me. I'm saving their husbands from the heartache that would have inevitably ensued. Those men deserve better." He examined his fingernails.

"What about the rest of the girls? Shawna? Kayley?"

"It was the same story with the other girls. Kayley led me on. Shawna turned me down after I took her on an expensive date. I took Shawna on the day she returned from her honeymoon. Kayley was really feisty, so eventually I just had to slit her throat."

He smiled to himself as though fondly remembering each kill. Claire gagged. Kayley had gotten married to another woman shortly before she had been murdered. No wonder she wasn't interested in dating Barney.

"And then there was Courtney! Of course she only went out with me so that I would buy her alcohol. But at least she was up front about what she wanted. She was a loathsome human being and really should have been first, but I had set a precedent. I had to wait until she finally settled down. I picked her up on a run after she left that idiot's car that morning and made sure she never saw daylight again."

She shuddered. She needed Barney to keep talking. What was left to discuss?

"Why did you take my underwear? The police only

found two pairs, and I know there were more." The cords around her ankles had loosened slightly, but not nearly enough for her to escape.

"Ah, the underwear. I needed it for a special project. A trophy, if you will."

"What kind of trophy?" Nausea and fear blended in her stomach.

He pulled out his phone and flicked his finger over the screen. He turned the phone around and held it up to Claire.

A picture showed what appeared to be a haphazard quilt. Fabric in every color of the rainbow stretched across the length. He zoomed the screen in for her, and she could see that each panel was made out of a different pair of women's underwear.

"I added a new corner down here just for yours." He zoomed in on the bottom.

She recognized several of her missing pairs of underwear. Bile rose in her throat, but she wouldn't give Barney the satisfaction of knowing how much he had rattled her.

"That's a nice quilt. Is that hand-stitched? I've been looking for a good tailor—"

He reeled back and slapped her. Her face stung, and her heart hammered in her chest. She didn't want to know anything else, but the questions kept tumbling from her mouth. She needed more time.

"Why am I wearing my wedding dress?"

He had touched her when she was unconscious, removed her clothes. The realization rolled over her like a wave. Dread clenched her stomach. What else had he done?

Barney looked down at the A-line gown, and she followed his gaze. The bottom was dirty where it had dragged on the floor. "I've been watching you since graduation, waiting for you to get married like the others. I followed your story. I know you had to break off your engagement because that idiot cheated on you. I was so furious the day that I found out."

"Is that why you planted evidence at Jason's? Because I was supposed to marry him?"

"He ruined everything when he walked into the bathroom with that hussy," he hissed. "I have standards. A system. And he compromised everything. He shouldn't have done that."

Was this sympathy from a serial killer? Now she'd seen everything.

Barney resumed his pacing. "I had to wait for you to have everything, and you made me wait even longer. And now I'm really upset because you're forcing me to break my precedent. If you had just shut your mouth and gotten married like you were supposed to, this would have been so much easier. But you drove your fiancé away just like you're inevitably going to drive this new guy away. What's his name, Luke? I don't have a decade to wait for you to die, Claire."

She spat at him.

His hand came out of nowhere, slapping her again. Tears sprung into her eyes, but she fought them back.

He bent down, ripped off a fistful of her dress, and used it to wipe his face. Son of a bitch. "Don't you dare do that again, you disrespectful little slut." He wound up and slapped her again on the other side of the face. The crack echoed in the depths. The impact stole her breath. Between Wendy and Barney, she had never been slapped so many times in one twenty-four-hour period.

"But what about Victoria, Barney? She loves you," she half-whispered after the shock of the blow passed.

"A pawn." He tossed the fabric to the floor. "I finally got the girl I deserved, but she means nothing to me. The story I told you about meeting her in the diner is true. But the only reason we met was because I was waiting for you."

She stared blankly back at him. What the hell did that mean? She didn't eat diner pie *that* often.

He paced in front of the pillar again, occasionally punctuating his sentences with a jab of the knife. "Around that time, you had started your business, and you would take late night runs, anywhere from one to three in the morning. I can still see you running past the diner in those tiny black shorts." He closed his eyes for a moment, smirking. "I was just watching, biding my time until you married that asshole. Why'd you stop running, Claire?"

She shuddered and ignored the question. "Victoria has no idea you're a complete psycho?"

Danger glinted in his eyes. "Don't call me a psycho," he hissed, getting so close to her that their noses nearly touched.

"I apologize," she whispered.

That seemed to appease him, and he took another step back, eyeing her up and down. "Victoria doesn't know anything about my extracurricular activities. And she never will." He kicked at a flounce on her dress. "I wanted to make sure you got to wear that wedding dress before you died. After all, that's all your pathetic, shallow life revolves around. Weddings. Proposals."

He put his hand on the concrete pillar and got right up in her face. "I could have made you happy. You could have married me in this dress." His fist closed around the knife handle. He brought the tip of it down and slashed through the sweetheart neckline, ripping it open down to her navel. The dress fell open to her waist, and she made a mental note that fluorescent underground lighting was incredibly unflattering to her areolas.

"Now," he said conversationally, "I'm going to kill you. I'm going to stab you right through the heart, like you and all those other girls did to me." He tapped his finger over her heart. "And I'm going to watch your blood spill all over your wedding dress until the light fades from your eyes. Then I'm going to bury you outside and let my men pour asphalt over you. You should be honored, you know. You're the very first guest of the Monroeville branch of Heirloom Hotels. In fact, you'll be with us forever."

Monroeville. She was twenty miles north of West Haven. How much time had passed? Surely someone had noticed she was missing. But who would find her here even if she managed to escape?

He pressed the knife to her neck, tracing what felt like initials on her skin.

She didn't allow herself to whimper as warmth trickled down her neck.

"Do you have any last words before I kill you, Claire?"

"Actually, I do." She stared at him for a moment, looking at the face of someone she had gently rejected half a decade ago. "I was wrong. You're a really shitty friend."

Before he could react, she whipped her hands out from behind the pillar and landed a jab squarely on his nose. A satisfying crunch split the night.

Barney howled and clutched his face. His knife clattered to the floor.

She leaned forward and snatched the knife from the ground, quickly sawing through the bonds around her feet. She was nearly free when he rushed her and kicked her square in the stomach.

Her knees gave out, and she clutched her belly. It was

surely going to fall out of her butt. Was a prolapsed stomach a thing? She took a gasping breath and cringed when a sharp stab of pain sliced her rib cage. She would bet her last dollar that several ribs were fractured.

Barney kicked the knife out of her hand next and darted after it. Adrenaline coursed through her veins, urging her to ignore the pain and crawl over the bone-cold floor and away from the madman with the knife.

He was laughing again, staring at her with wild eyes as he bore down upon her. "You're a feisty one. I always thought you would be. I wondered if that would be how you were in bed. Maybe I'll find out before I kill you." He lunged with the knife again.

She rolled, but not fast enough. The knife plunged through her skin and into her chest. Pain exploded in front of her eyes, and she mouthed wordlessly as Barney crouched over her, staring at her.

"It's about time you learned your place, Claire. I'm doing you a favor. No one could love a cold, selfish bitch like you." He gripped the ragged edges of her dress and was about to rip it from her body when she brought her knee up and rammed it directly into his crotch.

"That's for Rosie." She grunted with the effort.

Barney gasped, collapsing onto her knees.

She kicked him off and got up, sprinting for the exit. Yards of lace and satin billowed out behind her. Panic all but paralyzed her, but she forced herself to keep going. She would not die topless and bloody in a hotel basement.

A warm wetness gushed from her chest, and her vision began to blur. She tugged at the neckline of her dress, tried to press it to the wound.

Ignoring her increasing weakness, she shoved through a doorway and into a stairwell. Of course. She glanced behind her before the door shut and saw Barney running toward her in a bizarre, predator-like crouch.

There was nothing to barricade the door. Her only choice was to run. She lifted the hem of her dress and took the stairs up two at a time in bare feet. Her chest heaved as she ascended, sending the knife that was still sunk in her chest bobbing in and out of her peripheral vision.

No need to panic. It was just a very large, pointy statement necklace. She had totally seen one like it on *Project Accessory*.

Blood was slick under her feet as she ran. She glanced behind her. Had he made it to the stairs? A trail of blood marked her progress. Finding a place to hide was out of the question. The door at the bottom of the stairs smashed opened, banging off the wall, and heavy, desperate footsteps shook the stairwell.

"Get back here, you stupid bitch," Barney snarled.

She fought the urge to scream and leapt up the stairs as quickly as her failing body would allow.

He grabbed her ankle just as she reached the door to the first floor. She kicked him hard in the face. Strangled swearing and the sound of tumbling marked his fall to the landing below. There was no time to waste. She exploded out of the door and looked around. A dark hotel lobby greeted her complete with rich carpets and luxurious furniture. It was completely deserted.

She sprinted to the front doors and shook the handles furiously, but they were locked. Her heart pounded. So much wasted time. He would be upon her in seconds.

Another set of doors partway down the lobby was also locked. The door to the basement opened. Barney's labored breath echoed raggedly off the walls. Shit. She was out of time. A line of bar stools stood to her left. She picked one up and charged toward the large glass window that stood by the door.

Pain punished every inch of her body as she lifted the stool and sent it crashing through the window. Glass shattered everywhere, littering the lobby with glittering fragments. Without hesitation, she leaped through the window and ran on her tiptoes, crunching over the glass.

"Help!" She screamed as she ran. "A serial killer with daddy issues is trying to kill me!"

Piles of dirt stood next to an imposing patch of woods, but nothing looked familiar. A gravel driveway led from the front of the hotel into darkness. Somewhere nearby, cars rushed past on a highway. Help wasn't far away.

She clutched the ragged fabric of her dress to her chest as she ran, cursing her mother for handing down her voluptuous chest gene. Running was difficult at the best of times, and without a sports bra, it was only a matter of time before she took an eye out.

"Somebody help," she cried, her voice weakening. She ran through the night, ignoring the searing pain that radiated through every inch of her body. What remained of her wedding dress billowed out behind her, getting snagged in the weeds.

Were those footsteps? She risked a glance behind her. Barney climbed out of the window. Sparkling shards of glass crunched under his feet and caught in his pants. Please, god, let the glass slice an important artery or a sensitive body part. The moonlight shone on his face and revealed a bloody nose and a face contorted in rage.

Claire turned and sprinted faster, gasping with the effort. The entire bodice of her dress was drenched in her blood.

She tripped on the edge of her dress and fell, catching herself with her hands. Pine needles bit greedily into her palms, but she got back up and kept running. Her head was so fuzzy that she could no longer see straight, and she wasn't sure how fast she was going, but her feet kept moving forward in a direction that she desperately hoped would lead to other people.

Claire fell a second time and was about to give up and face her attacker again when a loud engine roared through the night. Headlights lit up the night and approached at an incredible speed. She ducked and rolled to the side just in time.

The car came to rest immediately next to where she had fallen.

A man in an all-black uniform jumped out of a truck.

"Miss? Are you okay? What the—"

"Get away from her!" Barney snarled as he rounded the corner, drenched in sweat. His bowtie was coming undone, and droplets of Claire's blood blossomed over his snow-white button-up.

"Mr. Windsor?" The man looked from Claire and the knife sticking out of her chest to Barney, who was charging over with a glint of crazy in his eye.

"I said get away from her! You work for me," Barney shrieked. He was nearly upon Claire.

The stranger pulled something from his belt, held it at chest-height, and fired.

A crackle of electricity split the air as two prongs from a Taser buried themselves in Barney's chest. He stopped dead in his tracks, doubled over and clutching his ribs, then fell to the ground, seizing.

Claire crawled on her hands and knees toward him, the wedding dress now pooling around her waist. It was incredibly annoying that he hadn't provided the strapless bra she bought for her wedding dress.

"You ruined my perfect track record. Thirty thousand volts straight to the nipples is going to be the least of your worries, you murderous asshole. Rot in prison." She landed one last weak punch to his face before she collapsed and rolled a few feet away, carefully avoiding shoving her statement necklace any deeper into her torso.

Numbness started to cloak her as her mysterious rescuer handcuffed the prostrate Barney. Sounds were getting fuzzy, but she thought she heard him call for help on his radio. Or maybe he was ordering tacos.

"Don't skimp on the guac," she called faintly in his direction. "I think I've earned it."

Sirens wailed in the distance. The voluminous skirt of her wedding gown cushioned her, and the night almost seemed peaceful as she lay in the cold grass. She bet she looked like a fallen angel cloaked in scarlet. It would probably make a great album cover or impressionist painting. Weariness dragged at her. Maybe she could close her eyes for a few minutes. Just a quick power nap, and then she should really check with the marching band conductor for her next proposal.

The sirens were louder now, drowning out the crickets in the nearby bushes. She pried her eyes open. The police would probably need to speak to her. Red, white, and blue lights flashed off the trees lining the dirt road. It looked almost like the Fourth of July. Very on-brand for Tyler's proposal.

A cop car skidded to a stop a few feet away, followed by Luke's pickup truck. A mass of bodies poured out as though it were a clown car. Luke, Nicole, Mindy, and Kyle jumped out of the truck. Officer Shiccitano threw his door open and sprinted toward her.

While Luke, Nicole, and Kyle rushed to Claire's side,

Mindy passed in a blur of black hair and metallic gold fabric. She launched herself at Barney, kicking him in the ribs with her second-best pair of black pumps. She was picking him up by the collar to punch him in the face when Officer Shiccitano grabbed her by the waist and forcibly held her back as she screamed obscenities at Barney. She took off her left shoe and threw it at him. It hit him squarely in the ear. More sirens were approaching.

"Hey, guys. You bring the guac?" Was that Nicole crying? Damn it. First, Claire had assaulted Wendy, then she had gotten kidnapped. The spotlight was supposed to be on Nicole. They would have to do a complete do-over.

"Oh, Claire," said a familiar voice.

She was dimly aware of someone with a sensational butt sitting beside her on the ground.

Luke drew her into his arms, disregarding the blood that was still seeping through her wedding dress. He pressed a tender kiss to her forehead.

Claire stared up at him as he cradled her. "You found me," she said in disbelief.

"I found you. Just too late," he said, clutching her tighter for a moment. He released her and immediately started assessing her wound. He barked an order at Kyle to get the first aid kit from the police car.

"Too late? Oh my god, am I dying? Never mind, I don't want to know. Don't tell my mom."

"You're not going to die. You're Claire Freakin' Hartley."

"Damn straight," she slurred as he pressed gauze to her neck, shining a flashlight at the pointy statement necklace that was still protruding from her chest. His face was grim.

"Luke," she said weakly. "Come closer."

"What is it?" He lowered his ear to her mouth.

"Are my boobs falling out of my dress?"

He was shaking beside her, and she couldn't be certain if it was because he was laughing or crying. His face swam in her mind as she allowed herself a brief power nap. Twenty minutes tops.

CHAPTER THIRTY-TWO

To Do:
- Buy lunch for the doctors and nurses at the hospital
- Apologize to Victoria for helping her get engaged to a murderer
- Pull B blog post down ASAP

MUFFLED VOICES CAME FROM SOMEWHERE IN THE CAVERNOUS depths of Claire's mind. She was paralyzed and weak, and the effort of listening was almost too much to bear. The dark edges of the world seemed to slowly recede as she opened her eyes.

Sandpaper scraped against her cheek. She swiped weakly at the source. An IV was sticking out of her arm. A blue and white hospital gown sagged around her. Her breathing was ragged and difficult.

"Not again," she grumbled. She was definitely going to

hit her deductible this year. "If there are creepy flowers here, I'm going to lose my shit."

A large wad of cotton was taped to her chest, and there was a warm presence next to her on the hospital bed. She turned her head and was greeted by the unmistakable fawn-colored fur of a corgi.

Rosie panted in Claire's face and nudged her chin with her muzzle.

"Rosie," Claire whispered, lifting her left hand with difficulty to pet her. Rosie let out a soft whine and snuggled in next to Claire, burying her nose in her armpit. Tears prickled in her eyes and rolled out, dampening Rosie's fur.

Nicole and Kyle sat in two chairs on her left, leaning against each other as they slept. Stilettos snapped in the hallway outside. Mindy paced back and forth, yammering into a cell phone.

In the corner of the room sat an unconscious Luke, partially obscured behind the biggest bouquet of flowers she had ever seen. His arms were crossed over his chest. His head lolled onto his shoulder, and occasionally a soft snore escaped. A tattered medical handbook lay face-down on his lap.

"Not today, Satan," Claire said as she sat up with extreme effort. Her chest burned. Her legs were jelly. She swung them stubbornly out of bed, ignoring the headache that threatened to split her head in two. She gripped the IV pole with one hand as she staggered over to the flower arrangement.

Seeing no card, she clumsily picked it up in one hand and dragged herself to the window. The sickeningly sweet smell of lilies engulfed her. Surely Barney had been arrested. How had he managed to send flowers to the hospital? She set the flowers on the windowsill and fumbled with the latch.

"What the hell are you doing?" Something hit the floor.

Claire turned and saw a panicked-looking Luke climbing out of the armchair.

"Creepy flowers," she explained, lifting the giant bouquet.

"They're from Nicole and Kyle, not the Widowmaker." He scooped her up and carried her back to the bed. "And you can't just keep throwing flowers out of windows. You're going to hurt someone."

"Are you seriously lecturing me on flower disposal safety procedures after I was almost stabbed to death?"

"Get back in the bed, Claire." He shook his head. Grumpy Luke was back. At least that meant she was most likely going to live.

"Where's Barney?" she asked as she settled back in, stroking Rosie's fur.

"In a different hospital, heavily guarded. And then prison, presumably for the rest of his life."

Claire bit her lip. Her life had somehow transformed into a soap opera. "Poor Victoria. I don't know how I didn't see it. I always thought he was a little creepy, sure, but not *murder* creepy."

He smiled. "You would be worried about someone else when you've nearly been stabbed to death." He leaned over and kissed her forehead. "I am so sorry, Claire."

"For what?" she whispered.

He took a deep breath. "For so many things. I'm sorry I didn't tell you about my suspicions right away. I should have figured it out sooner. I should have saved you. I knew it wasn't Jason. It was right in front of me."

She waved one hand weakly. Breathing was almost too

much of an effort. "I forgive you. Nobody ever suspects someone named Barney. How did you find me?"

"I went straight to his office after we noticed you were missing. We found your shoe in the hallway." He paused to take a sharp breath.

"We figured he could pull some strings, get the security tapes before the police even arrived. But when we showed up at the office, he wasn't there. I saw a diploma for Venor University hanging on the wall, and something just clicked. I knew it was him. We went to the security team, and they called him, but he didn't answer. We saw a sign for the new Monroeville branch of the hotel, and I figured that a partially constructed hotel would be the perfect place to take someone to kill them. A big, empty lot. No one around to ask questions. I called Officer Shiccitano, and we followed him there. We got there right after Sawyer incapacitated Barney."

"Who's Sawyer?"

"Kyle's groomsman, and the owner of Sanctum Security. Sanctum handles security for four of Barney's hotels. He was covering a shift at a gated community in Monroeville for one of his staff who called out sick. That's why he wasn't at the party. You tripped a silent alarm when you broke the window, and Sawyer was the one who responded."

Sawyer. The name from the guest list rang a bell.

"He saved me. Remind me to send him a gift basket."

Luke frowned. His eyes were stormy again. They sat in silence for a moment, listening to the beeping of Claire's monitors.

"Luke. How did he get pictures of my mom in Florida if he was here in Pennsylvania the whole time?"

"I have no idea. He had plenty of financial resources. I'm

assuming he hired a private investigator down in Florida and had him send the photos."

"He killed those other girls." Claire shivered in the thin hospital gown. "They all friend-zoned him. He told me he was going to bury me under the parking lot before they poured asphalt."

Luke climbed carefully into the hospital bed and wrapped himself around her.

"He will never be able to hurt you again. I'll make sure of it."

"Thank you," she whispered, relaxing into his warmth as she stroked Rosie's fur with her other hand. Rosie stood, shook, and climbed over Claire to settle in between them. They both laughed.

"You might change your mind about that 'thank you' in a minute."

"Oh? Why's that?"

"I had to call your mom. She's on her way here."

Claire glared at him. "You can't be serious."

"If I didn't do it, the doctors would have."

She groaned and turned over, cringing at the pain in her chest. "On second thought, bring Barney back in here. I want him to kill me. She will never get over this, and before you know it, she'll be making unannounced visits to my apartment and slowly moving my things to her house."

"She won't. We had a nice chat. She told me she had 'an intuition' that there was a man in your life. She also said she could tell through the phone that my aura is a bright blue. A perfect complement to yours, apparently. By the way, what the hell does she do for a living?"

Claire put a hand over her face and rolled onto his chest. "She's a psychic. She has her own TV show. If she offers to read your cards, do not accept," she said firmly.

He laughed and drew her closer. She relaxed into his warmth and felt truly safe for the first time in months. The Widowmaker (the real one) was locked up. Everyone she loved was safe.

Luke quieted, and he stroked her hair until her eyelids drooped.

———

CLAIRE AWOKE TO TWO MEN STANDING BESIDE HER BED. SHE jumped and recoiled until she recognized Detective Smith. The pain in her chest was excruciating, and she inhaled sharply.

"Good morning, Miss Hartley," he said kindly. "We were hoping to take a statement from you about what happened last night, if you're up to it."

She nodded and reached for a glass of water. Nicole and Kyle's chairs from the night before stood empty. Her reach jostled Luke awake. He climbed out of bed with Rosie when he saw the cops.

"I'll be right back," he whispered to her. He gave her a quick kiss before leaving the room.

Claire recited everything that had happened the night before, beginning to end. She felt sick to her stomach when she described the trophy quilt made out of the victims' underwear.

"I know, it's disgusting," she added. "I have so many questions. Was it machine-quilted or hand-quilted? Who taught him how to sew? Did he even wash the underwear? Does he sleep with it at night?"

Detective Smith took careful notes and asked questions throughout.

Luke returned a moment later with a hot coffee and a

panting Rosie. Her tiny feet were green. Someone must have just mowed the hospital's grass.

Detective Smith turned to Luke. "Were you present at the hotel last evening?"

"I was." Luke set Rosie down next to Claire. "At the end."

"We're going to need to take a statement from you. When did you realize Miss Hartley was missing?"

"After she didn't come back from the bathroom. She had been gone for maybe twenty minutes when Mindy went to check on her. The time was probably about seven forty. We noticed the lights were off in the hallway, and after we investigated, we found her shoe in the hallway. We knew as soon as we saw the shoe that she had been taken. Everyone went into crisis mode. That's when I called you."

Detective Smith nodded.

Great. She absolutely owed Nicole a do-over engagement party. Hurling someone into a buffet was one thing, but getting abducted and taking the limelight away from the bride-to-be was inexcusable.

"Unfortunately, since Claire's an adult, she couldn't really be declared a missing person right away. Kyle and I went to speak to hotel security, Kyle's parents checked the parking garage, and Mindy checked the ladies' rooms on each floor. Kyle's parents found Jason and Wendy having sex in her car, so we knew it wasn't him. Nicole called Claire's cell phone. We found it ditched in a trash can by the service entrance at the back of the hotel."

Luke took a breath and ran through a detailed account of what had happened after he went looking for Barney. He held Claire's hand as he spoke.

"Thank you, Mr. Islestorm. Claire, do you have any questions for us?"

"Did you find out who tampered with the carriage

wheel? Was it Wendy?" she whispered, fighting the pain that radiated each time she drew breath.

"The investigation is ongoing, but we will be happy to help you press charges when the time comes." He seemed to be fighting a smile.

"That bitch." She breathed shallowly. "I knew it. What happens now? With Barney, I mean."

"Once he's treated for his wounds, he'll be placed in the county jail. We have already referred the case to the district attorney's office. They'll be collecting more witness statements and checking for any priors on his record. Once they decide on the charges, they'll be presented at an initial appearance."

"Will I have to face him?"

Detective Smith nodded. "After he enters his plea, there will be a preliminary hearing. You might be called to present testimony. He'll be in the courtroom that day."

She shuddered. He may be behind bars, but the nightmare was far from over. Luke rubbed her arm.

"What about Jason?"

"Charges have been dropped against Mr. Goldman. He provided an explanation for why Mrs. Stevens was in his car the morning of her disappearance."

Right, the weed. Who knew that Courtney smoked pot? Her only vice in college had been liquor.

"We'll leave you to rest, Miss Hartley. If you think of anything else at all that might be relevant to the investigation, please give our office a call. You'll also likely hear from the district attorney's office."

Claire nodded as the two policemen left.

"How are you feeling?" Luke pressed his hand to her cheek.

"Like I've been stabbed in the chest by a damn madman."

"Huh. I wonder why." He crawled back into the hospital bed.

"Where did everyone go?"

"Nicole and Kyle went to change clothes and to get you some real food. Mindy is picking up your mom from—"

"MY CLAIREBEAR!" Alice Alejo burst into the room, dragging an oversized suitcase behind her. Her platinum blonde hair was flawlessly curled, even after a last-minute redeye flight from Florida. Her chest heaved as she flung her carry-on into the chair Luke had vacated.

Mindy followed behind, carrying a larger suitcase. She was panting as she reached the doorway. "I'm so sorry," she mouthed to Claire.

"Oh, Claire." Her mom leaned in to give her a hug. "My poor, sweet baby girl. I came as soon as I could. I just knew something awful was going to happen. I had a premonition."

Claire was smothered in the scent of patchouli. She coughed and pain stabbed into her chest. She exchanged a terrified glance with Luke.

"Hi, Mom. Listen, it's not as bad as it looks."

"Claire Aurora Hartley. I know you think you can lie to me over the phone, but a mother always knows when her daughter is lying. Oh, my baby." Her mom hovered a hand over the wad of gauze taped to Claire's chest.

"It's just a flesh wound," Claire said, laughing deliriously at her pop culture reference.

"And who is this?" Her mom extended a manicured hand to Luke.

"Luke Islestorm. We spoke on the phone."

"Claire," Her mom hissed as though Luke couldn't hear

her. "I can't believe you have a boyfriend that you didn't tell me about."

"He's not my boyfriend." She sat up to protest. "Ouch." Nope. That was too much. She quickly laid back down.

Luke tugged at the hem of her gown gently, inspecting the gauze. "I'll be right back." He climbed out of the bed and left the room.

"He's cute," her mom whispered as he left the room.

Mindy took Luke's spot by the bed and pulled out a makeup kit. "I know, right?"

"And holy cow, get a load of the rear end on him." Her mom gestured at the door with a hitchhiker's thumb.

"Mom. That's totally inappropriate. But I'm really glad you're here." Claire opened her arms for another hug.

Mindy descended on Claire and started applying eye shadow.

"Is this really necessary?" Claire asked, blinking as some powder slipped into her eye.

"Hold still. You look like a dead person."

"She's right, Claire. You really do. Your aura looks a little dull too, darling. I might have a sage and rhubarb poultice in here for that." Her mom slipped a manicured hand into her carry-on bag.

"My aura will be fine, Mom."

"You know, sweetie, if you would have just moved in with Roy and me, none of this would have ever happened."

"Please. If I had moved to Florida, something infinitely more insane would have happened to me. For example, last week I saw an article titled 'Miami Man Set Fire to His Wife After Game of Twister.'"

"Well, maybe it was an accident."

Claire groaned and leaned back into her pillows.

"Hey," Mindy said quietly as Claire's mother continued

to search her carry-on. She was now wielding a tube of mascara. "Remember that yearbook we were trying to get from Ariel's high school?"

"Of course."

"The mail carrier delivered it this morning." Mindy pulled her phone out of her purse and showed Claire a black-and-white picture of a smiling young man with acne and glasses. Beneath the untidy swoop of hair, steel-gray eyes burned. The name listed underneath the picture was Bernard Twigg.

"We were right," Claire whispered, feeling instantly nauseated. She turned away from the phone, unable to look into those cold and cruel eyes.

"I'm sorry I found it too late." Mindy tossed her makeup bag back in her purse and pulled Claire into a smothering hug. "I should have known Jason wasn't smart enough to be a homicidal mastermind."

Luke returned, followed by Nicole, who bore stuffed animals and balloons. She immediately descended on Claire, hugging her and asking a million questions.

Claire pulled Nicole in close and whispered her request. A moment later, Nicole walked over to Mindy and Claire's mother, and the three of them miraculously decided to get a coffee to catch up, leaving Luke and Claire alone again.

"Your mom's nice," Luke observed as he came to sit next to her.

Claire stared blankly at the ceiling.

"Don't look," he said as he tugged at the gauze covering her wound.

"You know they have nurses for that."

"They have enough to do."

He gently removed the gauze and applied a fresh piece before taping it down.

"Actually, I've been thinking you should move in with me," he said as he disposed of the used gauze in a biohazard bin. "You know, just for a little while."

She stared at him. "Whoa. Slow down, crazy."

"Just think about it. You're going to need a lot of care until you get better," he said, brushing her hair away from her face.

"It's a stab wound, not a crushed pelvis. I'll take care of myself." Despite her words, she wiggled tighter against him.

He chuckled, stroking her arm. "I give a mean sponge bath," he offered.

"You give a mean everything, you're like the grumpiest person I know. Besides, I can't live with you. I don't know anything about you. You won't even tell me what your favorite ice cream is." She yawned tremendously and stretched a hand over Rosie's furry body.

"It's teaberry," Luke whispered.

Claire smiled up at him. She soon fell into a light sleep, soothed by the soft beeping of her monitors. When she awoke from her nap, she was going to be ready for whatever the universe could throw at her, be it man, mother, or murderer.

BONUS EPILOGUE

"Where are we going?" Claire asked.

The sun hung low behind the evergreen trees flanking them. They hadn't passed a restaurant—or even a house— in miles. A two-lane highway meandered in front of them.

"To our date," Luke grunted.

She glanced at her phone. No service. "Are you sure? Or are you bringing me out here to murder me?"

Luke snorted. "Too soon."

He was probably right. It had only been two days since a former client had rudely kidnapped and stabbed her. But she wasn't thinking about that tonight. Tonight was about exploring the indescribable connection between her and Luke—and maybe she'd give up the sex embargo she'd enacted after calling off her wedding. Maybe.

But did she trust him? He *had* hidden the fact that he suspected she was being targeted by a serial killer. And that had only been like a month ago. Had he really changed? Or was he hiding more secrets?

"Are you sure you're feeling up to this?" he asked when she didn't respond.

She jumped. "What? Because of the stabbing thing? That was nothing. You should see the other guy."

He reached across the center console and rested his hand on her knee. "I'm serious. You went through a real trauma."

She straightened in her seat. "I'm not going to stop living my life and reschedule a very important date just because of a nearly fatal wound. Besides, you promised. Are you trying to get out of this? Mr. Cold Feet?"

Luke cracked a smile. "No, I'm not trying to get out of this. I told you I want to get to know you better, and I meant it."

His hand slid a couple of inches up her thigh. Her toes curled in her boots. The sex embargo was very much in danger.

What would a first date with Luke be like? He was unlike anyone else she had ever dated. Jason, her ex-fiancé, would throw in a frozen pizza and fall asleep with his hand down his pants during date night. But Luke was no Jason. He was caring, successful, charismatic. And definitely a bit egotistical.

She glanced down at her jeans, sweater, and boots. Whatever they were doing couldn't be too fancy. He had been very specific with his instructions on what to wear.

A sign caught her eye. Stone Valley State Park. Either he was taking her to her favorite park, or they were heading all the way through the woods to the college town on the other side.

Luke activated his turn signal and swung the car onto a road. Park it was.

Her stomach growled. Would there at least be food? The only food she knew of at Stone Valley was their dingy but loveable beachside concession stand. A two-dollar cheeseburger and a Rocket Pop wasn't exactly what she had envisioned, but the point was to get to know Luke better. The food didn't matter.

A line of police tape stretched across the lot when they approached. Uh-oh.

"It looks like it's closed," she said.

"No, it's not." Luke seemed completely unbothered, as always.

"Are you sure? Because it kind of looks like a crime scene."

"Trust me. It's fine."

He put the car in park and exited. A pocketknife flashed under the dying sun as he cut the tape. It fluttered to the ground. What the hell were they doing?

He got back in the car and pulled into a spot nearest the beach. "I'll be right back. Just going to fix the tape."

"Okay," she said slowly.

Of all the things she had on her bingo card for a first date with Luke, infiltrating a crime scene wasn't one of them.

A minute later, he reappeared and opened her car door. The police tape was back, strung across the entrance. The rest of the parking lot was deserted.

"Did you drive here early and stage a crime scene so that we would be alone?" she accused.

"No."

Claire heaved a sigh. Luke was never forthcoming with important details. If he said everything was fine, she was going to put her trust in him. Or at least try to.

She undid her seatbelt. It slid across her torso, and she flinched when it grazed the wad of gauze beneath her sweater. The sharp pain was creeping back in. Ibuprofen must be wearing off.

He extended his hand, and she took it. A pink-streaked sky warmed the world around them as they crossed the gravel lot to a small, rocky path.

"Do you think you're okay to walk? Maybe a quarter of a mile."

She scoffed. "It's a stab wound, not a broken femur. I can do it."

His grip tightened on her hand nonetheless. A thrill ran through her. Where were they going? And what exactly were they doing?

"Is there going to be food?" If not, she was going to have to break into the emergency granola bar stash in the bottom of her purse.

Another ghost of a smile cracked the marble façade of Luke's face. "You can't seriously think I would let you get hangry on our first date. I've seen what happens."

"If you're referring to the picture-hanging incident, I spackled and re-painted that section of the hallway."

He stayed silent, but the smile had grown. A rough hand snaked around her waist and pulled her closer. His warmth chased away all thoughts of decorating hazards. Her stomach flip-flopped and she snuck a look at him.

Why did she turn into such a simpering schoolgirl around him? Was it that chiseled jaw, or maybe the bulge of his biceps against her back? He did bear an uncanny resemblance to the members of boy bands she had plastered on her wall in middle school. Or maybe it was his rarely earned smiles? His quick wit and dreamy green eyes? Whatever it was, it was kind of pissing her off. This had never been a problem with Jason, even in the beginning.

Luke's phone vibrated in his pocket. He glanced at it, then withdrew his arm. They came to a stop in the middle of the rocky path.

Her heart fell. Had something happened? Was he about to end the date before she even found out what he had planned?

He reached into his jacket pocket and groped around, eventually withdrawing a bottle of ibuprofen. He fished two tablets out and handed them to her.

"What?" he asked when he saw her smile.

"You have an alarm set for my pain meds?"

He stiffened. "Pain management is very important. If you were in charge, you'd be nose-deep in proposal details and forget to keep up with it."

"Sure," she said, but the warm feeling was growing. Even her fingertips were tingling.

She swallowed the pills with a swig of water from her designated purse water bottle before setting off again.

Silence stretched between them as they went deeper into the forest, but it wasn't uncomfortable. They passed the pavilion where they had had a celebratory Jason's-Going-to-Prison brunch only a couple weeks before. He led her down the path that led to the lake, and when they emerged at the sandy beachfront, she gasped.

A low table was arranged on the sand near the water's edge. Pillows in pastel colors were nestled around it, and lit candles flickered softly. A strand of Edison bulbs stretched overhead. Sparkling wine bubbled merrily in champagne flutes. Color-coordinated napkin rings bound the silverware on the white tablecloth. Good lord.

"Luke," she began, but once he turned the full force of his gaze on her, all thoughts promptly spilled out of her head.

"Come on," he said and took her hand again.

He led her to the table and helped her down onto a pillow with a full view of the setting sun on the lake. He sat next to her, and she scooted an inch closer.

It was amazing. Almost too amazing. It was something she and Mindy would have set up for a client—sunset picnic in the proposal recipient's favorite place. She glanced over her shoulder to make sure there wasn't a photographer hiding in the woods behind them. Obviously Luke wasn't proposing. That would be insane. They barely knew each other, after all.

He lifted the lid on a dish in front of her. She had been so taken by the scenery that she hadn't even noticed the plates.

Fettuccine Alfredo and homemade garlic bread appeared. Her stomach growled audibly.

Luke smiled and picked up his champagne glass, then handed hers to her.

"I know it's not the real beach," he said, gesturing at the glass surface of the lake. "But I hope it's enough."

"It's more than enough." If she had been in an MRI machine, her heart would be visibly glowing and the rest of her organs would have transformed into piles of goo.

He raised his glass. "To you," he said simply.

"And to beginnings," she added. They clinked glasses. The bubbles hit her tongue like fireworks. Her whole body pulsated like she might fly out of her skin at any moment.

Golden light streaked across Luke's face. He turned to look at her, a smile in his eyes telling her he knew he had knocked it out of the park. The butterflies in her stomach were back. Her glass clunked onto the table, and she took one more long look at him.

She couldn't explain why, but she was certain she would

remember this exact moment for the rest of her life. The fresh scent of the pine trees around them. The cool breeze rolling off the lake. Goosebumps from the chill of the sand beneath them. Luke smiling back at her with one of his infamously infuriating grins.

She lunged for him before she could change her mind. Their lips met, and her heart hammered in her chest. One of his hands fisted in her hair while the other tugged her roughly toward him. The world disappeared. Heat washed over her as their tongues dance. It was probably a good thing she had instigated this before eating garlic bread.

A bird cawed somewhere too close, and Claire jumped. Her shin banged the table.

"Ouch," she grunted against Luke's mouth.

He pulled back. Disappointment washed over her. Stupid cockblocking bird.

The smile was still there. "You're supposed to wait until the end of the first date to do that, you know."

She rubbed her shin. "I'm sorry—am I not following your timeline?"

He glanced at his watch. "Speaking of timelines, we do need to eat. This isn't the last stop tonight. It's time sensitive."

She raised an eyebrow. The human stopwatch was at it again. What was next? Gondola on the lake? Tantric sex workshop?

He stared pointedly at her until she picked up her fork. She twirled some pasta around the tines and popped it into her mouth. Anything to move this date closer to more making out.

"So," Luke said nonchalantly, as if they hadn't been thirty seconds away from ripping each other's clothes off and committing a series of indecent crimes in a public park.

Maybe the police tape was a self-fulfilling prophecy. "I'm assuming you have a long list of questions and interrogation tactics for a first date. Is there a PowerPoint you want to pull up? Should I have installed a projector?"

She shot him a dirty look. If this pasta wasn't so delicious, she would have shoved him into the sand.

"Actually, I haven't been on a first date in a really long time." Aside from a handful of makeouts with sweaty strangers in clubs, there had been no one since Jason.

"I find that hard to believe," Luke said.

Claire shrugged. "That being said, I do have an extensive relationship questionnaire to tap into. You know, from the business."

"Of course. And I'm sure your first question is to ask how I pulled this off."

She narrowed her eyes. Was he a mind reader as well as an adult Abercrombie model?

He picked up his glass again and took a sip. "I befriended some park rangers."

"Park rangers with advanced degrees in atmospheric beach picnics?" She pointed at the ornate silver candlesticks.

"I drew them a diagram."

"You are something else, Luke Islestorm." She shook her head and sampled another forkful of pasta.

"Well, if you don't have any questions, I do have some for you."

Her curiosity was piqued. "Okay, shoot."

"Would you rather have the power of invisibility or flight?"

She considered for a millisecond. "Definitely flight. It would make getting to appointments so much easier. Just think of all the gas money I'd save. And you?"

"Invisibility."

She waited, but he was quiet. "Care to elaborate?"

"Mostly for work. It would be beneficial to uncover people's true natures. Find the real truth."

Claire frowned. "That's awfully unromantic."

"Maybe. Your turn."

The questionnaire they sent to clients scrolled through her mind like a prologue in a movie. "What's a goal of yours in the next ten years?"

"Easy. I'm going to win an Emmy. What about you?"

She considered for a moment. "There are so many things I want to do. Plan a mega proposal that's larger than life. Win the next Planner of the Year award. Adopt another dog. Get married. Start a family."

Oops, she was rambling now. Luke hadn't even mentioned anything related to his personal life. Wrap it up, you blithering idiot.

"What's the best gift you ever received?" she fired off before he could comment on her oversharing.

He stared into the dying sun. Pinprick stars were appearing in the darkening sky. Silence stretched. He looked like he was a thousand miles away.

"My dad got me my first camera. I must have been six or seven. Even back then I was obsessed with film, with stories. I filmed everything—our cat, my parents, the neighbors barbecuing next door. There's always a story if you look hard enough."

The thought of a young Luke with a camera pressed to his face brought another wave of warmth to her extremities. She smiled and scooted a little bit closer.

"So why did you join the military? If filming was always such a labor of love for you, I mean."

He shrugged. "It didn't feel like a realistic dream. My

mom was always on me about doing something concrete—
be a lawyer, be a doctor, go to pharmacy school, do something with a guaranteed paycheck that demands respect.
But I didn't want to be any of those things, and I definitely
didn't want to waste years of my life going to school for
something I had no passion for. The Navy got me out of
that bubble, gave me some skills. It was an easy way to
connect with people when I was discharged. A surprising
number of Hollywood elite are veterans, you know. Even
Betty White."

Claire gasped. "Did you meet Betty White?"

He smiled. "Just once. Her drink was a vodka on the
rocks, twist of lemon."

"Wow." She sat back. Her plate was empty, but her heart
was full.

"And you? Best gift?"

She paused. "When I turned sixteen, my mom gave me
the family car. It wasn't fancy—it was an old Toyota Corolla.
We had had it since I was little. She was embarrassed to give
it to me, I think. We had to sleep in it a couple times after
my dad left, so it was kind of a reminder of all the struggles
we had been through."

Luke made a sound, but she continued. "But there was a
lot more to it than that. I have so many amazing memories
of that car too. My first trip to the beach, singing at the top
of our lungs. Visiting Roy at his garage while they first
started dating. Spilling Mountain Dew in the back seat.
Racing rain drops on the way to my grandparents' house. I
took it to college with me, too. I drove it until it literally fell
apart on the highway. I'll always miss that car."

His hand found hers, and he rubbed a thumb over her
knuckles. She turned to look at him. An unreadable expression was on his face. His hand slipped up to cup her chin.

His eyes were soft. Was he going to kiss her again? Shit, she should have slammed down a couple breath mints.

His phone vibrated in his pockets, and a glimmer of regret flashed in his eyes. He pulled his hand back and slid it into his pocket.

"Come on. We're not done yet." He helped her up from the ground, and she winced at the movement of muscles. As much as she wanted to pretend the stabbing had never happened, her body insisted on reminding her.

"Do we need to clean up?" she gestured at the discarded plates.

He shook his head. "Don't worry, I tipped the rangers generously."

They fell in step beside each other as he guided her back to the car. While the walk had been romantic just an hour before, the forest was starting to come alive. Darkness stretched beyond the trees. What if a bear smelled the fettuccine Alfredo on her breath?

She dug a tin of breath mints out of her purse and shook a couple out just in case. Luke snatched the container from her before she put it back. Hopefully that meant more making out was on the agenda.

"What would you do if you won the lottery?" he asked in the dark.

"To be honest, I kind of feel like I already have," she blurted out. Shit, why did she say that? Calm down, idiot. It's a first date.

He raised his eyebrows and turned to look at her. "Even though you were stabbed a couple days ago?"

She nodded. "Yeah. But after I won the lottery, the universe cursed me and tried to take everything away. You know, that old hat."

Luke nudged her. "Serious answer."

"Fine. Depending on the amount, I'd pay off my mom's mortgage to thank her for everything she did for me when she was a single mom. And with whatever's left, I'd probably do something boring. Buy an office space instead of rent. Sponsor some underprivileged kids. A couple of scholarships at the local high school. Maybe set up an animal sanctuary if it was like a Powerball situation."

"Not more shoes?" He pointed at her fashionable brown boots.

She laughed. "I try to only buy shoes when I earn something. Unless I'm emotional shopping. That can't be helped."

Something rustled in the woods next to them. Claire screamed and jumped in front of Luke. Her mind ran a mile a minute. If it was a bear, she needed to make herself big. She put her arms out to her sides and puffed her chest out. Like the bear could tell.

"Get out of here!" She clapped, and the sound was like a thunderbolt.

A warm hand closed over her shoulder, and she whirled around, fingers curling into a fist. Had bears learned to mimic friendly gestures? But no, it was just Luke, amusement sparkling in his eyes.

"Thank you for being willing to lay down your life, but I think we're good. That branch fell out of a tree." He pointed at a large clump of sticks on the ground.

"Oh." Her arms fell to her sides. She had truly made an idiot of herself now. He'd probably cancel the rest of the date and call Kyle with all the details as soon as he'd dropped her off. So much for breaking her sex embargo.

"Come on. We have somewhere to be." He held out his hand, and she took it. Electricity crackled between them. Maybe the bear faux pas hadn't ruined everything.

"So," Claire said when Luke started the truck up. "You never told me what you'd do if you won the lottery."

He shrugged and put his arm around the back of her headrest. The truck backed slowly out of its spot. Where would they go next?

"I don't play the lottery."

Of course he didn't.

"Okay, unexpected windfall then. Deceased relative left you millions. What do you do?"

He considered for a moment. "Probably something boring. Invest, put an extra bump in my niece's trust fund. If I was feeling really irresponsible, maybe buy a lake house."

"I love that for you," she mused. He totally seemed like a lake house guy. She could practically see him stepping confidently down the dock in boat shoes, rolling a cooler full of brewskis behind him.

They trundled down the road. Luke paused to rip the police tape down. He rolled it up and put it in his pocket.

"Where to now?" she asked.

"Not far," he replied.

The truck wound up the mountain that loomed large behind the lake. Eventually, they came to a stop at an over-look. The very same overlook Claire and her mom visited when she was young.

From their new vantage point, they could see above the trees to the drive-in movie theater across the highway from the park.

A shiver ran through her that had nothing to do with the cool spring evening. Her past and present were colliding in a beautiful, unexpected way.

Luke backed the car into a spot and pulled right up to

the railing. He jumped out of the truck and came around to her side. She nearly stumbled while stepping out, but he caught her. Heat crept into her cheeks at his embrace.

He led her to the back of the truck. The stars were out in full force now. Previews were rolling at the theater across the highway.

Luke dropped the tailgate down and released the mechanism on his truck bed cover. It rolled smoothly back and revealed pillows, blankets, more sparkling wine, and another mysterious covered dish.

Her heart fluttered. The picnic alone had far exceeded any expectations she had ever had for a date. Never in her life had someone taken so much care in planning an evening, let alone for a first date.

"Luke," she started again. Her eyes watered.

He smiled. "You don't have to say anything." He held out one hand and helped her into the truck bed.

She took the opportunity to wipe away the stray tears that had leaked out without her permission. She crawled on hands and knees over the blankets to the back. Not the most dignified position. He followed her and picked up the champagne.

"This might have rolled around a little bit." He held it over the side of the truck and twisted the cork until it popped out.

He poured the liquid into two glasses and handed one to Claire.

She held it up. "To you."

"Aw, shucks," he said, then took a sip. He leaned against the back of the cab, and she snuggled in next to him.

"What are we watching this evening?"

"You'll see." A classic Luke non-answer.

He balanced his champagne flute on the edge of the

truck bed and lifted the lid on the mystery dish. Two small apple pies with expert latticework huddled together on a plate.

"Tiny pies?" she cooed. As if this night couldn't get any better.

Luke pulled a small cooler from nowhere and unzipped it. Vanilla ice cream appeared.

"Teaberry wouldn't pair well with a fruit pie," he said, a hint of defensiveness in his voice. He had even remembered her favorite ice cream.

Claire cracked a smile. "Trust me, it's fine. Did you make these yourself?"

He shook his head. "I ran out of time. These are from the bakery on Main Street. There are *some* limits to an Islestorm first date, you know."

"No judgments here," she said, hands held up in front of her to proclaim her innocence.

He handed a fork to her, then slid open the back window of his truck. He rooted around inside for a moment before withdrawing a handheld radio. The AM channels flicked by until he found the one that matched up with the video playing below.

"This is almost stupidly comfortable," she mused while pressing a hand into the truck bed. "What did you put under here, a memory foam mattress?" She lifted the corner of a blanket. "Oh my god. You literally dragged a memory foam mattress in here. I hope this was something you had lying around. You've gone through enough trouble already."

Luke looked at her. His face was half in shadow. "For you, nothing is too much trouble."

Her heart was doing a whole-ass jig in her chest again. A stupid grin spread across her face. She hid it with her champagne glass and moved closer to him.

"You didn't strike me as a pie guy," she said as a plop of vanilla landed on her slice.

"No?"

"Nope. More of a fussy, five-tiered cake guy," she teased.

"I hate cake," he said vehemently.

She inhaled sharply and choked on a piece of crust. The fork nearly tumbled from her hand when Luke beat her on the back.

"Sorry," she said after a cleansing sip of wine. "I've never heard anyone be so violently anti-cake before."

"It's kind of a sore subject. I'm a pie guy now."

"Good to know." The second she got home, she was going to make a gigantic note in her phone to never bring cake anywhere near him.

"It's starting." He pointed at the screen.

"Wait. Is that—" The beginning credits of her favorite movie, *Clueless*, rolled on-screen.

Luke smiled conspiratorially and ate a forkful of pie without comment.

"I can't believe they're playing this movie. It's been out for like thirty years."

"Ouch, way to make me feel old."

"It must be some kind of retro night," she mused.

"It wasn't," he said quietly.

"What? Did you befriend a projectionist too?"

"Something like that."

Claire settled back against the truck bed. How many strings could one man pull? What would a second date be like? Or was this all for show?

As the ice cream and buttery pie crust melted in her mouth, she decided that for now, it didn't matter. She would just enjoy this perfect, once-in-a-lifetime date. Unless a bear lumbered up the mountain and murdered them.

As the movie progressed, the sparkling wine disappeared. Without acknowledging their intent, they crept closer together until she was wrapped in the safety of his arms.

It was a feeling unlike any she had ever known. Even though feasibly danger could have been all around them—criminals hiding in the trees, coyotes and bears looking at them like a five-course dinner—every part of her felt safe and warm under this blanket of stars.

"I'm surprised you don't have more questions for me," she said into the fabric of his sweater.

"Well, I have to save some for the second date. Or tonight. You should come home with me."

Her eyebrows flew way up. That was a tad forward.

"Not for that," he said hurriedly. "No offense, but you're useless at changing your gauze."

The warm fuzzies were gone. She sat up and swatted him on the torso, practically bruising her hand on his stupid abs in the process. "Hey. I am capable of changing my own bandages."

He shook his head. "You're not trained. If I left you to your own devices, you'd have sepsis by now."

She spluttered, but he silenced her with his mouth. A rush of warmth hit her, and the retorts she had been ready to spit back died in her chest.

Alicia Silverstone mused about matchmaking in the background as Claire's hands explored the impressive topography of Luke's torso. She shoved the pie plate and empty wine bottle to the side and straddled Luke. He met her hungrily, rough hands sliding up her back. She ground against him, desperate to be closer. This was it. The embargo was toast. Were there cobwebs down there?

He sat up and flipped her over, lowered her gently to the

bed of the truck. His face was framed by an inky black sky. There was hunger in his eyes, but also softness. He dipped down and inched the hem of her sweater up, kissing as he went.

Her body was on fire. She reached down to tug her shirt off. Who cared if they were in a public park? There was no one around.

The sweater had barely cleared her midriff when a piercing pain hit her chest.

She gasped, and Luke backed off immediately. Which was a shame because something interesting had definitely been pressing into her leg a moment before.

"Are you okay?" His eyes searched hers. He brushed her hair to the side and inspected her wound as best as he could through a layer of fabric.

"I'm fine." She grabbed his sweater to tug him toward her again, but the same pain rippled through her like a live wire. She hissed through clenched teeth.

Luke's hands closed over hers. They both blew out a long, slow exhale. The pain had receded somewhat, but it had definitely short-circuited her horny brain.

"It's too soon. With your injury, you could have gotten seriously hurt. I got carried away. I'm sorry," he said.

"*You* got carried away? I was dry humping your leg."

"You don't usually hump legs on first dates?"

"I don't know. You're the expert on first dates, Mr. Fancy Pants Beach Picnic Who Bribes Everyone Under the Sun."

It wasn't her best insult. The sensation of annoyance was almost welcome after the all-encompassing wave of lust that had washed over her and then left her barren.

He sat next to her and gently pulled her back in to him. She tilted her head to look at him, and he kissed her again, more gently this time.

"You want to finish the movie?" he asked when they broke apart. "Or should I take you home?"

"Let's stay. I'm not ready to leave."

Even if she couldn't shake off the cobwebs in her downstairs department, it was still the most perfect evening. What would forever look like with Luke Islestorm?

It was way too soon to start thinking about forever. Who knew what other skeletons were hiding in his closet. Maybe he had an estranged wife living in the attic. Or an extensive collection of taxidermied penguins.

She would have to fight against every instinct to keep the wall she had built around her heart intact. But she had a feeling Luke had never met a wall he couldn't knock down.

ABOUT THE AUTHOR

Madison Score is the author of the Claire Hartley Accidental Mystery series (and the younger, weirder sister of Lucy Score). She lives in Pennsylvania with her husband, son, and perpetually shedding corgi. For some reason, her parents allowed her to get a degree in Creative Writing, which she now utilizes to craft stories with comedy, romance, and sometimes a hefty dose of crime.

When she's not writing, working at her real job in medical billing, or chasing after her tornado of a toddler (seriously, how many times can he upend our rubber tree?) you can find her blatantly ignoring recipes in the kitchen, flailing her body around in the gym, or bingeing true crime podcasts, TV, and movies.

Follow her on Facebook and Instagram if you want to see an excess of poorly photographed foods during her weekly Madison Tries It segment.

Website: madisonscore.com
Facebook: madisonscore
Instagram: madisonscore

ACKNOWLEDGMENTS

First and foremost, I have to thank my amazing husband, Mike. Without your patience, love, and extraordinary sacrifice, these books never would have been written. Thank you for putting up with my crazy requests ("Hey, can you lock me in the trunk of your car real quick?") and taking endless long walks with me while I pelted you with plot holes and story troubles. I love you always, forever, and longer.

Thank you also to my sister, Lucy. You paved the way for me and showed me that this crazy dream is possible, worthwhile, and life-changing. I am so proud of you and so grateful to be your sister.

The biggest of thank yous goes out to Mr. Lucy, publisher extraordinaire and easily the best brother-in-law of all time. Thank you for leaning into the nepotism and taking a chance on me. I hope I don't bankrupt us both.

To the publishing team: Jess, thank you for your compliment sandwiches and for gently urging me to be better. Lisa, for pointing out my brain farts. Rachel, for communicating my hare-brained ideas to designers. And to Audio Dan, for sending legendary memes and coordinating the big stuff.

And my TWSS girls—Avery, Stephanie, LJ, and Kathryn. Thank you for celebrating with me, commiserating with me, and giving the best advice.

Last but not least, thank you to my parents. For letting me major in Creative Writing, for encouraging me to be independent but letting me know I'm not alone. Love you guys.